Lakesly smiled seductively

"You've had a taste of Bernardo de Falcon and you've had a taste of Reed Lakesly. How do we compare?" he teased.

"You handle your liquor better," Michaela responded, trying to keep a straight face.

"And?"

"His cologne is worse than yours."

"What else?"

"Bernardo understands the importance of flowers. But you...have very nice eyes," she said.

Lakesly ran his finger down her forearm and across her hand. Then he took it and kissed her fingers.

"These macho affectations wear a little better from you," Michaela teased.

"Is that all?" Lakesly said with mock outrage.

"Well..." Michaela paused. "I have to admit you know your way around the bedroom...."

Dear Reader,

At last we can enjoy the flowers of May, and Superromance readers will particularly enjoy our perennials—perennially favorite authors, that is!

We're delighted to welcome prolific author Tracy Hughes back to Superromance. *The Princess and the Pauper* is the tale of a man and woman, brother and sister in name, though not in fact, forced to work together to put their father's ailing cosmetics company on its feet. *He* hasn't the slightest inclination; *she* is determined to succeed. And somehow, along the way, the inevitable happens....

Bobby Hutchinson has created wild and wonderful Sameh Smith, a klutzy, comic, endearing heroine who's somehow not quite from this planet. She meets her match in Adam Hawkins, a cynical P.I. who can't figure her out, but can't help loving her, either.

Lynn Erickson will take you from the glamour of the Big Apple to the haunting grandeur and sandy shores of Israel and Greece, where her wealthy heroine, Alexandra Costidos, travels with hired mercenary John Smith on a mission of love—to kidnap her son from the clutches of his powerful father.

Janice Kaiser always delivers a surprise, and in *The Yanqui Prince*, reporter Michaela Emory, bored with her beat, jumps at the chance to track down and interview the legendary Reed Lakesly, a modern-day Robin Hood whose territory is Central America. Naturally, Lakesly has a few surprises of his own, and suddenly, Michaela has more adventure and passion—and men—than she bargained for!

Happy spring!

Marsha Zinberg,
Senior Editor, Superromance

JANICE KAISER

THE YANQUI PRINCE

Harlequin Books

TORONTO • NEW YORK • LONDON
AMSTERDAM • PARIS • SYDNEY • HAMBURG
STOCKHOLM • ATHENS • TOKYO • MILAN
MADRID • WARSAW • BUDAPEST • AUCKLAND

ISBN 0-373-70597-2

THE YANQUI PRINCE

Copyright © 1994 by Belles-Lettres, Inc.

This edition published by arrangement with Harlequin Enterprises B. V.

® and TM are trademarks of the publisher. Trademarks indicated with ® are registered in the United States Patent and Trademark Office, the Canadian Trade Marks Office and in other countries.

Printed in U.S.A.

ABOUT THE AUTHOR

When Janice Kaiser wrote her first Superromance novel nine years ago, she had a theory that so long as her books had a darn good love story, her readers wouldn't mind also getting a mystery or a thriller and a three-hankie emotional read. Thirty romance novels later, her challenge is to continue to do something different in each book—to stretch a bit, to take risks. *The Yanqui Prince* is her first out-and-out comic adventure, and she has never had more fun writing a book. We hope you have just as much fun reading it!

Books by Janice Kaiser

HARLEQUIN SUPERROMANCE
494—THE BIG SECRET
541—CRADLE OF DREAMS

HARLEQUIN TEMPTATION
462—BETRAYAL
466—DECEPTIONS

Don't miss any of our special offers. Write to us at the following address for information on our newest releases.

Harlequin Reader Service
P.O. Box 1397, Buffalo, NY 14240
Canadian address: P.O. Box 603,
Fort Erie, Ont. L2A 5X3

For Margo Scofield

CHAPTER ONE

MICHAELA EMORY had a splitting headache. She rubbed her temple, only half hearing the chairman's voice as he droned on and on about the federal budget. No matter how hard she tried, she couldn't concentrate. Just once, she'd like to write about something she cared about. As it was, the only thing that mattered to her was how soon they'd break for lunch.

She glanced around the cavernous wood-paneled room. The lobbyists and staffers seemed interested in the proceedings, but then, they were free to leave whenever they wanted. Most of the other reporters looked attentive, though she spotted a couple of veterans who looked every bit as bored as she felt.

Michaela shut her eyes, hoping to bring back the fantasy that had been so soothing. She'd been on an island somewhere off the coast of Indonesia. The vegetation was lush, tropical. It was paradise.

She sighed. It was that travel magazine she'd picked up on her way home from work last night. That's what had set her off. There'd been a photograph of a beautiful girl standing under a waterfall as emerald spray pounded down on her.

Michaela simply couldn't get the image out of her mind. She wondered what it would feel like to stand in that pool as warm water caressed her body. If she worked at it, she could almost picture the face of a handsome stranger as he came upon the scene, catching her unaware.

She couldn't decide whether he'd be the heir to a major fortune who was a dead ringer for Alex Baldwin, or if he should be a debonair Frenchman living in exile on his nearby plantation after suffering a tragic love affair. Either would do, so long as she had an adventure. Michaela needed to escape—to see new sights, to meet new challenges. She was bored with her work and her life—and the men in it.

She had always been a dreamer, there was no denying that. As an only child, she'd enjoyed a rich fantasy life. As an adult, her heart told her that Mr. Right was out there somewhere. He'd be handsome and sexy and he'd share her love for adventure, yet have a sensitive, caring side, too. But as time passed, she was beginning to believe that the perfect man existed *only* in dreams since the actual specimens never quite measured up.

The microphone squawked, and the chairman tapped it to make certain everyone could hear. Michaela sat up straight, and told herself to stop daydreaming. She was there to work. Besides, by almost anyone's standards, she had few grounds for complaint.

Most young journalists would kill for her job. Furthermore, her personal life was full. She was dating three men—Mark, a lawyer with a downtown firm; John, a CPA; and Matt, a logistics specialist over at the Pentagon. All three men were intelligent, nice, and reasonably good-looking. And none of them did a thing for her. On the excitement scale, they managed a five or a six.

Michaela was having difficulty deciding whether she should kick herself for not being thankful for what she had, or if she should do something to change her life. But what did a woman do when her complaint was that she wasn't satisfied? The solution was to stay away from travel magazines!

She glanced at her notepad. During the two hours she'd been sitting there, she had only jotted down three notes, and one was a reminder to pick up her dry cleaning. The U.S. Congress might not be the most scintillating subject to write about, but Capitol Hill was her beat. It was her duty to do her best.

About the time she picked up the thread of the chairman's remarks, the rumpled little guy next to her bumped her arm. He apologized, grinning. Michaela had been vaguely aware of his fidgeting—pulling at his collar, clearing his throat, running his fingers through his thinning hair. When she glanced at him again, he was ogling her legs. Apparently all the fuss had been designed to get her attention. Dread washed over her.

It wasn't as if she wasn't up to handling yet another guy bent on making a pass. As a former Miss Arizona, she'd met more than her fair share of men who were interested in her solely for her looks. She'd learned to be both firm and polite in dealing with them. Mindful of her Aunt Gayle's warning that she would reap whatever she sowed, Michaela tried to be nice to everyone.

Still, every once in a while she encountered a real jerk who wouldn't take no for an answer. She agonized when that happened. It hurt to be wanted for what she looked like, instead of who she was inside.

Uncomfortable with the growing determination of the man next to her, she debated between retreating to her daydream or giving the hearings her unqualified attention. Indonesia beckoned, but duty had the more commanding voice.

Michaela recrossed her legs and tried to pay attention. The speaker was offering a dissenting view on the chairman's proposed schedule for the second session. She listened for thirty seconds before her brain darted off again. She hadn't had a vacation in two years. Maybe that's what was wrong. Maybe she needed a change of scene, a break from her routine.

The TV reporter bumped his knee against hers. When she glanced at him, he was checking out her breasts. She groaned. Wasn't it bad enough that she didn't have the slightest idea what story she'd file that evening, without having to deal with both a headache and would-be Lothario?

Michaela stared up at the ornately carved ceiling. She took a deep breath and smoothed the hem of her white linen skirt. No matter how hard she tried to concentrate, nothing registered.

Thank goodness it was almost noon. She was meeting Chelsea Osborne for lunch. Chels would give her a pep talk or a kick in the butt—whatever was required. They had known each other for years, having been in college together. And Chelsea understood her better than anyone, even Aunt Gayle.

The chairman brought down the gavel, announcing the recess. A few members of the press moved forward to buttonhole witnesses. As Michaela gathered her things, she felt an elbow nudging her.

"Hey, gorgeous, got plans for lunch?" The pesky reporter was at least six inches shorter than she was.

Michaela tried to look both pleasant and apologetic. "Yes, I'm meeting a friend."

"Sure you can't be tempted to eat with me instead? You could see your friend anytime."

"It's a working lunch," she said firmly. "My friend works on the Hill and is one of my better sources."

It was true. Chelsea was press secretary to the ranking member of the Senate Finance Committee, and a great source. When she'd called that morning, she'd said she had important business to discuss.

Michaela resolutely picked up her briefcase and headed for the aisle.

"If it's business, maybe I can join you," he said, following her. "No harm in sharing the wealth, is there?"

"I don't think that would be a good idea." Michaela moved into the crowd, but he was right on her heel, like a pit bull. She made it past the door and started up the corridor.

"You're Mike Emory, aren't you?"

She glanced back at him, surprised. "Yes. How did you know?"

"I noticed you and made a point of checking you out. Word is you'd like to do features, write a column, win a Pulitzer, et cetera, et cetera."

She stopped walking and gave him a searching look, stunned that he would know that she wanted to have her own column. She didn't talk much about her dreams and ambitions—except to Chelsea. "What are you, some kind of spy?"

He laughed. "No. I was interested in you, so I made it my business to ask a few questions and read some of your work. And I know good journalism when I see it."

Michaela couldn't help but be flattered. His approach was more refreshing than the usual "Aren't you the ex-beauty queen they hired over at the *Bulletin?*" She continued along the corridor, but at a more sedate pace.

"The name's Woodson, by the way. Dan Woodson," he said. "With WNTV news."

"Nice to know you, Dan."

"I know I've already stuck my nose in your business, Mike, but I'm curious about something."

"What's that?"

"You've got it all. You're gorgeous. You can write a mean article. So why do you seem to be such an unhappy lady?"

She blinked. "Unhappy?"

"Yeah, I sense you're restless. Like you're searching for something. Or maybe frustrated."

The observation struck a bit too close to home for comfort. Michaela felt a lot more ill at ease than she let on. Woodson had zeroed in on something that made her uneasy.

"Tell me, Dan, are your instincts equally good when it comes to investigative reporting?"

He grinned. "I do okay. Take you, for instance. I wanted to find out all I could about you, so I asked around. But to be honest, I guessed about your ambitions. Name a print reporter doesn't want a column and a Pulitzer."

A crowd had gathered in front of the bank of elevators. He beamed, then carefully brushed aside an errant hank of hair that had been swirled to cover a bald spot.

Michaela wasn't sure whether he was especially intuitive, or if her frustrations were obvious to everyone. She'd have to ask Chelsea. One thing was certain, though. Whether Dan Woodson was intuitive or not, his tenacious side was well developed.

"If you put as much effort into your work as you do in checking out women, Dan, you must be a darn good reporter," she said.

"The budget isn't nearly as stimulating as a sexy redhead with great legs," he said wryly.

Michaela scowled. She hated being objectified. The older woman in front of them turned and gave Woodson a meaningful look. Michaela couldn't help smiling at the rebuke. But the reporter didn't seem to care.

"So, what do you say? Have lunch with me. I'll show you a great time, make it worth your while."

"I'm sorry, but I'm already committed," she said. "Really."

Fortunately, the elevator arrived before he could come up with another plea. The crowd surged forward. Michaela squeezed in next to the woman who had given Woodson a dirty look. There was no room for Woodson. He looked crestfallen.

As the elevator door closed, Michaela rolled her eyes. She didn't mean to be unkind, but at the same time she was grateful she wouldn't have to endure further embarrassment. Yet a part of her couldn't help but feel sorry for Dan Woodson. At least *he* had the guts to pursue what he wanted, even if he'd been somewhat obnoxious about it. It made her wonder if there wasn't a message in it for her.

She exited the elevator at the basement level. She planned to meet Chelsea at the Capitol cafeteria, and in the middle July, using the tunnel was infinitely preferable to being out in the sweltering Washington heat.

As Michaela's heels clicked on the cement, she thought about Dan Woodson. How had he tuned in to her dreams, her restlessness? Had he picked up pieces of gossip, drawn some lucky conclusions and happened to hit the mark? Or could anyone who took the time to look see that she wasn't happy with her life?

Maybe being a beat reporter wasn't what she truly wanted. Michaela had always had a secret yearning for adventure. She'd gone into journalism sure she would roam the world, writing about interesting people and places. Washington had been a big step up from Tucson. Still, a year of writing about murders, robberies, and crises in the city's social-welfare department wasn't quite the dream she'd had in mind.

The Capitol Hill beat had been an improvement, but once she'd gotten used to the glamour of high-profile politicians, all that was left was humdrum. How could anyone get excited about the difference between a two- and three-percent cut in discretionary spending? Was it her? Was *she* the fish out of water? Was her predicament so obvious that even a stranger like Dan Woodson could see it?

"You know, Mike," Chelsea had once said after listening to her lament, "you really ought to write for travel magazines. Or be a foreign correspondent. Something like that is more you."

It was true. Exotic people, exotic places. That was her destiny. But one didn't become a foreign correspondent fresh out of journalism school. As for travel writing, who could afford to free-lance? As it was, she could barely make ends meet. No, she would simply have to pay her dues first, like everyone else. One step at a time, Mike, she told herself. One step at a time.

Chelsea Osborne was waiting at the entrance to the Capitol cafeteria. She was a petite brunette with large, scholarly-looking glasses and as always, wore a prim little suit. Her briefcase looked as big as a suitcase, and it was bulging with papers.

"Hi, Chels," Michaela said cheerfully, determined to improve her mood. "Sorry I'm late. I sat through Congressman Wilbertson's droneathon to the very end."

"I could have saved you the trouble. The hottest stuff on the budget is in my briefcase."

"Something you'll share?"

Chelsea grinned devilishly. "In this briefcase, my dear, is nothing short of political dynamite. And it's for your eyes only. Unless you decide to publish it, of course."

Chelsea loved the wheeling and dealing of Capitol Hill. She was bright and funny and had a real knack for putting things into perspective—a quality Michaela found useful, given her penchant for romanticizing.

"Should we transfer this meeting to the Watergate?"

Chelsea laughed. "It's not that hot, to be honest. But my boss wants to spike a few guns. You're the lucky lady I selected to plant the charge."

"Oh, thank you, thank you. This couldn't come at a better time. I'm brain dead today. I hardly heard a word this morning and I don't know what I'd have filed, unless it was my obituary."

Chelsea patted her shoulder. "Well, I've definitely got a story for you. Let's discuss it while we eat."

They went through the cafeteria line. Michaela selected a chef's salad, Chelsea a cheeseburger and French fries.

"How do you keep from turning into a porker, eating that fattening stuff?" Michaela asked as they sat down. "If I ate like you, I'd be able to play for the Redskins in six months."

"Genetics, I guess. Anyway, you're the last person who has to worry about her appearance. You attract men the way a gossip columnist gathers rumors."

Michaela laughed. "Thanks for the compliment, but there's a downside, believe me. Speaking of which, have you ever run into a TV guy named Woodson? Dan Woodson, WNTV?"

Chelsea had her burger poised at her mouth, ready to take a bite. She smiled. "Funny you should ask. He came by my office yesterday, asking about you. I think he has a crush on you."

Michaela rolled her eyes. "Tell me about it. He sat next to me this morning and proceeded to analyze me. He said I seemed unhappy. I think he saw it as his duty to cheer me up." She picked up her pepper. "I hope you weren't his source, Chels."

"I suppose I told him a few harmless things—nothing you'd have found objectionable."

Michaela eyed her. "Such as?"

Chelsea looked sheepish. "He wanted to know if it was true that you'd been Miss Arizona. But that's not exactly confidential."

Michaela took a sip of her iced tea. "I guess I'm being overly sensitive. To tell you the truth, it sort of got to me when he said that I was restless."

Chelsea put down her hamburger. "Maybe you should think about changing your life. You could use a vacation. It's been a long time since you've done anything new."

"You've got that right. I've been dreaming about going off somewhere exotic, where you can bathe nude in a waterfall."

"Did you say *nude?* In a *waterfall?* If I didn't know better, kiddo, I'd say you haven't been getting enough. Matthew, Mark and John aren't cutting it." She dipped a fry in catsup and popped it into her mouth. "In fact, now that I think about it, have you noticed anything in particular about this group?"

Michaela took a bite of salad as Chelsea chomped on another fry. "Not really. They think if they take me out to dinner I ought to cook breakfast, but you can say that about most men."

"I was referring to their *names,*" Chelsea said, feigning exasperation. "You've got a Matthew, a Mark and a John. All you're missing is Luke!"

Michaela groaned. Chels was into bad puns and dumb jokes. Oddly enough, though, she hadn't noticed it. It was funny, now that she thought about it. Luke would probably turn out to be the love of her life. Fate could be funny that way.

Michaela took another bite of salad, determined to stop moaning about her life. She pointed to Chelsea's briefcase. "Let's get down to business. Tell me about the evil deed."

Chelsea swallowed her last fry. "My boss plans to cut the legs out from under the House Committee on the discretionary-spending cut. He has White House backing. If it hits the papers before the House committee votes, it could change the outcome."

Michaela poked at her salad, nodding. "Very interesting."

It wasn't, actually. It sounded as dull as everything else had that morning. But she hated herself for thinking that. This was her profession, for goodness' sake. So why did she want to run from the room, screaming?

"I've made a copy of a key memo," Chelsea said. "We can go over it when you finish eating."

"Fine." Michaela stared at her salad, wondering if she could finagle a few days off, though she had no idea where she'd go. Over to the East Shore maybe. Lord knew she couldn't afford to go off to Indonesia in search of a secluded waterfall.

"Oh," Chelsea said. "I almost forgot. I brought along a letter I got yesterday, something you might find interesting."

"A letter?"

"Yes, from Susana Riveros. She was a journalism major in the class behind ours. A foreign student from Pangonia."

"Oh, I remember her. Short and dark and very pretty."

"That's right. Well, Susana and I got friendly during my last year. She let me practice my Spanish. We've written off and on since graduation. She'd been working for the major daily in Montagua, the capital."

"The congressional beat?" Michaela quipped.

Chelsea's expression turned serious. "At the moment, I'm afraid, Susana's in jail."

"Jail?"

"Yes, she wrote something that didn't please General Juan de Falcón, the president."

"And they put her in *jail* for it?" Michaela said.

"We tend to forget that in some places, freedom of the press is honored more in the breach, if you know what I mean."

Michaela shook her head. "I don't know much about Pangonia."

Chelsea pushed her glasses up off her nose. "Neither did I, before knowing Susana. But I've gotten a sense of the place from her letters." She opened her briefcase and removed an envelope. "This one's heart-wrenching. Susana's really in a mess."

"Surely they're not keeping her there indefinitely. I mean, how long is your sentence for writing an unpopular article?"

Chelsea held up the envelope. "According to this, she's been in the slammer three months, and there's no end in sight. Here, read it."

Michaela put down her fork and read. The letter was written in tiny, pinched script, apparently so that it could be squeezed onto a single sheet of paper.

My dear friend Chelsea,

How lucky you are to be in a country where the press is free. For three months I have been in the jail only because I question the policies of the government. If it wasn't so sad what these idiots are doing to my country, I would laugh. They are so crazy, and also stupid.

For several weeks I wrote articles about a fictitious country, making a satire of their policies. All of Pangonia was laughing and the buffoons who took over our country from our elected president did not even know I am writing about them. Then, when they discovered I made them the fool, they became enraged and put me in the jail.

It is especially embarrassing for them because Bernardo de Falcón, the son of our new dictator, is the editor of our paper. Only by giving money to a guard could I send this letter.

Nevertheless, my imprisonment is for a good cause, Chelsea. I have tried to rally the people of Pangonia behind the new movement to return our elected president, Ricardo Corazón de León, to power. We call ourselves the Movimiento Abril Primero—MAP. We are headed by our great patriot, Reed Lakesly. Perhaps you have heard of him. If his name sounds American, it is because his father is from your country. His mother is our countrywoman. Perhaps that is why his heart, it is with us.

I am writing, my dear friend, in the hope that from your important place in the American government you can bring pressure to bear against the general and his army of idiots to return our freedoms to the people of Pangonia. If you write about our struggle in your newspapers, perhaps the eyes of the world will fall on our small country.

Meanwhile I wish you good fortune and health.

Your friend,
Susana Riveros

Michaela folded the letter and put it back in the envelope. She stared at her friend. "I feel like crawling into a hole."

"Kind of puts things in perspective, doesn't it?" Chelsea said.

"You know something? I envy Susana, in spite of her hardship."

"Why?"

"She's doing something vital with her life. Sure, she's suffering, but at least she's relevant! At least she's living!"

"Mike, I just realized what your problem is."

"What?"

"You're a wide-eyed romantic living in a button-down world of bills and budgets and bull."

"I've known that forever, Chels. I ought to be digging up fantastic stories that move people's passions. I should be writing about revolutions, not budgets. I should be writing about revolutionaries like Reed What's-his-name." Michaela paused. "What was his name?"

"Lakesly, I think."

"That's right. Lakesly." She rubbed her chin. "You ever heard of him, or that MAP movement Susana talked about?"

"No, but then I don't follow the foreign news as closely as I should."

Michaela pushed leaves of lettuce around with her fork. "I try to, since it's always interested me, but I confess this is all new to me, too."

"Maybe Susana is right," Chelsea said. "Maybe Pangonia does need a champion in Washington."

"She was thinking of you, my dear."

Chelsea laughed. "Yeah, from my exalted position as press secretary to the ranking member of Finance. I can slip memos to you, but I can't turn the tide of the revolution in Pangonia."

Michaela stared off at the roomful of congressional employees, all jabbering away. Her mind was in Pangonia, a place she could barely place on a map. Her pulse hadn't risen this way in months—not counting her aerobics class and the occasional spirited tussle with Mark, John or Matt.

"Mike," Chelsea said, "you have the most deliciously wicked expression on your face. What are you thinking?"

"That maybe I should do a story on Susana and MAP and this guy, Lakesly."

"You?"

"Why not? I'm a journalist, aren't I?"

"One assigned to Capitol Hill. One, I might add, who's going to put my leak in tomorrow morning's paper."

"Don't worry, I'll take care of your leak."

"Then you're just talking, fantasizing again. Right?"

Michaela shook her head. "Nope. I'm going to talk to Jack Ellison. I'm going to ask him to send me to Pangonia."

"Mike, you're crazy. He wouldn't send you down there. Besides, you said the next time you asked Jack for a favor, you had to be willing to pay the price. He all but made a condition of you getting this job that you had to go to bed with him."

"Yes, but I've stayed clear of him for months. I never go into his office alone and I haven't so much as asked him for a box of pencils since I got this job."

"But now you're willing to beard the lion in his den?"

"Just because he asks me to go to bed with him doesn't mean I have to say yes."

"No, and he doesn't have to send you to Pangonia, either. I think you're off your rocker, if you don't mind me saying so."

"Maybe you're right. This could be the phase of the moon. By tomorrow I might have forgotten all about it," Michaela said. "But for the moment, my engine is running."

Chelsea shook her head. "By God, I think you're serious."

Michaela smiled happily for the first time that day. "I am, Chels. I am."

MICHAELA'S HANDS WERE shaking as she sat in Jack Ellison's office, watching him read a photocopy of Susana Riveros's letter. Jack was the managing editor and ran the *Daily News Bulletin* like a battleship. He had been a young navy officer once—a dashing one, undoubtedly, because he was now an attractive, charismatic man of fifty. There was gray at his temples, some wrinkles on his well-tanned face, but he was fit and his primary passion in life—besides the newspaper business—was chasing women. Mike knew she had gotten her original job over three or four equally talented reporters because of her looks. Jack had wanted another potential playmate out on the news floor.

He looked up at her over the rims of his glasses. He was in shirt sleeves, leaning back in his big red leather chair, his leg resting jauntily on a drawer of his desk. "What can I get out of her for this?" he seemed to be asking himself. "A room-service lunch at the Sheraton? Four or five days in Bermuda?" Alice Littleford, Michaela had heard, had opted for Bermuda and was now bureau chief in New York.

Jack finally put the letter down and engaged her pale blue eyes—"the color of an April sky" was the way he'd described them during her hiring interview. Finally he took off his reading glasses and laid them carefully on his desk.

"So you want me to send you to Pangonia?"

"Yes, Mr. Ellison. Don't you think there's a fantastic story there?"

"An interesting story, yes. I'll have to ask my bureau chief why I haven't heard more about MAP and Lakesly."

"I'd like the assignment," she said forthrightly.

"So you said." He studied her.

Michaela could see the wheels turning. How was he going to work into the question that was doubtlessly on his mind—"What are you prepared to offer me, Mike?" Instead, he opted to make her beg a bit more.

"You don't have the experience for this kind of assignment," he said. "That's the cold hard fact."

"I'm a damned good reporter," she argued. "That's what counts."

"I've got lots of good reporters, my dear. But I've been watching you, reading your pieces. Your work is solid, Mike, if a little uninspired at times."

"Capitol Hill isn't always exciting."

"But Montagua would be?"

"Yes."

Jack Ellison stroked his chin, a faint smile forming on his lips. "Have you had your vacation this year?"

Michaela gulped, sure she knew what was coming. "No."

"I try to sneak down to Bermuda now and then for a little golf. I'm going this weekend. Perhaps I'll take your proposal with me and give it some thought."

She shrugged. "Fine."

"Since you've got some vacation time, perhaps you'd like to come along, so you'd be available to discuss the matter. I may have some questions. Do you golf?"

"I don't golf but I'd be happy to give you my telephone number if you'd care to call me with your questions."

He stared at her without flinching. "I find supplicants much more persuasive when they make their case in person."

It was crunch time. Michaela decided to meet him head-on. "In other words, if I spend two or three days in bed with you, you'll send me to Montagua."

"Did I say that, Mike?"

"You may not have said it, but that's what I heard."

"You have a vivid imagination. I like that in my young reporters. Imagination is important to so many things."

"Well, I have an imaginative proposal for you. How about if I go to Pangonia on my own? I'll take a week of vacation."

"And the *Bulletin* provides the airfare?"

"Plus expense money," she said.

"My," he said with a grin, "you certainly drive a hard bargain. Maybe we ought to discuss this further over a leisurely lunch. How is tomorrow?" he asked, looking at his desk calendar.

"Mr. Ellison," she said sternly, "I'm flattered. But I am not going to bed with you. If that means I get fired, so be it. Just tell me if you're going to send me to Pangonia. Either you will, or you won't."

Ellison leaned forward, looking her dead in the eye. "Mike, there are five or six people I could have sent to Capitol Hill in place of you. A couple of them, anyway, would have been a good deal more grateful than you. Now you're asking me to give you something you haven't earned and aren't qualified to do. How do you think that makes me feel?"

"Only you are able to answer that, Mr. Ellison. But I have a backup proposal. I'd like permission to take a week off to fly to Montagua. If you like the story I write, you can reimburse my expenses. If you don't, I'll have had an expensive vacation."

Ellison sat thinking for a long time. Finally he slid Susana's letter across the desk. "Such a shame," he said. "The other way is so much more pleasant."

"For whom?" she asked, picking up the envelope.

"I've never had a complaint. Ever."

"Yes," Michaela said, getting up. "But this way I'll know what you think of my writing, not my body."

"But I won't know what you think of me . . . as a man."

"I can tell you that right now, Jack," she said pleasantly. "You're irresistible—almost, anyway."

He laughed. "If you didn't have balls, Mike, I'd fire you."

"If I did have balls, you would." Smiling, she left his office.

CHAPTER TWO

MICHAELA SAT ON THE EDGE of the worn vinyl seat as the taxi slowly crept through the crowded streets of Montagua. Despite the sapping fatigue of a long flight, she was excited. This trip would be a turning point in her life—she felt it in her bones.

As she looked around, she saw that Montagua didn't look all that different from the Mexican border towns she and her friends had visited during spring vacation when she was still in college. True, it was bigger and greener and there weren't as many twenty-year-old American-made cars, but there were obvious similarities. The downside was that not as many people spoke English. She had discovered that at the airport.

Her taxi came to a halt, stalled in the heart of what seemed to be a hopeless traffic jam. Already sweating, Michaela rolled down her window. The driver sat impassively listening to the rhythmic Latin music on the radio.

"What's wrong?" she asked, leaning forward.

The driver, a chubby man of forty, gestured toward the snarl of traffic. "Nobody moves," he said.

"That's apparent. Any particular reason? Is it like this all the time? I mean, this isn't rush hour, is it?"

"Maybe," the driver replied.

Michaela rolled her eyes. He didn't speak much English, after all. She had interviewed four different drivers before choosing this one. Apparently, she hadn't talked to him enough. Now she was stuck in traffic for heaven only knew how long, and dying to go to the bathroom.

She glanced at the children on the nearby curb, hoping to get her mind off her problem. But the more she tried to forget about going to the bathroom, the more uncomfortable she became. She cursed that last beer she'd had on the plane, and the fact that she hadn't taken time at the airport to find a ladies' room.

It had taken forever to get through Customs, and there had been a long wait before getting her press credentials. When she found herself outside the terminal building with nothing between her and a nice clean hotel but a fifteen-minute taxi ride, she'd decided to wait. That was half an hour ago. Michaela crossed her legs and groaned.

The children began circulating among the cars. Half a dozen gathered by Michaela's window, smiling at her and jabbering. One little boy reached in to touch her hair, marveling.

Men had always liked her hair. Jack Ellison had described it as "the color of pink champagne" during that infamous hiring interview. They'd gone to lunch to discuss her working for him, and when Jack had started getting effusive, she'd assumed it was the martinis speaking. By the time the formal interview was over he'd suggested still another drink—to get better acquainted. Naive twit that she was, Michaela had assumed that meant discussing hobbies, favorite books and authors. What a laugh.

It was too late now to worry about Jack, though. She'd taken her savings out of the bank, and borrowed another five hundred from Chelsea. Jack had let her take time off on short notice, but even so, she couldn't help but be resentful that he hadn't ponied-up for airfare. If she'd given him a weekend in Bermuda, the trip would have been all expenses paid. That wasn't right!

But by paying her own way, Michaela told herself she could preserve her dignity. Whatever happened, that was a victory.

She smiled at the children and tried to put Jack out of her mind. Though physically tired, she felt truly energized about her work for the first time in months. This is finally it, she told herself. I'm doing something that matters.

But the imperatives of nature weren't willing to allow her contentment. Not quite yet. Why hadn't she braved the public rest rooms when she had the chance?

Michaela leaned forward again. "What's going on?" she asked the driver plaintively.

"*No sé, señora.* Maybe it's the police."

"The police?"

"Sometimes they stop the cars to look for guns. It happens many times. I think maybe they got some. We must wait."

"Maybe *we* have to wait, but I'm not sure Mother Nature can."

The driver looked at her inquisitively.

"Never mind," Michaela said.

She watched the children, trying again to get her mind off her problem. A little boy stuck his hand in the window, palm up, his brown eyes imploring. Michaela couldn't resist. She reached into her purse, took out one of the packages of gum she'd brought along for this purpose, and gave a stick to each eager child.

The excitement brought more children clamoring to the cab. She dispensed gum until half her supply was gone, then leaned forward and looked up the street. There was nothing to see but cars and trucks jammed together, unable to move.

"This is ridiculous," Michaela said. "What if someone was in a hurry?"

"The police don't care," the driver said, turning down the radio. "They get paid if you are in a hurry or not."

Michaela knew she couldn't last long at this rate. She was hot and sticky, attracting more children than the Pied Piper, and she was about to float away.

"I'll go see what the problem is," she said, knowing bold action was required. "If the traffic starts moving before I get back, take my bags to the hotel. I'll walk there, if necessary."

The driver did not like the idea. She could tell by the way he shook his head. But her bladder was in charge now.

"How far to the hotel?"

"Maybe one kilometer," he replied.

"On this street?"

"Sí, señora."

"I'll either see you here or at the hotel." Michaela got out to the rising chorus of children's voices. She patted a few heads and stepped over to the sidewalk. It helped to be moving.

The clamor followed her and Michaela glanced back. There were at least twenty children in tow, dancing along after her. She felt as if she were leading a parade at Disneyland.

At the cross street there was a roadblock. The police were searching two buses. Baggage was spread everywhere, passengers were shouting and cursing, chickens in a large crate were cackling, policemen were giving orders and pushing people around.

Michaela surveyed the hubbub until she spotted a large, heavyset officer standing off to the side. He was observing the proceedings with an air of detachment. Deciding he was probably in charge, she marched up to him with her army of followers.

"Excuse me, officer," she said.

The policeman's thick mustache twitched as he checked out her bright yellow T-shirt dress that ended six inches above her knees. He clicked his heels. *"¿Señorita?"*

"I'm sorry to bother you, but my taxi is stuck in traffic. I was wondering how much longer this is going to last. I need to get to my hotel."

"Lo siento, señorita. No hablo inglés."

"Oh, great. Well, tell me this. Is there a public rest room around here?"

"¿Qué?"

"You know, a W.C., a bathroomo, a john."

"No comprendo."

"A john. You know, a *juan*. Is there a *juan* around here?"

"*¿Juan?*"

Michaela sighed with exasperation. "How do you tell a fat cop who doesn't speak English you've got to go to the bathroom?" she mumbled.

"Not by sayin' *juan*, lass. The blighter will think you're askin' for the president of the republic."

Michaela turned to see a priest standing in the middle of the children. He wore a long black cassock and a straw hat that seemed as big as a small umbrella. He wore old-fashioned wire-rimmed sunglasses and sported three or four days' growth of beard. He smiled benevolently. The accent was unmistakably Irish.

"Generalissimo Juan de Falcón runs this country, me child. The people affectionately, or not so affectionately, call him Juan. I don't think it's him that you be wantin', is it?"

A chicken squawked, making Michaela jump. The children laughed. The priest smiled. The policeman did not, though he did look at her legs.

Michaela studied the priest, who fingered a large wooden cross hanging on a leather thong around his neck. As best she could tell, he was in his thirties.

"No," she said, "that isn't the *juan* I had in mind."

It was only then that she noticed another priest standing nearby. He was similarly dressed, though without the sunglasses. He weighed about three hundred pounds, his ample stomach swelling under his cassock.

"Father Tucino and I observed you having difficulty with the language. We thought we might help," the first priest said. "I am Father O'Laughlin. Me parishioners call me Padre O. It's a construct, sort of like bathroom*o*." He grinned and extended his hand.

"Michaela Emory," she said, blushing. "As you may have surmised, I'm desperate."

"We priests are cognizant of the needs of the body, as well as the soul. Maybe Father Tucino and I can be of assistance.'' He glanced around. "This is not an ideal neighborhood in which to have need of facilities. It is a poor section, as you can see, and the bars are mostly for working men and prostitutes.''

"Prostitutes have to go the same as any other woman. And at this point, I'm not too proud to mind who I share with.''

"Aye, lass,'' the priest said. "In heaven we are all equal in the eyes of God. Nature accomplishes the same thing here on earth.''

Father O'Laughlin began speaking with the policeman. After an exchange or two, the officer grinned, drew himself up, clicked his heels and gestured for them to go.

The priest took her arm and guided her through the crowd of children. Father Tucino, who fell in step with them, shooed away the stragglers. The three of them headed toward what appeared to be a *taberna* on the corner.

"I can't tell you how much I appreciate this,'' Michaela said.

"You won't be havin' trouble in the company of a couple of priests,'' Father O'Laughlin said. "Besides, it's sparin' us the trouble of goin' through the security check, though I don't think the fat cop, as you so aptly called him, has figured that out yet.''

Father O'Laughlin's tone had taken on a not-so-priestlike air. Michaela knew she shouldn't be surprised. In many Third World countries, the clergy—especially at the lower echelons—sided with the peasants against the government. She'd learned that, among other things, during her intensive two days of research in the Library of Congress.

They'd come to the *taberna,* filled, as Father O'Laughlin had predicted, with working-class men. Heads turned as they stood at the entrance to the smoky room.

Father O'Laughlin stepped to the bar and had a word with the bartender. Then he returned to where Michaela waited with Father Tucino.

"The facilities are in back,'' he said. "The last door at the end of the hall. I'm afraid it's not set aside for ladies. They don't have one of those. If you can wait, he told me that there's a restaurant around the corner and down the street that might be a little better."

Michaela shook her head. "Thanks, but this one will be fine, I'm sure."

Without hesitating, she strode through the bar, watching from the corner of her eye as heads turned. She noticed the scent of perspiring male bodies, and she heard kissing noises that clearly were intended to be rude. She was in the world of machismo now—there was no doubt about that. It was amazing how benign, dear old sexist, predatory Jack Ellison seemed from this vantage point.

Several minutes later, feeling much better, Michaela walked back through the gauntlet of eyes. The sounds were louder and more assertive this time. She decided she was inappropriately dressed for a visit to a workingmen's bar. But she knew the men would have been even more overt if she hadn't been in the company of the two priests.

Fathers O'Laughlin and Tucino were seated at a small table near the door, a bottle of beer in front of each of them. Both men rose as Michaela approached.

"We were havin' a wee bit of refreshment while waitin' on you, lass," Father O'Laughlin said. "Would you care to join us?" He glanced out the window, in the direction of the roadblock. "Our bus is just gettin' ready to move on through."

"Don't you have to be on it?"

"No, it's better to stay here for a while. To run out now would only remind the police of our absence during the search."

Michaela considered his comment as she took her chair. Earlier the good father had made it clear his sympathies lay with the peasants, but this latest remark was tantamount to admitting that he had something to hide. She decided to probe a bit—to see if she could learn anything useful.

"Father, would it be impolitic to observe that you seem unduly concerned about the local authorities?"

The priests exchanged looks. "Yes, my child," Father O'Laughlin said firmly. "It would be impolitic." They watched the buses move on up the street.

Father O'Laughlin removed his sunglasses then, and Michaela had to swallow her astonishment. He had the most gorgeous deep blue eyes she'd ever seen in her life. When he took off his hat and unfastened the top two buttons of his cassock, his whole image was suddenly transformed. Michaela stared dumbly. If he shaved and washed his hair, the good father would be a very attractive man!

He saw her staring and smiled as he pulled on the front of his tunic to let a little air in. "The Church has us dressed this way to ensure humility," he said wryly. "Since we won't be goin' to hell, they figure we ought to experience a little of it right here on earth."

"You're Irish," she said, amused.

"Indeed I am, lass."

Suddenly the "lass" and "me child" routine seemed forced. When he was covered up, and his image more nondescript, it was easier to accept the terminology, though now that she thought about it, it really seemed more appropriate coming from a man twice Father O'Laughlin's age. In fact, this guy was not all that much older than, say, her triumvirate of gentlemen friends back home—Mark, John and Matt.

"You aren't Catholic, by any chance, are you?" he asked. Michaela shook her head. "No."

"That's good. I shan't be offendin' you so easily, then."

Father Tucino laughed. He hadn't said a single word, seeming to defer to his companion. But, as he picked up his beer, he gestured toward Michaela. "Maybe the *señorita* would like something to drink, *padre*," he said.

Father O'Laughlin gasped with dismay. "Aye, brother, you're right to mention it. I'm a terrible host. Forgive me, Miss Emory. Would you be wantin' a cola, perchance?"

Michaela smiled, thankful for the excuse to stick around for a while. Getting to know these priests could prove to be useful. She needed friends—people who knew the country and might give her a good tip for her story. And with Susana in jail, she had no one in Montagua to turn to for help.

"Is a cola my only choice?" she asked.

Father O'Laughlin chuckled, giving her a decidedly secular smile. "No, Miss Emory. Beer is permitted. Especially in the company of two men of the cloth." He signaled for another beer.

"Dos," Father Tucino added eagerly.

Michaela could see where the good father had gotten his potbelly. She watched Father O'Laughlin take a long draw on his beer, the muscles in his neck rippling as he drank. She sensed a strong, very masculine physique under the priestly garb.

She shifted her gaze to the second clergyman. Father Tucino kept a wary eye on the street while he waited for his drink. His behavior added to her growing conviction that the priests were involved in more than just saving souls.

"Tell me, Miss Emory— It *is* Miss, isn't it?" Father O'Laughlin asked.

"Yes."

"Tell me, what are you doin' in Montagua, if you don't mind me askin'?"

The bartender brought the beers. Michaela tapped her bottle with her fingernail, studying the priests, trying to decide how candid she should be. She figured it couldn't hurt to be cautious.

"I'm a reporter, Father," she began. "I'm on assignment. Just arrived today."

"A reporter, are you? Very interesting. Very interesting, indeed. And who might you write for?"

Michaela took a long drink. The beer wasn't cold, but it was wet. "The *Daily News Bulletin* in Washington."

"Really, now? And what is it you're writin' about, if you'll forgive me curiosity?"

She observed him, getting a very strange feeling. Something about the good father wasn't ringing true. The accent had a way of fading. Could it be too many years away from Ireland, or might there be another explanation?

"I'm doing a story on the politics of Pangonia," she said, carefully choosing her words.

"And what is it about the politics of a little country like ours that would interest you, lass?"

Michaela picked up her beer and took a swallow, wanting to give herself time to think. She decided not to mention Susana, yet she knew if she didn't give out some information, her chances of gaining his confidence would be nil.

"Not a lot has been written on the April First Movement back in the States. My paper thought it justified looking into."

"Ah, you know about MAP," he said.

She decided to crank it up a notch. "I know a little. But tell me, what do you think of Reed Lakesly, Father?"

He gave her a long hard look before he spoke. "That is a very sensitive question, as you must understand. And I am but a simple priest, Miss Emory."

Michaela took another swig of beer. "Perhaps not so simple as you might like to appear, Father," she said.

He gave her a lazy grin. "Aye, but it's hard to know when you're among friends. If you get me meanin'."

She considered the situation. She was positive now that the priest knew more than he was letting on. "I've got the least to lose, Father O'Laughlin, so maybe I should state my theory."

"I like a woman who's not afraid to take the bull by the horns, as you might say. You don't see a lot of that in Pangonia. Please proceed."

"They way I figure it, you and Father Tucino are probably both sympathetic to the April First Movement, if not actually involved in it. Why else would you want to avoid dealing with the police? Frankly, I hope you are with MAP because I want to interview Reed Lakesly. What I'm saying, Father O'Laughlin, is that I'd like your help."

The priests exchanged looks. "You don't mince words, do you, lass?"

"I don't expect you to divulge any secrets," Michaela said, "but if you could pass the word on to Mr. Lakesly that I'd like to interview him, I'd be most grateful."

"You're makin' some pretty big assumptions. As I understand it, Reed Lakesly doesn't hold press conferences."

"I respect that. But I'm in a position to help him get his story out to the rest of the world, if he's willing to help me in return. Any help you could give me would be appreciated. I'd like the name of somebody I can contact. I need an address, a telephone number, someplace I can go stand with a flower in my lapel. Whatever it takes."

Father O'Laughlin smiled, his eyes drifting down her. His gaze froze for a long second where her thighs protruded from her skirt. "I can't promise anything, Miss Emory, but let me look into the matter. There may be a few places around Montagua where I can inquire on your behalf."

"I would be eternally grateful," she replied. She opened her purse and took out a twenty-dollar bill. "Perhaps, as a sign of good faith, I can make a small donation to the Church." She handed the priest the bill.

O'Laughlin took the money, handing it to Father Tucino, who promptly tucked it into his purse. "You are indeed most generous. Bless you." He stroked his stubbled chin thoughtfully. "Could I ask a question, lass?"

"Certainly."

"Why is it so important you talk to Lakesly?"

"I need a story, Father. My career, maybe even my solvency, is turning on it. If Reed Lakesly is the leader of the movement, he's the man to talk to."

"I see."

"How long do you think it will be before I might hear something?" she asked.

"If I'm able to be of help, I'll get word to you soon. Where are you stayin', Miss Emory?"

"At the Hotel El Presidente."

O'Laughlin nodded, storing away the information. He stared at her, his deep blue eyes watching her every expression. Then he smiled. Suddenly he seemed like a completely different man—not carnal, exactly, but he didn't look pastoral, either.

"This has been an interesting conversation," he said absently, fingering his wooden cross.

Michaela had trouble meeting his gaze. Again, something wasn't ringing true. Was it because he was so good-looking, so...unpriestly?

Father Tucino, who seemed unduly nervous, leaned close and muttered something in Spanish. Michaela couldn't hear what was being said, and probably wouldn't have understood it if she had.

"My brother suggests that we should be on our way, lass. And he's right," Father O'Laughlin said. He turned to Father Tucino and they exchanged a few more words in Spanish. The hefty priest then produced some bank notes from his purse.

"Here, let me get the beer," Michaela said, opening her purse. "I changed some money at the airport."

Father O'Laughlin looked at the crisp bill. "You're most generous, me child."

"You did me a kindness," she said. "I'd like to return the favor."

"Avoidin' the search benefited us as much as you. We're beholdin' to *you*, Miss Emory, for giving us the excuse."

She gazed into his deep blue eyes, feeling a momentary sense of helplessness. Michaela was trying hard not to think of him as a man, even though it was proving extremely difficult to think of him as a priest. What was Father O'Laughlin like in the pulpit? Funny, but it was as hard to imagine him there as...say, Jack Ellison. The thought made her chuckle out loud.

"You find our gratitude amusin', my child?"

"I find everything here in Pangonia a bit unreal."

"This isn't Kansas."

"No, you're right about that."

He signaled the bartender, who came to the table. Michaela handed the man the Pangonian pesos. Father Tucino went to the door to study the street while they waited for her change. When it arrived, Father O'Laughlin put on his sunglasses and his hat. They got to their feet and went out the door under the watchful gaze of dozens of eyes.

"It has indeed been a pleasure talkin' to you, lass," he said, his eyes twinkling. "You'll be hearin' from me soon."

"I hope so."

He glanced at the traffic, slowly moving through the roadblock. "Do you have transportation, Miss Emory?"

"I'm sure my taxi's gone on to the hotel."

"Let us get you another, then. I don't think you'll be wantin' to walk alone."

Father O'Laughlin said something to Father Tucino, who went to the curb. After some emphatic arm waving he attracted an empty taxi. As it pulled up to the curb, Michaela shook Father Tucino's hand, then Father O'Laughlin's. "Thank you so much," she said.

The younger priest smiled with devilish satisfaction, then took her by the shoulders and kissed her cheek. "God bless you, me child. Be careful." With that, he helped her into the taxi.

Michaela was stunned by his affection, caught completely off guard. She wasn't quite sure what had happened, or what it might have meant, but she was absolutely certain of one thing—the scent of Father O'Laughlin's cologne. It was Giorgio!

As the taxi pulled into traffic, she glanced back through the window at the smiling priests, both waving goodbye. Now what in the world, she wondered, would an Irish priest living in Pangonia be doing wearing an American cologne?

CHAPTER THREE

AFTER THE PORTER HAD gone, Michaela looked around her hotel room. It was old-fashioned, with solid furniture, high ceilings and a gracious, but not-quite-elegant air. Finally she would be able to relax. She tested the bed. It was soft and inviting, so she took off her dress and stretched out, sighing with relief.

Michaela glanced out the tall windows at the ornate architecture of the building across the street. She'd eschewed the larger modern hotels on the outskirts of the city in favor of the Hotel El Presidente. Situated in the old quarter, it seemed closer to the action—though it wasn't clear what the action was going to be. One thing was certain, though: If she wanted a good story, she would have to dig for it.

Running into the priests at the roadblock had been a stroke of luck. Whether they'd end up helping or not, remained to be seen. Still, she was hopeful.

Thinking about the good fathers, Michaela conjured up a vivid image of Father O'Laughlin. She visualized him rubbing his stubbled chin as he looked at her in that terribly unpriestly manner of his. Well, she told herself, priests were human, too, so his reaction shouldn't have come as a surprise—even if it wasn't completely admirable.

O'Laughlin certainly was an interesting character, though. His awareness of her—his easy charm, his wryness and sexual presence—were clearly beyond the norm for someone of his vocation. If he was involved in MAP, as she suspected, his life had to be terribly fascinating. How did he balance his politics and his religion, his concerns for this life and the next?

Though their encounter hadn't been particularly dramatic, Michaela had enjoyed every minute of it. Being stopped at a roadblock might be commonplace in Pangonia, but beside budget hearings and playing footsie with Jack Ellison, it was the stuff of adventure. It had gotten her journalistic juices flowing.

But logic told her that she couldn't place all her faith in a chance encounter. Her funds were limited. Every day had to count. Back in Washington, she had spent hours trying to decide how best to focus her efforts. Gaining access to Susana Riveros was a top priority, but her friend's plight was intertwined with Reed Lakesly and the MAP. As Jack Ellison had pointed out, to find the truth about Susana, she would have to uncover the larger truth behind the revolution.

Michaela had talked over strategy with Chelsea, too, wanting to be absolutely certain in her own mind that publicity generated by a story on Susana wouldn't do more harm than good. Chelsea convinced her that writing about MAP was precisely what Susana wanted. Nothing, she'd argued, gave a nefarious government pause like the eyes of the world looking over its shoulder.

The real question was how to get to Susana. Chelsea had suggested petitioning the president. Michaela thought a better approach might be to work through Susana's paper, *La Pensa*.

"If the editor is the son of the president of the country," she'd argued, "he's got to have some influence."

"Lord knows, you've had experience manipulating difficult editors," Chelsea had agreed.

The prospect wasn't an appealing one, but Chelsea was right—she'd been down that particular path before. It didn't stop her from hating the struggle, though.

Any woman alone, even a professional doing her job, faced dangers and unpleasantness that were perhaps even more ominous in a society like this one, where men's attitudes toward women were antediluvian. Michaela had had a taste of what that felt like already, when she'd walked the gauntlet in the bar.

She deeply resented being objectified, but she also knew that she wasn't going to change things. Machismo was a way of life here, and not always unappreciated by the women who lived with it. In any case, she hadn't come to Pangonia to be a social critic; she was a reporter after a story. Her only recourse was to cope as best she could and stay focused on her work.

Michaela drew a long breath and tried to relax. It was midafternoon, when people in this part of the world had their lunch and a siesta. She wasn't hungry, so she decided to take a nap before heading over to *La Pensa*.

Letting the tension drain from her body, Michaela was surprised at how readily Father O'Laughlin's image came to mind. She pondered why that would be. It horrified her to think there was a sexual thing at play, because if not sick, being attracted to a man of the cloth was at the very least unproductive. Could it be the combination of his reaction to her—the unmistakable awareness on his part—and the fact that he was forbidden, which had made such a deep impression on her?

Had he felt something special, too? It was idle curiosity, but she was intrigued by the possibilities, if only as a mental game. They came from worlds apart, but they did speak the same language and they'd definitely connected at some level. In a way it was too bad he was a priest, yet in another way she liked the psychological titillation, knowing it couldn't go anywhere.

As Michaela began to get drowsy, she wondered if she might not be missing a good bet. If she couldn't get an interview with Reed Lakesly, then the roguish priest would make a good human-interest story. He was an alluring person, a man of many contradictions.

The questions she could ask him filled her head: What had led him to a life in the priesthood? How did he come to care so much about the people of Pangonia? How did he cope with the temptations of the temporal world? Thinking about him, Michaela felt a strange contentment. Her eyes closed and she drifted off.

An hour later, she was awakened by a tapping on her door. She opened her eyes and looked around. It took a moment for her to figure out where she was. She'd been dreaming. That island in the travel magazine again. And she hadn't been alone. Of all people, she'd been with the Irish priest!

Again there was a rap on the door. "Yes?" she called out as she got up, looking around to figure out what to put on.

"It is the maid, *señorita.*"

Michaela grabbed her yellow terry robe and went to the door. Opening it, she found a tiny woman with dark eyes, olive skin and well-defined, strong features.

"Sorry," she said, "but I have brought more towels."

"Oh, okay." Michaela stepped back. The woman took an armful of towels from her cart and carried them to the bathroom.

On her way out the maid stopped to look at Michaela. Her expression was not hostile, but it had a critical air about it. "So you are the American lady who writes in the newspaper."

Michaela's brows rose. "How did you know that?"

"There is talk, *señorita.* One hears these things."

Michaela remembered that on the hotel registration form she'd put down "journalist" as her occupation. Hotel gossip. That's what it probably was. Or was it?

A paranoid thought struck her. Maybe the maid wasn't simply another curious person. Maybe she was with MAP. Or perhaps even a government spy. Either was possible. It would be very useful to know where the maid's sympathies lay. After all, if she, like the priests, was a supporter of Lakesly, this might be another chance to put out feelers for an interview.

"So, you've heard that I'm a reporter, have you? Has anyone told you what I've come to Pangonia to write about?"

"It is not for me to say."

Michaela seized the chance to ask a few questions. "I'm here to write about MAP," she said, watching the maid's reaction.

The woman frowned. "What is this, *señorita*?"

"The Movimiento Abril Primero."

"*O, sí, sí.* I know it, but not by those words."

The response seemed honest. "What do think about it?"

"I am the maid, *señorita*, not the president."

Michaela laughed. "Don't you have any ideas, though?"

The woman appraised her. "You are no longer in America, *señorita*. Here we are careful with the words. Understand?"

Michaela knew she was being warned, but she wasn't sure what against. Perhaps she was overreacting. It was possible that the woman simply didn't want to talk about a sensitive issue. "I didn't mean to put you in an awkward position."

The maid shrugged.

"Can you tell me how the people generally feel about MAP?"

"Some think one way, the others think another."

Michaela could see that she wasn't getting very far, but to get a feel for conditions in Pangonia, she had to talk to as many people as possible. She decided to try another tack. "Surely some people support the president."

The maid smiled. "He has a large family, *señorita*."

Michaela laughed, suddenly liking the woman. She gestured toward two armchairs. "Do you have time to sit and talk?"

"They pay me for half a day's work, but I work a day and a half, so perhaps I can talk for a little minute."

Once they'd settled, Michaela asked, "What is your name?"

"Rosita."

"Mine is Michaela."

"It is pretty," the maid said. "Do you have a husband?"

"No."

"Are you rich?"

"No," Michaela replied.

"Then you are very brave."

"Why do you say that?"

"You are far from home. This country is not the place for a girl alone."

"What about you, Rosita? Do you have a husband?"

"*Sí,* but Julio is in the country."

"Then you are alone in Montagua, too?"

"Yes, *señorita.*"

"Then maybe we are not so different."

Rosita appraised her. Michaela could tell the woman was being cautious. She wished she knew why. The more she thought about it, the more she realized that this encounter couldn't have been completely accidental.

The maid slowly got to her feet. "Forgive me, I must go."

Michaela was disappointed. She also rose.

Rosita went to the door. Michaela considered asking if she knew Father O'Laughlin, but if Rosita worked for the government, bringing up his name could be dangerous. Besides, she didn't want to draw attention to herself unnecessarily.

"I enjoyed talking to you, Rosita," she said. "I don't have a lot of time here in Pangonia, and I want to learn as much as I can. What you think is important to me."

"Be careful who you speak with, *señorita,*" the woman said, giving her a meaningful look. "Maybe we will talk again, no?"

"I'd like that," Michaela told her. "Anytime you're free."

"*Adiós, señorita.*" Rosita left, closing the door.

Only one thing was certain—caution and secrecy seemed to be a way of life here. But she'd made a fairly good start. If luck was with her, Rosita might drop by again. And it might be clearer the next time they spoke whose side she was really one. Trust came slowly in a society like this. One step at a time, Mike, she told herself. One step at a time.

She checked her watch. If she was going to get over to the offices of *La Pensa* that afternoon, she had to hurry. Every nonproductive hour was costing her.

MICHAELA'S TAXI TOOK her to the newspaper's offices. She had changed into a cotton summer dress that was scooped in the front, but not too low. The hem of the slim skirt came to just above her knee. After her experience in the bar, she'd decided that a more reserved image would serve her better. After all, even the Irish priest had noticed her short skirt, though admittedly not altogether with disapproval.

After paying the driver, she got out of the taxi and peered up at the ornate three-story building. Its heavy front door was guarded by two policemen. Michaela wondered whether they were there to keep the truth in or out. If Susana Riveros's experience was any indication, it could be both.

She hadn't been as close to Susana at college as Chelsea, but the Pangonian reporter's plight disturbed her. Although journalists were trained to probe the truth, not champion causes, they were people, too, and Michaela couldn't help letting her feelings guide her. Still, she knew she'd have to be careful. Even the maid, Rosita, had said as much.

Michaela had no appointment, but she'd already decided she'd go right to the top and ask to speak with Bernardo de Falcón. If she was going to make the most of her limited time, she'd have to be assumptive. A good reporter made things happen.

She got past the policemen by showing her press card. Once inside, she encountered a receptionist who spoke only a couple of words of English. Eventually, after explaining that she wished to see Bernardo de Falcón, Michaela was shown to a room on the third floor. She waited ten minutes, not knowing whether the editor had agreed to see her or not.

Eventually the door opened and a bald, bearded man in his mid-thirties entered the room. He wore wire-rimmed glasses and was dressed in an expensive Italian suit. Seeing her, his face registered first surprise, then growing admiration. For a long moment he didn't speak. Michaela instantly had him pegged.

His facial expression told her the most—the lilt of his brow, the slowly-forming curl of his lip—but there was also the flower in the lapel of his jacket, and the way he held himself. Bernardo de Falcón clearly fancied himself a Latin lover, a real lady-killer, Señor Amor of Montagua.

Meanwhile his look had turned steamy and languorous. "Miss Em-or-y?" he finally said, lowering his voice and stretching out the syllables, letting the *r* roll off his tongue.

"Yes."

He elevated his chin slightly. "I am Bernardo de Falcón. I understand you wish to see me."

Michaela got up. "Mr. de Falcón," she said, extending her hand. "I'm so pleased to meet you."

Michaela towered over him by two or three inches. Bernardo took half a step back, drawing himself up. The questioning look on his face slowly turned to admiration once more. As he stared into her eyes, his delight grew. "The pleasure is mine, I assure you," he said, clutching her hand. "How can I be of service?"

Michaela glanced around. "I'd like to discuss a very confidential matter with you."

Bernardo pounced on the opportunity. "Then come to my office, please." Guiding her through the door, he pressed his hand against her waist. As he drew close, she could hear him inhaling her scent, almost murmuring, but not quite.

Michaela's first instinct was to be wary, but at the same time she couldn't help but be amused by his effusiveness—the theatrical show of self-importance. She might have been a bit unsure where Father O'Laughlin had been coming from, but this guy left nothing to the imagination.

They went into the editor's formal, antique-filled office. Bernardo showed her to a sitting area with a love seat and two Louis XIV chairs. She sat on the love seat. There were Persian carpets on the floor, a vase of flowers on a nearby table. The room smelled of roses and tobacco smoke.

Michaela glanced around. There were hardly any papers or files, no sign of work being done. The antique desk was clear. Jack Ellison's office, while neat, was filled with evidence of journalistic activity. Michaela immediately wondered if Bernardo was just window dressing, a dilettante who left the real work to others.

"I appreciate you taking the time to talk to me," she said.

"Not at all," he replied, sitting in one of the chairs. "Can I offer you something to drink? Coffee, perhaps, or tea?"

"No, thank you."

"Something a tiny bit stronger? I have a lovely champagne I keep for special guests." He twitched his eyebrows and smiled.

"No. Thank you very much, but I don't care for anything."

He checked out her legs in an obvious, unabashed manner. Then he folded his hands on his knee, trying to look pensive. "What is it you wish to discuss, Miss Emory?"

Michaela didn't like playing the coquette, but time was of the essence, considering her limited finances, and Bernardo de Falcón was obviously the kind of man who opted for only one type of communication. "May I be direct?" she asked, lowering her voice as he had, and pronouncing the words breathlessly.

"Most assuredly, Miss Em-or-y." Again he drew out the pronunciation of her name, as though by stroking it, he was stroking her.

"I would be grateful...eternally grateful...if you would help me get an interview with Susana Riveros."

Her statement hit him like a splash of cold water. His look turned icy. "How is it you know about her?"

"Susana was a classmate at the University of Arizona. We weren't really close friends, but when I heard what happened to her, I became most concerned. I want to visit her."

Bernardo de Falcón appeared unsure what to say. He shifted uncomfortably. "What makes you think I could be of help? Miss Riveros was an employee of *La Pensa*, it is true, but her case is in the hands of the government now."

"I was given to understand you have influence with the government, Mr. de Falcón." she said coyly.

"I am the son of the president, as you surely know, but my responsibilities are solely with the newspaper."

"My last assignment was with the U.S. Congress," Michaela said sweetly. "I observed that men with power are often able to accomplish impressive things, even outside their major area of responsibility. Surely it is the same in Pangonia."

Bernardo eyed her, considering her words carefully before answering. "This is true, of course. But I, like others, take my responsibilities most seriously."

"I know," she said. "Even before I left the States, I heard you were a man of considerable integrity."

His wariness turned to delight. "Ah, I am known there?"

"In certain journalistic circles. My boss mentioned you most respectfully."

He allowed himself a moment of satisfaction, then grew serious again. "What is it you wish to accomplish with Miss Riveros, may I ask? Is your interest personal or professional?"

Michaela sensed she might be on the right track. Bernardo's pride was apparently his weakness. With luck, she thought, it could also be his downfall. "I would like to write her story."

"Then it's professional."

"It's both."

He looked unhappy. "I can tell you with confidence that the government has no interest in having you do a story on her. Miss Riveros was a traitor to our cause. The president does not wish to give currency to her ideas."

"Surely the president wouldn't want the world to think there is no room in Pangonia for dissent."

"With all due respect, Miss Emory, what the world thinks is secondary to our domestic tranquillity. We are a happy people in a happy country. Those who seek to destroy our tranquillity are traitors to us all."

Was he thinking exclusively of Susana when he said that, or could there be a warning to her in his words? Michaela wasn't absolutely sure, but somehow Bernardo didn't seem capable of that sort of subtlety.

"That may be, Mr. de Falcón, but surely the government is not so insecure that it is afraid for outsiders to look into its jail cells. If Susana Riveros is a false prophet, what do you have to fear?"

Bernardo smiled. "You are very eloquent and very clever, Miss Emory, but I am unsure of your passion for writing on this subject. Surely there are other things in our country that could be of equal interest. What about our culture—Pangonian art, for example?"

"If that was my interest, I would have gone to the ministry of culture. I came to you, Mr. de Falcón, because I want to write a vital, important story, and you are the heartbeat of journalism in this country."

He was unable to repress his smile. "You are very astute," he said. "What you say is true, of course. Personally, I have no objection to you interviewing Miss Riveros, but unfortunately the matter is not in my hands."

Michaela blinked with dismay. Bernardo seemed suddenly to realize that the truth did not reflect well on him. He shifted uncomfortably, looking unhappy. She decided to change her tack.

She recrossed her legs, instantly drawing Bernardo's eye. "What are the chances I might be able to speak with your father?" she asked. "Would he grant me an interview, do you think?"

"No. It is impossible," he replied without hesitation.

"I'm terribly disappointed."

Bernardo weighed the situation, obviously trying to find some course of action that would give him an advantage. Michaela let him stew over it for a minute. As he thought, he checked out her figure again, evidently finding the potential benefits worth some extra effort.

Michaela had trouble maintaining the pleasant expression she'd affected. She thought back on her days as a beauty contestant, days she'd worked hard to put behind her. But this was war, a battle of survival that Bernardo de Falcón couldn't begin to understand.

He tapped his chin with his finger, deep in thought. It was easy to see that visions of romantic weekends were going through his head. Jack Ellison, Latin-style, she thought.

She decided to pull out all the stops. "I must be honest, Mr. de Falcón," she said, imploringly. "I badly need a good story. My job probably depends on it. If I can't interview Susana, I'll try to find Reed Lakesly."

Bernardo drew himself up. "This man is of no consequence, Miss Emory. He is not worthy of your attention. Basically, he's a bandit."

"I thought he was popular with the people and had their support."

He smiled. "That's a romantic notion, one you North Americans are always so ready to embrace."

"But he'd make a great story. As a journalist yourself, you must see that."

"This is not a matter for a woman to become involved in. Believe me, you do not wish to pursue this."

Michaela had to bite her tongue. This jerk was posing the greatest challenge to her self-control she'd ever faced. But she held her smile. "Why do you say that?" she asked, trying hard to sound innocent.

"You will never find Lakesly, no matter how hard you try. I can name half-a-dozen army colonels who would gladly give you their daughters in slavery for the information of how to locate him. Lakesly is not a man to be taken lightly."

"You are not encouraging me, Mr. de Falcón," she said with obvious disappointment. "You give me no hope."

He tapped his fingertips together as he contemplated the remark. "Miss Emory, I do not mean to be inhospitable. I have been thinking how I can be of help to you, and I believe I have an idea."

Michaela felt a tiny surge of hope.

"The president is having a press conference in the morning," Bernardo went on. "It is not open to all the media, but only to a few select journalists. Perhaps I can arrange for you to come with me. Would this be of interest?''

Michaela was elated. "I'd love to go!"

Bernardo beamed. "Then I shall see that you are able to attend, Miss Emory."

"Please call me Michaela, if you wish," she said, signaling her gratitude.

He liked that. "I am honored. And to you, I am Bernardo."

It was getting harder and harder, but she gave him her prettiest smile.

"Our acquaintance is very brief," he said, "but there is no reason it can't be an amicable one. Don't you agree?"

"You've been very kind, Bernardo."

"I'm sure we can find a good story for you—one that doesn't involve revolutionaries."

"I'd be grateful for any help you can give me."

The editor puffed out his chest, apparently pleased with himself. "The press conference is at ten. I will pick you up at nine, if I may. Where are you staying, Michaela?"

"At the El Presidente."

"Excellent."

She'd gotten her foot in the door, though it was possible Bernardo would turn out to be all talk and no do. He might also want his payoff before she produced hers, but that was routine with men. Michaela sighed. It was the same old thing, but with some finesse, a slightly different spin than what she was used to. She'd simply have to find a way around it. She'd dealt with it before, though admittedly, not Latin-style.

"Well, I've taken a good deal of your time, Bernardo," she said. "I'll be running along."

She got to her feet and so did he. They went to the door, and he escorted her to the entrance of the outer suite, where they shook hands. This time Bernardo insisted on holding hers for an extra-long time, grasping it in both of his. He gave her a penetrating look, filled with a machismo that

definitely fell short of being sexy. In some men, she could
see, it played better than in others.

"I am so glad you came to me first," he said, again lowering his voice to suggest intimacy.

Michaela could see the game was already defined. Mask-
ing her true feelings, she gave him a vaguely coquettish look
and said, "So am I, Bernardo."

She turned to go, but he reached out and took her arm,
stopping her. He plucked the flower from his lapel, sniffed
it, then pressed it into her palm. "Until tomorrow," he
purred.

Her teeth grinding, Michaela drew the blossom to her
heart and turned to go, rolling her eyes as she went out the
door. She hated having to choose between principle and
survival, but fate seemed to have given her little choice.

Michaela found a taxi and climbed into the back seat,
telling the driver to take her to the El Presidente. Despite the
heat, she was covered with goose bumps. When women
ruled the world, she said to herself, guys like Bernardo de
Falcón would be the first to be sent off to the reeducation
camps.

But as she rode along, the sticky tropical air wafting in the
window, a smile crept over her face. She was making progress and, in the end, that was what mattered most.

Between her contact with Father O'Laughlin and Bernardo—and if luck was with her, even Rosita—Michaela
had done all right for her first day in Montagua. The trick
was to capitalize on those opportunities.

The doorman at the hotel opened the door of the taxi as
she paid the driver. Stepping onto the sidewalk, she noticed
a boy of about eight standing at the entrance. He stared at
her with soulful eyes. He was wearing shorts, sandals and a
badly worn shirt.

Michaela considered rummaging through her purse for
another package of gum or a few coins, when the boy
marched up to her and said in a firm voice, "Señorita
Emory?"

She was surprised. "Yes."

He took a tightly folded piece of paper from his pocket and handed it to her. Michaela carefully unwrapped it and found a message written in pencil in block letters. It said, "This is Pablo. He will be at the fountain in the square at the end of the street that runs along the side of the hotel at seven o'clock tonight. Go where he takes you." It was signed, "O."

When she looked up, the boy was gone.

CHAPTER FOUR

MICHAELA WAS NERVOUS and excited. She left the hotel early, unsure what to expect from her clandestine meeting, but hopeful that whatever transpired would lead eventually to an interview with Reed Lakesly.

The rendezvous place Father O'Laughlin had indicated in his note proved to be less than a hundred yards from her hotel. The square itself was surrounded on all four sides by colorful old stucco-and-wrought-iron structures. A tall fountain stood in the center of a flower-filled garden.

It was dusk and everything was in shadow, but Michaela immediately saw the boy, Pablo, waiting. The shops were open and there were a number of people milling about. Though this was an older section of town, it was one of the better neighborhoods. Michaela attracted admiring glances, but she wasn't bothered.

Uncertain what she was getting into, she made a circuit of the area, alert for anything suspicious, though she wasn't sure what kind of danger to be on the lookout for. Michaela figured she was taking a chance in trying to contact Reed Lakesly, but she'd known from the first that this assignment wouldn't be like covering the White House Easter-egg hunt.

As nearly as she could tell, there was nothing amiss, so she crossed to the middle of the square. When he spotted her, Pablo rose.

"*Buenas noches,*" she said, as the boy nodded.

With a tilt of his head, Pablo indicated for her to follow him. They set off at a brisk pace, ducking down a side street. Michaela was glad she had worn flats, because she never could have kept up with him in heels—not over cobble-stones.

"You training for the Pangonian Olympic team, kid, or is this a way to avoid getting mugged?"

Pablo ignored her question and she figured that he probably didn't understand much English. They wound through the maze of narrow streets in an older quarter. She'd have liked to slow down enough to enjoy what she was seeing, but Pablo's gait made it impossible.

They were soon in a residential area. Most of the buildings were apartments. Lights were on and windows open, allowing music and cooking smells into the streets. Older children were still outside, laughing and talking in small groups. Old men sat on stoops. Young men smoking cigarettes watched Michaela hurrying along with the boy.

She was into aerobics, but Pablo's pace managed to get her heartbeat up. She wondered why he was in such a hurry.

Rounding a corner, she soon found out. The boy grabbed her wrist and pulled her into a dark alleyway between two buildings. He put his finger to his lips, indicating she should be quiet. Pablo listened, probably for the sound of footsteps.

After a minute or two they continued their trek, this time at a more leisurely pace. Michaela glanced at the kid, knowing there'd be no explanation. But then, one wasn't necessary. This was no ordinary little boy doing a favor for a priest. She was in the hands of the Movimiento Abril Primero.

They came to another small square, dominated by a parish church—a likely place to meet a priest, she decided. They waited in the shadows long enough for Pablo to survey the situation. Then they proceeded to the church.

The interior was dank and lit only by candles. A couple of parishioners were kneeling at the front of the nave, apparently praying. An old woman stood by a bank of votive candles. She stared at Michaela, then beckoned her forward. Michaela turned to Pablo, but he was gone.

She stepped toward the woman, who handed her a prayer book. Michaela slipped into a pew. Nothing happened. Then she glanced down at the prayer book, noticing a tiny slip of paper sticking out from between the pages. There was a brief message printed in the same block letters as the note Pablo had given her that morning. It read, "Confess your sins."

Michaela rolled her eyes, wondering if it was a joke or an attempt at a religious conversion. What was she supposed to do? Throw herself prostrate at the altar? Looking around, her gaze eventually fell on the confessional. Then it struck her. That's where she'd find Father O'Laughlin!

Michaela moved toward the confessional. She could hear the hushed voice of a woman and the more muted tones of the priest. A moment later, an older woman dressed in black pushed the curtain aside and left.

Glancing about to make sure no one was watching, Michaela slipped inside and closed the heavy curtain. It was dark. She couldn't see through the screen separating her from the priest, though she sensed his presence.

A flash of whimsy struck her. Michaela said, "Father, I have sinned."

There was a low chuckle, then a familiar voice with a thick Irish brogue said, "I wouldn't exactly call a visit to *La Pensa* a sin, lass, but it's pretty close."

"You've been spying on me," she said with indignation.

"You can't be too careful in this business."

"Why didn't you tell me you were with the MAP?"

"Shh!" he admonished. "Careful."

"Well, what are we supposed to do? Speak pig Latin?"

"Did you have the same smart mouth this afternoon, when you talked to the boys at *La Pensa*, Miss Emory?"

The barb angered her, but she told herself she had to keep her cool. Thus far, Father O'Laughlin was her best contact, and her main hope of interviewing Lakesly. "What's with this snoopy stuff, Father? What's going on?"

"That's what I'd like to know. What were you doing, going to the government press?"

"I went to get some help."

"With what?"

"A story."

"Be more specific," he said.

The Irish accent had lapsed. In spite of her resolve to be diplomatic, she considered challenging him, but thought better of it. "I want to interview Susana Riveros," she said, "and I asked *La Pensa* for help."

"You might as well ask the devil for advice on getting into heaven, lass," the priest replied, his accent returning.

"That may be. But I'm getting help from whatever source I can find."

"Well, if you want my help, you're going to have to make clear whose side you're on."

She sighed. "I'm not on anybody's side, Father. I'm a reporter. I convey the facts to my readers."

"Who did you talk to at the newspaper?"

"Bernardo de Falcón."

"Well," he said. "Went right to the top, didn't you?"

"I prefer not to deal with intermediaries," she said, her voice ripe with innuendo. "Present circumstances included."

"The government is one thing, the MAP is another," he shot back. "Tell me, what did Bernardo have to say?"

"Hey, Father, I'm the one who's supposed to ask the questions. I'm the reporter, remember?"

"In the confessional I ask the questions, me child."

"Then maybe we should meet on neutral ground."

"You're lucky we're talking to you at all," he whispered.

"Look, Father O'Laughlin, I'm not interested in getting into skirmishes between you and the government, the Pangonian press or anybody else. I'm a simple reporter who wants an interview. Are you going to help me or not?"

"I . . . That is, we . . . haven't decided yet."

"Well, what do you need to make a decision? A sworn affidavit? A vaccination certificate? Just tell me what you want and I'll try to deliver it."

"How do you know about Susana?" he asked.

"More questions," she said.

"I need to know." The accent had lapsed again, making her wonder.

Michaela told herself there was no sense letting the priest get on her nerves. He still could turn out to be a help. So she calmly explained how Chelsea had received the smuggled letter telling of Susana Riveros's plight.

"We need to talk," Father O'Laughlin said after a pause.

"I thought that's what we were doing."

"Not here," he said. "Leave the church. As you go out, turn left. About fifty yards on the right you'll see a small restaurant. It'll be closed, but knock. They'll admit you if it's safe. If they don't let you in, return to your hotel and I'll be in touch later, when it's safe. Otherwise we'll have dinner together. You haven't eaten, by the way, have you?"

"No."

Father O'Laughlin suddenly sounded as American as Jack Ellison. And she'd picked up the scent of Giorgio again. What was going on?

Sitting there, with nothing but his voice to relate to, Michaela recalled his eyes—his beautiful deep blue eyes—and rugged good looks. She also remembered the way he'd regarded her in the *taberna*. "Father O'Laughlin," she said, lowering her voice, "can I ask a personal question?"

"What, my child?"

"You aren't really Irish, are you?"

There was dead silence.

"Are you really a priest?" she asked.

He cleared his throat. "My, you *have* sinned," he said dryly. "I think thirty Hail Marys ought to take care of it, though. Go in peace."

MICHAELA STOOD just inside the front entrance of the church, wondering what she'd gotten into. Had she worked her way into the very heart of the Pangonian revolution? Or had she happened upon a few people on the fringe of the *movimiento* who were taking advantage of her for their own interests, whatever they might be? Was Father O'Laughlin for real, or merely a fraud?

More than once she'd wondered if she was a fool not to have stayed in Washington and contented herself with reporting the Byzantine undertakings on Capitol Hill. Even Chelsea had been skeptical about her plan, though she'd tried to be supportive. But Michaela had been determined to press ahead. Not that many stellar opportunities came along in a reporter's lifetime. Now she was more than ever convinced that this could be her shot.

But if she was to succeed, it would take more than writing talent. With Bernardo de Falcón she'd have to rely on her feminine wiles. With Father O'Laughlin the issues were less clear. It might come down to street smarts. One thing was certain: The good father liked to play games. The trouble was, she didn't know what kind of games and to what end.

She turned to look back down the aisle of the church before she stepped outside. As she did, she'd caught a glimpse of the priest leaving the confessional, the skirts of his cassock flying as he disappeared out a side door. Though her doubts about his authenticity had grown with each encounter, Michaela couldn't imagine him hearing confession unless he was really a priest.

With any luck at all, she'd ferret out the truth soon. Father O'Laughlin seemed eager to talk to her. And though she wasn't exactly comfortable with the idea of walking along the streets of a strange city at night, she was determined to find out just what the priest had in mind.

She headed along the narrow street that turned off from the square at a point just left of the church entrance. About fifty yards along the way she came to a cubbyhole restaurant, exactly as he'd told her. A sign in the window said Cerrado. The curtains were drawn, but there was a light on inside. She glanced around to make sure no one was watching her. She didn't see a soul, so she knocked on the door.

When no one answered, her heart sank. She knocked a second time. Finally the door opened and a pretty young woman with black hair and gleaming dark eyes stood there, looking her over.

"I'm—"

"Yes, I know," the woman said. "Come in."

Michaela stepped inside. The room was so small that there was room for only five tables. The walls were whitewashed and the floor was wooden. There were a couple of pictures on the walls, but no other decoration except a ceiling fan that revolved slowly, circulating cooking odors. She turned to the woman, who'd double-locked the door.

"I am Cecilia," the girl said, looking Michaela over. "Sit wherever you wish." She was tiny, though she had large breasts that amply filled her tank top. Her loose skirt came to below her knee. "You want a beer?"

Michaela started to decline, but changed her mind. "Yes, I would, thank you."

"Lucas said you drink it."

Michaela would have asked who Lucas was, but before she could, Cecilia had gone out the door toward the kitchen. Michaela glanced at the tables before going to the one against the back wall. Above it was one of the four sconces that dimly illuminated the room. She sat down and waited.

There were hushed voices coming from the back room and the faint sound of music. Cecilia returned, putting a bottle of beer on the table. The woman looked neither friendly nor particularly pleased by Michaela's presence.

"You want a glass?" Cecilia asked.

"No, the bottle's fine. No need to be formal," she said with a wan smile.

Cecilia found no humor in the remark. She pulled out a chair from another table and sat down, crossing her legs. She stared at Michaela. She hadn't yet smiled.

Michaela took a drink and put the bottle back down. "So you're from Washington, eh?"

"Yes."

"A reporter."

Michaela nodded. "Funny how everybody seems to know all about me, even before we meet."

"Lucas tell me everything."

"Who is Lucas?"

"The priest."

"Father O'Laughlin?"

Cecilia smiled for the first time. "Yeah, him."

"You find that amusing," Michaela said.

"I like Lucas as a priest. He's a very pretty one, no?"

Michaela appraised her. "Are you saying Father O'Laughlin is not really a priest?"

"He is and he isn't."

Michaela was annoyed with the obfuscation. Since coming to Pangonia, no one had given her straight answers. Not the maid, not Father O'Laughlin, and not even this woman. "Does the Church consider him a priest, or not?"

"No, *señorita*. To have a priest like Lucas would be a great scandal. He understands too much the heart of the woman."

Michaela blinked, suddenly understanding why the sexy priest had seemed so sexy. He wasn't a man of the cloth at all. The news pleased her, in a way. She hadn't been at all comfortable feeling an attraction toward a man of God. Yet at the same time she was annoyed that he'd deceived her. It was understandable that he'd want to carry on the ruse at the roadblock where there was immediate danger, but why in the confessional?

"Let me guess. Lucas is not Irish, either," she said.

"Lucas is Pangonian in his mind and in his heart," Cecilia said with a fervor that Michaela did not quite trust.

"How about in his birth certificate?"

The woman gave her a look of disapproval. "What matters besides the heart, *señorita?*"

"I take it he's American."

Cecilia rose to her feet. "I have things I must do. You want another beer, you call to me."

With that she walked out, swinging her hips in a way that could only be interpreted as hostile. "Lucas"—if that was his real name—seemed to arouse either passion or suspicion in most everyone. And the way Michaela figured it, that probably meant he wasn't a lightweight in the organization. He might even be one of Lakesly's lieutenants. She could only hope.

Michaela glanced around impatiently, wondering how long he intended to make her wait. He'd left the church the same time she had. What could be keeping him?

Several more minutes passed. Michaela heard voices in the back room, but there was no sign of the erstwhile priest. She was starting to get really annoyed, though she wasn't sure there was a lot she could do about it. Finally, her frustrations got the best of her, so she called Cecilia. The woman appeared.

"¿Sí? You want another beer?" she said tersely.

"No, I'm getting concerned that... Lucas isn't coming."

"If you're hungry, I bring you the food now."

"It's not that."

"Then what you want, *señorita?*"

Michaela sighed. "I'll have another beer."

The woman nodded. "Yes, Lucas said you like beer." She turned and disappeared into the back. Several moments later she returned, putting the bottle on the table and taking the empty one. "You want something else?"

"I'd like to know exactly what's going on. Is this normal to keep somebody waiting like this? I mean, are there security concerns or something of the kind?"

"Lucas is very important. Maybe you are not so important, *señorita.*"

That certainly put her in her place! "Yes. I'm beginning to see that."

Cecilia folded her arms under her ample breasts and gave another of the critical looks that seemed to be her trademark. "You not married?"

"No."

"Got somebody?"

"Does it matter?" Michaela asked.

"Not to me." With that she turned and walked from the room, leaving Michaela wondering.

She checked her watch. Half an hour had passed since she'd left the church. This fellow Lucas, or whoever he was, obviously ran on Latin time. She recalled his gorgeous eyes and magnetic presence. A fascinating man, she decided, if somewhat glib and discourteous. Where was he? She reached for her beer.

"I see they've not neglected you." It was a man's voice.

Michaela looked up, startled, not realizing anyone had come into the room. It was Father O'Laughlin—or Lucas, if Cecilia was to be believed.

The man was totally transformed. All evidence of his clerical identity had been swept away. He had on a pure white shirt with large, full sleeves and dark trousers. The shirt was unbuttoned to midchest; his dark hair was damp and combed back. His deep blue eyes, the ones she'd been recalling so fondly only moments earlier, were framed by incredibly thick lashes.

"My God," she said.

CHAPTER FIVE

MICHAELA FORCED HERSELF to close her mouth. The fact that she was flustered seemed to amuse him.

"You look surprised," he said. "Haven't you ever seen a priest out of uniform?"

"You're no priest, *Father.* You deceived me," she said.

"For a good cause." The Irish brogue was completely gone. The accent was straight American. "Sorry to keep you waiting, by the way," he said. "May I join you?"

"Of course." As Michaela grandly gestured for him to take a chair, she tipped over the bottle, dumping cold beer into her lap. She instantly jumped to her feet. "Damn," she said, brushing the front of her skirt.

Lucas quickly grabbed a napkin and handed it to her. She rubbed the growing spot on the front of her skirt, then tried to wipe herself dry where the beer had run down her legs. Fortunately, none of it had gotten into her shoes.

"Good Lord! Now I'm going to smell like a brewery," she said, glancing up at him.

Lucas was smiling, though more with sympathy than amusement. "Are you all right?"

"Yes, I suppose so."

"It doesn't look too bad."

She was mortified and still hadn't gotten used to the man's transformation. But there wasn't much she could do about either, so she finished drying herself off, then put the wet napkin on the table. They stared at each other.

Lucas was clean-shaven. He had a slight cleft in his chin that drew her eye. It was the first time she'd noticed it—he'd had several days' growth of beard that morning, and at the church he'd been hidden behind the screen. She became aware of his tangy clean smell, and the hint of Giorgio.

"I'd have been here earlier except I wanted to get cleaned up," he said, sounding genuinely apologetic for the first time.

"That's all right." She stared at him, wondering if she'd ever seen such an attractive man before.

"Let's get you another chair so you don't get more beer on you," he said, setting aside the one she'd been in and replacing it with a chair from another table.

Michaela slipped into it, mumbling her thanks as Lucas sat down across from her. He gave her a wide ironic smile, his teeth showing white in the dim light of the small room.

"I'll be glad to order you another drink," he said.

"No, no. I'm fine. I really don't want another."

"Hope you haven't said your Hail Marys yet." He chuckled.

She gave him a tight little smile. "Only fifteen."

"That's fifteen in the bank, then."

"I'm not Catholic," she said.

"I'm not, either. Will you forgive my pretense?"

"Is that what it was?" she asked, offended that he should toss it off so easily.

"When we met I was already in costume. I couldn't very well break character in the middle of the street."

"True. But you didn't have to continue the hoax. That confession business was totally unnecessary—not to mention sacrilegious."

"I thought it was fairly clever. Besides, you aren't the first person I've met in the confessional."

"Maybe. But I can't believe the Church sanctions you doing that. What about that old lady who was in there before me?"

"I listened with a compassionate heart, which is what she wanted. I suggested she pray, but didn't offer to forgive her."

"Where was the priest who was supposed to be there?"

His expression turned serious. "In the hospital. That usually follows one of General Juan de Falcón's interrogations."

Michaela was taken aback. She'd been so involved with his sexy transformation, and their bantering, that she'd forgotten the reality. Lucas was involved in a deadly game, and the stakes were high. Even now, Susana's life might be in jeopardy. If a priest would be beaten, even tortured, what would they do to her?

"I'm sorry, Lucas. I wasn't thinking. I guess I was offended by the idea that you were using the Church for your own ends . . . that seemed disrespectful to me."

"I understand. But we're a better friend of the Church than the government. And friends help each other out. It can be a very effective cover, as you yourself saw."

"Your point is well taken. So...am I to assume now that Lucas is your *nom de guerre?*" she asked, arching a brow.

"If you wish."

She sighed. "I *wish* to learn the truth. I've come here for a story. I need facts to write it and I'm prepared to help the MAP and Lakesly by publicizing your cause. But like any reporter, I don't relish being used. We journalists are funny that way."

"I'm not using you, Ms. Emory. The fact is, we all have to be careful, especially Reed. And forgive me, but you've already shown a propensity for playing both sides of the street."

"A good reporter doesn't play either side of the street. She looks for the truth wherever she can find it."

He contemplated her for a long time, his blue eyes at once challenging and seductive. "Then let's get down to business. I'd like to talk to you about Susana Riveros."

"That's fine, because I want to talk to you about Lakesly."

"I believe I asked you first, Miss Emory."

She rolled her eyes. "If we're going to play children's games, you may as well call me Michaela."

"Is that what your friends call you?"

"My close friends call me Mike."

"May I call you Mike?"

"For now, Michaela would be more appropriate," she said with a hint of sarcasm.

He gave her a most provocative grin. "I trust you'll tell me when it's time to call you Mike."

She nodded. "Oh, I'll let you know. It'll be somewhere around the time I start calling you by your real name, *Lucas*."

"You haven't forgiven me."

Somehow he managed to sound wounded, like an innocent child unjustly accused. She wasn't quite sure how he managed that—beseeching forgiveness with his eyes, though underneath she was sure he was mocking her. Michaela sighed, looking away.

He took the opportunity to call Cecilia from the back room. She entered, casting a hard glance Michaela's way. The two spoke in Spanish, giving Michaela a chance to look him over carefully.

She again noted the matted hair under the opening in his shirt, the broad shoulders and muscular physique. His cheeks were smooth and well tanned. For the first time she noticed a silvery scar running from his sideburn a quarter of the way across his cheek. Had he gotten it in combat? Perhaps an ambush by hostile government troops? She could picture him dragging off an injured comrade, himself bleeding from his wounds. Lucas, the guerilla hero and—yes—dashing ladies' man.

Cecilia had said he understood women, and watching the two of them, the thinly disguised admiration on her face, Michaela could visualize the whole scenario—women idolizing Lucas, men fearing and respecting him. She could almost write his story now. The classic man of action, with a corresponding penchant for adventure between the sheets, of course.

The conversation finished, Cecilia gave her another dark look and, lifting her chin, sashayed out of the room. Lucas turned to her, smiling. Michaela smiled back.

"She's rather fond of you, isn't she?"

"Members of clandestine organizations are close by necessity," he said.

"Giving the term 'comrades in arms' new meaning."

He chuckled. "Ah, a quick wit. You're not one to be taken lightly."

"Then let's hope you don't."

"Indeed." Bemusement touched his lips. "I ordered dinner for us. I hope you don't mind."

She studied him. "Fine. But while we're waiting, maybe we can have some straight talk."

"Good. Since you don't want to talk about Susana until I talk about Reed, why don't we start with Bernardo de Falcón?" he said. "What's going on between you two?"

Michaela paused, weighing her response carefully. "Sorry, but I can't discuss my sources."

"This is Montagua, Michaela. You may not have a choice."

She blinked. "What are you saying? That you intend to torture me if I won't talk?"

Before he could respond, Cecilia returned and put two beers on the table. Lucas picked up his, clinked it against hers in salute, then drank, the cords in his neck rippling as they had that morning in the *taberna*.

He put down his bottle and looked at her. "Torture, Michaela, is their game, not ours."

"Well, I'm not here to pass judgment either way. I'd like to interview Reed Lakesly, and all I want to know is whether or not you'll arrange it."

"Persistent, aren't you?"

"I'm here to do a job."

"So am I," he said. "The question is if we are willing to help each other in the process."

"I'm not partisan."

"That might work in Washington, but it won't wash here. General Juan de Falcón does not recognize neutrality. You're either for him or agin him."

"And what about you, Lucas? Are people either for you or against you?"

"I like to think the enlightened see the virtue of our cause."

"How do I know you aren't working for the general and this whole thing is a sham, a test?"

"For all I know, *you* work for the general, my dear Ms. Emory," he shot back. "And between us, who do you suppose stands to suffer more by the uncertainty?"

"Well, I can assure you, *my dear Lucas,* I do not work for the government of Pangonia, or any other government, for that matter."

"Hmm," he said. "We seem to be at an impasse. There must be some way to develop mutual trust." He fingered his beer bottle, looking her over.

Michaela knew where this was headed. Cecilia's remark about him understanding women so well was a major clue. His method of operation was obvious—seduce first and ask questions later.

She picked up her beer and nervously took a sip, aware that being on to his game gave her an advantage. But she also knew that even the most enlightened bird found the snake fascinating. "So where are we left?" she asked.

Cecilia entered with a tray and another icy look.

"I'd say we're about to eat," Lucas replied.

Cecilia stood by Lucas, close enough that her hip rubbed his arm as she placed the dishes on the table. After she'd finished, he put his arm around her waist. Michaela immediately discerned a history between them.

"You want something else?" Cecilia asked, hurt in her voice.

"I think this will do it, *pequeña,*" he said.

As she went off, he glanced up at Michaela, smiling.

"She's a sweet kid. Very dedicated. Very loyal."

"Apparently so." Michaela took another sip of beer.

Why she was drinking so much, she didn't know. Maybe it was that she wasn't used to dining with pseudo-Latin revolutionaries. Or maybe it was because the guy was just so damned appealing that she felt off-balance.

He had a really nice mouth, especially when he smiled. It was sensual, promising...so much. His long sooty lashes made those deep blue eyes stand out. She knew women who used a pint of mascara to get that effect.

"So you plan on interviewing Susana Riveros," Lucas said, handing her a serving dish of *arroz con pollo*. He picked up a bowl of beans and helped himself.

"I'd like to," she said, spooning some of the chicken-and-rice dish onto her plate.

"Is your interest personal or professional?"

She considered the question. "Both."

"Susana is important to us," he said. "Her imprisonment has been a cause of great concern."

They exchanged dishes.

"For me, too," she admitted.

"Then we have something in common, after all."

They each took some braised green beans and began eating.

"What makes you think they'll let you in to see Susana?"

She took a bite of chicken. It was delicious. "I don't know that they will."

"But I take it you expect Bernardo to help you."

"Yes. I accept help in getting a story wherever I can."

"At what price?"

"What do you mean?" she asked, putting down her fork.

"Bernardo de Falcón is not one to let a needy young lady prevail upon him without exacting a price...usually in bed. I would be very careful with him, Michaela."

She gave him a tight smile. "I appreciate your concern, but I can take care of myself."

"Don't be too sure about that. Bernardo is slippery. Has he offered to help you?"

She frowned. "In a manner of speaking, yes."

"You expect me to believe that you didn't offer something in exchange?"

"How dare you!" she retorted. "What happened between us is none of your damned business!"

"If you expect my help, it is."

Michaela was so enraged that she threw her napkin on the floor. Lucas picked it up.

"That was a move worthy of the most fiery Latina. I seem to have struck a nerve."

"You have no right to talk to me that way," she seethed.

"Look, I'm sorry," he said, handing back her napkin. "I was just testing you."

"I don't appreciate being tested any more than I appreciate being insulted."

He shrugged. "Well, I had to know how far you'd go."

"I'm considering getting up and walking out of here, Lucas. Would that be far enough to impress you?"

"Don't take it personally, Michaela, please. Think of it this way. A number of people have their lives on the line just because I've taken the risk of talking to you. For their sakes, I can't be cavalier. I have to be certain who I deal with."

She felt somewhat mollified, though part of her was annoyed by his ploy. She picked up her fork and took a bite of chicken, not at all certain what Lucas was up to, though she was inclined to accept the fact that he'd been testing her. She decided two could play that game. If she didn't get a few straight answers of her own, it would be obvious that he was using her.

"What's your relationship with Reed Lakesly?" she asked.

"Cordial."

"Do you report to him, or what?"

"I'm afraid I can't answer that. For security reasons."

"The old stonewall," she said cuttingly.

"All right, I'm a front man. Does that satisfy you?"

"But you work closely with him?"

"Yes."

"Will you arrange for me to meet with him?"

"A face-to-face meeting?"

She sighed. "That's usually the way interviews are done."

He nodded and rubbed his chin. "Well, Michaela, that's going to be very difficult to arrange."

"Why?"

"Because Reed rarely ventures far from headquarters."

"No problem. I'll go to him."

"Only the most trusted of the cadre go to headquarters. The location is top secret."

"I won't tell anyone."

"Not even your friend, Bernardo?"

She contemplated him, her eye lingering at his open shirt. Lucas, she had to admit, made one hell of a front man. She found him nearly as irresistible as he was annoying. Fortunately, though, she was smart enough to keep her guard up.

"You aren't going to cooperate with me unless I tell you what happened at *La Pensa* this morning, are you?" she said.

"I know it raises your journalistic hackles, but I insist."

"And if I refuse?"

"Your experience with the MAP may be limited to dinner with me."

"And if I do tell you about my meeting with Bernardo, will you get me the face-to-face meeting with Reed Lakesly?"

"I'm afraid it will take a little more than a report on your conversation," he replied. "We'll need an ongoing account of what happens, especially if you're able to see Susana."

She blanched. "In other words, you want me to spy for you."

"Is the prospect so abhorrent?"

"What about my journalistic integrity, not to mention my safety?"

"You have guts, Michaela. Otherwise you never would have come down here. And you must also want your story very badly. I'm prepared to give you Reed Lakesly for your cooperation."

She took the last bite of her dinner, thinking.

"Are you ready for coffee?"

"Yes, I suppose so."

Lucas called to Cecilia and she came to clear the table. After she'd gone he leaned back in his chair, eyeing her as he drained the last of his beer. Michaela was not quite sure what to make of the cocksure grin on his face, but by the looks of him, he was aware that he was beginning to get the upper hand.

"Maybe if we proceed one step at a time," she said.

"What are you proposing?"

"Bernardo made me an offer," she began, deciding to play out her hand. "Before I tell you what he said, I'd like to know who you really are. The truth."

"You like to bargain, don't you?"

"Is it too much to ask to know who I'm dealing with?"

He stroked his jaw. Michaela was aware of the cleft in his chin, the way he sized her up with his eyes as he thought. He was shrewd, she decided, as well as sexy.

"Your point is well taken," he said at last. "My name is Luke Hammond. I'm Canadian. I've been down here for a number of years. Originally I worked for a humanitarian-aid mission, in full cooperation with the government of Ricardo Corazón de León. When he was deposed by the military coup and chased into exile, everything we were working for fell apart. Under Corazón the country was making good progress, both socially and economically. When General de Falcón took over, the best people in the country were arrested or forced into exile. The few who stayed organized the Movimiento Abril Primero to resist the military government and work to reinstate Corazón in power.

"I sympathized with their efforts right from the start, but it wasn't until after I was arrested and rather brutally interrogated that I decided to join up. I went underground right before they tried to deport me." He gave her his crooked grin. "There you have it, Michaela. The story of Luke Hammond."

"Well," she said, half mesmerized, "that's quite a tale, if somewhat general. I'd like to hear the details sometime."

"Perhaps as we get to know one another better." He leaned back in his chair. "Now, I believe you were going to tell me about Bernardo's offer."

"Ah, yes, the quid pro quo."

Cecilia came in, silently putting a small pot of coffee and two mugs on the table before leaving. Luke poured each of them some coffee before sitting back to listen.

Michaela began recounting her conversation with Bernardo. She had just mentioned she was going with him to the presidential palace when there was a commotion in the kitchen. A moment later a slender young man came running into the dining room from the back. Words were exchanged in Spanish and Luke abruptly got to his feet. He gestured to Michaela.

"Come on, we've got to get out of here."

"What's the matter? What's happened?"

"There are half-a-dozen military patrols in the district. One is coming down the street."

She rose. The alarm in Luke's voice was unmistakable. He took her by the arm and they went into the kitchen. Cecilia was there, her eyes wide with fear. She had a semiautomatic pistol in her hand. A heavyset woman, evidently the cook, stood beside her with her hands clasped prayerfully.

Luke, Cecilia and the young man conferred in low, anxious tones. Cecilia evidently was taking exception to something Luke was saying. He seemed annoyed at first, but appeared to relent. He turned to Michaela.

"This is Santos Moreno," he said, gesturing to the slender young man. "He'll escort you to your hotel. It would be best to avoid the patrols, but if you're stopped, your story is that you met Santos in a bar and he's walking you back to your hotel."

"All right," she said, her heart racing. "What about you?"

"We'll have to split up. I don't think you'd like an extended vacation in our national prison as a reward for being caught in my presence. I'll be in touch." With that he reached out and tweaked her chin, grinning broadly. "We have unfinished business to discuss, I believe."

He signaled to Santos Moreno, who took Michaela's arm and led her out the back door. Michaela glanced behind as they stepped into the dark alley. Luke was drawing a pistol from his belt at the back of his trousers. The cook was wrapping a shawl around her plump shoulders. Cecilia was looking at Luke with shining eyes. He smiled and pinched her cheek. It was Michaela's last glimpse of him before the door closed.

CHAPTER SIX

THEY HURRIED DOWN the dark alley, the only sound the clicking of their heels on the cobblestones. When they stopped at a street corner, not far from a lamppost, Michaela was able to see plainly for the first time. She glanced up at Santos Moreno, not having taken a good look at him in the restaurant.

He was a handsome young man with fine features and sensitive eyes. He did not seem like a revolutionary. A drama student or high-school teacher would have been a better guess. There was fear in his expression, but not panic. He took her by the arm and they left the alley, walking in what seemed like the wrong direction for her hotel. He still hadn't spoken and Michaela began to wonder if he knew any English.

"Is this the way to my hotel?" she whispered.

"Indirectly," he replied without looking at her.

The street was empty. What sounds she heard came from the apartment buildings on each side of the street. At some distance she could hear traffic. They walked steadily, but not rushing as they had in the alley.

"Soldiers!" he said, under his breath.

Michaela looked up and saw five men in fatigues under the lamppost on the corner across from them. They had rifles slung over their shoulders and were smoking and talking. Santos put his arm around her.

"Ignore them," he said. "Maybe they won't bother us."

At first the men didn't see them. Then they turned to stare. The light was good enough for them to tell she was a foreigner. She didn't know if that was an advantage or not.

"Perhaps if you laugh to show you enjoy my company," Santos murmured.

Michaela swallowed hard and tittered, trying to sound natural. She now wished she'd accepted one of the many offers she'd had to act in plays at school.

One of the soldiers shouted something, but it sounded more like a catcall than an order. Santos ignored them and so did Michaela. She put her arm around his waist instead.

They rounded the corner as the whistles and calls continued. Santos sighed with relief.

"I was afraid they were going to stop us," Michaela said as Santos dropped his arm from her shoulders.

"Yes. I, as well. Sometimes they do and sometimes they don't. It depends upon their mood. I thought our chances were good since you are so pretty."

"Your English is very good," she said.

"I studied it in the university."

"You're a student, then?"

"I was. Now I do this."

They walked on for a time. Santos pointed up the street.

"There is a large patrol ahead," he noted. "It would be better if we went into the park until they pass."

They crossed the street and entered a small square that was dark except for a lamppost at each corner. They found a bench and sat down. Michaela glanced at her companion.

"You lead a rather exciting life, don't you?"

"Exciting perhaps, but not happy. I cannot be happy until our president is returned to power. Many people suffer." He turned to her. "I have a question, Miss Emory. Is it true that you will speak to Susana Riveros?"

"I hope to. Why?"

"I do not wish to be presumptuous, but could you tell her that Santos Moreno sends his best wishes. And tell her I pray for her."

"If I see Susana, I'll tell her, Santos." She saw the emotion on his face. "I take it you are friends."

"As children, Susana and I knew each other well. Our families were close. She has always been . . . dear to me."

Michaela heard more than just friendship in his voice. "Do you love her?" she asked gently.

"Very much," he said.

"Then her imprisonment must be especially hard for you."

"It is. But the prison is not what keeps us apart."

She watched him stare off. "What do you mean?"

"Susana does not love me in the same way I love her. She cares for another. She is in love with Reed Lakesly."

Michaela nodded. "I see."

"Of course, Susana is not the only one. Many women love him. He is very strong and very brave. He is adored."

"You must have many of those same qualities, Santos. You shouldn't feel unworthy. Look at Lucas—he's charismatic and he seems to be greatly admired."

Santos smiled sadly. "It is very obvious, isn't it?"

"I haven't met Reed Lakesly, but Lucas proves Reed doesn't have a monopoly on . . . machismo. I don't know anything about your relationship with Susana, but I see no reason for you to feel dejected or inadequate."

"You are kind to say this, Miss Emory. I wish Susana was equally aware. Now I can only pray for her safety. Her love is not nearly so important as her life."

"I don't know how they're treating her, but if I speak with her, I'll give her your message. I'm sure it will cheer her."

"Thank you, Miss Emory." He looked toward the street. "The patrol seems to have passed. I think we can go now."

They returned to the street and continued on their way, until they came to a boulevard. Santos told her that it would be better if she went alone in a taxi back to her hotel. That way, if the hotel was being watched, suspicions would not be aroused. She agreed and he flagged down a passing cab and put her in it. Michaela took his hand, thanking him and promising again to pass along his message if she was to get the chance.

Her promise seemed to lift his spirits. "Until we meet again," he said. He saluted her as the taxi pulled away.

Michaela settled into the back seat, able to relax for the first time in hours. There had been some tense moments, but the excitement had left her feeling alive. And even though she'd been afraid, the adventure appealed to her soul. In retrospect, she realized what a stimulating experience her encounter with Luke Hammond had been. It certainly made a Saturday evening in Washington with John or Matt or Mark pale in comparison.

Michaela sighed happily. She'd finally found her true calling. A taste for adventure had always been in her blood. And being in Pangonia had only served to prove she'd been right.

BACK AT THE HOTEL, nothing seemed amiss. The doorman, the bellhop and the concierge were oblivious to the fact that she'd had a clandestine rendezvous with one of Reed Lakesly's chief lieutenants. Oh, the glorious thrill of it all!

When Michaela approached the desk to get her room key, the clerk advised her that a floral delivery had been made. The bouquet had been put in a vase and was in her room.

On the ride up to her floor, Michaela decided that the flowers had to have come from Bernardo de Falcón. The only other possibilities were Jack Ellison or Luke Hammond. Jack's only conceivable motive was guilt, and her boss wasn't the guilty type. Luke seemed an unlikely candidate—first, because there hardly had been time to contact a florist, and second, because he would more likely be the type to *receive* flowers than send them. Hammond might be Canadian, but he'd acquired a Latino machismo. No, it had to be Bernardo.

The slippery editor of *La Pensa* held no allure for her, but Michaela did feel a certain excitement about receiving flowers. That didn't happen much in Washington these days, or anywhere else for that matter. Maybe that was one of the benefits of the Latin culture—men were men, in the most traditional sense, and women expected to be courted.

The notion did have some appeal. But if she was wise, she wouldn't forget that both Bernardo de Falcón and Luke Hammond were predators. Their politics might be different, and in a purely physical sense the revolutionary had buckets of animal magnetism, but when push came to shove, the two men weren't all that different.

When Michaela unlocked the door to her room, she was surprised to find that it was dark. She invariably made a point of leaving a light on in hotel rooms when she went out at night. She hesitated. When she didn't hear anything, she decided the lamp had been turned off by whoever brought the flowers to her room. She fumbled for the light switch.

The first thing she saw was an enormous bouquet on the table by the window. She headed toward it, then sensed a presence. Seated in the easy chair in the corner was a man. It was Luke Hammond in his Father O'Laughlin disguise.

"My God," she said, clasping her hands to her chest. "You scared me to death."

"Sorry, me child," he said in his phony brogue, "but I couldn't advertise me presence."

She looked at him with exasperation. "What are you doing in my room, *Father* Hammond? And why are you dressed like that?"

Luke put his finger to his lips as he got up. "It's better if you call me either Father O'Laughlin or Lucas. The background information I gave you was confidential."

Michaela managed to collect herself. "I wasn't planning on splashing your real name on the front page of the *Daily News Bulletin*."

"I think it would be best if you pretended you never heard it. And, to answer your question, I'm dressed like this because it's easier to get around undetected in the clothes of a cleric."

"Even into ladies' hotel rooms, *Padre?*"

"There are souls to be saved just about everywhere, my child. Anyway, I wanted to make sure that you said your prayers before going to bed."

"I appreciate the saintly concern," she said dryly, "but I'm not pleased with the liberty you've taken. Why *are* you here?"

He removed his cassock and tossed it over the chair. The clothes underneath were those he'd worn in the restaurant.

"I know I'm intruding, Michaela, and I really am sorry to have startled you. But we need to talk before you and Bernardo go to the palace." He gestured toward the flowers and smiled. "Since he's become a full-blown admirer, further discussion is all the more important."

"How do you know they're from Bernardo?"

"The envelope wasn't sealed."

Michaela put her hands on her hips and glared. "You come to my room uninvited, you read my mail, and you even try to coopt me to spy for you. Anything else you'd like?"

He gave her a provocative look. "It might be a little early in our relationship for that, tempted though I may be."

"That's not funny," she said, heading for the table. Her cheeks were crimson as she snatched up the envelope that had accompanied the flowers. She read the card.

It said, "For the flower of American journalism. I look forward to tomorrow. B. de F."

"The guy can really turn a phrase, can't he?" Luke said.

She whirled to face him. "Bernardo may not be every woman's dream, but he at least understands common courtesy."

"Is that what turns you on?"

"That's none of your business."

He managed to look wounded. "I'm still out of favor, I see."

"Look, Lucas, I'm tired. Say what you want to say, then please leave so I can get some rest."

He acted disgusted. "I appreciate how taxing it is to fly all the way down here to see a revolution close up and personal, Miss Emory. Believe me, if I could show you what it's been like for most Pangonians since de Falcón took over, from the back of a comfy limousine, I would. But those of

us not yet in jail have our hands full just trying to survive—
not to mention doing what we can for our comrades who
have been less fortunate. So, let me be direct. I'm trying to
think of anything, anything at all, we can do to help Susana. Is that okay by you?"

Michaela felt the full power of his rebuke. She lowered her
head, ashamed that she'd been so derisive. What was it
about the man that put her on the defensive—or more ac-
curately, the offensive?

"I guess I was sharper than I intended to be," she said
apologetically. "As I told you at the restaurant, I'm concerned about Susana myself. Did you have some advice?"

"From what you said earlier, I assume you're going to use
your meeting with General de Falcón to press for permission to see Susana."

"That was my intention."

"Good. The general is very sensitive about his reputation outside the country. He doesn't like to be seen as the
tyrant he is. You can exploit any show of openness he might
make by asking to see Susana. If you seize the opportunity,
Michaela, you might finagle your way into the prison for a
meeting with Susana."

"That's what I'd hoped for, and I do appreciate the tips
on General de Falcón. But I'm not sure I understand why
you're so eager for me to see Susana. Is it to publicize her
situation?"

He gave her his crooked smile—the one that seemed to
make the cleft in his chin even more prominent. "Not entirely. But let's take it a step at a time. If you arrange to see
her, we'll discuss what to do then. You're taking a risk even
talking to me, so the less you have to hide, the better."

"You seem to have an agenda for me all worked out,
don't you, Lucas?"

"Revolution is an opportunistic undertaking." He arched
a brow. "And in you I see . . . an opportunity."

She ignored the innuendo. "And you, evidently, are the
revolution's foremost opportunist."

He chuckled. "Is that a complaint or a compliment?"

"Take it any way you like."

They were staring at each other, the nonverbal messages flying back and forth, when the lights went out. "Now what?" she said, exasperated.

"That's ours."

"Your what?"

"Blackout. We pull the plug at a relay station and knock the power out now and then."

"What for?"

"Partly to remind everyone that we're here, partly for tactical reasons. It's easier to move around undetected in the dark. I'll take advantage of it to get from here to a safe house, for example."

"So, you're leaving?" She sensed him moving toward her, though only the dimmest of silhouettes were visible.

"Shortly." He was near her now. She could tell by his voice, but also his scent.

He touched her arm and she jumped. Luke slid his hand down her arm until he reached her fingers. Taking them, he led her to the window and pulled back the heavy drapes.

"The city is quite lovely during a blackout. It has the stillness and the obscurity of the forest—until the candles and lanterns come on, anyway."

"Candles?"

"Look. People are beginning to light them. See the glow in some of the windows?" He hadn't let go of her hand.

"Yes, I can see now. It's a reminder of all the life out there. Don't people resent you for the inconvenience, though?"

"They understand. And we try to be considerate. Whenever possible we avoid blackouts at dinnertime, or during popular TV programs. Our favorite time is when the government is putting on the news."

She chuckled. "An interesting form of censorship."

"A free press can say whatever it wants. In this country it's not free, though."

Michaela was very cognizant of him toying with her fingers. He seemed to be doing it absently, as if he was unaware of the intimacy. She considered pulling her hand away, but decided he meant nothing by it. Anyway, to resist would be to make a point of something meaningless.

Luke turned to her. He seemed to inhale her scent, to want to draw her close.

Just then there was a knock at the door and she flinched. Luke put his arm around her shoulders and gave her a reassuring squeeze.

"Don't worry," he whispered. "If it was the police they wouldn't have knocked. Anyway, I'd have been warned they were coming. Ask who it is."

"Who is it?" she called with a shaky voice.

"The porter, *señora*. I have candles for the light," the man replied through the door.

"Take them from him," Luke whispered.

She instinctively followed his command, though she didn't open the door until Luke had gathered his cassock and stepped into the bathroom. The porter had an apologetic smile on his face. He was holding a large candle, and smaller ones in a box.

"Sorry for this, *señora*," he said. "Sometimes it happens."

"Reading's difficult without lights, otherwise it doesn't matter," she said vacantly.

"Please take some candles and I will light the first."

Michaela took two or three candles from the box, then lit one of them from the one in his hand. "Thank you."

"A pleasure, *señora. Buenas noches.*"

She closed the door and turned. Luke was standing at the bathroom door, his cassock over his arm, watching her hold the flickering candle. He studied her a moment.

"It's an inconvenience having to rely on a flame," he said, "but it's for a good cause."

He took one of the other candles from her and lit it, using the flame of the first candle. Standing close to him, Michaela felt a sense of intimacy. She was still wary, but there were strong positive impulses, as well. Maybe it was because they shared a common goal of helping Susana.

Luke started to speak, caught himself, and then went ahead anyway. "Would it be inappropriate to tell you that you look lovely by candlelight?"

"Considering I still think of you as a priest, it probably is," she replied.

"Maybe I've been too convincing in the role," he said. "What if we think of each other as 'comrades in arms'? That was your phrase earlier, as I recall."

"The reference wasn't meant to be complimentary." She gazed at the shimmering flame reflected in his eyes.

"Can't comrades in arms be friends?"

"In the sense that we're devoted to the same cause, yes, I suppose we can. For Susana's sake."

"You see it as strictly business, in other words."

"You aren't suggesting otherwise, are you, Lucas?"

He grinned and so did she.

"Well?" she prompted.

Before he could answer, the telephone rang.

"You get a reprieve," she said, and went to the phone. "Hello?"

"How's my favorite cub reporter?" came the man's voice. It took her a moment before she realized it was Jack Ellison. "Jack..." she said, dumbfounded.

"Well, have you got a story for me?"

His brash manner brought her back to reality—to her life in Washington. She'd only been away for a day, but for the past several hours she'd been in an entirely different world, sparring with the likes of Father O'Laughlin and Bernardo de Falcón. She glanced at Luke. He still stood in the middle of the room, holding a candle.

"I'm hot on the trail of one hell of a story, as a matter of fact," she said into the receiver. "Tomorrow I'm going to the presidential palace with a select group of reporters to interview General de Falcón. And I've made steps toward getting interviews with both Susana Riveros and Reed Lakesly." She glanced over at Luke and noticed there was a touch of amusement on his face.

"Is that true?" Ellison asked her.

"Scout's honor. I'll be faxing my first story by tomorrow evening."

"I eagerly look forward to reading it," he said. "You seem to have hit the ground running, Emory. I was afraid you'd find getting through Customs a challenge."

"Thanks a lot," she said, miffed.

"No offense meant," he quickly added. "It's just that you're new to the international game. I was fully prepared to give you time to get your feet wet."

"Does that mean I'm going to get my expenses covered sooner rather than later?" she asked, taking the opportunity presented her.

Luke Hammond moved over to the easy chair and sat, crossing his legs as he listened. Michaela stared at the flame of the candle she held as she listened to her boss.

"Frankly, Mike, I've been thinking I was a little unfair to you. If you get your story, all your expenses will be covered. If the work is top quality, there may even be a bonus."

"I'll hold you to it, Jack."

"If you uncover something really big, maybe I'll send help."

"If I'm big enough to find the story, I'm big enough to report it. I don't need help."

"Don't get your back up, kid. It's your show. I recognize that. Nobody else in my organization turned it up. But you wouldn't be offended if I came down myself, would you? It might not be a bad idea if I witness your triumph firsthand."

"I'm surprised you'd have time, Jack."

"It wouldn't be an extended stay. Just long enough to...shall we say...give you a pat on the back?"

"Thanks for the vote of confidence, but I'm at a delicate point in my work. Too many chefs could spoil the broth."

"You may be right, Mike. Maybe a better use of my time would be to bestow the accolades after your triumph. When you get things wrapped up down there, you'll need a few days' rest. We can meet in Bermuda. A bureau-chief slot is not beyond the realm of possibility, Mike.''

She grimaced, but held her tongue in check. "I'd like to wrap up this story before I start thinking ahead," she said.

"Just give it some thought, kid."

"Yeah, Jack, I will." She hung up and looked over at Luke, still holding his candle as he watched her.

After a while he said, "You seemed to be getting offers of help from all quarters. I take it that was your boss."

"Yes. Jack Ellison."

"Does he hit on everybody in the organization, or just you?" he asked, getting up.

"Jack is especially fond of female reporters. There's a well-defined promotion route, if you know what I mean."

Luke approached her. "You seem a reluctant participant."

They stood facing each other, candles in their hands.

"Being a woman can be a challenging proposition. A lot of men think that any female is fair game. Even unlikely types, like clergymen, can hit on you when you least expect it."

"Did Father O'Laughlin do anything improper?"

She repressed her smile. "He may have sinned in his heart."

"Father O'Laughlin is, after all, but a man."

"Most women are able to control their libidos."

"That's the beauty of God's creation, my child. He made somebody willing to take the initiative. But for that, the species would spend a lot of time looking and not much time doing. A sure path to extinction."

"Propagating the species comes far down the list of most men's goals," she said. "You're being too generous to your sex."

"Maybe you're being too hard on us," Luke replied.

They sized one another up.

"It's been a long day," she said. "I've got to get to bed."

"My cue to leave."

Michaela nodded. "Good night, Father. I'll say my prayers."

Luke blew out his candle so that only hers remained lit. "Say a prayer for Susana and one for me," he said softly.

She saw emotion in his eyes. "All right."

"And good luck tomorrow. Be careful, Michaela."

"I will."

They stood facing each other, neither of them moving. "Forgive my mortal weakness," he murmured. With that he leaned forward and, taking her jaw in his hand, kissed her lightly on the lips. "Good night, Michaela."

She stood frozen, mesmerized, as he took his cassock and slipped quietly from the room.

CHAPTER SEVEN

MICHAELA HAD A good night's sleep, dreaming of Luke Hammond, and waterfalls, and warm tropical islands. She ordered juice and a pastry from room service and, when she'd eaten, she decided to have a leisurely soak in the big old-fashioned tub. That was a real treat, since her apartment had only a tiny shower.

As she slid into the warm water, Michaela thought about her progress. In a little over an hour Bernardo was due to take her to the presidential palace. She was excited about the prospect, but she didn't want to think about the slippery editor just then—not when it was so much more pleasant to recall Luke Hammond's kiss. In truth, he had been on her mind since she awoke. That could have troubled her if she'd let it, but she preferred to think of it as symbolic—a gesture of allegiance to the MAP for the sake of Susana Riveros.

Michaela was sure Luke had something a lot more personal in mind than politics—and under a different set of circumstances her priorities might have been personal, too. But she had come to Pangonia to do a job, not to have an affair with a swashbuckling revolutionary.

Still, she derived a certain amount of pleasure from their encounters. It was fascinating to watch him in action, even if he annoyed her at times and put her on the defensive. Luke was different from the men she'd known—larger than life, somehow.

That made her wonder. If Luke Hammond was so charismatic, what would Reed Lakesly be like? He was considered a ladies' man. He was half Pangonian and half American. Would that mean he was macho or liberated?

Might he be an enlightened romantic, or a pain-in-the-butt traditionalist?

Michaela added more hot water to the tub, unsure of the answer. Regardless, the Pangonian-American combination was intriguing. Was it the profile of a revolutionary leader? Or... a shocking thought struck her! What if Luke wasn't Canadian? What if *he* was Reed Lakesly?

He'd proved himself a master of multiple identities. He'd been an Irish priest, then a Canadian. Could he have a third identity? How many North Americans could there be in the MAP anyway?

A cold shiver went down Michaela's spine. Had she been face-to-face with Reed Lakesly almost from the moment she'd arrived in Pangonia? She didn't know.

Of course, it was possible that Luke was who he said he was. There might be two North Americans in the movement. Yet she was almost sure she'd been duped. Call it intuition, even paranoia, but Michaela suddenly saw what she'd been unable to see before.

She climbed from the tub, her mood changed. She'd gone from wistful to annoyed, even angry. If Luke was really Reed Lakesly, how could he have let her go on and on about how badly she wanted to interview him? The rat! How could she have been so stupid?

As Michaela dried off, she recalled her Aunt Gayle cautioning her not to go off half-cocked. She knew her instinct was to jump to conclusions—a dangerous trait for a journalist. A reporter should always check and double-check her facts. Above all, never assume anything.

For the most part she'd managed to bridle her excesses, but this was different. This was between her and Reed, or Luke, or whoever he was.

She dressed, feeling a newfound determination to seek the truth. If Luke had made a fool of her, she'd call him on it. After all, what had she gotten out of the evening? Empty words, idle promises. He'd given her lip service—so to speak. She'd let the machismo crap blind her. Even worse, she had compromised her journalistic integrity, agreeing to be an informant. How could she have been so naive?

In deference to her aunt, Michaela resolved to proceed cautiously. One thing was certain, she wasn't going to end up as Father O'Laughlin's patsy again. It was back to square one. She was a free agent and she was going to play this independently, in proper journalistic fashion.

As she twisted her hair up off her neck and pinned it into a loose chignon, she told herself that her first opportunity would be coming up shortly. Bernardo might be everything that Lucas had told her he was, but that didn't mean she couldn't use him to her advantage—the same way Luke Hammond had tried to use her. From now on, she'd have only one allegiance: the truth.

She'd finished her hair and had just put on gold hoop earrings when the telephone rang. She looked at her watch. Bernardo was punctual if nothing else. Sure enough, it was the desk, informing her that the editor was in the lobby. She told the clerk she'd be right down.

Bernardo de Falcón sported a boutonniere in his lapel and a broad smile on his face. His neat beard was freshly trimmed, his bald pate shiny.

"Ah, a vision," he said as she approached him, "a vision." He held out his hands and, taking hers, kissed them.

Bernardo's cologne was strong, pungent, overpowering. Underneath, he vaguely smelled of cigars.

"Your flowers were lovely, Bernardo," she said. "Thank you."

"A token," he said, looking her over.

Michaela had decided to wear her pink linen suit. With a white shell and white heels, she looked fresh and sexy. It was her favorite business outfit for summer. She'd worn it to her only White House press conference. It had produced admiring glances, though not a chance to ask the president a question.

Bernardo de Falcón was enraptured. "Your beauty leaves me speechless," he said, looking as if he wanted to throw his arms around her.

"I hope not," she replied sweetly. "How will we communicate?"

He still had her hands clasped in his. "You are right, my dear Michaela," he said, squeezing her fingers. "I must blind myself to your charms." Then, looking her dead in the eye, he took a deep breath and added, "For the sake of our friendship."

Michaela smiled, easing her hands from his. "Yes, I think that would be a good idea."

"Well." He drew himself up. "My limousine is waiting. Shall we go?"

A sleek white limousine was outside. Michaela looked it over as the driver opened her door. Was this an indication of Bernardo's status as editor, or as son of the president?

Bernardo climbed in behind her, sitting very close, making her aware, once more, of his overpowering cologne. She scooted away a few inches. Bernardo scooted close again, so that his beefy leg was up against hers. She cringed inwardly, hoping this wasn't a sign of what was to come. She'd resolved to endure him, but she had her limits. She could only hope he wouldn't try to push her to that point too quickly.

On the other hand, it occurred to her that Bernardo would be inclined to make hay while he could. Once she'd interviewed his father, his leverage would be gone. She would have to string the game out as best she could.

They were soon on their way. Bernardo continued to scrutinize her, his thoughts completely transparent, though he hadn't said a word. Michaela looked out the window. Bernardo drummed his fingers on his knee.

"Forgive me for being so blunt, Michaela, but I simply must know. Is there a man in your life?"

She considered telling him there was someone, in hopes that it would put an end to his inveigling. But that was also risky. Her use for him might not end with the press conference. She decided on a middle course.

"There are several men I see in Washington," she said.

"But they are only friends," he said hastily. "I mean, there is no one special?"

"No," she said reluctantly, "no one special."

"Excellent."

"Why is that important, Bernardo?"

"I will not attempt to make a secret of my very high regard for you, Michaela. It is my wish that we become better acquainted . . . apart from our journalism."

"I see."

"I hope you are not shocked."

"No, but it's only fair if I know about you too, Bernardo. Are you involved with anyone?"

He chuckled. "I'm married, of course, but that is of no consequence. I mean, as far as you and I are concerned. Matters of the heart have a separate . . . shall we say 'life' . . . from one's family. I'm sure it is not much different in America, unless perhaps we in Latin America are more honest about it." He gave another self-satisfied chuckle.

Michaela would have liked to tell him where to get off, but he had a point, in the philosophical sense. Jack Ellison was married, too. If they differed, it was in style. But with Jack, she could make her feelings known without completely jeopardizing her position. With Bernardo, she wasn't so sure.

The editor put his hand on her knee. "You are being very quiet, my dear. Has what I've said upset you?"

"It's very important that you respect me, Bernardo. I'm a serious journalist and I hope that you understand that. I am determined to get my story."

"Indeed," Bernardo said. "I have the utmost respect for you. But I hope that my respect for you and my regard are not mutually exclusive. I see no reason why we cannot have our cake and eat it, too, as it were."

"Surely you aren't putting conditions on our friendship, Bernardo."

"Michaela," he declared solemnly, "I am above all a gentleman."

She allowed him a smile. "I can't tell you how much better I feel, hearing you say that."

Bernardo seemed pleased with himself, while Michaela knew *she* was the one with cause to be pleased. She'd maneuvered him into a corner—for the moment. She peered out the window again, knowing that her companion was trying to figure out where things stood, and that he was less than thrilled with the conclusions he was reaching.

She decided it might be a good time to press for information. "I know you think the MAP and Reed Lakesly are of little consequence, but I'm curious about them. What can you tell me about the leadership of the MAP?"

"What do you wish to know?"

"Who is there besides Reed Lakesly?"

"Military intelligence is not my area of expertise, Michaela. Frankly, I know very little about them."

"Is there a Canadian in the inner circle?"

"A Canadian? Why do you ask?"

She shrugged. "I heard rumors. I'm curious about these people."

"Now that you mention it, there was a Canadian we tried to deport for aiding and abetting the MAP," he replied. "I'm not sure, but I think he joined up with them."

Michaela was shocked. Was Bernardo talking about Luke? "What was this Canadian's name?" she asked.

He threw up his hands. "I don't remember."

She wondered whether she dared volunteer the information. It could arouse suspicion. And yet, she wanted to know who she'd been dealing with. "What sort of name was it, Bernardo? Anglo?"

He considered the question. "As I think about it, I recall a Biblical connotation. Yes, it was a Biblical name."

"Joshua? Abraham?" she asked disingenuously.

"No," he said. "New Testament, I believe."

"Matthew? John?"

"No."

"Luke?"

Bernardo's eyes widened. "Yes, that was it. Luke. Luke...uh...Luke Hanford! No, not Hanford. It began with an *H,* as I recall."

"Hammond?"

Bernardo blinked. "You know him?"

"No, but in doing my research before coming down, I ran across the name in a Canadian paper."

"I see."

For a moment Michaela feared she hadn't been subtle enough. But Bernardo seemed to take her explanation at face value.

"I don't hear much about Hammond," he said. "I don't think he's all that important."

"No," she said, wistfully, "maybe he isn't." She turned her attention back to the cityscape, but not much registered. Had Luke told her the truth? Bernardo's statement threw cold water on her suspicions. Maybe he wasn't Reed Lakesly, after all. No, she thought, he *probably* wasn't Reed Lakesly. She'd gotten a bee in her bonnet and she'd gone off half-cocked. Again.

They pulled up to the gate of the presidential palace, a classical structure built in the very heart of Montagua. Other government buildings lined the surrounding streets, though the palace stood out. It was more heavily fortified than the other buildings and was surrounded by a low wall topped with a heavy wrought-iron fence. One guard looked in the windows of the limo while another checked under the vehicle for bombs, using a mirror on a pole. A third guard held a German shepherd on a tight leash.

"Security seems awfully heavy," Michaela remarked.

"The rebels make life difficult at times," Bernardo replied casually. "Sometimes they are a real pain."

"The MAP?" she said, letting the surprise in her voice show.

It took a moment, but Bernardo saw he'd been caught in a contradiction. "It's amazing how only a very few can create problems for the majority in a law-abiding society," he said, recovering.

The limo proceeded to the entrance, and Michaela was aware of her building excitement. It wasn't so much a matter of celebrity—she had, after all, been to the White House—but rather it was the circumstances. Despite her misgivings about Reed Lakesly or Luke Hammond or whoever he was, she regarded the government of General Juan de Falcón as an adversary—if only because of her sympathies for Susana Riveros.

As she and Bernardo climbed from the limo, the weightiness of the occasion struck home. Chelsea, after initial reluctance, had encouraged her to travel to Pangonia on the off chance she could help Susana. The opportunity had arrived. She could only hope that she wouldn't let Susana down.

An officer hurried down the steps to greet them. They were escorted to a heavy wooden door that was being held by a footman. Bernardo, who had Michaela's arm, led her into to the cool marble entry. They were greeted by the commander of the presidential guard, a gray-haired colonel with a black mustache. They shook hands and the three of them proceeded casually through the palace to an ornate reception room.

A large antique Louis XIV writing desk stood at one side of the room, just in front of a massive fireplace that didn't look as if it had ever been used. The yellow-and-green Pangonian flag was at one side of the fireplace and military colors were at the other. Facing the desk were two rows of antique armchairs, six to a row. Behind them and on either side were camera crews. All but four of the chairs were occupied.

Bernardo led her to the two empty chairs in the front row. Before sitting he glanced over the assembly, nodding his greeting to those in attendance, swelling his chest with pride. Michaela realized she was being displayed.

"It seems like a small group for a press conference," she said in a low voice.

"The president does not like speaking to large groups of reporters, so only a select few are permitted to attend his conferences," he said. "The television is allowed, as you can see."

"Is the conference shown live?"

"No, no. It will be edited before broadcast tonight."

"Edited?"

Bernardo immediately saw the negative implications of his comment. "The people have a low tolerance for politics," he explained lamely. "We give them only the important nuggets."

"I see."

It was obvious that she was not attending a news conference with a free press. Rather it was a propaganda exercise. For her purposes, it probably didn't make much difference. Her goal was to be able to ask a few questions of General de Falcón.

Michaela worried about having problems with the language, though she was certain Bernardo could translate, if necessary. She was genuinely sorry now that she'd studied French instead of Spanish. Growing up in Arizona, she had been able to pick up a little Spanish, but certainly not enough to converse with the general.

"Does your father speak English?" she asked Bernardo.

"Yes, but I hope you aren't planning on asking questions."

"Why not? It's a press conference, isn't it? And I *am* a reporter, aren't I?"

"Yes, but all questions are submitted to the press secretary in advance," he replied in a hushed tone. "You can't just stand up and ask a question. It isn't done."

Her heart sank. What was the point in her coming? For Bernardo's amusement? The more she thought about it, the angrier she got. "Bernardo," she said, struggling to remain civil, "why did you bring me here if I can't ask any questions?"

"I thought you might like to observe," he answered weakly, aware now that he'd miscalculated. "I might be able to arrange for you to meet my father after the conference. But please, Michaela, only on the condition that you do not bring up the MAP. It is not a subject that my father will discuss publicly."

"Not even with his own press?"

"We talk, of course," he said, lowering his voice still more. "My reporters get what they need for their stories."

"I imagine they do," she said glumly.

A glance at him told her he'd already figured out that she wasn't pleased. If this turned out to be a waste of time, she was at least glad she hadn't endured more of an indignity than having Bernardo pat her knee.

The editor squirmed, apparently wrestling with the same realization. While he struggled with his problem, Michaela tried to devise new strategy. They were both deep in thought when a side door swung open and a smallish, barrel-chested man in full dress uniform entered the room, followed by an aide carrying a leather-bound folder.

Everyone rose until the general was seated and the folder was placed in front of him. He signaled for everyone to sit. General de Falcón was baldish, like his son. They looked much alike in the face, though the father was clean-shaven and even shorter in stature. He also had a more severe demeanor.

He began by reading a statement in Spanish. One of the secretaries brought Michaela a translation, which Bernardo whispered had been prepared at his request. He evidently was desperate to get credit in any way he could.

Glancing over the document, Michaela saw that it was a self-serving propaganda piece. General Juan de Falcón was singing his own praises.

Once the statement had been read, the reporters stood in turn, reading their prepared questions. The general replied to each question by reading a prepared answer. Michaela couldn't understand a word, but she didn't need to. The whole thing was rather sad. She could see what Susana Riveros had been referring to in her letter to Chelsea.

Listening to the general drone on, Michaela began feeling twinges of sympathy for Luke Hammond or Reed Lakesly or whoever he was—not so much for him personally, as for what he stood for. But at the same time, she was frustrated. What good did it do to witness a spectacle like this without having the liberty to unmask it, to expose it to the world for what it truly was?

The longer Michaela sat there, the more she seethed. What kind of journalist was she, to sit on her hands and let this go on while Susana rotted in jail? Finally, she couldn't take it any longer. During the lull after what appeared to be the last question, she got to her feet. Bernardo gasped.

"Forgive me, General de Falcón, for addressing you in English," she said. "Unfortunately I do not speak Spanish, but if I may, I'd like to ask a question."

The man appraised her, seemingly as intrigued by the interruption as disconcerted by it. "You are the American journalist," he said in halting English.

"Yes, General. I am Michaela Emory with the *Daily News Bulletin* in Washington."

The general cast a glance at his son. "What is your question, Miss Emory?"

"There is a Pangonian journalist who's been imprisoned for several months at the direction of your government. Her name is Susana Riveros. With all due respect, sir, I'd like to know if you plan to charge her with a crime and try her, or if she will continue to be held without being tried and convicted."

A gasp of surprise rippled across the room. General de Falcón did not look pleased.

"I am not familiar with the details of the matter," he replied. "It is in the hands of the minister of justice and I am sure it will be handled according to the laws of our country."

Bernardo touched her arm to indicate she should sit down, but Michaela ignored him. "If I may interject a personal note," she went on, "Miss Riveros was a friend of mine in college. We were classmates. I wonder if you would grant me the opportunity to interview her."

"You wish . . . to talk to her?" he asked, frowning.

"Yes. Surely there is nothing your government wishes to hide from the press."

"I'm sure the particulars have been made available. You may ask the press secretary for the information."

"I would like to speak with Miss Riveros directly, sir. Would that pose a problem for your government? The world is already well aware that she will have a different view than yours. You aren't afraid to have it heard, are you?"

"Certainly not," the general answered, bristling.

"When might I speak with her, then?"

The crowd mumbled. Michaela already knew she'd gone beyond the bounds and that her impudence could get her hustled onto the next plane out of the country, but dammit, this was her only opportunity. The general again looked at his son. Michaela knew she'd embarrassed Bernardo, but his goodwill meant nothing if she couldn't see Susana.

"Perhaps your request could be granted, Miss Emory," the general said. "If you would be so kind as to speak with my press secretary after the conference." Reverting to Spanish, he asked if there were any other questions.

No one else had the temerity to get to their feet, so the general closed the press conference. Rising, he cast a faint smile in Michaela's direction, then strode from the room. She heard Bernardo issue a sigh of relief. She glanced at him as he took a handkerchief from his pocket and dabbed his brow.

"You are not without courage, are you, Michaela?" he said.

"I had a perfectly reasonable request."

Bernardo rolled his eyes.

"Where do I find the press secretary?" she asked.

"Come, I will accompany you."

They went off to the press office, where the secretary advised Michaela that arrangements would be made. In due course, she would be told when she could see Susana. Bernardo exchanged a few words with the man, who then said to her, "Señor de Falcón will tell to you the time when we know it."

Drawing himself up, Bernardo said, "I shall be honored to accompany you to the interview, Michaela."

She looked back and forth between the men. "It will be soon, I trust. I can't stay in Pangonia forever."

"Very soon, *señorita*." The secretary clicked his heels.

Michaela smiled. "Good. I feel much better."

"Then we shall go?" Bernardo said, taking her arm again. As they headed for the entry, he added, "I am happy I could arrange that for you. As I think about it, it is a very good idea that you talk to Señorita Riveros."

They left the palace and descended the steps to their limousine. Once they'd climbed inside, Bernardo took her hand.

"I am even a greater admirer of you than before," he said, as he toyed with her fingers. "I must take you to dinner this evening."

Obviously, Bernardo was going to strike while the iron was hot. With the particulars of her interview with Susana in his control, he had the upper hand, and he knew it. She could hardly afford to alienate him.

Quickly calculating how onerous it would be to indulge him, Michaela could see she would have to endure some unpleasantness. The question was how much. Bernardo was lecherous and self-indulgent, but fortunately, he was also a buffoon. She would simply have to outsmart him, keep him at bay until she'd had her interview with Susana.

"Shall I pick you up at eight?" he persisted.

Michaela saw there was no avoiding him. "If you wish."

Bernardo put his hand on her knee, proving once more he lacked all subtlety. "I'm sure it will be a delightful evening."

"Yes," she replied, "it should be very interesting." She cringed as he squeezed her knee. Lord, she thought, this guy makes Jack Ellison seem like a saint.

Then, unexpectedly, another man entered her mind. Michaela thought of Father O'Laughlin, longing for his protective presence and good-natured chiding. Ironically, though, the charming priest had only been an illusion—whose real name was Luke Hammond.

On reflection, she decided that maybe that wasn't so bad. Luke had the same genuine concern for her well-being as had Father O'Laughlin. And he'd done something the priest couldn't have done—without dishonor. He'd kissed her.

Taking Bernardo's hand, she removed it from her knee and put it on his own leg, patting it in a friendly way. "You don't want to make me feel cheap, do you, Bernardo?" she said.

"But of course not, my dear. I have the utmost respect."

"Then be the gentleman I know you to be."

Bernardo de Falcón sighed, and Michaela's mind turned to happier thoughts—like the way Luke Hammond had kissed her the night before.

CHAPTER EIGHT

WHEN MICHAELA GOT to her room, she found the maid, Rosita, cleaning the bath. Michaela dropped her purse on the bed and sauntered over to the door to talk to her.

Rosita, on her knees, looked up with a friendly grin. *"¡Hola!"* she said. "How are you today, *señorita?*"

"I'm fine, Rosita. It is a good day."

The maid studied her. "Yes, I can see that on your face. Is it the satisfaction of work, or... something else?"

"You read palms when you not working in the hotel?" Michaela said, gently teasing her.

"A new man brings a special look to the face of a lady, *señorita.*" Her expression slowly turned sober. "But forgive me for saying this, I hope it is not the snake, Señor de Falcón, who makes you so happy."

Michaela blinked. "You knew I was with Bernardo today?"

"You left with him in the big limousine. The whole hotel knows this, *señorita.*"

"So they do. What else does the whole hotel know, Rosita?"

"Señor Snake is not your only admirer."

"Oh?"

A smile twitched at the corner of Rosita's mouth. "To say more would not be wise," she said, making the sign of the cross.

Michaela was fairly certain now that the maid's sympathies were with the MAP. Even so, that didn't mean Rosita was aware that the surprise visit from "Father O'Laughlin" was in reality a meeting with a lieutenant in the revolution.

"I hope you know I would never do anything...indecent or improper," Michaela said, concerned that Rosita might be under the impression she'd been cavorting with a priest.

"It is not my affair, *señorita.*"

"It's not mine, either." Michaela spoke forcefully to make her point. "I mean to say, it was strictly business."

Rosita repressed a smile.

"I'm referring to my work as a *reporter,*" she explained, blushing.

"Personally, *señorita,* I think you should worry only about the bald one. The world knows the kind of man he is."

"Oh? What kind is that?"

"He is without honor. He has a wife and three daughters, but all his time he spends with the *señoritas.*"

"Bernardo has three daughters?" Michaela felt a stab of guilt—not that she'd actually done anything to warrant it.

"*Sí, señorita.* Three."

Michaela hated him even more. "You're right, Rosita. He is a snake."

"Do you see him again?"

"Yes, we're supposed to have dinner tonight. But it's really for business reasons. I need him to help me with my story," she added.

"Maybe that is true. But the business of Señor Snake may not be the same as the business you prefer." Rosita got to her feet. She started to speak, then stopped, as if she had a hard time considering whether she should say more. "As a kindness, I will tell you something very important about Bernardo de Falcón. Come," she said, pointing to the bedroom. "It is more easy to talk in a chair than on the knees."

They went to the armchairs and sat. The maid's expression was serious, her manner reflecting almost a maternal concern.

"A friend of my cousin is the maid of Señor de Falcón's mistress."

"His *mistress?*" she sputtered.

"There are two or three, but one is the favorite. From my cousin I know all the important informations."

Michaela blanched. "Like what?"

"He has a weakness, *señorita*. It is champagne. He loves to drink it and when he drinks *mucho* he cannot—how do you say?—be a man in the bed with a woman." Rosita held up her finger, then bent it at the first joint. *"Comprende?"*

Michaela blushed, nodding. "Yes, I understand."

"It is very good informations for a woman to know," Rosita said. A big grin filled her face. "So remember, *señorita. Mucho* champagne."

"Thank you, Rosita, but I hope that information won't be needed."

The telephone rang and Rosita went off to the bathroom to finish her work. Michaela answered the phone.

"How's our foreign correspondent?" It was Chelsea Osborne.

"Chels," Michaela said. "A voice from the past. God, I'm glad you called."

"Everything okay?"

"Except for the fact that I'm about to be carried off into bondage by Señor Snake, everything's great."

"Mike, what are you talking about?"

"He's my date for dinner tonight."

"Have you been drinking too much tequila?"

"No, I've squeezed three weeks of adventure into two days, and I'm just getting started."

"Who's Señor Snake?"

"The Pangonian answer to Jack Ellison. But it's a long story. The main news is I'm getting in to see Susana."

"When?"

"I don't know for sure, but they promised it would be soon."

"That's wonderful, Mike. How'd you work it out?"

"By agreeing to play footsie with Susana's old boss, the editor of the government paper. That's what it boils down to, anyway. But I'm hoping it won't be as bad as it sounds. I've got a secret weapon that the hotel maid told me about—champagne. Too much and the snake wilts."

"Forgive me for saying this, Mike, but I really think you are drunk."

"Nope. Honest Injun, I'm sober. It's just that the situation down here is pretty crazy, Chels. Honestly. I can't go into it now, but I'm also hot on the trail of Reed Lakesly."

"My God, you have been busy."

"And are you ready for this?"

"I don't know," Chelsea said. "You've already got me overwhelmed. What?"

"Remember the missing disciple?"

"What?"

"You commented that I was dating three of them, remember? You claimed all I needed to do was meet the fourth."

"Oh, yeah. Matt, Mark and John. Don't tell me you found Luke."

"Well, it's early in the relationship, but it's gotten off to a rather auspicious beginning. He shows promise in a crazy kind of way, if you get my drift."

"I don't, but I'll take your word for it."

Michaela felt a little dazed, just recounting everything that had happened in Montagua. "The funny thing, Chels, is the next few days should be even more exciting."

"I hope you took your Valium with you."

"Frankly, a nice hot bath wouldn't be bad. I've got to be rested for tonight. Unless I'm quick with the champagne, it could end up like a sumo wrestling match. It's the one part I'm not looking forward to."

"I wonder if you aren't overdoing it, Mike," Chelsea advised. "Nobody said you've got to win your Pulitzer your first day as a foreign correspondent."

"I'm not so worried about myself as I am about Susana," she said. "The jailers here aren't kindergarten teachers. What's worse, I'm still not sure there's a lot I can do to help her, even if I do get in to see her.''

''Sometimes publicity is the most effective way to fight abuses.''

''That's what I've been thinking. But I'm not so sure we should be discussing this over the phone, if you know what I mean. So, tell me. Any news from the home front?''

''Same ol', same ol','' Chelsea replied. ''I'm sure you don't want to hear the latest back-room developments on the budget.''

''You're right about that. Creepy as it may seem, I'd rather worry about keeping my tail feathers out of the soup tonight.''

Chelsea laughed. ''Something tells me I'm beginning to see the real you, Mike.''

''Yeah. It's early, but I'm thinking the same thing. The excitement appeals to me.''

''You *are* coming home, aren't you?''

''If I can stay out of jail, I am.''

There was a long silence on the line.

''Chels?''

''I'm going to worry about you,'' her friend said.

''No need to. I'm having a ball.''

''Keep smiling,'' Chelsea told her. ''And don't let down your guard.''

''I'll be packing a week's supply of champagne tonight.''

They said goodbye. Michaela hung up, feeling better. Just talking to Chelsea Osborne picked up her spirits. They always managed to do that for each other. It was one of the reasons they were such good friends.

Rosita came out of the bath carrying her bucket of cleaning supplies. ''I'll go now,'' she said. ''But if you feel better for it, I will work late tonight. I can be here when you come back to the hotel with Señor de Falcón.''

''That's kind of you, Rosita, but I'm sure there won't be any problem.'' Then she winked. ''I'm good at pouring champagne.''

"Even so, *señorita,*" Rosita said, "I pray for you. The pretty ones always need a little bit extra help."

BERNARDO DE FALCÓN arrived promptly at the appointed hour. He was wearing a black suit and black tie and had a fresh boutonniere in his lapel. Michaela had packed a black silk dress with a slim skirt and cap sleeves on the theory that she could dress it up or down, depending on her needs. She decided to wear that, along with her fake pearls—the *good* fake ones she'd gotten when she was Miss Arizona.

When Michaela got downstairs, and noticed that both she and Bernardo were in black, it occurred to her they looked more like they were going to a funeral than to dinner. She hoped it wasn't an omen.

"*¡Bella, bella!*" he said, ceremoniously taking her hands. He added a kiss on her cheek. "I am totally captivated, Michaela. I could stand here the whole night looking at you." He puffed out his chest a bit and elevated his chin.

She swallowed a giggle. "You're too kind, Bernardo."

He touched her hair, looking thoroughly entranced. Then he turned and took a bouquet of roses from the chair nearby and gave them to her. "For you, my dear."

"How lovely," she said. They were beautiful, but getting them from Bernardo was creepy, especially after what Rosita had told her. Michaela had a sudden craving for champagne.

"Shall we go?"

"Maybe I should have these put in my room. It would be a shame for them to wilt."

"As you wish." Bernardo snapped his fingers and a bellman promptly presented himself. After extracting a single bud from the bouquet, Bernardo gave the bellman explicit instructions in Spanish. Handing Michaela the single rose, he took the bouquet from her and gave it to the bellman. Then he ushered her to the door and out to the waiting limousine.

Bernardo scooted close to her and gave her a quick hard kiss. Michaela was caught completely off guard. Before she knew what was happening, he had pressed her head back against the seat and slipped his meaty hand around her waist. He drew her body close to his. His mouth tasted of cigars and repulsed her. She finally managed to push him away.

"You told me you were a gentleman."

"A gentleman, yes, but also a romantic. I have never known a woman so lovely as you, my dove."

Michaela was dismayed. Could there be something more than an excess of Latin hormones at work, or was he merely overdoing the sex bit? "Try to control yourself. Please."

The limousine pulled away and as it did, she glanced out the window. A man on a motor scooter across the street was watching them. As they whisked by, she saw that it was Santos Moreno.

"Have you heard when I'll be able to visit Susana?" she asked sweetly, hoping to get Bernardo's mind off romance.

"Perhaps tomorrow afternoon."

She was happy with the news. "When will I know for sure?"

"Let's see how things go this evening," he said craftily.

He didn't even have the grace to try to be subtle. The message was clear—if she went to bed with him, she'd see Susana. His brazen assumption was too much. Her first impulse was to give him the what-for, but she held her tongue. Bernardo was as every bit as much an idiot as he was a predator. Still, it would do her no good to tell him so.

They drove through dark streets and Michaela sniffed her rose, preferring it to the sickly-sweet scent of Bernardo's cologne. She wondered if Santos Moreno was following them. She didn't know what difference it would make, but she was secretly hoping he was. She was experiencing a small crisis of confidence and needed every friend she could get.

Bernardo drew his fingers along her bare arm. She shivered with revulsion. "I'm taking you to Montagua's finest French restaurant," he said. "I hope you like French cuisine."

"Do they have champagne?" she asked breathlessly. "I love champagne."

"Ah," he said, kissing the tips of his fingers and tossing it heavenward, "the woman of my dreams."

Michaela sighed, thanking God for Rosita's timely advice.

A few minutes later they arrived at Chez François, a French restaurant located on an elegant street filled with jewelers and designer boutiques. They disembarked from the limo, stepping under a blue-and-white canopy. A doorman in a blue uniform and white gloves held the door for them. As they headed inside, Michaela glanced back up the street, seeing Santos Moreno on his motor scooter at the corner.

The maître d', with slicked-back hair and a pencil-thin mustache, greeted them effusively, speaking French with a heavy Spanish accent. *"Bon soir, monsieur et madame,"* he said, as he clicked his heels. *"Je suis très content de vous voir, Monsieur de Falcón. Comme toujours. Comme toujours."* He gave Michaela a little smile of recognition, then Bernardo a grin of approval. The editor's chest swelled.

They were shown to a quiet corner table. Their chairs were covered in a rich blue damask that matched the wallpaper. The carpet was also blue. There was a single candle on their table. The maître d' beamed at them.

"C'est une occasion spéciale," Michaela said in her best college French. *"Soyez certain qu'il y en a assez de champagne, s'il vous plaît."*

"Bien entendu, madame," he replied. *"Comme vous voulez."*

"Le meilleur que vous avez."

He bowed and left the table.

"Ah," Bernardo said to her, "you speak French."

"A little."

"What was that about?"

"I told him it was a very special occasion and that we had to make sure you were completely happy."

Bernardo beamed. "You are a woman of many graces."

"I value our friendship, Bernardo." She sniffed the rose.

Almost immediately a chilled bottle of Dom Pérignon champagne was brought to their table. Bernardo's eyes rounded.

"Aha, so that was what you were saying," he said with delight. "A woman who understands the passions of a man, is a woman indeed."

Michaela silently muttered another prayer of thanks to Rosita. She could only hope that Bernardo's appetite for French champagne exceeded his appetite for her. The bottle was opened with a flourish. They picked up their crystal flutes to drink.

"May the evening end as auspiciously as it has begun," he said, flicking his brows suggestively.

Let's hope it ends in a drunken stupor, Michaela thought as she gave him her best plastic smile. "Also to friendship and the spirit of cooperation," she said aloud.

"An excellent word, *cooperation,*" Bernardo said. "The mutuality much appeals to me." He lifted his glass to his lips and guzzled half the wine.

Michaela let the amber liquid touch the tip of her tongue. Bernardo gazed at her, his eyes twinkling with expectation. He quaffed the rest of his champagne, and Michaela took the bottle and refilled the glass for him. It was the least she could do.

Several minutes passed in which Bernardo drank and waxed rhapsodic about the joys of the good life. "I can imagine nothing so pleasurable as being able to enjoy the sight of you and the taste of a good champagne at the same time," he said.

Michaela watched him closely. Though he'd single-handedly drunk two-thirds of the bottle, it hardly seemed to have an effect on him. That worried her.

The waiter came for their orders. "Hearing you speak French is such a pleasure," Bernardo said to her, "I'll defer my duty as a gentleman and ask you to order, if you'd be so kind."

Michaela did as he asked. When she'd finished, she requested another bottle of champagne. Bernardo, who'd beamed through the entire process, impulsively took her hand and drew his fingers down each of hers. It was all she could do to keep from snatching her hand away.

"Do you have children?" she asked.

He did not much like the question, but admitted that he had daughters.

"They must adore you," she said.

"They do," he conceded. "But this is hardly a topic for us to discuss," he said, giving her a seductive look. "This is a night for romance."

Michaela wondered if a conversation about his mistress would be suitably romantic, but she knew she'd be wise to confine her sarcasm to her thoughts. Even so, the resentment she felt toward the man was considerable. Bernardo had but one objective in mind and he'd chosen to attain it by coercion—sprinkled with wine and roses, to be sure, but coercion nonetheless.

Just as their soup course arrived, the electricity suddenly went out. The candles on the tables afforded just enough light that shapes and silhouettes could be seen.

"Ah, wouldn't you know," Bernardo said, gulping some more champagne. "A bit earlier than usual tonight."

"Does this happen often?" Michaela asked.

"Our electrical system needs modernizing," he replied ingenuously.

After a tiny sip of the wine, she picked up her soupspoon. Her mind was turning. Was this just another routine power outage arranged by the MAP, or could it somehow have been connected with her date with Bernardo? Knowing that they'd been followed by one of Luke Hammond's compatriots made her wonder. It was an egocentric notion, but it pleased her to think it might be some sort of signal. She even flirted with the idea that Luke was jealous, but that was probably wishful thinking on her part.

They had finished their soup and Bernardo was enjoying an intermediate glass of champagne, "to clear his palate," when she noticed two men in clerical vestments enter the restaurant. One was quite large, heavyset. The other was Father O'Laughlin.

Michaela was astounded. Bernardo saw the surprise on her face and glanced vacantly in their direction. She immediately diverted his attention, asking him if they should order more wine.

"We still have some," he said, slurring his words ever so slightly.

At last, the alcohol seemed to be having some effect. She'd worried that he'd developed an immunity. But her eyes quickly shifted to Luke. He was following the maître d' to what appeared to be the empty table next to them! She tensed, thinking he was surely subjecting himself to needless danger. Why had he come? For her sake?

The other priest was Father Tucino, the man who'd been with him the first day. Their garments were much finer than the rough cassocks they'd worn when they'd been in the guise of country priests. Even Tucino was well-groomed and presentable.

Michaela assumed it wasn't unheard of for clerics to dine in a fine restaurant, though it was clear they were less conspicuous in the virtually dark restaurant than they would have been before the power went off.

They settled at their table. Michaela watched them from the corner of her eye. Fortunately they were behind Bernardo and she was able to see Luke by glancing over Bernardo's shoulder. She didn't know whether she was nervous out of concern for his safety or because of his proximity. Either way, Michaela couldn't help but be struck by the irony that she was dining with the son of the president of the republic while a prominent revolutionary was sitting only a few feet away.

Luke caught her eye just then, and nodded a subtle greeting, betraying no more than the faintest of smiles. Bernardo was watching her, too, so she had to look away.

"Michaela, my dear," Bernardo said, his voice loud, and his tongue seemingly growing thicker by the minute. "I've had a delightfully wicked thought."

She quailed. "What's that?"

"I'm wondering what it would take for your paper to put you on permanent assignment here in Montagua."

"I don't know that there would be any justification for it," she said. "We have bureaus in Caracas, Rio de Janeiro and Buenos Aires. I doubt there's need for still another. As you know, I'm here on special assignment."

She shifted her gaze to Luke, knowing he could easily hear the conversation. He was perusing his menu.

Bernardo drained his glass. "I'm convinced you should stay longer," he said.

"Oh? Why's that?"

"Because I may be falling in love with you," he said, his Dutch courage starting to show.

She noticed a smile touch Luke's lips. "You've let your romantic nature overwhelm you, Bernardo," she said.

"Don't you think it's a good idea?" he asked, really beginning to sound tipsy.

"I'll be interested to see how it goes with Susana tomorrow," she said pointedly.

The editor gave her a drunken grin as he refilled his glass. "And I'll be interested to see how it goes tonight."

Luke's smile broadened, though he didn't look up from his menu. Michaela still didn't know what to make of his presence. Was he amusing himself? Was he there out of concern? Or some more important purpose? Could it be that he didn't trust her?

That seemed unlikely. Knowing he was only a few feet away, she would have guarded her words if she was harboring any nefarious intent. If he was truly suspicious, he would have sent someone she didn't know to spy on her. There had to be some other reason.

Bernardo drained another glass of champagne and was well approaching the point of no return. Michaela felt a sense of relief, though Luke's presence still made the situation tense.

Bernardo hiccuped, surprising even himself. "Hmm," he said, savoring the sensation in his head. "Perhaps you will excuse me for a moment, Mich-ch-aela," he said, butchering her name.

"Certainly."

He got to his feet, pausing to rake his fingers across her cheek. Then he lurched off in the direction of the facilities. Luke chuckled, looking directly at her. "The things a dedicated journalist must do," he said, almost sounding sympathetic.

"What are you doing here?" she whispered, loud enough for him to hear.

"Having dinner."

She glanced at "Father" Tucino, who wore the same wary grimace she'd seen the first day. But Luke Hammond appeared as unconcerned as could be. She shook her head. "How can you sit three feet away from the son of General de Falcón and casually eat dinner?" she asked, as dismayed as she was exasperated.

"You're closer to him, *my dear,* in more ways, it seems, than one."

"If you think I'm enjoying this," she flared, but still in a whisper, "you're nuts."

"Maybe you're too friendly," he said.

"I could insult the man and it wouldn't make any difference. Thank God he loves champagne."

"Yes, I thought that information might come in handy." Michaela blinked. "That came from you?"

"Ever since you came to me in the confessional, I've felt a special responsibility toward you, my child. Body *and* soul."

Michaela colored, but couldn't say anything because the waiter had arrived. After placing their entrées on the table, he left. She glanced toward the door where Bernardo had exited.

"If you're hungry, I wouldn't wait," Luke said from the adjoining table. "He's trying to sober up. You'll have to get another bottle down him to be safe."

"Is anyone in this country safe from your prying eyes?"

He looked surprised. "You aren't unhappy with me, are you?"

"Does Rosita spy on me?" she asked curtly.

"Think of her as a guardian angel."

"And what are you?"

"Besides father confessor? Well...not big brother—that's more the government's style. Let's say a friend and admirer—though it seems you aren't without other admirers, my child."

Michaela proceeded to eat, not looking at him as she spoke. "You really get off on this, don't you, Father O'Laughlin?"

"You're worried about Susana," he said. "And so am I."

"You heard I may see her tomorrow."

"But as I understand it, at a price."

"Not if the champagne works," she replied.

"And if it doesn't?"

"I may be in the confessional again...confessing murder."

Luke chuckled, then turned serious. "I must say, I'm torn over this. I feel responsible for you."

The sentiment moved her. She looked at him in the candlelight, thankful that his priestly image was but a mask. She liked him very much, even as she continued to be distrustful.

"Look alert," he said under his breath, "The buffoon is returning."

Michaela glanced up and saw Bernardo heading back to the table, his gait slightly more steady than before. She sighed regretfully. How much more enjoyable it would have been to share this meal with Luke Hammond.

"We must talk before tomorrow," he said hastily.

Michaela looked at him for the last time before Bernardo arrived. His words somehow gave her heart.

"A thousand pardons," Bernardo said, dropping into his chair. "Perhaps the champagne didn't agree with me." Then he looked at his plate. "Ah, the entrées have arrived."

"Perhaps we should try a different brand of champagne," she said, trying not to sound too anxious. "The last bottle didn't seem quite right to me."

"You think not? Well, perhaps we should, then—if only for you, my dear."

Michaela gave a silent sigh of relief. Looking over Bernardo's shoulder, she saw Luke give a subtle wink. It was a small gesture, but one she found infinitely endearing. *Lord,* she thought, as she watched Bernardo dig into his dinner, *what am I doing with Señor Snake?*

CHAPTER NINE

THE LIMOUSINE PULLED UP in front of the hotel and Bernardo lurched from his drunken stupor. Michaela held the half-empty bottle of Dom Pérignon in her lap, waiting to give him what she hoped would be the last slug before saying good-night.

She felt guilty, like a pusher selling drugs to children. Not that Bernardo had needed pushing, exactly, but he might have controlled himself better without her encouraging. And yet, if she hadn't, she'd have been in for an evening of hand-to-hand combat. As it was, she'd had to get tough a couple of times.

Fortunately he was far too drunk to fully comprehend the character of her rebuke. He knew that sex was the issue but booze had leveled the playing field, and Bernardo was largely oblivious as to why.

He looked out the window, bleary-eyed. "*¿Dónde estamos?*"

"We're at my hotel. The time has come to say good-night."

"Good night? I can't say good-night, *pequeña*. Don't you remember, Mich-ch-aela, we're *supposed* to come to the hotel. *¿Hay algún problema?*" He took her chin, his head weaving as he tried to focus his eyes. "I love you, remember?"

"And I'm fond of you," she said, patting his cheek. "But now you have to go home and get some sleep. We've got a big day tomorrow. We're going to visit Susana Riveros, remember?"

"Who?"

"Susana. My friend, the one who your father has in prison."

"*Seguramente*. She is your friend and I am your friend. And I love you."

The driver had gone around and opened the door.

"Good night, Bernardo," she said. "I'm going now." Escaping his grasp, she slipped from the limousine. But Bernardo was not going to be defeated so easily. He staggered out behind her.

"You can't leave. You can't leave," he protested as he drew himself up, struggling to maintain equilibrium. "Anyway, I am a gentleman, and a gentleman always sees a lady to her door."

"*This* is my door."

"Not the door to your bedroom," he said, wagging his finger.

Michaela began to lose patience. "Honestly, Bernardo." The half-full bottle of champagne in her hand, she turned and marched into the hotel. She asked for her key at the desk but Bernardo snatched it from the clerk's hand.

"A gentleman always takes the key," he insisted.

She headed for the elevator, wondering if it would be better to make a stand in the lobby or at her room. She couldn't give him much more slack. Deciding not to make a public spectacle, she let him follow her. As the door closed, Michaela handed him the bottle.

"Chug-a-lug," she said. "We might as well enjoy this."

Bernardo shook his head. "Drink is a hindrance to my manhood. I'm a better lover if I don't have too much champagne."

"Sweetie, there's never too much champagne." She took the bottle from him and took a sip. Then she tried to affect a sexy expression. "See, it makes a person amorous."

Bernardo pondered the comment, shrugged, and took a long drink. Michaela wondered how many more until he was unconscious.

They arrived at her floor. She headed down the hall, with Bernardo staggering along behind. She came to her door, stopped and faced him.

"Well, here we are, Bernardo. Give me my key," she said, holding out her hand. "It's time to say good-night."

With a struggle, he drew himself up. "I'll open it."

Gently pushing her aside, he began fumbling with the lock. He managed to get the key in, but couldn't make it work. In exasperation, he put his shoulder to the door and gave a shove. It burst open and Bernardo went flying. He ended up sprawled in the middle of the floor, spilling the champagne all over himself and the carpet. He lifted his head and looked up at her, dazed.

"Perdón," he mumbled.

"Oh, Bernardo," she said, "I wish you weren't so pathetic. It would be easier to be angry with you." She helped him into a chair. "Sit here and let me get a towel to clean up the mess." Tossing her purse onto the bed, she went into the bathroom.

As she flipped the light switch, she caught a glimpse of a robed figure. She almost screamed before realizing it was "Father O'Laughlin." "Oh, my God," she said. "You scared me to death."

"Yes, I know. We've got to stop meeting like this."

Michaela looked back over her shoulder at Bernardo, who was too dazed to know what was going on. She closed the door. "You said it, Father, and I couldn't agree more."

"I didn't know you were going to bring lover boy here. What happened? Did he suddenly become irresistible?"

"No, just immovable."

"Shall I send him packing?"

"Of course not. He's drunk, but not so far gone he'd forget being thrown out of my room by a priest."

"Are you sure?"

"Well, I can't take the chance. And neither can you."

"So what are we going to do?" he asked.

"I'm tempted to get another room and let you and Bernardo spend the night together. What is it about men in this country that they think they have a right to enter a woman's bedroom whenever they wish?''

"I can't speak for Bernardo, but I've got business to discuss with you."

"In the middle of the night?"

"It's difficult conducting a revolution during normal office hours, and I've got to speak with you before you see Susana."

"First, I've got to get rid of Bernardo. I'd better get out there." She grabbed a towel from the rack and left the bathroom.

Bernardo was sitting on the bed in his underwear.

"Where have you been, Mich-ch-aela?"

"Bernardo! What in the hell are you doing?"

He frowned. "*Querida*, what's wrong? Aren't we lovers?"

She marched over and picked up his trousers and tossed them to him. "Put these on immediately!"

"But you don't understand," he said, getting to his feet. "I love you. Surely you know this."

Before she knew it, he had her in his arms.

"Bernardo!" she screamed. "Let go of me!"

As she fought him he lost his balance and they toppled onto the bed, Bernardo landing on top of her with a thud. He reeked of champagne and tobacco and he weighed a ton. He struggled to focus his eyes and kissed her anyway. The next thing Michaela knew, he was being pulled off her. Lucas gave a sharp blow to the back of Bernardo's neck and he dropped to the floor.

"God, he's obnoxious."

"Lucas," Michaela said, sitting up, "what am I going to do now? How am I going to explain this?"

"He's too drunk to know what hit him. If he asks, say you were kissing and he suddenly passed out. Believe me, it won't be the first time ol' Bernardo has failed to answer the bell."

"But what do I do with him now?"

"Have hotel security take him to his limo. It won't be the first time he's been driven home in a stupor, either."

"Is there anything about him you don't know?"

Luke smiled. "One principle of war, *querida,* is to know thine enemy. He's one of the men responsible for raping this country, though you've only seen the warm-up act. The *generalísimo* is bent on abusing a lot more than just alcohol and women. Bernardo is a child by comparison. Susana was able to use him until Daddy put a stop to it. *That's* what this is really all about."

"I guess I'd better call hotel security."

"When they come I'll step into the bathroom."

Michaela phoned the desk. Within minutes three security men knocked at her door. They dressed Bernardo and carried him off. When they'd gone, she turned the dead bolt. Luke appeared at the door to the bath. He'd removed his vestments and was in dark trousers and a plain white shirt with full sleeves and open at the neck. They stared at each other.

"I'm sorry you had to endure all that," he said solemnly. "This isn't the sort of evening a woman looks forward to, I'm sure."

"I can't hate Bernardo. He's more misguided than evil."

"I wish I were as generous." He sat on the corner of the bed and sighed. "Maybe I've been at this too long. Revolution is not fun when you come right down to it."

"Then why not go back to Canada? Surely your involvement isn't essential to the cause."

"No one is indispensable, but I have an obligation to finish what I've started. I care about this country and these people."

"I admire you for feeling that way."

He looked at her intently. "I am sorry you've been put in the middle of this, though. I feel responsible. That's why I was at the restaurant tonight and why I came here."

"I appreciate your concern, Lucas, but I would have gotten into this even if I'd never met you. You aren't responsible."

"I shudder to think where you'd be now without the rabbit chop I gave Bernardo."

"It wasn't a fun date, but as you well know, Señor Snake has his limitations." She held up her finger, then bent it as Rosita had done. "I assume you can relate to that," she added.

"Not from personal experience." The corners of his mouth twitched. "Though I can't prove it unless we get to know each other a lot better than we do now."

"A *whole* lot better," Michaela said, crossing her legs.

"It was a statement of fact, not a proposition."

He answered calmly, his voice light and unruffled. He was smooth, she had to give him that. "Well, I believe you wanted to discuss Susana," she said, changing the subject.

"Yes. If you see her tomorrow, it'll give us a perfect opportunity to contact her. I know I'm asking you to take a risk, but we need you to help us help her."

"She was one of the reasons I came down here, so if there's a message you want me to pass along, I will."

"I'm afraid it's a bit more complicated than that, Michaela. I want you to hand deliver a coded message." He reached into his pocket and produced a pill-size capsule, holding it between his fingers. "Just give this to her. If you're compromised, swallow it. The paper is digestible. The danger is in getting caught with a coded message from the MAP."

Michaela contemplated him. "I understand."

"I don't know if they're suspicious of you, but if you were caught, it's only fair to tell you that it wouldn't be pleasant."

She nodded solemnly. "You're asking how far I'm willing to go to help a college friend."

"Essentially."

"How important is it that Susana gets your message?"

"Naturally, I'm going to tell you it's very important. But I think you're really asking how important this is to her well-being. The truth is, it could be critical to her survival."

"I can hardly say no under those circumstances," she said.

Luke held out the capsule. Michaela went over to him and he dropped it into her palm. She looked down at it.

"I guess I've become a revolutionary, haven't I?" she said.

"A fellow traveler, at least."

"Why do you trust me, Lucas?"

"At a certain point it becomes a leap of faith, I grant you But for now, let's say I feel your rapport with us is better than your rapport with them."

Michaela was still gazing down at the capsule. Luke lifted her chin and made her look into his eyes.

"Am I right?" he asked.

"Your cause seems just."

"That's not all I meant by rapport."

Her eyes moved back and forth between his. "What else?"

"Something much more personal." With that, his mouth moved toward hers. The kiss was tender, and he lingered, drawing out the caress, his lips barely grazing hers. Michaela was tantalized, wanting more, but he pulled back.

"Was that a test or a statement?" she whispered, staring at his mouth.

"A kiss. Nothing more. Nothing less."

"What does it have to do with Susana?"

"Nothing. It has to do with us."

Her expression turned wary. The spell was broken. "You're as bad as Bernardo. A bit smoother, but otherwise no different."

"I plead guilty to sharing an appreciation of you. But you shouldn't hold that against me."

Michaela slipped from his circle of intimacy and stepped to the dresser, where she put the capsule down. Then she went to the open window to inhale the balmy night air.

"*Do* you hold that against me?" he asked.

She turned to face him. "I'm always suspicious of men who want to kiss first and get to know you later."

"We're living on borrowed time, Michaela. And if I don't know you well, I certainly know how I feel about you."

He moved so close that she felt the warmth of his breath. It was seduction, pure and simple. But it was so hard not to like the sensations, so hard to control the loping beat of her heart. He was about to kiss her again when the lights went out.

"Our timing is superb." Luke chuckled.

"I think that's your signal to go home."

He took her jaw in his hand. "To the contrary, it means I'm off duty."

Before she could speak, before she even had time to think of something so say, Luke was kissing her. Michaela responded at once. She arched against him as his thigh slid between her legs. She rubbed against him, feeling his heat right through her silk dress. She felt herself moisten and knew that if she didn't stop then, she never would.

"You really believe in...making your point...don't you?" she said as she pulled her mouth free.

Luke drew his tongue along the side of her throat, all the while keeping his thigh between her legs. "We seem to speak the same language," he said.

"In a way you're worse than Bernardo," she murmured. "You don't fight fair."

"Is giving pleasure unfair?" He kissed the corner of her mouth.

"I'm not out of control, Lucas," she said, looking directly into his eyes. "You aroused me, I admit, but I can walk away."

"If I let you."

She narrowed her eyes, but Luke pulled her closer anyway. Her breasts pressed against his chest. And he was right, she didn't have the will to pull away. Before either of them moved, there was a knock at the door. Michaela stiffened.

"It's only the porter with your candles," Luke said. "The question is do you want light or do you want dark?"

"Light." She seized the opportunity to make her getaway.

Having the routine down, she went to the door, opened it and took the candles, one of which was already lit. Closing the door behind her, Michaela began placing the candles about the room, lighting them and the ones from the night before as she went.

"You aren't planning on having a service in here, are you?" he asked. "This is starting to look like a church."

"You came dressed for it, *padre.*"

"Celestial thoughts are the furthest thing from my mind right now."

She laughed. "I think you've identified the problem."

He went over to her. She looked into his shadowed face, seeing a desire very much like her own. She knew then that the control she thought she'd regained was only an illusion.

"Would it be a sin if I were to make love to you?"

She gazed at him, unable to say they shouldn't make love, though she knew that was what she ought to do. "You know what I think, Lucas? I think making love with you is a rite of the revolution—the ultimate recruiting technique."

He ran his finger down the side of her neck and across her chest. "We're united in the cause whether we make love or not."

"Would you leave if I asked you to?"

"Yes."

Michaela touched the shallow cleft of his chin. "Perhaps it would be better if we had an affair of the spirit, Lucas. Who knows, when we're better acquainted, maybe…maybe we…"

"You're not joking, are you?"

She shook her head. "The Father O'Laughlin I know is a man of utmost rectitude."

He grinned. "The Father O'Laughlin you know is a phony."

Michaela leaned forward and kissed him. Luke did not move, though he inhaled her scent. "Good night, Lucas."

He gave her a long, appraising look. "Then I'd better go before I change my mind about being honorable." He went into the bathroom to fetch his robes. He reappeared with them over his arm.

"Aren't you going to put on the cassock?"

"I'll dress downstairs, before I go into the street." He approached to within a foot of her, looking for all the world like he wanted to take her into his arms. He didn't touch her. He simply shook his head. "I'd forgotten *norteaméricanas* could be so hard-hearted."

"You're used to the *señoritas* eating out of your palm."

"You're enjoying this," he chided. "Don't deny it."

Michaela didn't, really. From the moment she'd asked him to leave, she'd had misgivings. It was the same old conflict—the one between her heart and her mind. "I'm not enjoying this at all," she said softly.

Hope returned to his face. "Is that because you want to be with me as badly as I want to be with you?"

They stared at each other for two or three minutes. Luke didn't say anything. He didn't have to. Michaela knew she was doomed. Some things simply couldn't be denied.

Sighing, she reached back and slowly unzipped her dress. Then she slipped her arms out of the sleeves she let it slither to the floor.

"Are you sure, Michaela?" he whispered.

"Mike," she corrected. "I guess it's time you call me Mike."

MICHAELA STOOD in the bathroom, undressing. As she thought about making love with Luke, part of her was excited and part was embarrassed. She had never offered herself to a man before—at least, not so blatantly. In fact, it was rare these days that she slept with anyone, and certainly never before forging a deep bond of friendship. Even then, she had misgivings because sex, she'd always felt, was meant to go with love.

And yet there were a couple of times when, out of loneliness or a need to be close to someone she cared for, someone who cared for her, she had gone to bed with a man for whom she felt no romantic love. This wasn't like that.

It was difficult to say why she wanted Luke Hammond. She didn't really know him. Reason told her she couldn't love him, but she didn't want to think the attraction she felt was simple lust, though she couldn't prove otherwise. Perhaps it was an impulse from deep within her—the same sort of impulse that had brought her to Pangonia. Some things seemed so destined to be that you made them happen. Giving herself to this *norteaméricano* revolutionary with the Latin-style machismo was like that.

Michaela freshened up, then put on the silk wrap she'd left on the back of the door. When she stepped into the bedroom, she saw that all but one of the candles had been extinguished. Luke was sitting in bed with a couple of pillows fluffed up behind him. The sheet was across his waist. His chest was matted with dark hair. Seeing it, she imagined the way it would feel against her breasts.

Luke watched her walk slowly to the bed. He seemed content, though there was no trace of triumph in his eyes. She suddenly found it difficult to look at him.

Her first inclination was to tell him she'd never done anything like this before—not with a man she hardly knew. But that seemed weak, and she didn't want to give that impression.

"This must happen to you all the time," she said. "Getting propositioned, I mean."

"I believe I asked you, Michaela, before you asked me."

"Don't feel you have to make it look better," she said.

"That wasn't my intention. I only wanted to take credit for having such an excellent idea."

Michaela laughed, grateful that his sense of humor had eased the tension. She didn't exactly regret her decision, but she was tentative.

"Does each *señorita* who joins the revolution get initiated this way?" she asked.

"The MAP is not a sex club, Mike."

"Perhaps not. But I imagine you can have anybody you want."

He took her hand. "It's not too late to change your mind. We can just talk if you're having second thoughts."

"I appreciate that, but I'm really not trying to back out."

"I think you need some reassurance," he said, rubbing the back of her hand with his thumb. "Come on, get in beside me."

He looked so appealing with the shadows from the candlelight playing on his face. Luke wasn't easy to resist. She hadn't known anyone like him before—not anyone who had this sort of effect on her.

He lifted the sheet so she could slide in next to him. Her hip and leg came up against his warm skin. She was aware of his scent—vaguely Giorgio, but mostly him. He laced his fingers with hers and rested them on the sheet draped across his waist. Michaela closed the V of her wrap, smoothing it over her chest.

"I have a confession to make," he said. "Before we decided to take you into our confidence, we checked you out through some friends in Washington."

"Oh?"

"I know a good deal more about you than you might think. It seemed only fair to make you aware of that."

"And what, exactly, did you find out?"

"That you came down here on your own, all but quitting your job. You're highly regarded. A journalist with a great deal of unrealized potential—that's how you were described."

"I don't know whether to be surprised or not. None of what you said is a secret," she said. "But it does feel odd to know people have been checking up on me...that I've been discussed."

"We got some information on your personal life, as well, but it wasn't complete. The main point, I guess, is that you are a former Miss Arizona."

"Oh," She rolled her eyes. "It's followed me all the way to Pangonia."

He squeezed her hand. "It's hardly a black mark."

"I don't want to sound ungrateful, especially since the scholarship money helped educate me, but once you've been in a beauty pageant you get classified. People tend not to take you seriously. It seems like I've always been the student who was the beauty queen, the journalist who was Miss Arizona, the girlfriend who was a runner-up in the Miss America contest."

"If it makes you feel any better, Mike, I won't hold any of that against you."

She chuckled. "Thanks."

"But I am curious. If the beauty-queen business bothers you so much, why'd you get into it in the first place?"

She looked down at their hands, liking the way her fingers meshed with his. "It's not easy to explain. I had a difficult childhood. I was poor and an orphan, and I wanted desperately to be somebody. I discovered early on that it was easy to trade on my looks, so I tried to take advantage of that. Later I learned that caused more problems than it solved. Once you're typed, it's not easy to change people's thinking."

"I can think of worse handicaps, Mike."

"I don't mean to whine, but people can become very insistent about how they want to regard you. They can ignore the things that truly matter."

"I promise I'll never mention it."

She glanced at him, feeling a little self-conscious. "And I promise not to complain."

He toyed with her fingers. "How old were you when you lost your parents?"

"Mother died when I was a baby and Dad when I was eight. I was raised by an aunt. Gayle was mother, father and big sister to me, though she was only fifteen years older than I. We had a rough time of it financially. I grew up figuring that if I got to be somebody my struggle would be over. Gayle did her best. She's a very principled person. But my dreams were a lot bigger than her world. I strove for more, took risks, and worked up some guilt along the way, I suppose."

"Guilt?"

"Maybe it's harder for women to throw caution to the wind, the way men do. I'm constantly asking myself what's important. I often find that my principles and my desires are at war."

"You wouldn't be talking about now, would you?"

She smiled. "How'd you guess?"

"I wouldn't want you to feel guilty about this," he said, sounding like he might actually mean it.

"I don't know why I even brought it up. I usually don't talk this way with people."

"I'm glad that you feel you can be so honest with me." He rubbed her hand in an affectionate way. "You've never married?"

"No."

"Come close?"

"Not really. It's difficult to develop feelings for anyone when you're at war with yourself—trying to figure out who you are. But I'm belaboring the point. Everyone has problems." She turned and looked into his eyes. "How about you, Lucas? Ever been married? Or maybe I should ask if you're married now."

He chuckled. "No and no."

"You've had a few proposals, I imagine," she quipped.

"Surely not as many as you."

"I tend not to get that far into relationships."

"Nor do I," he said. He regarded her thoughtfully. "Actually, there've been some similarities in our lives. I lost my father when I was young also. The impact of that is greater than most people realize."

"No question," she agreed. "Losing parents when you're little affects your self-confidence. I know I always felt I had to try harder." She fiddled with the opening of her wrap. "What an odd conversation we're having."

"I like it. It feels good. Right, somehow."

"Why?"

He thought for a moment. "I've gotten a glimpse of the woman you really are."

"And is knowing the person you're in bed with important?" she asked, hoping she didn't sound as insecure as she felt.

"Yes. It's very important, Mike. You interest me. I'm curious about you."

She laughed nervously. "You mean you're curious why anybody in their right mind would get in bed with you and proceed to tell you their life story?"

He kissed her hand. "I consider it a compliment that you wish to share your feelings. Especially at a time like this."

"Maybe it's because I'm nervous."

"Speaking from the heart is a form of intimacy. No matter what the reason behind it."

Michaela nodded. "You're right."

"And it's a lot better than getting drunk on champagne."

"Yes," she said. "Much better."

Luke kissed her, as if savoring the tenderness of the moment, the sharing. She sighed, thinking how much she liked it that he was being sweet, gentle. She slipped her hand behind his neck and kissed him back.

Luke gathered her into his arms then. Her shyness melted as he sprinkled kisses over her nose and eyes, drawing in her scent. And as he kissed her, he slipped his hand inside her wrap and took her breast. He weighed its fullness in his palm, then ran his thumb over her nipple. It was already hard, but it tightened under his touch, sending a tremor through her.

By the time he pushed aside her wrap to kiss her nipples, Michaela was quivering with expectation. She watched silently as he flicked his tongue over the tip once, twice, before he drew it into his mouth. A pang of desire went through her. She felt a rush of warm liquid between her legs.

As Luke sucked her breast, she leaned back against the pillows and parted her legs. Luke's hand immediately slid under the sheet and he began caressing her, tracing the edge of her plump folds, teasing her.

Michaela opened her legs a little wider. Luke understood her need. He slipped a finger inside, stretching her, probing deeply, all the while sucking her breast.

She put her hand on the back of his head and rubbed his neck as he moved back and forth between her breasts. In only a minute or two she was on the edge. When she stiffened, he pulled away. His fingers slid out of her. She looked at him, dazed, noticing a bubble of moisture at the corner of his mouth.

"Luke . . . don't stop. Not now."

"You'll like this better. Trust me."

Before she could say a word he wedged her legs farther apart and slipped between them. He kissed her belly and she moaned, knowing what was coming. When she felt the warmth of his breath, she nearly cried out with joy.

Luke flicked out his tongue and barely touched her. The sensation was so strong, so intense, that Michaela almost came. She moved forward just a bit as his tongue flicked out a second time, and she got more of him then. He teased her a third time, a fourth and fifth, before finally crushing his face into her.

His raspy tongue felt warm. She moved her hips, grinding against him, wanting more, always more. But every time she found herself about to come, Lucas pulled back. He'd kiss the inside of her thigh, or reach up to rub her nipple. He fondled her, but he wouldn't give her the touch she wanted, the touch she needed.

She was at the point of telling him she couldn't take it any longer when his mouth began caressing her again. She spread her legs still wider and tried to relax, tried to commit the pleasure to memory. She was nearly there when Luke slid his finger inside her, all the while making love to her with his mouth. That sent her over the edge.

"Oh, Luke. Oh, my God."

He pulled back to watch her in her ecstasy. It took a couple of minutes before the pulsing began to fade. When it finally subsided, Michaela looked at his face. Luke smiled, but there was something in his eyes that surprised her. It was the promise that their night of love had just begun.

CHAPTER TEN

THE PALE GRAY LIGHT of dawn was coming through the window when Michaela awoke. Lucas was dressing, preparing to slip away. She watched silently, savoring the chance to linger over the memories of their lovemaking and put it all into perspective.

It wasn't the first time she'd spent the night with a man she wasn't in love with, and yet, in a way, Michaela had felt loved. She'd been desired, to be sure, but there had been something extra, too—an intangible caring. She felt a real bond with him, as though their lovemaking mattered, as if it was only the beginning of many more nights together.

Lucas was a superb lover. No one had ever turned her on the way he had, made her feel as if she could spend the rest of her life touching and being touched, soaring to the heights and then coming to earth only to soar again.

They had made love three times. The first time he had been dominant, demanding more from her than she thought she had to give. Later it was slower and more gentle. The last time, she had been on top, looking into his eyes as she rocked over him. She'd felt warm and creamy then, as if she had the rest of her life to be like that. And when they had finally come, she'd looked into his eyes and seen his pleasure.

Lucas had pulled her mouth to his, then, and kissed her hard. She fell asleep like that, on top of him, with him still inside her. That had been only a couple of hours ago, but she wasn't tired.

Now, as she watched him dressing, she felt tentative again. They had shared so much...and yet so little. What did it mean? People made love all the time without expectation or commitment—why should this be different? And yet Michaela felt it *was* different. She wasn't sure how, but she knew it was special, at least from her perspective.

The real question was how Lucas felt. Was it routine as far as he was concerned? When she had asked if making love with him was a rite of passage—an initiation—he had scoffed. But his reputation belied that. And even if he didn't move from one woman to another as easily as he moved from one safe house to the next, it was hardly proof that he had felt the same way about it as she did.

No promises had been made. Perhaps that is what brought the reality home. The conquest was over. It was time to return to the real world. And that was sad.

As she thought about it, she imagined that he probably had as much trouble recalling the women he'd slept with in the past month as recalling the meals he'd had. Of course it was possible she was blowing things out of proportion, but the details hardly mattered. The tension between them had been inexorable. It had been inevitable that they would make love. Now they could go on with their work, without the distraction.

Michaela wondered if he would leave without saying goodbye. Nothing needed to be said, really, except for form's sake. In a way she hoped he would slip away quietly. It would be just as well if the entire episode was forgotten.

Michaela closed her eyes, hoping that the next sound she would hear would be the click of the door closing. Instead, she felt him sit down beside her.

"Are you awake, Mike?" he asked softly.

She opened her eyes. "Yes."

He touched her cheek. "I have to go now. I don't want to leave like this, but the patrols will be out soon."

There was enough light that she could make out his features. He'd put on his clerical garb. "I understand," she said. She managed a weak smile.

"It was a wonderful night, Mike. Being with you was fabulous, very special."

"Don't feel you have to say anything you don't really mean. It's not necessary. We knew what we were doing."

Luke stared at her. He didn't say a word but she saw by the look in his eye that she'd wounded him. She immediately felt guilty, realizing she'd been unfair. Just because she was feeling insecure didn't give her the right to take it out on him.

"I'm sorry. I shouldn't have said that."

"Did I do or say something wrong?" he asked quietly.

"No, I suppose I'm uncomfortable."

"Do you regret it?" he asked quickly.

Michaela shook her head. "No. I'm trying to cover my embarrassment. Ignore what I said."

"It's not easy to ignore it," he replied. "I care about you, what you feel and how you think."

"It's kind of awkward for me, knowing what to say. But the last thing I need is to be the cause of you getting captured." She patted his cheek. "You're a wonderful lover, Lucas. I know it wasn't fair to start something without finishing it, but it *is* getting light. You should go while it's safe."

His expression told her he wanted to discuss the matter further, but knew she was right about him leaving. "I'll see you later, after you've talked to Susana," he said. "Meeting here again is too dangerous. We survive by being unpredictable. I'll make other arrangements and get word to you."

"That's the most interesting formulation of 'I'll be in touch' that I've ever heard."

He pinched her cheek. "You're a difficult one, aren't you?"

"Was I snide again?"

"You don't trust easily, do you?"

Michaela lowered her eyes. "I suppose I don't."

Luke leaned over and kissed her tenderly. "It's probably because you were orphaned. Give me a little time, Mike," he whispered. "I can be very reassuring."

His tone was so gentle and understanding that it brought tears to her eyes. "You *are* reassuring. And I'm sorry to have been like this. Now go, Lucas. Please. You'll have me worrying about you."

"*I'm* the one worrying today. Remember what I said about the capsule. Swallow it immediately if you run into trouble."

"I'm sure everything will be fine, Father. If you wish to pray for someone, pray for Susana."

He gathered her into his arms a final time, holding her close. She took in his scent and tears welled in her eyes, though she wasn't quite sure why. That sadness again.

"Goodbye, Lucas," she whispered.

He got up and went to the door, pausing to look back at her. Michaela bit her lip. Her eyes shimmered so that she could no longer see him clearly. Without another word, he slipped from the room.

She stared off at the window. "Damn you, Luke Hammond," she muttered.

He'd been gone for two or three minutes before it occurred to her that she'd neglected to ask him about Reed Lakesly—whether or not she was going to get her interview. What an idiot she was. She didn't even use her leverage to exact a promise for a meeting. She wondered how long it would take for her to learn to play the game like everybody else.

MICHAELA SPENT THE morning writing her account of the news conference with General Juan de Falcón, though she'd decided not to file her story until after she'd spoken with Susana. The writing came easily, as inspiration burned bright inside her. She had a sense of purpose for the first time in months, and yet, in spite of her enthusiasm for her work, distracting thoughts of Luke Hammond entered her mind.

She kept thinking of his remark that she wasn't trusting, and his speculation that it might have something to do with the fact that she was an orphan. It would have been easy to blame every problem that came along on her unfortunate childhood, but Michaela had long since decided that nothing was to be gained by worrying about the past. Still, Lucas had been sensitive to pick up on that. Why didn't that square with what reason told her about the man?

At midmorning Michaela got a phone call from Bernardo's secretary. "Mr. de Falcón, he wishes that you are ready to go to the prison this afternoon at two," the woman said. "He will send a car for you at the hotel."

"Won't Bernardo be going with me?" she asked.

"He say to tell you that he will meet you there at the prison, *señorita.*"

"Okay. Thank you."

Michaela hung up, wondering if Bernardo had had his secretary call because he was still suffering the effects of the night before, or if something was up. Did it mean anything that he'd decided to meet her at the prison, rather than escort her as he had before? Or was he upset by what had happened in her room? She didn't know whether or not to be concerned. It was possible she'd embarrassed or offended him by having him carried off so ignominiously. Surely he hadn't remembered Luke pulling him off the bed and knocking him out. If so, she was in real danger. It could even be that she was being led into a trap.

There was no point in getting paranoid. She would simply have to concentrate on the task at hand—her interview with Susana. Michaela gave careful thought to how she would transport the message capsule. She needed to be prepared to swallow it if she was compromised. That meant being able to get to it quickly. Perhaps a dress with a pocket. There would be no time to fumble through her purse.

Just before she went downstairs for lunch, another bouquet arrived from Bernardo. The sight of the pale yellow roses eased her concern somewhat. His note said, "I'm sorry that I became ill last night, Michaela. I hope you will give me another chance.''

She sighed with relief and actually felt gratitude toward her would-be paramour. Of course, it could still be a trap. The note and flowers might have been designed to give her a false sense of security. But again, Bernardo didn't seem capable of such subtlety. Michaela could only hope she was right.

By the time the car arrived to take her to the prison, she had managed to work herself into a nervous state. Maybe she'd been a bit too cavalier in agreeing to be a spy for Luke, not fully appreciating how nerve-racking the task could be.

Good journalists, Michaela knew, needed moral courage, panache and bravado. Though their work could be dangerous, they always had the prerogatives of their craft on their side. But by becoming partisan, she had sacrificed the protective cloak of her profession, exposing herself to the vicissitudes of the political battlefield. If caught, she would have to pay the consequences. It was a sobering thought that seemed all the more weighty by the light of day.

Michaela didn't want to think that she'd taken the risk for Luke Hammond or even for the MAP. She told herself that she'd done it for Susana, a fellow journalist and a friend. If Susana could sacrifice herself for important ideals, then so could she.

Michaela went out to the waiting limousine, her heart pounding. The innocent-looking capsule Luke had given her felt like a time bomb ticking away in the pocket of her olive linen camp shirt. She climbed in the back seat, clutching her briefcase and purse. The chauffeur, a stony-faced man, took his place and they headed off to the prison.

Michaela was surprised to discover that the facility was so near the presidential palace. She glanced at General Juan de Falcón's residence. It seemed like a week since she'd stood up to challenge the little tyrant, though in fact it had only been a day. Strange to think that in the interim she'd rejected the general's son and gone to bed with his enemy.

The prison was a squat stone building, four stories high. It was predictably grim looking. Michaela glanced up at the facade as she exited the limousine. No bars were visible on the windows at the front of the building, but it did not give the appearance of a place that one could easily escape from.

Two policemen guarded the heavy metal door. One asked to see her passport before letting her enter. The guards inside inspected her briefcase and purse. She walked through a metal detector. Michaela sensed no undue suspicion. If she was being invited into a trap, it wasn't evident.

Once she'd passed through Security she was taken to a small waiting room. She'd no sooner sat down than Bernardo appeared at the door.

"Michaela," he said, his expression crestfallen, "have you forgiven me?"

"Forgiven you?"

"For my despicable behavior last evening. I am terribly humiliated for leaving you as I did. I had a bit too much champagne and became quite ill."

"I knew you weren't feeling well, Bernardo, and I knew you'd be more comfortable at home in your bed, so I instructed them to help you to your limousine."

"Ah, that was it. I wasn't sure. I recall going to the hotel, but not much more. I must have had a fever." He went to her, taking her hands. "Did you receive my flowers?"

"Yes, they were lovely. Thank you."

Peering into her eyes beseechingly, he asked if she would give him another chance. "Dine with me tomorrow," he implored. "I would see you tonight, but it is the birthday of my youngest daughter. I must be with her to celebrate. But tomorrow I have reserved for you, my dear."

Michaela wanted to tell him to go to hell, or at the very least to stay home with his family every night, but she knew she couldn't afford to alienate him—she hadn't yet gotten in to see Susana. "Perhaps," she replied. "If you call me tomorrow we can discuss it."

"I pledge to you on my honor as a gentleman that I will not drink any champagne if you'll dine with me, Michaela."

"Well, there's no need to overdo it," she said. "I don't think it was the champagne, anyway, to be frank. More likely it was the food. I felt a little funny myself."

"Really?"

"Yes, definitely. And it would be such a shame to give up something you enjoy so much. We had such a good time, and I do like champagne myself."

"Then last night wasn't the disaster I thought."

"Not at all, Bernardo."

He thought for a moment. "Tell me, Michaela, how good a time did we have? I mean, the food poisoning left my memory hazy. Did we...uh...did we *really* enjoy ourselves?"

"I can't speak for you," she said, smiling, "but it was one of the best nights of my life."

"Aha!" he said triumphantly. "I thought so!" Then he twitched his eyebrows. "You are as eager for tomorrow night as I am, undoubtedly. I mean, since we had such a good time...the prospect of another...delightful evening must...well..." He was suddenly so overwhelmed that he grabbed her and kissed her passionately.

"Bernardo!" she exclaimed, pushing him away. "This is a prison, not a nightclub."

He clutched her hands to his chest. "But Michaela, my little dove, we have shared so much, I can hardly wait to again experience your love."

"This is not the time or the place."

"Tomorrow is an eternity."

"Time apart can only make it better," she said, feeling very uncomfortable with the direction of the conversation.

"I live for the hour."

"Do have lots of champagne available," she said. "That may be the secret of our...success."

He considered that. "All the same, I must be careful what I eat. It's so much better to be able to remember."

There was a light rap at the door and they looked over at a uniformed guard. *"Perdón, Señor de Falcón,"* the man said. *"El señor Gómez Mateo está aparejado."*

"Muchas gracias, señor," Bernardo replied. He took her elbow and looked into her eyes. "Michaela," he said, "my father was not enthused that you wished to see Susana Riveros. He is concerned that you will use the opportunity to attack the government."

"My job isn't to attack anyone, Bernardo. I report the facts as objectively as I can. Surely, as a respected journalist yourself, you understand that and can explain it to your father."

"But he does not see how you can be objective if you only talk to Susana. Accordingly, he asks that you listen to the evidence against her collected by the ministry of justice. One of the prosecutors, Mr. Gómez Mateo, is here to brief you before you interview Susana."

Michaela could see the intent was to brainwash her, which, for professional reasons, she didn't appreciate. But she was relieved that they were still concerned what she thought. It probably meant they didn't suspect her of being in complicity with the MAP. Otherwise, she probably would have been questioned, if not arrested.

"I have no objection to hearing what the prosecutor has to say," she answered calmly.

"Excellent," Bernardo said, beaming. "I told them you would be reasonable."

He took her arm and led her down the hall to a small office where a slender man of forty-five stood waiting for them beside a desk. Señor Gómez Mateo was dark and gaunt, but had a commanding, self-assured manner. Bernardo introduced him. Michaela shook his hand.

"I am happy to have the opportunity to discuss with you the case of Señorita Susana Riveros," he said in correct but stilted English.

"Knowing nothing about the case, I'm happy to hear what you have to say," she replied.

"Excellent," he said, nodding politely. He smiled at Bernardo. "Before we begin, may I offer to you a refreshment? Coffee or a cold drink, perhaps?"

"Something cold would be nice," Michaela said.

"*¿Señor?*" Gómez Mateo asked to Bernardo.

"*Café sòlo, por favor.*"

"Excuse me, *señores.* I will ask the servant to bring the refreshments." He walked from the room.

Bernardo gestured toward the leather couch against one wall. "Please sit, Michaela."

They went to the sofa. On the coffee table were a stack of files and a small pile of newspapers. She noticed the banner heading, *La Pensa,* and realized it was the first time she'd seen a copy.

"Oh, this is your paper," she said.

"Yes," Bernardo answered, "I selected a few issues containing the news stories about Susana Riveros's arrest. I wanted you to see that the coverage was fair."

"My Spanish is hardly good enough to judge."

"I will be happy to provide translations," he said.

Michaela idly picked up the top paper. In the lower right corner was a picture of the attractive young woman she'd known in Tucson. The caption read Susana Riveros, *Periodista Acusada.*

"I believe there is more on the back page," Bernardo said.

She turned the paper over and there was a picture of a man—Luke Hammond. Michaela nearly said something before she realized that Bernardo might have planted the photo to get her reaction. She glanced at the editor out of the corner of her eye, but he didn't seem to being paying any particular attention to her.

She casually examined the picture, thinking how incredibly good-looking he was, marveling that she'd made love with him the night before. When she looked at the caption, however, she was startled to see that it read Reed Lakesly, *Jefe Revolucionario.*

"Bernardo," she said, her eyes wide with disbelief, "who's this?"

"Lakesly."

"Are you sure?"

He laughed. "Of course, I'm sure. You would recognize a picture of Fidel Castro, wouldn't you?"

She was almost too stunned to speak. Bernardo noticed, but Michaela didn't care. Her shock was beginning to turn to anger. The bastard had deceived her! He'd let her go to bed with him, thinking he was somebody else.

"Haven't you seen this picture before?" Bernardo asked. "We usually run it when there is a story about the MAP. My father has offered a substantial reward for his head, so we have the whole population on the alert."

"Is it possible there is a mistake?" she asked, risking delving further into the subject. "This looks very much like the description of that other North American, the Canadian—what's his name? Hammond. Luke Hammond."

"No, Michaela, Hammond is very fair. They don't look at all alike. I think there may be a picture of the Canadian somewhere in these issues."

Bernardo began riffling through the stack of papers, finally coming up with a story about the MAP in which pictures of prominent members of the organization were shown. Michaela spotted the same photo of Reed Lakesly, identifying him as such. Bernardo pointed to another picture in the bottom row. It was of a thin-faced blond of about Lakesly's age. The caption indicated it was Luke Hammond.

"My God," she muttered.

"You asked about Hammond the other day," Bernardo said. "Does this man mean something special to you? Does he look familiar?"

"No," she replied with assurance. "I've never laid eyes on him before in my life."

"That's good. Pangonia is not the place to socialize with revolutionaries. Journalists who break the trust of our people are dealt with harshly, as you will soon see," he added gesturing toward the files.

"Well, *señores,* I am sorry for the delay," Gómez Mateo said, entering the room. "The waiter was away from his post. The refreshments are coming promptly."

Michaela sat back on the sofa and crossed her legs, unsure where her incredulity ended and her rage began. She hated being made a fool of, and if she had the chance to let *Reed Lakesly* know, she certainly intended to do just that. The gall!

Michaela took her tape recorder from her briefcase, turned it on and listened as Gómez Mateo began explaining Pangonian law and the charges that were being prepared against Susana Riveros. He made reference to press freedoms, but it was evident that Chelsea had been right when she'd said that in Pangonia they were honored primarily in the breach.

The prosecutor was articulate within the limits of his knowledge of the language, but it was obvious that Susana was being held captive essentially because she disagreed with the government. Her greatest sin was challenging its legitimacy.

After a while, Michaela began tuning out the lecture, her mind turning instead to Reed Lakesly. She'd had a flicker of suspicion that Lucas was the fabled revolutionary himself until Bernardo had told her there was an the MAP leader by the name of Luke Hammond. Why hadn't it occurred to her that Lakesly had simply assumed the identity of his Canadian lieutenant? Was it because he seemed so sincere and trustworthy? The thought made her laugh out loud.

"*¿Por favor, señorita?*" Gómez Mateo asked, surprised.

"Excuse me," Michaela said. "Your account reminded me of another criminal I know."

"You are a personal friend of Señorita Riveros, no?"

"We were in college together, but I can't say we were especially close. Still, her case interests me personally as well as professionally."

"Can you be objective, *señorita?*"

"Certainly as objective as you are, Mr. Gómez Mateo." She gave Bernardo a little smile, then turned back to the prosecutor. "But tell me, when do you plan to charge and try Susana?"

"Within a month."

"If she is convicted, what kind of sentence could she receive?"

"If convicted of treason, the punishment could be death. In my professional opinion, she will be charged with a lesser violation and would likely receive a prison term if convicted. Five years, perhaps. Please understand, *señorita*, it is only a guess."

"I have another question, Mr. Gómez Mateo. If General de Falcón's coup had been unsuccessful and he had been arrested by the elected government, what might have been the charge against him."

"Well, treason, of course."

"Right and wrong seems to be determined by the barrel of a gun, then. Is that a fair assumption?"

"Revolution is not unknown in most countries, *señorita*, including your own."

"The more free the press and the people, the less violent revolution is necessary."

"In this case, the people of Pangonia will decide."

"Will they?"

"Perdón," Bernardo interjected, "but is there something to eat? Are you hungry, Michaela, or is it only me?"

"I'm not hungry, thank you," she replied.

"Perhaps a pastry, Señor Gómez Mateo," Bernardo said. "All this talk brings on an appetite."

"I will see, Señor de Falcón. *Con permiso.*" The prosecutor got up and left the room.

Bernardo took Michaela's hand. "Why do you concern yourself with revolution, my dear? There are so many more interesting things to think about."

"Such as?"

He twitched his eyebrows. "Last night you weren't thinking about revolution, were you? Not at the moment of ecstasy."

"No, Bernardo, I wasn't thinking about the revolution, or revolutionaries, either."

"You see, a beautiful woman has better things to occupy her."

"Susana is beautiful, too. Politics mattered to her."

"Yes," he said sadly. "And revolution was her downfall."

"Because she wrote about it?"

"That and because she loved Reed Lakesly, and let him use her so shamefully." He shook his head. "Very sad. The man cost her her career and her freedom."

Michaela thought of Santos Moreno. He, too, had said that Susana was in love with Reed. "Are you quite sure that she is in love with Lakesly?"

"They all seem to be. I don't understand his hold on women. They seem willing to die for him, do anything he wants. Lakesly must be an interesting fellow." Bernardo glanced around. "But don't tell anyone I said that."

She shook her head dumbly. "No, Bernardo, I won't."

Gómez Mateo entered the room with a plate and a pastry. "Here, *señor*," he said. "I brought it myself."

"You're very kind. *Gracias.*" Bernardo regarded the pastry with relish. "Care for half, Michaela?"

But she was off, lost in thought, trying to assimilate everything that had happened. How could she have gotten into such a mess? How could Lucas have used her like that, knowing that both she and Susana would be hurt? Maybe the man didn't care about anyone or anything except his precious revolution.

"Michaela?"

"Huh? Oh, no, thank you." And what was worse, at Lakesly's request, she was carrying a secret message to Susana. Her cheeks burned at the thought that she had actually risked her neck for him. Chances were, the note was a love letter. Didn't the man have any scruples at all?

Bernardo stared at her. Michaela gathered herself.

"Well," she said, "when do I get to see Susana?"

"As soon as *el señor* has finished his snack," Gómez Mateo said dryly.

Bernardo chomped away. "I'm nearly finished. *Por favor, señor,* tell them Miss Emory is ready to see Señorita Riveros."

"*Sí, señor.*"

Gómez Mateo left the room again. Bernardo popped the last piece of pastry into his mouth and licked his fingers, then wiped them on his handkerchief. "A word of advice, Michaela," he said soberly. "I know Susana is a friend. But be careful. The room in which you meet will be bugged."

"Why are you telling me this, Bernardo?"

He gave her a devious smile. "Because I am thinking we should go to my country house for an intimate weekend together and I wouldn't want anything to interfere. We are, after all, lovers. What could be more important than our pleasure?"

Gómez Mateo returned. "Please come with me, *señorita,*" he said. "You may interview the prisoner now."

Michaela gathered her things and slowly got to her feet.

"It is a wonderful place, my country home," Bernardo said under his breath as he stood beside her. "You'll love it there. Believe me."

Michaela had a terrible sinking feeling. She felt as though she didn't have a friend in the world.

CHAPTER ELEVEN

MICHAELA WAITED IN THE small conference room where the prosecutor, Gómez Mateo, had taken her. It was the sort of room where prisoners met with their lawyers. It was plain, the walls bare, the ceiling high. There was a wooden table and two chairs. Natural light came from a high window. There was also a ceiling lamp with a metal shade hanging from a long cord.

Though Michaela hadn't seen the cellblock, she knew it was nearby because she heard the clank of metal doors in the hallway. When they clanked again, she shivered, thinking how terrible it must be to be confined in a place like this.

A moment later the door opened. A female guard peered in, then stepped aside to admit Susana Riveros. Susana stood still, staring at her. Michaela got to her feet and Susana suddenly recognized her. Her eyes widened.

"Michaela Emory!" she cried, moving toward her.

They embraced.

"You didn't know I was here, did you?" Michaela said.

"They said that a foreign journalist was to interview me." Susana pulled back to see her face. "How wonderful to see you!"

Michaela felt a well of emotion—the compassion and concern that had brought her to Pangonia. Susana was both a friend and colleague. She needed her help, whether she was Reed's lover or not. Michaela regarded her carefully.

Susana was pale and tired looking. She wore a gray prison dress; her dark hair was pulled back in a ponytail. Though she wore no makeup, her natural beauty was evident. Susana had aged more than the intervening years could justify, but it was hardly surprising, considering the ordeal she'd been through.

"How *are* you, Susana?" Michaela asked.

"They've left me alone the past month or so. The bruises have faded. At first it was very difficult. They made me tell them everything I knew. Fortunately it wasn't much. It hasn't been a happy time," she said sadly.

Michaela touched her cheek sympathetically. "Chelsea and I have been concerned. That's why I came. Frankly, I was hoping that by interviewing you, I might be able to help."

Susana pointed to the ceiling, to indicate they were being monitored. Michaela nodded. They sat down.

"I haven't made a secret of why I'm here," Michaela said.

"How did you persuade them to let you in to see me?"

"Your old boss, Bernardo de Falcón, and I have become good friends. It afforded me the opportunity to ask the general for permission to interview you."

"I'm surprised they let you," Susana said.

Michaela casually extracted the message capsule. She took Susana's hand and said, "I'm investigating the entire political situation here. I'd even like to meet with the leaders of the MAP." As she spoke, she slipped the capsule into Susana's hand. "The government wouldn't appreciate it, I'm sure," she went on, "but it's the only way to get a balanced story."

Susana, evidently a veteran of such situations, did not acknowledge what had happened. "The people in the MAP would probably not cooperate with you," she said easily, "if only because of the possible danger to them."

Michaela sighed. "Yes, I've come to realize the work of a reporter is different here than in the States. But my personal experiences aren't important. I'm here to learn about yours."

"I'll tell you everything," Susana said, fingering the capsule. "But first give me the news about Chelsea."

Michaela started talking, knowing that Susana wanted to be reminded that there was a free world out there somewhere. As she spoke, Susana nervously opened the capsule and removed the ultrathin paper. She unfolded it, and read the cramped inscriptions.

Michaela saw a glimmer of pleasure on Susana's face, a faint smile. She read the message a second time before popping it into her mouth, chewing and swallowing.

"Well, I'm happy for Chelsea," Susana said. "And grateful to you both for this visit. I am so pleased to see a friend."

Michaela got out her tape recorder. "Your story's the one the world needs to know," she said. "Tell me what happened."

Susana explained how she got around the prohibition against sounding antigovernment by slipping in political commentary in the guise of satire. Humiliated, the government made an example of her. She was accused of working in complicity with the MAP.

"Were you?" Michaela asked.

"I was sympathetic with their cause and in the course of my work I interviewed their leaders. I told my interrogators that. But I did not engage in revolutionary activity or break any laws, except perhaps those that limit freedom of speech and the press."

"In other words, you did what any good journalist would do."

"Yes," Susana said. "I was telling the people the truth."

"Did you interview Reed Lakesly?"

"Yes," Susana replied. "They told me it was a crime not to report this to the police, but I insisted I was a reporter, not a police informant."

"What is Lakesly like?" Michaela asked, closely watching Susana's reaction.

"Michaela," she said, her eyes shining, "he is wonderful. I cannot begin to tell you how much I admire him. He wants for the country what the vast majority of the people want—the return to power of our elected president, Ricardo Corazón de León."

Michaela pushed the stop button on the tape recorder. She looked Susana in the eye. "What do you think of him personally?"

"I love him," she answered, her voice tremulous.

Michaela couldn't be absolutely sure that Susana's love had been reciprocated, but intuition told her that it had been. She felt a twinge of jealousy. "He seems to arouse passions?"

"If you ever met him, Michaela, you would see."

She nodded. "Yes, I'm sure that's true." She knew it was not a topic to be pursued just then. "Apart from writing about what's happened, is there anything I can do to help you?"

"Probably not. But seeing you has given me hope. Locked up, you lose touch with the world. It's easy to feel forgotten."

"You aren't forgotten, Susana. And I don't just mean by me and Chelsea. As a matter of fact, I had an unusual experience soon after I arrived in Montagua. I met a man in a restaurant who got very excited when I told him I was a journalist and that I hoped to be interviewing you. He claimed he knew you, that he was a childhood friend."

"Who was it?"

"His name was Santos Moreno."

"Ah, dear Santos," Susana said. "Yes, we have known each other since we were children. He is my dear friend."

"He loves you, Susana. He told me I should tell you that. He loves you very much and he is praying for you."

The words brought tears to Susana's eyes. She became very emotional. "Wonderful Santos," she whispered. "If you should happen to see him again, tell him his love cheers me and that I am forever grateful."

"Yes, if I see him I will tell him."

Michaela looked into Susana's eyes, certain that words of love from Reed Lakesly would have warmed her heart even more. Perhaps the joy she'd seen on her friend's face when she read Reed's note were because of love that was expressed.

Worse, Michaela didn't know how she herself felt. There was compassion in her heart for Susana, but some jealousy, too. And resentment toward Reed—a lot of resentment. For all she knew, he was using them both. She couldn't believe he'd actually slept with her, using an assumed identity, and then had had the cheek to send her off with a personal message for his lover.

But nothing was to be gained by exposing him to Susana. She was suffering enough. Better to leave her with her illusions.

Thankfully, *she* wasn't laboring under the same constraints. There was no reason why she couldn't give Reed Lakely a piece of her mind, and she fully intended to do so.

She took Susana's hands. "I don't know if they'll let me come back, but if they do, I certainly will."

"Thank you so much, Michaela. I know you took a risk and I shall be ever grateful for it."

"It was nothing. I have a good story and if I can help you by writing it, so much the better."

They both stood and embraced.

"The world prays for you, Susana," Michaela said.

"Give the world my love."

Michaela knew what she meant. "I will."

Susana went to the door and knocked. The guard came and took Susana away. In a minute or so, Gómez Mateo came into the room and escorted her to the reception area.

"Was it a productive interview?" he asked.

"Yes. Susana sees the situation very differently from you, as you might expect."

"Perhaps the difference is that my side won."

"That's the way life works, Mr. Gómez Mateo. Sometimes you win, sometimes you lose. There's a lesson in it, though. Things always change and it's a mistake to get too complacent."

"Are we talking about politics or something else?" he asked.

"That's for you to decide," she replied coolly.

In truth, Michaela was not thinking about the tug-of-war between the MAP and the government of General Juan de Falcón so much as she was thinking about the Reed Lakesly she hated and the Reed Lakesly she'd made love with the night before. It brought home the truth of the old saw that love and hate weren't as far removed as they often seemed. In this case they were separated by a few hours and a couple of newspaper photos.

"Señor de Falcón had to leave," the prosecutor said, "but he asked me to see you to your limousine."

"Thank you."

They went to the entrance, then down the steps to the limo. Gómez Mateo opened the car door. Michaela shook his hand.

"I hope you won't be too hard on us, *señorita*. A little moderation will make future cooperation much easier."

"I find truth to be the only reliable friend," she told him.

"There are many truths," he said.

"That's the nice thing about freedom. The various truths can compete for people's hearts and minds."

He smiled. "I see you are a romantic, Miss Emory."

"In some matters. In others I am a cynic." She climbed into the back of the limousine.

Gómez Mateo leaned down for a final word. "Señor de Falcón asked that I tell you he will call to make arrangements for the weekend." A tiny smile curled at the corners of his mouth. "He said that at the beginning of the week a private interview with General Juan de Falcón might be arranged." He gave another smile.

Michaela flushed, knowing the man was thinking she was a whore. "Thank you," she said quietly.

He grinned. "Good luck, Miss Emory." He closed the door.

Michaela sighed, relieved that the ordeal was behind her, though she was uncertain what would happen next, or even what she wanted to happen next. They hadn't moved and she wondered what was going on. Then the chauffeur turned around and smiled. It was Santos Moreno.

"Good Lord!" she exclaimed. "What are you doing here?"

"The other chauffeur became sick. Besides, I know where you must go and he did not."

"You aren't taking me back to my hotel?"

"No. Lucas wants to see you, *señorita.*" He started the engine and pulled away. "It is important. We must go directly."

Michaela was tempted to say the hell with Lucas, that she had no desire to see him. On the other hand, she did want to give him a piece of her mind! But that was her pride speaking, not her reason. Besides, there was Susana to think of. There was no point in making things worse for her friend.

They drove for a minute before Santos spoke again. "Did you see Susana?"

"Yes, Santos. And I gave her your message."

The eyes in the rearview mirror looked delighted. "Truly?"

"Yes. She was very happy to hear from you. She told me to tell you that. And she asked me to give you her love."

"Oh, how wonderful!" he said. "What a beautiful day."

"It's all a matter of perspective, Santos," she said under her breath. "All a matter of perspective."

THEY DROVE ACROSS Montagua, through poor neighborhoods and rich. Santos had been cryptic about their exact destination, which Michaela had expected, but she became curious anyway and asked if they were leaving the city.

"Yes," Santos replied. "Lucas wanted to go to the country where the danger is not so great and it is possible to relax."

She wondered what sort of relaxing "Lucas" meant. He had said he wanted to debrief her after her visit to the prison, but she couldn't help wondering if he had something else in mind. After all, Susana was in prison, and as an American, Michaela was a change from the local *señoritas.* "Seize the opportunity at hand." That was a philosophy that Reed Lakesly, Luke Hammond and Father O'Laughlin could subscribe to. "Lucas" had certainly lived it in the few days she'd known him.

"Why does Reed Lakesly cling to that ridiculous *nom de guerre?*" she asked. "Is he ashamed of his real name?"

Santos looked into the rearview mirror. "You know?"

"Yes, I know. It took me a while to figure it out, I'm ashamed to say. Does he always play games?"

"Lucas is the name he is known by in the revolution. It is not only for you, *señorita*. That was the name of his mother's father, a famous democrat in Pangonia who was also the mentor of our president, Ricardo Corazón de León."

"I see." Michaela was not going to get into a debate with Santos over Lakesly's multiple personalities. She would save that for the *jefe revolucionario* himself.

They drove for a few minutes in silence before the limo began to slow. "Oh, damn," Santos said.

Michaela leaned forward in her seat. "What's the matter?"

"A roadblock."

"Won't they let us through?"

"I don't have the papers to be driving a government car, *señorita*. It could be trouble for me."

"Maybe we should turn back."

Santos glanced into the rearview mirror. "It is too late."

A dozen vehicles were stopped ahead at the roadblock. There were other cars behind them. They were on a two-lane highway at the edge of the city, with no cross streets to turn onto.

"We must hope for the best," Santos said, as he came to a stop.

Michaela had been so preoccupied with her pique that she'd lost her sense of personal danger. But seeing the soldiers and military vehicles, and knowing she was in the company of one of Reed Lakesly's most trusted foot soldiers, her heart raced.

If they were caught, what was the best strategy? To claim she'd been kidnapped? To plead ignorance? Neither scenario was plausible. She had to hope they would get through the roadblock unchallenged. Otherwise she might end up in a cell like Susana.

The vehicles moved forward and a soldier with an automatic rifle slung over his shoulder approached. Santos lowered his window. A brief conversation in Spanish followed. Santos was evidently trying to explain why he lacked the proper papers. The soldier glanced at Michaela, then called over his sergeant. Santos was asked to get out of the car. It was not a good sign.

Michaela knew she had to act. She opened the car door. The soldiers turned toward her. She strode to where they stood and the sergeant brought himself to attention, saluting her.

"What seems to be the problem?" she asked.

"The papers of your driver, they are not correct, *señora*."

"I'm not surprised. He was assigned to drive me at the last minute."

"Just the same, *señora*, he must not take the car without the papers. This is not right."

"Not right?" she said indignantly. "You are stopping me for a stupid technicality? Do you know who provided this car for me? Bernardo de Falcón. Do you know who he is? If not, perhaps you know his father, General de Falcón. You know who the president of the republic is, don't you, sergeant?"

"*Sí, señora.* I know very well. But I have my orders."

"Well, this man was given the order to drive me to a private rendezvous with Señor de Falcón. Is it necessary for me to spell out what that means? Señor de Falcón wanted an intimate meeting with me, and you're ruining everything! I suppose you are going to tell your commanding officer. Or maybe call up the television station, as well."

"Oh, no, *señora. Por favor.* It is not what I am thinking at all. They tell me what to do and I do it."

"Well, sergeant, if someone has to tell you what to do, perhaps I can borrow your radio to call General de Falcón. I can ask him to order you to let me proceed. Would that satisfy you? What is your name, anyway?"

"*Por favor, señora.* I want no trouble. You are right. The papers are not significant. You are clearly an important lady. There is no need to disturb *el general.* Please go. I beg you."

"That sounds reasonable," she said. "I don't know why you didn't think of it sooner."

She and Santos returned to the car. He held the door for her, then took his place behind the wheel. He wiped his face with his handkerchief.

"Thank you so much, *señorita,*" he said, starting the engine. "You are a genius, if I may say so."

"No, Santos, I'm just a woman. We've had to think on our feet for centuries. Men have tended to make the rules, so we women have learned to bend them to our purposes. Believe me, if you worked for a while in Washington, you would understand that."

They were moving slowly through the roadblock. The sergeant was at attention, saluting as they passed by.

"I take your word for it, *señorita,*" Santos said. "However you wish to say it, you saved my neck."

"I probably saved mine, as well," she replied, aware of the perspiration on her own brow. "By the way, where are we going?"

"To the country house of Señor Bernardo de Falcón."

"What!"

"*Sí, señorita.* Lucas thought it would be a good place to meet you."

"In God's name, why?"

Santos shrugged. "I don't know, for sure. Perhaps because there is a very good supply of champagne."

CHAPTER TWELVE

REED LAKESLY LEANED against a tree, staring at the heavily wooded hills that rolled off into the distant countryside. It was a hot, humid day, but there was enough breeze to make it pleasant in the shade.

He'd needed to be alone, so left the villa knowing he had time to kill before Michaela arrived at the Rancho Delgado. It had been a while since he'd come to the estate he'd visited so often as a child, and he wanted to reacquaint himself with it, and with his past.

His maternal grandfather, Lucas Mejia Delgado, had loved to walk across this land. When Lakesly was young, he'd often gone with his grandfather on his jaunts. He particularly recalled an occasion not long before the old man died when they'd come to this very spot to talk and take in the view. He'd been thirteen, and was about to leave Pangonia for the States.

"Lucas," his grandfather had said, "I want you always to remember this country. I know you are as American as Pangonian, but you have two peoples, two cultures and two heritages in your blood. Do not sacrifice one for the other. They can both live in your heart."

They had spoken in Spanish that day, though his grandfather spoke excellent English, having received an advanced degree from Harvard. But Lucas Mejia Delgado had wanted his only grandson to know the Spanish of an educated man.

"You heard English on your father's lips," his grandfather had said, "and you should hear Spanish on a man's lips, as well—not just from the women." At the time, the

comment had struck him as curious, considering his mother
was well educated and had often discussed intellectual matters with him in Spanish. But Grandfather Mejia Delgado
was of the old school. He was a proud man and he believed
in machismo, which to him meant something more associ-
ated with honor than chauvinism. For him, dignity and
honor in a man were largely a matter of philosophy and
culture, just as grace and beauty were feminine virtues.

By his mother's generation the old ideas had become di-
luted. Her attitudes had been further transformed when she
married Hale Lakesly. Still, the philosophy of Lucas Mejia
Delgado lived on in Reed's heart. He'd loved his grandfather and admired him greatly for his strength of character.

The old man had been sexist until his dying day, though
he had a benign form of the disease. "There are inherent
differences between men and women," his grandfather had
told him. "One is not better or smarter or braver than the
other, but there is a difference in the blood. You will feel it
when you hold a woman in your arms. Never forget this, my
son. No matter what a woman tells you, including your dear
mother, women want machismo in you as much or more
than you want it for yourself."

His grandfather's words had stuck. And though they
seemed far less relevant to his life in the States, they clearly
helped him to live successfully in Pangonia. Through the
influence of his grandfather, he'd developed the Latin side
of his soul. He understood intuitively the Latina's heart.

But he was his father's son, too. Hale Lakesly had, after
all, won his mother's heart. "You have the best of both,
Lucas," she'd assured him years before. "You have both
your father and grandfather in you."

The split identity had proved to be a source of strength.
He capitalized on it whenever he could. But there was one
area where his natural instincts didn't serve him well—in his
dealings with North American women. He had never quite
figured out the source of the problem—whether it lay in
him, in them, or in his mixed blood and mixed identity.

Since returning to Pangonia he hadn't given the issue much thought. It had been years since he'd talked to a woman from the States, much less made love with one—that is, until Michaela had come along. It didn't take long for him to realize she was a completely different kettle of fish from what he was used to.

Not that North American women were an anathema. To the contrary, he'd grown up among them, had spent his teenage years and most of his twenties in Chicago. His love life in the early years had been satisfactory. He'd had more relationships—many of them quite fulfilling—than most young men. But it wasn't until he'd returned to Pangonia at twenty-nine that he'd realized his full prowess with the ladies. Everything fell into place.

But Michaela Emory had knocked his legs right out from under him. And what frustrated him most was that he didn't understand why. She was beautiful, intelligent, compelling, mesmerizing in her way, and yet that hardly explained what he felt. He'd known other exceptional women, but she did something to him that the others hadn't.

The night before, when he'd told Carlos Tucino he was going back to the hotel, his lieutenant had shaken his head.

"How can you take such a risk?" Tucino had asked in disbelief. "So much is riding on you, Lucas. Don't take the chance."

"Susana is important to us, Carlos. She has given much and must know we haven't abandoned her."

"There are other ways," Tucino had protested.

"The American woman will meet with Susana in private," he had explained. "It is the perfect opportunity to get a detailed message to her."

Carlos Tucino had stroked his heavy jaw. "If that is the truth, it is only a half truth, *mí amigo*. This woman has you hypnotized."

"Carlos, you know me better than that."

"Yes, I know you, Lucas. Better than anyone, perhaps. But Santos tells me Cecilia is jealous over the *norteaméri-*

cana. A woman knows when she has a competitor to be feared."

"Cecilia is jealous of everyone," he'd replied with less than full conviction.

"I know the world is changing," Tucino had insisted, "but I also know when a man thinks with his balls and not with his head. You go to see the vixen with the red hair too often to be safe. Know your weakness, my friend, and guard against it."

"What are you saying, Carlos? That you should go in my place?"

"I'm saying we should think twice before we take her into our confidence. She is friendly with Bernardo de Falcón."

"De Falcón is an idiot. You know that as well as I."

"Yes, but the father is not so much an idiot. If you are seen in the hotel too often, someone is bound to notice. I don't have to tell you this, Lucas."

"This will be the last time," he had told him. "In the future I will have her brought to me."

"You see a use for this woman in the future, *jefe?*" Tucino had barely repressed his smile. "Besides for your pleasure, I mean."

"She could be very useful, my friend."

"For what purpose? There is no shortage of girls for you, Lucas. Why this one, the dangerous one?"

"I don't know," he had answered candidly. "Maybe because she *is* dangerous."

"You want danger, *amigo,* you can ambush a patrol."

"That's not the kind of danger, Carlos. When a woman makes your heart stop, when you know you would do anything within your power to have her, when you know that to have her will only make you hunger for more, *that* is danger, my friend."

"Maybe I should shoot you now and save General Juan the trouble," Tucino had said.

"Let me have this night with her, Carlos. Then I'll know."

"You'll know what?"

"Whether the danger is one I can walk away from, or whether it is a danger I cannot resist."

"You are saying that the revolution hangs by the thread of a woman's sorcery."

"The revolution is bigger than I am. What I don't know is the size of my love. And I must find out."

In retrospect the conversation seemed so naive, his words betraying the innocence of a boy. But now, a day having passed as well as a magical night, he was even more beguiled. The only way to survive was to have himself bound to the mast. It seemed crazy, but it was exactly what he'd done.

"Lucas!" came a voice from the direction of the villa. "Where are you?" It was Carlos Tucino.

"Here, *amigo,* by this tree."

The giant of a man came through the undergrowth, pushing the branches aside like a battleship cutting the waves. He wiped his damp brow with his hand.

"We've had a report," he said. "The army put up an unscheduled roadblock on the highway leaving Montagua."

"Before or after Santos was to come through?"

"Before."

"Damn. He had no papers."

Tucino smiled. "No, *jefe,* he didn't. But somehow he made it through. We have another report of the limousine passing by the lookout twenty kilometers from here. They should be arriving in perhaps fifteen minutes."

"Good," he said, getting to his feet. "I'll just wash up before they get here."

Tucino arched his brow. "Since when do you wash up for a debriefing, Lucas?"

"Since last night, *amigo.*" He grinned and moved past his friend, punching him playfully in his considerable gut. "Come on, you could use a bar of soap, yourself. It is a question of putting the best face on the revolution."

"No, *jefe.* It is a question of red hair and long legs."

He laughed. "Ah, so you noticed."

"I noticed, but like the priest, I think of it as a sin. With all due respect, the revolution is in the best hands when you are in the robes of Father O'Laughlin."

"I'm afraid, my friend, that it's much too late for me to become a priest. I'm beyond salvation. Well beyond salvation."

AFTER WASHING UP AND putting on a clean shirt, Reed Lakesly stepped out the front door of the villa. One of the local MAP cadre, a man named Domingo, sat on the veranda in a chair tilted against the wall. An automatic rifle lay across his knees. He gazed off at the wooded terrain that sloped down the hillside. Reed looked down the gravel drive, following it with his eye until it disappeared into the woods.

"No sign of the limousine, eh?" he asked.

"No, Lucas."

"I wonder if they ran into another roadblock."

"More likely a brick was thrown through the windshield as they went through a village. It is dangerous to masquerade as de Falcón in the countryside. That is why the fat one usually comes with an armed escort."

"Maybe we didn't appreciate how dangerous our friends can be," he said, not completely in jest.

"I don't think any serious problems will arise, Lucas. It is a warm day. Maybe they stopped for a beer."

"Let's hope so."

It was too early to be genuinely concerned, but he couldn't help worrying. He'd had mixed feelings about involving Michaela in their plans, and yet she afforded them a unique opportunity. Even now, there was much she could do to help—she might even play a critical role in the final operation. But that would mean she had to ingratiate herself with the de Falcóns even more. The risk in that—not to mention the inherent distastefulness of the notion—did not sit well.

Carlos was right—he couldn't let his personal feelings cloud his judgment. But it was a tall order to put his feelings for Michaela aside. Maybe an impossible one.

Descending the steps, he walked along the drive, listening to the quiet of the countryside, hoping to hear the distant sound of a vehicle coming up from the highway that ran up the valley a mile or so from the villa. A small pickup used by the cadre was parked under the trees nearby. Two armed cadre members sat in the bed of the vehicle, talking and smoking.

It was sad that his first visit to Rancho Delgado in years had to be under these conditions, in the company of a dozen armed men. He'd often chafed at Bernardo de Falcón using his grandfather's beloved estate as a weekend getaway for his whores. Fortunately, de Falcón had kept the place in good shape. Had he despoiled it, Lakesly would have gone after him with a castrating knife.

With the general's days in the presidential palace numbered, Reed drew comfort in the knowledge that the proud old estate would soon be back in his hands. The de Falcóns stood between him and so much he held dear—that was nothing new. But putting Mike in their hands for the sake of the revolution *was* new. It caused him a great deal of anxiety.

He turned and walked back along the drive. As he neared the villa, the caretaker, a thin, wizened old man named López, came around the corner of the building.

"Señor Lakesly," he called. "A word with you, please." As he approached, López removed the large straw hat. He had a very worried look on his face.

López had been caretaker of Rancho Delgado since the early days of Lucas Mejia Delgado's ownership. He was practically an institution. Lakesly had known him as a boy and had played with his grandchildren when he visited the estate. Bernardo had kept him on under the theory that if it wasn't broken, it shouldn't be fixed. The approach had worked well for all concerned—López's loyalty to the heir of Lucas Mejia Delgado was not in doubt.

"What's the problem, my friend?" he asked.

"Señor de Falcón, he just telephoned to me. He says he will come to the *rancho* this weekend. He comes with a special guest, an American lady. I am to have the maids clean especially well, put flowers in the house, and a chef is coming from Montagua on Friday to prepare French cuisine during the visit.''

"Hmm," he said, rubbing his chin. "Sounds like Bernardo has quite a party planned."

"There are many women who come here, but he says this one is the most special of all. What am I to do, *señor?*"

"Don't worry, López, we'll be gone well before de Falcón and his guest arrive, though I wouldn't be surprised if his guest comes to the *rancho* well before Bernardo."

"*¿Señor?*"

"You'll have plenty of time to ready the villa for him."

"I will do what you say, Señor Lakesly, but I am old and I do not want trouble."

Reed put his hand on López's bony shoulder. "You will always have a place here, my friend. Nothing can change that, even if it means throwing the entire government out."

The old man grinned a toothy smile. "Blessed be the day, *señor.*"

"Blessed the day is right."

Just then, they heard the sound of a vehicle in the woods and they turned to see Bernardo de Falcón's limousine appear, the sun gleaming on its windshield.

"*¡Dios mío!*" López exclaimed. "Señor de Falcón!"

"No, *amigo,* it's his guest. Actually, not *his* guest. She's *my* guest. Don't worry."

The limo pulled to a stop in front of them. Santos Moreno immediately jumped out.

"You're late," he said. "What happened?"

"Sorry, Lucas," Santos replied as he came around the car. "We had a flat tire and also we had to deal with some unhappy peasants. Miss Emory is not in a very good mood."

The rear passenger door flew open before Santos could get there to open it. Lakesly went over to greet Michaela, but she was out of the car and standing, her hands on her hips, glaring, before he could help her. The front of her blouse was spattered with mud and there was a smear of it on her cheek.

"Michaela, what happened?"

"I'm not sure what the word for *slut* is in Spanish," she seethed, "but I believe it was invoked numerous times when the locals welcomed me to this godforsaken place."

"Godforsaken?" he said with mock dismay, as he looked out at the lovely vista. "Michaela, this is God's country. If you were rudely treated, it had to be because you were mistaken for somebody else."

"Mr. Lakesly," she said, her hands still on her hips, "will you kindly tell me why I was brought here, and why in the hell you've been playing games with me as though I were a child who couldn't be told the truth? In case you haven't guessed," she said, her face growing red, "I'm pissed. I'm *really* pissed!"

"I see we need to talk," he said calmly.

"Talk! You're lucky I don't slap your face! You deceived me, Reed Lakesly! You deceived me in a cynical, heartless, insensitive way, and I'll never forgive you."

"Does this mean you no longer wish to interview me?"

"Interview you? Luke—I mean, *Mr. Lakesly*—how can you say that with a straight face, after last night?"

"What does last night have to do with it?"

Michaela rolled her eyes. "Honestly," she said, "sometimes I think when we women left the caves, we should have left you men behind. The world would be a much better place."

"If underpopulated."

She gave him a stern look, but not as hostile as before. "You don't get it, do you? You really don't understand."

"You're obviously upset, Michaela. And if I've done something unreasonable to cause it, I apologize."

"If," she repeated. *"If?"*

He sighed. Obviously, having kept his true identity a secret was proving to be a federal case. It was unfortunate she'd found out before he'd had a chance to tell her. He'd planned to come clean that day, but he could see now that he'd waited too long.

In spite of his regret at her unhappiness, he was having trouble focusing on his remorse—not because he didn't care about her feelings, but rather because the sight of her, the affection he felt, was simply overwhelming. Something about her mud-streaked face, the perspiration forming on her lip, even her scowl, made him want to take her into his arms and kiss her. Unable to help himself, he did the only friendly thing he could do. He smiled.

"You think it's funny that I'm upset and humiliated, don't you?" she said angrily. "It's entertaining to see me this way?"

"No, Michaela, of course not. I feel terrible that you've been through an ordeal. Come on inside," he said, offering his hand. "You can get cleaned up and we'll have a cool drink and discuss this. I guarantee you'll feel much better."

She shook her head. "You think that's all that's required—a cool drink, some sweet talk, and I'll be pacified? Luke...I mean *Reed,* you're as much a male chauvinist and condescending lout as Bernardo. The only difference is *he* has integrity and doesn't pretend to be anyone other than he is. *You* show no more respect for me than if I *was* one of Bernardo's sluts."

"You have grounds for complaint," he said, "but you're going too far, saying I think of you as a slut. That's not true."

"*I'm* the one to decide that," she retorted. "After all, I'm the victim of these little sex games you and Bernardo have concocted to amuse yourselves. I feel like the shuttlecock in a badminton match, if you want to know the honest truth."

"That's never been my intent—not for one second."

Michaela took an angry breath, seeming, for the moment, to have run out of ammunition. She suddenly became aware of López, and looked at him curiously.

The caretaker was standing with his hat in his hand, not understanding a word. Santos had lingered for a few moments before going up to the veranda. Lakesly noticed her looking at López and introduced him.

"This is my caretaker. He's looked after the place for years."

Michaela glanced up at the house, becoming aware of her surroundings. "Santos said this was Bernardo's country home."

"Bernardo is sort of a subtenant. He's allowed to use it weekends until his father is deposed and has to flee into exile."

She looked perplexed. "You mean this is your place and you allow Bernardo to use it?"

"It's a bit more complicated than that, Mike," he replied, taking her arm. "We can go into it later. The first order of business is to clean you up. I haven't found a girl with mud on her face sexually appealing since I was in the third grade. I have to admit, though, it's sort of a turn-on."

She gave him an elbow in the gut, taking him by surprise. It took a moment for him to catch his breath and straighten up.

"You're slow to forgive, aren't you?" he said.

"That may be the first of many. You'd be smart to change the subject, Mr. Lakesly. Sex is the last thing on my mind."

They climbed the steps and went inside the villa where it was cooler. Michaela seemed relieved to get out of the heat. She took in the plantation-style furnishings.

"Nice place," she said. "Whom do I compliment, Mr. Lakesly? You or Bernardo?"

"I know you aren't feeling very friendly right now, Mike, but you really can call me Reed."

Michaela looked him dead in the eye. "Call you Reed, only to find out tomorrow that you're really Ricardo Corazón de León, or maybe the Pope?"

"Would you care to see my driver's license?"

"That's not funny," she said coldly.

"Perhaps not. But I kept my identity secret for your own protection. The less you knew, the less the danger you were in."

"Oh, that's convenient. And when, pray tell, would you have told me the truth? When I boarded the plane to Washington?"

"No, Mike. I'd planned to tell you today. One of the reasons I brought you here was to give you the interview you wanted."

"Seriously?"

"Yes."

She scrutinized him for a long time. "I don't believe you." Then, glancing around, she asked, "Where's the bathroom?"

"Follow me," he said. He led her to the master suite, where her suitcase and laptop computer were lying on the bed.

"What are my things doing here?"

"One of my people got everything from Rosita. I thought the *rancho* might be more conducive to an interview than a safe house in Montagua." He poked his tongue in his cheek. "I understand, though, Bernardo had the same idea."

"Yes." She cocked her brow sardonically. "Great minds work alike." She turned toward the doorway. "I take it the bath is in there."

"Yes," he said, feeling chastened.

"Thank you, Mr. Lakesly."

He watched her go, appreciating the pleasant curve of her hips. But her sexual allure wasn't on his mind so much as the rather deep hole he'd put himself in. How, under the present circumstances, did you tell a woman she was the most wonderful creature on earth, without having her laugh in your face? He didn't know, but he had a feeling he was going to find out.

CHAPTER THIRTEEN

REED LAKESLY WAITED. It had been twenty minutes. He'd been nursing his beer, thinking that Michaela would return to the main salon at any moment. Was she punishing him or simply in no rush to see him? Or had she decided the hell with him, and taken a nap? He fingered his beer bottle, debating at what point he might go to see what was detaining her.

Before a decision was necessary, Michaela appeared at the doorway. She had washed her face, redone her makeup, combed her fiery hair. The mud spots were gone from her blouse. Evidently she'd washed them off.

She was lovely—a vision, cool and collected in her olive camp shirt and crisp white linen skirt. She regarded him without speaking. Lakesly slowly rose.

"I apologize for the temper tantrum earlier," she said. "I let my emotions get out of hand."

"Am I forgiven?" he asked, not fully betraying the relief and hope he felt.

"Not necessarily." She walked into the room.

He gestured for her to sit in the easy chair across from him. She did, crossing her long legs. She looked so fresh and delectable, he had another urgent desire to kiss her.

It had been like that the first time he'd seen her at the roadblock. He'd been sweating under the coarse robes of Father O'Laughlin, with three days' growth of beard and badly needing a bath. She'd been hot and tired from her flight, but she seemed like an angel—flawless yet real. How did a man explain such gut-wrenching attraction? It wasn't just hormonal, the allure of the female body, and yet he couldn't say why her effect on him was so powerful—why it should be this woman, this beauty over all the others.

"I was having a beer," he said. "Would you care for one, or would you prefer something else?"

"I'd rather have some juice or a soft drink or even water."

Lakesly arched a brow. "They weren't serving champagne at the prison this morning, were they?"

"I'm sure Bernardo could have arranged it."

"How was Susana?" he asked.

"In good spirits, considering. She sends her love, by the way."

Her gaze was steady and Lakesly looked back at her, knowing instinctively it was a test. There was an implied message in her words—an accusation, though he wasn't sure which sin she'd intended to address.

"You had no problems?" he questioned, moving on.

"No. Message delivered. Message read and consumed. All evidence destroyed."

Lakesly nodded. "Thank you."

"Anything for the April First Movement," she said, her sarcasm showing once again.

"Was Susana happy to see you?"

"Not so happy as she would have been to see you, but that's another story. If you don't mind, I'd like to clear up a few things before we talk about my service to the MAP."

"All right, but let me get your drink first. Ana!" he called toward the back of the house."

An elderly woman with frizzled gray hair appeared. She was wearing an apron and a plain gray dress that came nearly to her ankles. *"¿Sí, señor?"*

"What do we have to drink that's cold?" he asked in Spanish.

She went down the list. He turned to Michaela. "Orange juice, lemonade and cola seem to be the principal choices."

"I'd like lemonade, please."

Lakesly transmitted the request and the woman went off. He turned his attention to Michaela. She glanced around the room, no longer appearing eager to spar. "Is this really your place?"

"It was my maternal grandfather's before the coup. It will be mine after the countercoup. Your friend Bernardo thinks he owns it, but it's a delusion that I allow him to have."

"Isn't it difficult for you?"

"Yes, but many things are difficult to endure these days, Mike. I content myself with the knowledge that I could have him killed in his bed, if I wished."

"Why don't you kill him? He's evidently stolen your house and generally been a bastard."

Reed smelled a journalist's ploy. He wasn't surprised. He'd known from the beginning that dealing with reporters had its inherent dangers. It was another reason he'd wanted to know her without divulging his true identity.

"I don't believe in unnecessary brutality. We defend ourselves, and it's led to some deaths, but our revolution is strong because of the cause and the support of the vast majority of the people. As regards Bernardo specifically, he's as useful to me alive as dead. When the time comes, he and all the rest of them will get their just reward."

"I see."

"You said you wanted to clear up a few things," he said. "What did you have in mind?"

Michaela folded her hands on her knees. "I'd like to speak to you off the record, as a woman, not a journalist."

He felt a real dressing-down coming. "Fine with me. I prefer to think of you as a woman."

"That's precisely the problem."

"How so?"

"You took advantage of me and I very much resent it."

He returned her hard look with one of his own. "You say I took advantage of you. In what way?"

She seemed displeased that he was making her spell it out. "You slept with me under false pretenses," she said under her breath, but angrily.

"I withheld my real identity, it's true. But I've already explained it was for your protection. Surely you aren't saying that if you'd known I was Reed Lakesly, you wouldn't have gone to bed with me.''

''That isn't the point.''

''What *is* the point?''

''That you were dishonest, deceptive, and you took advantage of my ignorance. You played with me, Reed, like I was a toy—one of your *señoritas* to be used and cast aside at will.''

''Wait a minute. You're saying I took advantage of you because I was Reed Lakesly, but that if I was really Luke Hammond, as you thought, it would have been just fine?''

''No, of course that's not what I'm saying.''

''Michaela, I was under the impression that you went to bed with me willingly. I didn't get you drunk first. I didn't make promises that only Luke Hammond could have kept. To the contrary, you were better off sleeping with me than Luke.''

''Better off? Better off?'' she retorted, her voice turning shrill. ''What's that supposed to mean? That I should feel honored to have been bedded by so illustrious a personage as the great Reed Lakesly, revolutionary hero?''

''I didn't say that at all. Nor was I suggesting it.''

''What were you suggesting, Mr. Lakesly?''

''That if you came to Pangonia to find me, you got what you were coming for, not some stand-in!''

''Ah!'' she exclaimed, jumping to her feet. ''Now I'm a whore. You think I slept with you to get a story? That I write my articles on my back. Is that it?'' She began pacing.

''That's not what I'm saying and you damned well know it,'' he rejoined. ''You went to bed with me even though I wasn't Lakesly, which meant you were going to bed with me, *not* getting a story! Hard as it may be to believe, I'm rather pleased by that.''

She paused to glare at him. ''The trouble is that you're so used to women throwing themselves at you, you don't know what it is to have a normal, mutual relationship.''

"To the contrary, that's precisely what was so good about last night. Don't you see that, Mike? You didn't think I was Lakesly, and I didn't think you thought I was Lakesly."

She looked befuddled. "You should have been a polemicist, Reed. You're making cowardly deception sound like virtue, and you know as well as I do that what you did was wrong."

Ana returned with a small pitcher and a glass filled with ice. They watched her pour juice into one of the glasses, then leave the room. Michaela picked up the glass and took a sip.

"To the extent I hurt you, it *was* wrong," he confessed. "But that wasn't my intent. My motives truly weren't bad."

"You're still an opportunist. You lack integrity. It's only my opinion, I know, but given the fact we...slept together, I feel I have a right to make my feelings known. The point is, I want this behind us. Forgotten. From now on, I'm a reporter and you're a news story. I want that clear."

"I certainly will respect your wishes," he told her. "But I'm a person in addition to being a news story, as you put it, and I have feelings of my own. The fact of the matter is that I like you very much. I consider last night to be special, and I'm sorry you can't see me—or are unwilling to see me—simply as a person, a man."

Michaela had stood still as he spoke. Once he finished talking, she returned to her chair and studied him. He studied her in return, feeling an irrational warmth toward her, despite her obvious displeasure with him, despite her hostility.

"I'd like to believe you," she finally said, "but I can't."

"Because I lied about my identity?"

"Because of who I sense you are."

"Would you care to elaborate?"

"There's no point in throwing any more stones," she replied. "I've taken my shots. You've allowed me to vent my feelings and salve my pride. I appreciate that." She smiled. "Not that I didn't deserve it. But now I'd like to move on."

"Just like that? Last night swept under the carpet like it never happened?"

"Luke Hammond is gone," she said. "Not forgotten, admittedly, but gone. I'm going to do my journalism straight and professional from here on out. No more sleeping with anyone."

He gave her a hard look, unwilling to disguise his displeasure.

"Do you have a problem with that?" she asked.

"With all due respect, I don't think we're talking about journalism. I don't even think we're talking about last night. Let's get the cards on the table," he said. "We're talking about Susana and me."

She lowered her eyes. "I was hoping we wouldn't discuss that."

"Your sarcasm earlier about Susana sending her love did not go unnoticed."

"Your personal life is none of my business. I'd prefer to turn on my tape recorder and talk about the MAP."

"I'd prefer to talk about your misimpressions of me."

"Misimpressions?"

"I am not a philandering monster, Michaela."

"She loves you. That woman is in jail. She's been beaten and she's suffered because of her love for you."

"Because of her love for her country," he shot back.

"She did it for you!"

"Did she tell you that? Did Susana tell you that?"

Michaela frowned, unhappy with the question. "Not in so many words, no. But she didn't have to say it—I could tell."

"You could tell what? That she cares for me? Well, that may be true. But I can't control how people feel about me any more than a rock star can control the feelings of his fans. If that sounds egocentric, I'm sorry, but I can't legislate Susana's feelings any more than you can legislate mine!"

"All right," she said, growing angry. "If you're going to make me say it, I will. You used Susana, just like you used me and God knows how many others. I have no idea if you slept with her to get her to write her stories, but I do know you seduced me to become your courier pigeon.''

His blood surged at the accusation, but he forced himself to remain calm. "I think maybe we're finally getting down to what's troubling you.''

"I don't know whether you do it for gratification or if you grit your teeth and do it for the liberation of Pangonia, but I do know when I've been used, and believe me, I was used!'' With a trembling hand she picked up her lemonade and took a long drink.

"You put me in an impossible situation," he said. "Your mind is closed, so there's no way I can prove you wrong. You don't trust me, you see me as you want to see me— though God knows why it's got to be as an insensitive brute—and so I'm damned for all eternity.''

There was a look of marvel on her face. "You are incredibly smooth, you know that? You almost have me feeling sorry for you.''

"I hate to cast blame," he said, "but I wonder if *you* might have a problem, Michaela—a problem with men and trust.''

"So now the victim is the cause of her own suffering. Isn't that your point? Women have had to deal with that one forever. 'It had to be her fault that he attacked her. Why else would he have done it?' Sorry, Mr. Lakesly, that doesn't cut it with me.''

"So now I'm a rapist?" he challenged. "Maybe I should have folded when I was a simple philanderer. I still think you should look into your own heart. Whether you like it or not, what happened last night was not a common occurrence. I won't tell you it's love, Mike, because I don't know you well enough to call it love. But it's clearly infatuation—obsession, maybe—though I must say, your attitude tries my devotion.''

She stared at him blankly at first, but as the moments passed with nothing being said, her anxiety began to show. A minute went by, then she spoke softly. "I do have a problem trusting men, you're right about that. But sometimes people with paranoia do have cause to be paranoid."

"If *I* wanted to be paranoid, I could tell myself that you slept with Luke Hammond to cull his favor so that you could get your prized interview with Reed Lakesly. And if I were cynical I could look at you and say, 'Michaela Emory came to Pangonia for herself, not the truth. She used the son of the dictator to get an insider's view. She used the plight of an old college friend to sell newspapers and win kudos back at the office.' I could say all that, Mike, but I prefer to think you're a sincere individual who wants to succeed, yes, but who also cares about the truth and the lives of the people you write about."

She sat watching him silently.

"And I would like people to believe that in asking others to help me in a cause I care deeply about, I neither do it cynically nor with disregard for their needs and safety. I'd like people to understand that I agonize over the risks I ask them to take, that I share the burdens as best I can, and that any suffering that results is my suffering, as well as theirs.

"And finally, I wish you could understand that balancing my responsibilities and my desires, my duty and my feelings for you, has not been easy. Caring about someone while trying to decide what's truly fair and reasonable and honest is not easy. I make mistakes, Michaela. I made some with you, but that doesn't mean I'm insincere in what I feel."

She steepled her fingers and pressed them to her lips, contemplating him. Then she sighed and looked off toward the window across the room. Her mood had taken on an entirely different cast. She was agonizing, he could see, but she was also afraid, wary, unsure.

After a time, she turned back to him. "You are so damned convincing, Reed Lakesly, I almost want to cry."

"Does that mean you believe me?"

"It means that I want to, but that I'm afraid to."

He picked up his beer, fingering the bottle before draining the last of it. "Is there a bottom line?"

"You're asking if I intend to sleep with you again."

"It is a question of more-than-passing interest to me, I admit. But it's not the immediate issue. More important, I need to know if you'll forgive me and allow me to be your friend."

"That's a deft formulation," she said, picking up the pitcher of lemonade and pouring herself some more.

"It seems a reasonable starting point."

"I'll take that as an honest expression of your feelings," she said. "I owe you the same in return. I would like us to be friends. I'm prepared to give you the benefit of the doubt. But beyond that, I'm not willing to commit myself."

"I can live with that," he said. "Considering I was about to be thrown to the lions, it's a definite improvement."

She chuckled. "With Father O'Laughlin in your corner, you'd have survived."

"Father O'Laughlin never regretted his vow of chastity so much as the day he first laid eyes on you."

"Father O. was a very nice man. We got along quite well. Maybe he should be my contact in the MAP instead of you."

"That's a heartless suggestion," Lakesly said. "The poor man would be driven to torment."

"At least he'd let me leave here with my virtue intact."

"I wouldn't count on it," he said, stroking his chin. "He belongs to an order that isn't very orderly. Never can tell what that man might do."

"Sounds to me like I should interview you, Mr. Lakesly, and get the heck out of here."

"I owe you an interview and will answer your questions. How would you like to stroll around the estate while we talk? This is a beautiful place, and we might as well enjoy it while Bernardo isn't here."

"I'd like that." Michaela took a last sip of lemonade and they got up. "My tape recorder's in the car. I can carry it over my shoulder while we walk."

They got her tape recorder and he led her along a path that followed the ridge line. Michaela asked him about his life before the MAP.

He told her about his family, his father's death when he was still a boy, and how he'd been close to his maternal grandfather. His mother had died five years earlier, shortly before the coup that drove Corazón de León from power.

"Mother remarried when I was thirteen," he said. "A banker from Chicago, which is why we returned to the States. I went to high school in Flossmoor and then on to Dartmouth. After getting a master's degree at Wharton I worked in New York as an account executive with an investment firm. I was reasonably successful, but essentially miserable.

"When Corazón de León was deposed and things here started going bad, I came down to help with my family's business affairs. Most of our holdings, including Rancho Delgado, were confiscated because of my grandfather's ties to Corazón de León. I soon found myself a spokesman for the antigovernment forces. When they decided to arrest me, I went underground. Before I knew it, I was leading a revolution."

They'd come to a bench nestled under some trees at the edge of the wood and offering a perspective of the valley below. He suggested they sit and rest for a while. It was midafternoon and quite warm. Michaela wiped her brow with the back of her hand. He handed her his handkerchief.

"Thank you. It's difficult to be dainty when you're sweating like a horse," she said.

A thought entered his mind and he smiled, taking her in with appreciation. She was aware of his scrutiny.

"What's so amusing?"

"I was just thinking of that urgent look on your face that morning we first met. You were quite desperate, weren't you?"

Michaela pushed the stop button on her tape recorder. "Thanks for bringing up an embarrassing moment. Nothing like reminding a lady of the time she almost wet her pants.''

"I found it endearing. You were one of the most beautiful women I'd ever laid eyes on, so desperate, vulnerable, human. If there's such a thing as love at first sight, that must be what it's like.''

She blushed and dabbed her brow with the handkerchief. "There was nothing remotely romantic about that encounter, Reed. When your eyeballs feel like they're floating, you can't think of much else.''

"What about after you'd availed yourself of the facilities?''

She thought for a moment. "You were a scruffy priest who looked like he'd been sleeping with the chickens and pigs, but I admit to noticing a certain...I don't know...presence about you.''

"A priestly presence?''

"No, it definitely wasn't priestly. Frankly, I didn't like being attracted to you. I actually felt guilty about it.''

He reached over and stroked her forearm with his finger. "That's a rather candid admission.''

"I don't think it's a secret I find you attractive, Reed.''

He could see she was thinking about the night before. He thought about it himself, feeling the first stirrings of arousal. "But you don't trust me. Is that it?''

"The longer you're on good behavior, the more I'll trust you.''

He brushed her cheek with his knuckles. "That puts me in the unenviable position of being at war with myself,'' he said. "I want you, but I also want your respect and your trust.''

"That's what a woman's life is like all the time,'' she told him. "Self-denial is a big part of living successfully day by day.''

"Not a lot of fun, though,'' he said.

"Not for a man who's used to having his cake and eating it, too. Any cake.''

"That's an exaggeration.''

"Close enough for my purposes," she said. "But this is not what my readers in Washington want to hear about." She pushed the record button on her machine. "Tell me about the future of the MAP and the future of Pangonia. What's your prognosis?"

He reflected a moment. "The tide is in our favor. The days of the government of Juan de Falcón are definitely numbered."

"*How* numbered?"

"You don't expect me to outline our strategic plan and timetable, do you, Mike?"

"Are we talking years, months, weeks—what?"

"In my opinion the government will collapse under its own weight in the near future," he replied. "But you've been talking to both sides. You've been inside the presidential palace. I know you've only gotten a limited view, but what's your reading of the situation—as an objective observer?"

"You consider me objective?"

Lakesly smiled. "You've had a taste of Bernardo de Falcón and you've had a taste of Reed Lakesly. Besides Bernardo's inestimable integrity and my penchant for perfidy, how do you compare us?"

"You handle your liquor better."

"And?"

"His cologne is worse than yours."

"What else?"

"Bernardo does understand the importance of flowers." Reed nodded.

"But that odor of cigars is less than appetizing."

"Uh-huh."

"You . . . have very nice eyes," she said.

Reed ran his finger down her forearm and across her hand. Then he took it and kissed her fingers.

"These macho affectations wear a little better on you."

"Is that all?"

"Well, I have to admit you know your way around the bedroom," she said.

"Doesn't Bernardo?"

"Most of the time he was in my room, he was unconscious."

"His propensity for passing out is one of his more endearing traits," Lakesly said. "It doesn't make him a worthy adversary, but it's made it easier to entrust you to his care."

"Bernardo pledged that when he brings me here this weekend he won't overindulge in champagne," she said. "I tried to assure him I liked it every bit as much as he, but I'm not sure I can count on him being dead drunk for the entire weekend."

"It sounds to me like we'll have to give a lot of thought to letting you come here with him. I'm inclined to have you pass."

She gave him a penetrating look. "Bernardo implied that I might get a personal interview with his father if..."

"You cooperate in bed?"

"That's what he's had in mind from the first," she replied.

Lakesly gave her a long, thoughtful look. "Friday evening there's going to be a state dinner at the presidential palace," he said. "Your name is tentatively on the guest list."

"How do you know?"

"A little bird told me."

She shook her head, laughing. "How often does Juan de Falcón change his underwear, Reed?"

"Give me until tomorrow and I'll let you know."

"I have to admit it, I'm impressed."

"Much as I'd like to take credit, our success is really due to the hard work and dedication of a lot of people who care about their country and are willing to take risks. But that's a topic for another day. We need to talk about that state dinner."

She looked back and forth between his eyes. Lakesly could see the wheels turning; questions, doubt and uncertainty returning.

"Why do I have a feeling something ominous is coming?"

"Nothing ominous."

"You brought me out here because you have another mission for me," she said. "This state dinner was on your mind before you had Santos pick me up."

"I won't lie to you, Michaela. You're right." He saw her stiffen, though she looked like she hadn't quite decided if she should be angry or not. "But I wouldn't have brought it up unless we were friends again. I'm assuming I have your trust."

"I suppose whatever it is you have in mind will benefit Susana," she said. "That is the bait of choice, isn't it?"

"It will benefit us all," he told her. "But I'm not going to coerce you or charm you or beg you to help. I'm mentioning it up front so there won't be any surprises."

She reflected on that. "I guess that's an improvement from seducing me into compliance."

"My feelings for you are the same," he said. "I still find you one of the most appealing women I've ever known. Definitely the most irresistible." He waited for her reaction, knowing she was wary.

"I'm flattered," she said, "but I've never thought mixing personal feelings with business was a good idea." She looked at her watch. "In fact I should probably get back to town. If I'm gone too long, suspicions might be aroused."

"I was thinking you could stay and have dinner with me—a relaxed candlelit dinner on the terrace. Just the two of us."

"I have a feeling you don't have a business dinner in mind."

"I am transparent, aren't I?"

"You apparently don't share my qualms about us getting involved."

"I kind of felt we already were involved, Mike."

"Yes, but you're talking about more spying for the MAP now."

"You aren't going to make me choose between you and my country, are you?"

"You're the one who got us into this mess, Reed Lakesly. I was perfectly content being a journalist, doing my job. You seduced me, I didn't seduce you."

"I couldn't help myself," he said, more candidly than she could fully appreciate. "In fact, I'm every bit as torn as you. But I do want you to have dinner with me. Anyway, I've never understood what was so bad about mixing business and pleasure."

"I can certainly believe that."

He gave her the most charming look he was capable of, sensing he had her on the ropes.

"I should really say no. You deserve to fail occasionally, Reed. That way, you'll appreciate your successes more."

His heart lifted, but he didn't smile. He hoped her emotional momentum would carry her.

"If I thought you'd continue your honorable ways, I'd consider staying for dinner," she said.

"I was a Boy Scout before I became a revolutionary."

"An Eagle Scout?"

"No. An Explorer."

"That figures," she said dryly. "I think we'd better go back to the house. If there's time before dinner, I'd like to work on my story. I may have more questions for you."

"Agreed," he said, allowing his mouth to curve into a happy grin. "It will work out well because I've got some staff meetings this afternoon and meetings with my commanders."

"Here, in Bernardo's house?"

"They tend not to look for you in their own closet. Besides, it won't be Bernardo's for long," he said with a wink.

"You know what you're doing. I just report events." She got up and, slinging her tape recorder over her shoulder, started walking along the path, back toward the villa.

Lakesly watched her derriere as she strode ahead of him. He followed along, happy; but he also knew he was in for one hell of a test of willpower. How did a man stay on good behavior around a woman like Michaela?

CHAPTER FOURTEEN

LAKESLY SPENT THE afternoon conferring with some key staffers who came to discuss matters in their various areas of responsibility—supply, finance, communications, intelligence and operations. The three chief regional commanders—José Asuna, Ramón Cardón and Gloria Fernández—arrived late in the afternoon. Reed briefed them on developments during the past week, mentioning Michaela and her connections in the presidential palace.

Gloria Fernández, a short, solidly built woman of thirty-six with a penchant for military fatigues and cigarillos, listened as she blew smoke toward the ceiling. "Lucas, would this new agent of yours happen to be a gorgeous redhead who types?"

"Types?"

Gloria chuckled, her cigarillo between her teeth. "Yes. Earlier I saw this beauty out on the terrace typing away on a little computer. I watched her and said to myself, Lucas has gotten nostalgic for his executive suite in New York—he's got himself a new secretary with a short skirt."

The men laughed. "Fernández, what bothers you about Miss Emory? Her short skirt? The fact that she is a woman? Or the fact that she is here?"

"Naturally I don't hold the fact that she is a woman against her, Lucas. Some of our best cadres are women." She glanced at the others. "Most assuredly, our best commander is a woman."

Asuna and Cardón hooted good-naturedly. Gloria Fernández winked at Lakesly.

"The short skirt means nothing," she went on. "Every woman has her style. The question, I suppose, is why is she here?"

"Miss Emory is not typing for me, Fernández. She is working on a story for her paper. I told you she was a journalist."

"You're saying she is here with us, at the heartbeat of the revolution, because she is a reporter, Lucas? I do not question your judgment, but there is much at stake. Many lives."

Lakesly nodded. "I understand your concern. Miss Emory is a friend, I admit that. But you want to know if we can trust her. If I didn't trust her, she wouldn't be here."

"What you do is your business, *jefe*," José Asuna said. He was a portly man with very thick hair and a fat mustache that he constantly twisted with his fingers. "But I don't understand why you take the risk, unless there is something she can do for the revolution that you have not told us."

"As a matter of fact, she can be helpful," Lakesly replied. "Michaela has gotten closer to our enemy than any of us have."

"But not too close?" Gloria Fernández said.

"She was a friend of Susana Riveros back in the States. She has already helped Susana by passing along a message from us. I see an opportunity to make even better use of her."

"How?" Ramón Cardón asked.

"I believe Michaela can help us deceive Juan de Falcón. But it may mean moving up the time schedule for the final offensive."

"Change the plan because of the woman?" Asuna said. "Why, Lucas? What can she do?"

"If she can convince the government she is on their side, we would have a tremendous advantage."

"You are talking of making her a double agent," Fernández said, blowing smoke toward the ceiling.

Lakesly nodded. The commanders exchanged looks.

"Is she willing to do it?" Asuna asked.

"I don't know, but it will be my job to convince her."

Fernández inhaled her cigarillo, smiling as a thin stream of smoke issued from her nostrils. "If a woman needs convincing of anything, you are certainly the man for the job, Lucas."

Lakesly looked into Gloria Fernández's eyes, knowing her chiding was intended good-naturedly. But the reference to his machismo, his *fuerza masculina*, was not the source of pride it had been. Since knowing Michaela, he was looking at things differently—not seeing the world through the filter of his ego. He had begun seeing himself as he wanted her to see him, as the man she wanted him to be.

THE SUN WAS LOW OVER the Santa Teresa Hills when the last of the visiting MAP cadre climbed into their vehicles and left the Rancho Delgado. Only a rump force of a dozen men from the local revolutionary militia stayed on. Lakesly stood on the veranda, watching the last vehicle disappear down the drive.

He turned toward the door. Domingo was in his chair, still leaning back against the wall. The stubble on his jaw seemed heavier in the late-afternoon sun. He nodded a friendly greeting as he shifted his automatic rifle from one knee to the other.

"How long will you need us tonight, Lucas?"

Lakesly leaned against the doorframe. "That depends on how persuasive I am," he replied with a wry grin.

"I understand. With legs like those on the *norteaméricana*, I, too would want to be persuasive."

"Believe it or not, *amigo*, she is here for important business."

"My sincere condolences, *jefe*."

Reed arched a brow. "Which is not to say a time won't come when one needs to kick back and relax."

Domingo grinned. "We should prepare to spend the night?"

"No, it isn't necessary. Once it is dark, take your men and return to the village," Reed answered. "Carlos Tucino, two of his men and Santos Moreno will stay. If you can have a man watch the road for us to warn of army patrols—that will be sufficient. I don't want to keep you from your homes unnecessarily."

"As you wish, Lucas."

"Well," Lakesly said, "I'd better get inside. Before you go there will be brandy for everyone from de Falcón's cellar."

Domingo's eyes widened. "It will be a good night."

"I hope so, *amigo.* I hope so." Winking, he went inside.

He found Michaela sitting at a table on the terrace, still laboring over her laptop computer. He paused to watch her, as the rays of the setting sun turned her hair to fire.

She was incredibly lovely—her profile almost perfect, her pale skin as smooth as a swan's egg. But her looks were only the frosting on the cake. It was the woman behind the facade who affected him so—her smart mouth and intelligent, supple mind. Why he felt such rapport with her he didn't know, but he was completely in tune with her. He had known there was something special about her right from the start, though perhaps she hadn't seen it yet—not as fully as he.

Michaela continued to labor over her work but, unexpectedly, she turned toward the door. She smiled when she saw him.

"Are you spying on me, Reed?"

"Yes," he said, gathering himself and walking over to the table. "Your secret admirer."

His comment seemed to embarrass her a little. She stared at her computer screen. Reed pulled out a chair and sat opposite her, where it was hard for her not to look at him.

"Actually, of the forty or fifty men who were here today, I don't think there was one among them who wasn't an admirer."

"You're exaggerating."

"No, there was a consensus you'd make a wonderful mascot. Our Lady of the Revolution."

"Somehow I don't think you conferred with Cecilia and some of your other female cadres before coming to that conclusion."

"Maybe," he conceded. "But the point is I'm not your only admirer."

"I'm flattered. Thank you for the compliment."

"How's the *opus magnus* coming along?"

"I got a lot done, actually," she replied. "I'll be ready to file the first installment in the morning."

"You won't print anything that might be used against us, will you? Any names or places you include could be dangerous."

"I was careful. I haven't mentioned you yet. I'm saving it for one of my final dispatches. I don't imagine Juan de Falcón would appreciate knowing I'm playing both sides of the street."

"No, he wouldn't be as understanding as I."

They exchanged long looks.

"Are you getting hungry?" he asked. "I have a feeling it won't be long till dinner is ready."

"I noticed the wonderful cooking smells," she said.

"Ana is a fabulous cook. She's making something special."

She gave him a skeptical look, like she might be reading his mind. Maybe it *was* impossible to hide his feelings. Maybe he shouldn't even try.

"Would you care for a cocktail?" he asked.

She hesitated. "I don't think I should."

"I am not Bernardo."

"No, you are much more dangerous than Bernardo."

"Dangerous?"

"Don't think I'm not tempted, Reed, because I am. But I'm trying to think what's best for me—as well as for you."

"Something about that formulation troubles me," he said.

"It's self-denial. That's not easy. Life isn't easy."

"It may not be easy, but it needn't be grim."

"Am I grim?" she asked.

"You are cautious."

"People get conditioned, Reed."

"Why do I feel such a strong need to save you from your caution and your fear?"

"Maybe you don't like me as I am," she said.

"Or I like you too much."

She considered that. After hesitating, she turned off her computer and got up from the table. She walked to the edge of the terrace. He went to stand beside her.

"If I were still in New York, and you had come up from Washington, and we met, what would you say if I asked you to have dinner with me?" he asked.

"I'd probably accept."

"And if I wanted to spend a second night with you, what would you say?"

"I would be afraid, just as I am now," she said, staring out at the deepening hues of evening.

"Why are you afraid, Mike?"

She looked at him. There was a quiet desperation in her eyes that made him want to take her into his arms. Unable to help himself, he touched her face, his heart welling with affection.

Her wariness returned. "We aren't in New York," she said softly. "We're here. This is what's real."

There was a shuffling behind them. It was Ana. *"Perdón,* Señor Lakesly. Dinner is ready soon. May I prepare the table?"

"Thank you, Ana," he replied. He glanced at Michaela. "Saved by the dinner bell."

"Yes," she said, smiling faintly. "Saved."

THEY HAD A QUIET MEAL on the terrace, discussing a number of things, mostly growing up. By the time Ana had cleared the dishes, dusk had come and gone. The terrace was illuminated only by the candle flickering between them.

"I was several years older than you," he said after Ana poured the coffee, "but I think I'd have liked you back then."

"What makes you think so?"

"You are bright and you have a sense of humor, but there is a touch of sadness in your soul that appeals to me. I'm not sure I understand why that is, but whenever I sense it, I want to take you into my arms."

"I've never had anyone say that to me before," she said, fingering her cup. "Is it true?"

He nodded.

"I like hearing it," she told him, "and yet I resist."

"Why?"

"I think because I'm afraid of my baser impulses."

He laughed. "Why not call them your more noble impulses?"

"You'd prefer to think you inspire me," she chided, "rather than scare me. But the truth is, my instinct is to run away."

"I see I still have a way to go before I earn your trust."

"Probably."

"The air is nice this evening. Let's walk." He took her hand and they went off into the garden.

The air was rich with the scent of blossoms from flowering shrubs and beds of flowers. He could smell the damp earth and Michaela's perfume. He squeezed her hand.

At the foot of the garden they stopped. A faint light was visible in the west, though it was quite dark. In time their eyes adjusted enough for them to make out each other's features.

"It's been an exercise in self-control to be around you and not take you into my arms," he said.

"You're giving me fair warning that you want to kiss me."

"Yes."

"I appreciate your consideration."

They both smiled as he leaned over and kissed her. It was a tender kiss, cautious. He resisted the impulse to crush her. She touched his cheek, seeming to repress her impulses, too.

"I've got to tell you something, Mike," he said. "I'm torn. I have strong feelings for you, which I'm struggling to control, but at the same time I've planned an operation in which you could help us. They're two separate things—my plan and my feelings for you—and I don't want them mixed up."

"I'm not sure I understand."

He took her hands and kissed them. "I want you to stay the night," he said, "but first I want you to know that I'm going to be asking for your help. I don't want you thinking I seduced you to secure your cooperation."

"I see. You're giving me the option of saying no to either or both of your propositions."

"I want you to know they're unrelated."

"What do you want me to do for the MAP?"

"A decisive operation is in the offing, Mike, and I think you could be a big factor in its success—a very big factor."

She asked quietly, "Another message to deliver?"

"No, it's much bigger than that. It's dangerous, as well. Even telling you about it puts you in jeopardy."

Her expression turned serious. She searched his eyes. "So I have to decide if I even want to hear about it."

"Yes."

Michaela moved a few steps away where she smelled blossoms on a flowering bush. Lakesly watched her. She turned to him.

"When would you tell me what it is that I'm to do?"

"I can give you a general idea now, if you're open to the possibility of helping."

"And if I refuse you?"

"Then I'll ask if you'll stay with me tonight," he said.

"What if I say no to that, too?"

"I'll see that you're taken back to Montagua and I won't trouble you again, unless you wish to see me."

"You're putting quite a burden on me, Reed."

"It's the only way I know to be forthright. It's important that you don't doubt my motives, because what you think of me is more important than anything else."

"Not more important than your cause," she said softly.

"As between us, it is."

She thought for a moment, fingering the blossom on the bush. "Give me an idea of what it is you want me to do."

"You could disseminate misinformation to de Falcón. Once his forces were destabalized, we could launch a countercoup."

"You're not talking about months or weeks from now. You're talking about the very near future," she said.

"Yes. It would be a matter of days."

"And Susana?"

"Freed," he said. "If all goes well."

She reflected. "How can I say no to that?"

"Revolution is not for everyone, even those who believe in the cause. I don't want you to feel pressured."

"What's your plan?" she asked. "What would I do?"

"General de Falcón and the army are well aware that we are preparing a final offensive to take over the government. They have defense plans, though they obviously don't know where and when we will attack. They also are unaware that we know those plans down to the last detail."

"You know their plans? How?"

"We have spies everywhere, Michaela."

"Then you should be successful."

"Knowing their defensive strategy and taking advantage of it are not the same thing. At a critical moment, I want you to tell General de Falcón that you have learned his defense plans, having secretly gotten them from us. They'll panic, knowing that their plans were compromised. We'll attack then and run them out of Pangonia."

"What makes you think he'll believe me?" she questioned. "Why wouldn't he suspect you put me up to it?"

"That, of course, is the critical element. We have to find a way to convince de Falcón that your sympathies lie with him and his son."

"What are you suggesting? That I sleep with Bernardo?"

"It's true you have to keep him on the line and make him think you're interested in him," Reed said. "But there's no reason the affair has to be consummated."

"Wouldn't it be more convincing if it were consummated?"

Lakesly took her chin in his hand and peered deeply into her eyes. "Let's not get morbid. You've handled Bernardo well to this point. Just continue toying with him."

"He's going to tire of being put off. At some point I'm going to lose my credibility if I don't accommodate him. He's not as easy to fight off as you might think."

He let go of her chin, feeling uncomfortable about what he was hearing. "You aren't suggesting you'd actually go to bed with him, are you?"

"Would it matter?" she asked, almost sounding sincere. "Would you care?"

"Of course I would," he snapped.

"But isn't the success of the coup what counts? Isn't the revolution more important than anything, Reed? Look how Susana has sacrificed for the cause. A little champagne and some hanky-panky with Bernardo wouldn't be the end of the world—and it's not a lot to ask, considering what's at stake."

He flushed, though he knew she couldn't see it in the dark. "You almost sound like you want to go to bed with Bernardo."

"You want me to succeed, don't you?"

He turned away. "I don't find this amusing," he said.

"I'm not trying to amuse you," she replied. "I'm trying to please you. The whole thing was your idea, don't forget."

He looked back at her angrily. "I don't want you *actually* going to bed with him."

"Why not?"

"Would you want *me* going to be with . . . somebody you found disgusting . . . just so you could gain an advantage?"

"That would be up to you. I couldn't complain if I were the one asking you to get involved in the first place. Could I?"

"Maybe we should forget the whole thing. True, I've asked for your help, Michaela, but I did not intend to sell you into prostitution. A little friendly deception is one thing, but..."

"Oh," she said, "so now it's friendly deception."

"Look, if you don't want to do it, just say so," he said. "I told you from the beginning, only do this if you want to."

"I want to," she said tersely.

"Why?"

She hesitated. "For Susana. For the sake of the people of Pangonia. Because I don't like what General de Falcón has done."

"That's certainly reason enough," he said.

"I think it is."

They stood in silence. Michaela rubbed her arms. He looked at her face in the obscurity. It was an uncomfortable situation and he didn't like it at all. Nor did he understand what she was doing, unless it was to shame him.

What was it about this woman? One moment he felt weak with infatuation for her, the next he felt guilty, then enraged. And now he wanted to embrace her, possess her.

"Maybe we should go inside, Reed," she said. "It's chilly."

They walked back toward the house. They didn't speak, but the discomfort was palpable. When they got back to the terrace, the candle was nearly burned out. Lakesly leaned on the back of the chair, staring at the flame.

"This double-agent idea may not be such a good one," he said. "Maybe we should forget it."

"Because I might have to end up sleeping with Bernardo?"

He turned to her, taking her bare arms in his hands. "In case you haven't figured it out yet, Mike, I care for you."

"I care for you, too, Reed."

"Well, there's no mystery, then, why I feel the way I do."

"You're willing for me to risk going to prison, but you won't risk me ending up in Bernardo's bed."

"I'm not comfortable with any of it. If I had my way, we all would be living happily and free. But that's not possible, yet, so I do what I have to do," he said. "That doesn't mean I don't have feelings—including feelings for you."

She stared back at him, her eyes shiny in the flickering candlelight. He couldn't help himself. He kissed her fiercely, crushing her against his chest, wanting her.

It was a long kiss, arousing him, making him desire her even more. When it ended, they clung together, their breathing heavy, anxious. He spread kisses over her face, wanting to take her to bed, to have her, to possess her. To love her.

She drew her fingers across the back of his neck as her breasts pressed against his chest.

"I'd better be getting back to Montagua," she murmured.

The comment was a shock, surprising him. "You're staying here with me tonight, Michaela. I can't let you leave."

She shook her head. "It won't look good if they find out I've been off somewhere all night. A ride in the countryside. A flat tire. Getting home late in the evening. I might be able to sell that. But not being gone all night."

"I want to be with you." He kissed the end of her nose, inhaling her scent. "Stay."

"It's better if I go."

"Better for whom?"

"For us," she said. "It's a mistake to try to be soldiers of the revolution and lovers at the same time."

"One has nothing to do with the other," he insisted.

"Oh, but it does, Reed."

"How can a night of making love interfere with tomorrow? It can only make things better."

"I haven't forgotten last night," she replied with a trembling voice. "I never will."

"Then stay."

She kissed his lip. "I have to go."

They exchanged a painful look. He made no attempt to hide his displeasure.

"Will you arrange for the limousine?"

"Yes," he said. "If you insist."

While Michaela gathered her things, he found Santos. A few minutes later they were out on the veranda, saying goodbye. He put his arms around her and they clung together. The moon was just coming up over the eastern hills.

"I'll be in touch in the next day or so," he said, "as soon as things crystallize. If you need me, slip a note to Rosita."

She put her head on his shoulder. Holding her, he became aroused again. He didn't want her to leave.

"Reed," she said softly, "I want to ask you something, but I don't want an answer unless you're one-hundred-percent honest. I don't want less than the whole truth." She looked into his eyes.

"What? What do you want to know?"

"What was in that note you had me deliver to Susana?"

He hesitated, then said, "You put me in a difficult spot."

"The whole truth, or nothing at all."

He agonized, suspecting what was in her mind, though it wasn't true. "It's not what you're thinking," he said.

She put her finger to his lip. "Don't say anything else. Please."

"Michaela."

She shook her head. "It's really all right." She turned then, and ran down the steps to the limousine.

Santos started the engine. Lakesly felt powerless. It was not a feeling he was used to; it was not a feeling he liked.

The car made a wide circle and went down the drive. He watched the taillights disappear. Then he turned and went into his grandfather's house. The master suite was lit with half-a-dozen candles. An ice bucket holding a bottle of Bernardo's best champagne was by the bed.

Lakesly stared at it, knowing the editor's plan was to bring Michaela to this very house for the same purpose. His blood rose at the thought. He would not permit that to happen.

He went to the bed and lifted the bottle from the silver ice bucket. It was the finest French champagne. But Bernardo de Falcón would not be drinking it with Michaela. Not if he had anything to say about it.

With that, he walked to the open window and heaved the bottle into the night. He heard it crash into the brush, far down the slope of the hill. After blowing out the candles, he went to find Carlos Tucino. He wanted to get the hell out of there. And he wouldn't be coming back—not until he could reclaim his grandfather's house as his own.

CHAPTER FIFTEEN

IT WAS AFTER TEN by the time Michaela and Santos arrived back in Montagua. They hardly spoke during the drive, though she would have liked to question him about Reed's relationship with Susana. But given Santos's feelings, that would not have been either politic or considerate.

She was glad she hadn't stayed with Reed at the rancho—and not only because she was unsure how important Susana was in his life. In spite of that—in spite of everything, she'd been tempted. But weakness was a poor reason to spend the night with a man. It was no way to have a relationship.

Things were simply too muddled for her to feel good about a love affair. She and Reed both had been irresponsible. They'd let their desires get in the way of common sense. Worse, she'd been lax in getting her dispatches back to Washington. This way, she could take care of business first thing in the morning.

As they stopped in front of the hotel, Michaela patted Santos on the shoulder. "Thanks," she said. "I know you took a big risk today."

"It is you who should be thanked, *señorita,*" he replied. "But for you, I could be in jail."

"Maybe both of us," she said with a laugh. "I hope when I see you again, it will be under better circumstances."

"*Buenas noches, señorita,*" he said.

Michaela was helped from the limousine by the doorman. She walked into the lobby, exhausted. The tension suddenly catching up with her.

"Good evening, Miss Emory," the desk clerk said as she approached. "You have had a number of telephone calls from Señor de Falcón. And he came by earlier. He was most anxious."

Michaela had a sinking feeling. She'd completely lost perspective on the challenges she'd left behind in Montagua. Bernardo was like a dog on a scent. She told herself that she couldn't let down her guard again.

She took the the key, then headed off toward the elevator, leafing through her sheaf of messages.

In addition to Bernardo's phone calls, there had been one from Jack Ellison. It simply said, "So where's my story?" She winced, knowing she was on the verge of blowing it. Fortunately, she'd gotten in some writing that day. In the morning she would print up the first installment and fax it to Washington.

On the way up to her floor, Michaela leaned against the side of the elevator, weary, but also vaguely depressed. She didn't like the way the evening had ended. Her head told her she'd done the right thing, and yet in her heart she yearned to be with Reed, to throw caution to the winds and follow her desires.

For once, her room was devoid of flowers and priests. It was exactly as it should have been—a place of refuge. She took a look at the bed, knowing it would feel wonderful. But before she hit the sack, she wanted a hot bath.

She put some bubble bath in the tub and ran the water. As she undressed, she looked at herself in the mirror, trying to see herself as Reed had. She wanted to believe he might be falling in love with her, but her fears made her skeptical. He was the wrong man, at the wrong place, at the wrong time. What better reasons did she need to keep her distance?

Michaela climbed into the tub and settled back. She was on the verge of falling asleep when she heard the outer door to her room open. She was alarmed at first, until she realized it was Father O'Laughlin. Who else paid late-night calls on her?

Part of her was annoyed that he wouldn't accept a simple no. Another part of her was pleased. But she definitely wasn't going to give him the satisfaction of seeing the pleased side.

There was a timid rap on the bathroom door. She ignored it. The knocking grew bolder.

"What's the matter? Can't you take no for an answer?"

"Michaela . . . can I come in?" came a muffled voice.

"I don't do confession in the tub," she said. "Go away."

The door opened a crack. "Are you decent, my dear?"

Michaela's mouth dropped open. "Bernardo!" she exclaimed. It was practically a shriek. "I'm in the tub!"

"Oh," he said, opening the door wide. "Then you won't mind."

"You can't come in while I'm bathing!" she cried, sinking into the bubbles.

Bernardo ignored her, hurrying to the side of the tub and dropping to his knees. "Michaela, where have you been? I've called, I've come by. You disappeared. I was terribly worried. What happened to you?"

"I . . . I went for a drive," she stammered. "I couldn't come to Pangonia without seeing a little of the country."

He reached over and pressed the backs of his fingers to her cheek. "I'm so relieved, my little one. I notified the police. I was certain something terrible happened." Then, without warning, he leaned over and planted a big kiss on her mouth. "My angel. My love."

"Bernardo!"

"You don't know the torment I've felt. I was certain you were lost forever. That I would never have you again. Oh, what heaven it was . . . that night."

Michaela groaned, drawing herself deeper into the water. Why had she told him they'd made love? Now he felt as if he owned her.

Bernardo got to his feet. "But here you are. My blossom. My dove." He stared at her with wide-eyed awe.

Michaela wanted to pull the plug and go down the drain with the water. What did she do now? Bernardo didn't remotely smell of champagne and there wasn't a drop of booze in the room. She had a horrible feeling of doom.

"How did you get in here, anyway?" she asked. "A woman is hardly safe if anyone can come walking into her room at will."

"I bribed a porter. But I'm hardly anyone, my dear. We are *amantes,* lovers. We were as one, and we shall be as one again." He took off his suit coat and began unbuttoning his shirt.

"Bernardo, what are you doing?"

"I'm going to join you, my darling," he said, jerking his shirttail from his trousers.

"You can't!"

"Why not?"

"Because...I'm very shy. I don't take baths with...men."

He smiled and unfastened his belt. "You act like a virgin, dearest one. Alas, we know it isn't so, don't we?" He chuckled and pulled down his pants, which left him in baby-blue boxer shorts, a sleeveless undershirt, shoes and long black socks that came to just below his knees.

"I have a better idea," Michaela said, starting to panic. "Why don't you order some champagne? Then I'll get dressed and come and join you. This is a very small tub, Bernardo."

"Fitting together as hand and glove, we will find room."

"I'd much rather have some champagne first," she insisted. "Champagne and making love go together. Don't you remember how terrific it was last time?"

"Of course it was terrific, but I would like to remember it better. The best parts are rather fuzzy." He removed his shoes.

"Bernardo," she said sternly, "I must insist that you wait in the bedroom. I'll not be stampeded into anything."

He put his hands on his hips. "Stampeded? Am I a cowboy?"

"Don't you see? I have been having lovely thoughts about our weekend. Expectation is half the pleasure. But thrusting yourself on me like this will only spoil our time together."

"But *pequeña,* I have been so hungry for your charms. To deny me is torture." He removed his glasses and set them on the basin. Then he dropped to his knees and peered desperately into her eyes. "I beg of you, my love. Take pity."

"I would rather respect you, Bernardo."

"Alas, I believe I know the problem. You are not as aroused as I. Forgive the inconsideration." With that he thrust his hand into the blanket of bubbles and grasped her entire breast in his hand. Michaela gasped, her entire body going rigid.

Bernardo sighed, turning his face toward the ceiling. "A melon from heaven," he purred. "So full and succulent."

Michaela grabbed his wrist and pulled his hand away. "Bernardo, you're a pervert! Now get out of here!"

"But you love me," he said, dismayed. "I know you love me."

"I love you when you let me decide when and how—like last time. You have completely lost your sense of romance. You were such a gentleman before!"

He gave her a tragic look, a wounded look. "But my heart swells with love for you, Michaela. It is cruel to deny me."

"The weekend. Wait until the weekend."

He sat back on his heels, thinking. "None of the others are this way. I don't understand how you can resist me so."

"I'm different, Bernardo."

He considered that. Then his eyes widened as if he'd been struck by a realization. "I understand! You wish to be taken! You admire a man with *fuerza!*" He laughed gleefully. "I bet you like to be tied up! Ropes! Why didn't I think to bring ropes?"

"Oh, my God, don't be an idiot, Bernardo!"

Leaping to his feet, he pulled off his undershirt, revealing a mushy chest covered with long hairs. In a flash he dropped his undershorts. Michaela stared at his stubby little penis, erect beneath his protruding belly. Bernardo drew himself up, sucking in his gut. "Your conqueror!" he exclaimed proudly.

Forgetting to remove his socks, he stepped into the foot of the tub. Michaela sat up abruptly. As Bernardo sank into the water, he stared at her breasts, grinning with delight.

She only hesitated a moment before jumping to her feet and vaulting out of the tub. He lunged for her, managing to grab her wrist. Michaela pulled as hard as she could. Bernardo whooped with delight at the game, and tried to reel her back into the water.

Bracing herself with her foot against the side of the tub, she pulled as hard as she could. He rose to get better leverage, but slipped on the wet porcelain and toppled toward her, letting go of her arm. Michaela went flying, sailing through the door, landing on the carpet in the bedroom. Bernardo fell in a splat on the tile floor, his head clunking the edge of the bidet.

Michaela scrambled to her feet, but saw he wasn't moving. She crept into the bathroom and knelt beside him. He was breathing all right, but he was out cold. Michaela sighed with relief. The last thing she needed was to have the son of the president of the republic dead on her bathroom floor. If she'd been Catholic, she would have made the sign of the cross.

UPON AWAKENING in the morning, the first thing Michaela did was call the desk to inquire if there had been news of Bernardo. Though he'd come to before the ambulance arrived, he'd been incoherent and the decision had been made to take him to the hospital. Michaela had asked the night manager to check with the hospital and leave word for her of his condition.

"Señor de Falcón, he is fine, *señorita*," the clerk on duty informed her. "They say he will have the tests and then go to his home in the afternoon."

"That's good." She was relieved. "Can you tell me which hospital?"

The clerk gave her the name and the address.

When she went to the bathroom to get cleaned up, she found Bernardo's glasses on the basin. She stared at them as if they were dinosaur bones. What would have happened if he hadn't clunked his head?

After she dressed, she went downstairs for breakfast. Then she returned to her room to do a final edit of her story on the revolution. She'd inquired and had been told the hotel had a fax service, so she sent her dispatch to Jack Ellison.

Having gotten that behind her, she decided to pay a visit to Bernardo as a goodwill gesture. She had no idea what he might be thinking, or even if he would recall what had happened. He had not been himself when they'd wheeled him off, covered with a sheet, his wet stocking feet hanging out the end of the stretcher.

After putting his glasses in her purse, she went downstairs. It was a short taxi ride to the hospital. Seeing a small florist's shop near the reception's area, she bought a bouquet. The porter, an elderly man, took her to Bernardo's floor.

As they approached the door to his room, a prim, horsey-faced woman with a decidedly unhappy look on her face exited with three little girls in tow. They passed her without a glance. Michaela paused until they'd gone around the corner before proceeding to the door. The porter nodded and went off.

Michaela looked back in the direction Bernardo's family had gone, feeling guilty though she was morally without culpability. And yet, in a sense she *had* seduced Bernardo and encouraged his wayward behavior. She knocked lightly, then stepped inside.

He turned at the sound of her entering the room, squinting at her shortsightedly. She moved slowly toward the bed.

"Michaela!" he said excitedly when she'd approached close enough for him to recognize her. "A healing angel!"

She was relieved that he wasn't angry. "Hello, Bernardo. I came by to cheer you up. I hope you're feeling better."

"Oh, it was nothing. A little bump on the head. The doctors . . . Well, you know how doctors are."

She handed him the flowers.

"How lovely." After sniffing them perfunctorily, he set them on the table. "I should be bringing flowers to you, my dove. How can you possibly love a man who is as clumsy as I?"

"I worried that you were seriously hurt."

"The injury was not bad, but I confess, I scarcely remember going to your room." He lowered his voice. "No one here could tell me what happened, of course, so perhaps I should ask you."

"You fell in the bathroom."

"The bathroom?"

"Yes," she said, wondering if his apparent memory lapse was something to be taken advantage of. "We were being frivolous."

His brows rose with delight. "Having fun, were we?"

"Yes, you seemed to be enjoying yourself."

"Was this before or after the . . . uh . . . real fun?"

"Before."

He frowned. "You mean we . . . uh . . . didn't . . ."

She shook her head.

"Bad luck, then," he said glumly. "But we have tonight and tomorrow night and the night after. I'm having a few more tests this morning and then I'm leaving the hospital." He twitched his eyebrows. "I'm a new man, my dear."

"Bernardo, I think you need to rest for a few days."

"Nonsense. I've never felt so amorous before." He gave her a salacious grin. "If I could lock that door, I would."

"But last night you didn't talk this way."

"What?"

"We discussed it and I told you I didn't wish to make love with you like some cheap prostitute, that I—" she bit her lip, forcing the words "—wanted a romantic weekend with you where we could behave like lovers, not a couple of sneak thieves."

"Oh?"

"Yes," she said. "You were a real gentleman. You promised we'd do it right, with lots and lots of champagne."

"I did?"

"You were very sweet. I was impressed with your thoughtfulness and understanding."

He smiled weakly. "Well, I try to consider your... wishes."

"You also promised me something I want very much," she said, seizing the opportunity.

"What's that?" he said warily.

"To arrange an interview for me with your father."

"Did I really?"

"Yes. I told you how important it was to me. You said you'd spare no effort." Michaela knew she was being conniving, but she was dealing with a man who was utterly without scruples. Her cause was just, but it was still hard to lie—even to a fraud like Bernardo de Falcón.

"I suppose I should talk to Father, if I promised I would." He stroked his chin, clearly looking for a way to wiggle out of it. He brightened as another thought entered his mind. "Did I tell you about tomorrow night?" he asked.

Michaela shook her head. "No. What about it?"

"You are invited to a state dinner at the presidential palace as my special guest."

"As *your* guest? You mean we'd go together?"

He looked sheepish. "No, I must escort my wife. Protocol, you understand, my sweet. But afterward I told her I must attend a conference of top officials—a retreat that will occupy the weekend." Twitching his eyebrows again, he added, "Of course, the truth is you and I will steal away to Rancho de Falcón."

"Rancho de Falcón?"

"My country home. A lovely, romantic spot. You'll love it, my darling. I promise you."

She quailed at the thought, but managed to maintain a blissful look. "Your wife isn't upset?"

"She understands that I have responsibilities. With such burdens, a man also needs his pleasures."

Michaela couldn't help resenting Bernardo for his wife's sake. She didn't know the woman, but she felt sorry for her. "Mrs. de Falcón is evidently a very understanding woman."

"The kind of wife every man should have," he said smugly.

"How did she feel about you not coming home last night?"

"Naturally, she was concerned. I must confess she was also a bit suspicious. But when she learned that I had to work late—as I often do—and tripped coming down the steps from my office because I'd lost my glasses, she was consoled."

"Maybe you work too hard, Bernardo," she said, wondering if he would catch the irony of the remark. "Maybe you should spend more time at home."

"You've said that before," he replied, not altogether pleased. "Whose side do you take, anyway?"

Michaela knew she should shut her mouth, but she couldn't help herself. She had to point out the error of his ways. "You are a friend, Bernardo," she told him. "I value your help with my work, but if I had to choose the interests of anyone over all others, it would be those of your family."

He looked at her quizzically. "Michaela, are you not well? Lovers don't talk this way."

"I guess I have a conscience."

"Perhaps you think too much," he said. "If you must think, think about this weekend. What could be more pleasant?"

"Yes, it's a matter of getting my priorities straight," she said ironically.

"Pardon?"

"Nothing." She opened her purse. "I brought your glasses."

"You are so very thoughtful, my love. I wondered if perhaps I lost them in your bed."

"No, you left them in the bathroom."

He grimaced. "Not nearly so romantic." Then he grinned. "Bed seems so much more appropriate, considering love is blind." He chuckled at his pun, appreciating it much more than she.

"I should go," she said.

Bernardo clutched her hand. "I abhor the thought that we won't be together until this weekend. Are you sure I shouldn't come by the hotel this evening?"

"If you want to please me, arrange an early interview with your father. If I talk to him before the weekend, then I won't have anything else on my mind. No distractions."

"I worship you, Michaela. How can I not try to grant your every desire?"

"Then you'll talk to your father?"

"Let me think about it."

Michaela knew that if she was to pass on the misinformation that Reed wanted her to convey, she would have to see General de Falcón in person. But Bernardo was so obsessed with his desires that he would hardly listen. Somehow she *had* to get the job done before the weekend. There was a great deal at stake. Still, the thought of a tryst with Bernardo was too much to bear. It would take a carload of champagne to survive it with her virtue intact.

"Don't fail me, Bernardo," she pleaded.

He kissed her hands. "At worst you will have your interview next week," he murmured.

She had a horrible sinking feeling. Perhaps, just perhaps, she had outsmarted herself. "I must go now," she said, pulling her hands free. "I have to shop. If I'm to attend a dinner in the presidential palace tomorrow, I'll need a dress. I didn't pack anything formal, not thinking I'd have such an opportunity."

He looked at her fondly. "Michaela, it will be such torture to see you at the palace and pretend we are strangers."

"Talk to your father," she said. "Things will go much better this weekend if you do."

"For you, I will do my best," he replied.

In her heart she knew he didn't mean it. She could already see that she'd maneuvered herself into a corner. But with a lot of luck, and a little help from her friends, she might manage to save herself one more time.

CHAPTER SIXTEEN

As soon as Michaela got back to the hotel she requested that Rosita come to her room. "I've got to send a message to Lucas," she said.

"*Sí, señorita*. Whatever you want."

The maid waited while Michaela wrote a note explaining that she had been invited to the state dinner and Bernardo planned to take her to Rancho Delgado afterward, exactly as Reed had anticipated. She went on to say that she had asked to interview General de Falcón before the weekend, but had little confidence in Bernardo's willingness or ability to deliver.

Her words were matter-of-fact, unemotional. She assumed it would be obvious that the notion of spending more time alone with Bernardo was the last thing she wanted. But in apprising Reed of the situation, she hoped to put the burden of finding a solution squarely on his shoulders. She was, after all, undertaking the mission at his request.

When she finished writing, she handed the note to Rosita. "How long, do you think, before I can expect an answer?"

"*No sé, señorita*. I am but the bee who carries the honey."

"I understand."

Rosita gave her a broad smile. "I heard that there is much excitement last night. Señor Snake, he finds a bird to eat, no?"

"Señor Snake was doing his best to make a banquet of me."

"The wine, it works good, *no, señorita?*"

"Yes, it was good information and I'm grateful to you for it. But I can't always rely on him passing out. What do the others do if they can't get him drunk?"

Rosita shrugged. "I guess it cannot be avoided sometimes. The bird does not always escape from the snake, no?"

Michaela shivered. "That's not very reassuring, Rosita."

"It depends what you want, *señorita*. There is bad with the good in every case. No man is perfect. Each woman must decide what she wants more—what he offers or avoiding his demands."

"Well, there's little about Señor Snake that I want. I can assure you of that."

"Pray to the Virgin. Sometimes she is your only hope."

Michaela nodded. She didn't want to offend anybody, but somehow a shotgun seemed the more appropriate response to the danger posed by the likes of Bernardo de Falcón. And yet, what could she do? Rosita was right—she had to decide what was most important. Whatever she did ultimately, she simply couldn't picture herself sleeping with Señor Snake.

The maid got up and went to the door. "If there is anything you want that I can do, please call me, *señorita*."

"Right now there is nothing, unless it would be to pray for me. But thank you, Rosita. Thank you."

She left and Michaela suddenly felt very much alone. A visit from Father O'Laughlin would have been welcome. Actually, Reed would have been welcome in any of his personas. A part of her regretted now that she'd so cavalierly turned him down when he'd asked her to stay with him. But she'd been convinced at the time that leaving was the right thing to do, and it probably was. Still, being strong and self-reliant had its drawbacks. It meant that when you fell, you often fell alone.

By the same token there was nothing to be gained by moping around. She had the power to decide for herself what she should do. She could only hope she wouldn't be left with a Hobson's choice. Many people were relying on her.

At the moment, though, there was nothing to be done about Bernardo. She had work to keep herself busy, and she also had to do something about finding a dress for the state dinner. Once she had that problem solved, writing would be the best use of her time. Jack would be expecting another installment, particularly if he liked the initial one. First, though, she had to make sure she had something to wear to the dinner.

Michaela phoned the concierge to ask about the more elegant dress shops. Armed with the names of three, she took a taxi to the first. She found nothing that was suitable. She had bad luck in the second, too, though there was a black taffeta number that she would have bought had it fit.

The third shop was the charm. There she found a strapless chiffon dress in seafoam green trimmed with silver that looked sensational with her hair and eyes. It needed alteration, but the seamstress promised it would be ready by noon the next day. The price was six hundred and fifty American dollars. The silver heels and bag were another two hundred. Michaela's problem was figuring out how she was going to pay for it all. She had enough cash, but buying the dress would leave her without enough money to pay for the hotel when it was time to check out.

On the way back to the El Presidente, she decided to call Jack Ellison and try to hit him up for it. Ironically there was a telephone message at the desk, indicating that her boss had called. Michaela went to her room and phoned him in Washington.

"Fabulous work," he said. "Just fabulous."

A surge of joy went through her, though she wasn't a hundred-percent sure she'd been complimented for her work. "Are we talking about my story, Jack?"

"We are indeed. It's first-rate, Mike. I especially liked the piece on Susana Riveros. When am I getting more?"

Her heart soared. "I'll be working on it all afternoon, so you'll have it first thing in the morning."

"Excellent. I want to run it as a series, but I'll hold off until I have most of the installments in hand. I want to be sure I know what I'm dealing with. How's it coming with Lakesly?"

"You'll be getting a detailed piece. I can't say more."

Ellison hesitated. "Am I to take it I shouldn't be asking questions about it over the telephone?"

"That might be a good idea."

"I see. Can I assume the coming installments will be as hot as what I got this morning."

"That was just an hors d'oeuvre, Jack."

He gave his sinful laugh, though for once he was thinking about journalism, not sex. "Emory, you have outdone yourself."

"The talent's been there all along," she replied. "I only needed the opportunity."

"Well, if what I've seen is any indication, big things are in your future, my dear, with or without my personal input . . . so to speak."

He chuckled, but Michaela didn't dignify the remark with a rebuke. Anyway, things seemed to be rolling her way for a change and she wanted to take full advantage of what she had going.

"I look forward to talking about it after I wrap things up here," she said. "But I do have one little administrative problem."

"Administrative as in money, I presume."

"I'm attending a state dinner at the presidential palace tomorrow evening and I need a dress."

"Didn't you take anything with you?"

"Nothing formal. I didn't anticipate having this kind of opportunity. I'm a guest of the son of the president, Jack. I've got to look good."

"How much?"

"A thousand."

"A *thousand?*"

"I can't dine with the president in a linen camp dress."

"A *thousand?*"

"Well, I might be able to get by with nine hundred. But I had to get evening shoes and a bag, too."

"Evening clothes are not a normal expense for a reporter."

Jack Ellison was known for being tightfisted, and at the moment Michaela cursed that fact. "How about you pay half and advance me the other half against salary?" she said.

"Seventy-five percent against salary over three months," he countered.

"All right, but I want a two-hundred-and-fifty-dollar-a-month raise, retroactive to the first of the month."

"Hey," he protested, "I'd have been better off to give you the thousand."

"I would have hit you up for the raise anyway. And the point, is I deserve it."

"All right, you've got the raise, but I'm not paying for more than twenty-five percent of the dress."

"Done."

"Anything else?" He sounded grumpier than he really was.

"Wire the money by morning," she said.

"That it?"

"If the rest of my installments are as good as I think they're going to be, you might have to make that raise five hundred a month."

"They'd have to be pretty damned good."

"You can decide for yourself." She hesitated. "But you'd be straight with me, wouldn't you, Jack?"

"They'd have to be *really* good."

She giggled happily. "I knew you were a man of integrity."

"Is this call on my nickel?"

"Yes."

"Then we've talked enough. Get your sweet little ass to work, Mike."

Michaela hung up. The conversation had inspired her and she got out her computer and prepared to write part 2 of "The Quiet Revolution in Pangonia."

IT WAS STARTING TO GET dark before Michaela realized she'd worked right through lunch. If she didn't stop soon, she would miss dinner, too. The hours she'd put in had been productive. She'd hammered out nearly five thousand words. Some rewriting was all that was needed before sending it off to Washington.

Getting up from the small table where she'd been working, Michaela stretched her stiff limbs and tried to decide whether to go down to the restaurant for dinner or have a room-service meal. As she stood at the window, watching the color fading in the western sky, there was a knock on the door.

It was Rosita with fresh towels. The maid went into the bathroom and, as she was leaving, she slipped a folded-up piece of paper into Michaela's hand. Winking, she left the room.

Michaela immediately read the note. It was written in block letters and said, "Be at the fountain at nine tonight. If you think you're being followed, return to the hotel." It was signed, "O."

A surge of adrenaline shot into her blood. It wasn't the intrigue or the thrill of adventure. It was the prospect of seeing Reed Lakesly again.

Michaela showered and washed her hair and put on one of her favorite summer outfits—a sleeveless beige cotton dress with a very short skirt—then went downstairs to dinner. She was so keyed up that she scarcely tasted the light pasta and salad she'd ordered. She kept wondering what was up—whether Reed had felt the need to respond to her note in person because he wanted to see her, or if there was trouble.

The admonition about being followed had given her pause. Reed had told her the MAP had spies everywhere.

That probably meant that the government did, too. Had she become a suspect now? Was General de Falcón on to her?

After leaving the restaurant, Michaela strolled aimlessly out the front door of the hotel and along the street, trying to look as though she'd decided to get some air before retiring. She casually checked to see if anyone might be following her, but saw no one suspicious. Before rounding the corner to head up the side street, she stared into a shop window, waiting to see if someone in the street would give him or herself away. Nothing.

Proceeding, she went to the small square where she'd met the boy. There was a young couple at the spot where Pablo had been last time. Michaela casually approached them, but saw no sign of recognition. She went to the other side of the fountain and waited. Ten minutes passed and nothing happened.

Then a boy on a bicycle rode up to the fountain. Michaela didn't recognize him at first, but then, when he looked at her, she realized it was Pablo.

"Follow me, *señorita*," he said in a low tone and immediately began walking away, pushing his bike toward a dark side street.

Michaela strolled off in the same direction, trying not to be obvious. Pablo waited for her in the shadows.

"Come," he said, and they hurried off at a slow trot.

Michaela wasn't sure if they were retracing the route they'd followed the first time or not. Occasionally she saw a building that seemed familiar, but she wasn't certain. Then they came out onto the square where the church was located.

"Go confess, *señorita*," Pablo said, then hopped on his bike and peddled off.

Michaela went inside the church. There were two women kneeling in prayer near the front of the narthex. She went to the aisle on the side, where the confessional was located, and moved as quietly as she could, though her heels clicked on the stone floor.

Tiptoeing to the booth, she listened at the curtain for voices, but heard none. "Father?" she said softly.

"Michaela," came a man's voice from behind her.

She turned and was startled to see a hooded figure in priest's robes, standing in the shadows. She gasped.

"Come, me child," he whispered.

It was Father O'Laughlin's voice, but his face wasn't visible. Her heart beat heavily as she moved toward him. The padre extended his hand and took her fingers. Without a word, he led her past the transept and along the ambulatory. The first apsidiole they passed was lit with candles. The second was dark. After glancing back to make sure they hadn't been seen, he pulled her into the alcove.

Reed pushed his hood back, but she it was too dark to see his face. His cologne was familiar, though. They looked at each other without speaking.

Michaela was aware of the musky smell of the church and the smoky, pungent scent of candles and incense. Reed grasped her bare arms and held her close, though not quite against his body. As her eyes adjusted, she was able to see that he had a day's growth of beard on his jaw. For the moment, anyway, he was Father O'Laughlin again.

But he was also the same man who hadn't been able to answer her question about the note she'd carried to Susana Riveros. She thought of him on the veranda at Rancho Delgado, telling her that it wasn't what she thought.

She'd tried to put that from her mind, to focus on her work and her desire to help Susana, but being with him again like this brought it all back. How did Reed Lakesly *really* feel? What and whom did he really want?

"Why did you have me come here, Reed?" she murmured. "Is something wrong?"

He brushed her cheek with the backs of his fingers. "I guess I shouldn't be surprised to see the face of an angel in church," he whispered, "but it's awe-inspiring just the same."

"Thanks for the compliment, but that's not why you had me come here."

"No. I had to talk to you before the state dinner."

That gave her pause. "Is there a problem?"

"General de Falcón has decided to keep a close eye on you. We have to be very careful. I couldn't chance coming to see you at the hotel. This seemed the safest way to do it."

"Does he suspect me?" she asked, fear washing over her.

"I don't think so. Bernardo asked for an interview on your behalf, and the general's natural paranoia makes him cautious. You're going to have to play it straight, Mike. Be careful what you say at all times, even on the telephone in your room. We'd probably know if they bugged your room, but it's best if you're careful anyway. Do all your communicating with Rosita by note."

"All right. What about the misinformation you want me to give to General de Falcón? When are you going to tell me what you want me to say?"

"I'm working on it."

"But what if Bernardo arranges the interview before I talk to you again? Shouldn't I have something to tell the general?"

"I'll know what they're going to do before you do, Mike," he replied. "Don't worry. Besides, before you can go to him with secret information about the MAP, we'll have to build a credible case for you. Otherwise it could fail, and you'd be in trouble."

"So I'm supposed to go on as I have, blithely ignorant?"

"For the moment. Bernardo likes you just as you are." Reed smiled. "He and I have that much in common. But it's important that the world should think you're fond of him and don't like me. So, should we meet in public, particularly with the enemy looking on, use the opportunity to show your hostility toward me. We want de Falcón to believe you're sympathetic with his side."

"He knows I have sympathy for Susana," she said.

"Personal feelings for someone out of friendship are one thing. But the main thing is that Bernardo should think you love him. Politics is secondary. The way they have it pegged is you love Bernardo, but want to help your friend. That is, after all, the way women think, isn't it?"

"You're the expert," she said. "How *do* women think?"

"That wasn't sarcasm, was it?"

She sighed. "Sorry. It's just that I've been hearing that crap from Bernardo and would rather not hear it from you, too."

He smiled and caressed her cheek. "The difference between me and Bernardo is that he's obsessed with your body, whereas I love you for you mind, as well as for your heart and soul."

Michaela wanted to believe that; she wanted to believe it badly. But politics was a reality. Reed had his priorities and she couldn't be sure where in the list she fell. She believed that he hungered for her, but she also knew that he needed her help. "You said I should be hostile toward you if we meet in public," she said. "Does that mean we will be seeing each other soon?"

He gave her a half smile. "There's a good chance we will."

"When?"

He touched his finger to her lip. "For security reasons, it's better that it comes as a surprise. But in any case, it's important that you play along with Bernardo."

"You mean, go with him to the rancho?"

"Hopefully that won't be necessary."

"It sure as hell—excuse me—it certainly better not be."

He chuckled. "I would find you having to spend the weekend with him every bit as onerous as you, Mike. Believe me."

"I sincerely doubt that," she said dryly.

He took her jaw in his hand. "Trust me, honey."

Despite her doubts, Michaela had a strong desire to be in his arms. Her heart was pounding hard. She had a growing feeling of desperation, of being torn to the point of panic.

Reed took her face in both his hands. She read the same emotions in him—an intensity, a stirring deep within.

He kissed her then, pressing his mouth to hers. Michaela savored it, even as her longing for him, her excitement, rose. Reed folded her into his arms, the coarse weave of his robe rough against her skin. She became aroused. That seemed wrong, given where they were. She eased from his embrace.

"This is no place to get carried away," she whispered.

"You should have stayed with me at Rancho Delgado," he said, drawing his fingers along her jaw.

"I was tempted, but..."

"But what?"

"I thought of Susana, and how much she means to us both."

"Michaela, I don't want you getting the wrong idea about Susana and me."

"She loves you, Reed."

He was silent.

"You don't owe me any explanations," she said. "Let's just do what we have to do for her."

He put his hands on her waist and stared into her eyes as though he'd like to devour her. "It's you I care about, Mike."

"Don't, please," she whispered.

"I would come to your room tonight to prove it, but I can't take the chance. You're taking a tremendous risk already."

"Please, Reed. It's better if we stick to business."

He thought for a moment, agonizing as she had. "Perhaps you could come with me to the safe house where I'm staying tonight."

Michaela shook her head. "You're not thinking clearly. That's taking an unnecessary risk. If they're suspicious of me, I can't be gone until late for a second night in a row."

"You're right," he admitted.

"This is the way it's meant to be," she said. "If we've been brought together, it's for a higher purpose."

He kissed the corner of her mouth. "You're talking like a revolutionary. I thought you were a levelheaded journalist."

"I guess I'm a human being, first."

"In my eyes, you're a woman first. A beautiful, intelligent woman, whom I can't get out of my mind."

Michaela touched the cleft in his chin. "I'd better go."

"I don't say this to every woman I get involved with. And this is the first time I've ever felt like this."

She gave him a hasty, uncertain kiss. "I'm going now."

He sighed, but there was resignation in his tone.

"How do I find my way back to the hotel?" she asked.

"Wait outside the church at the foot of the steps. The boy will take you back to the fountain."

Michaela started to back away, but Reed held her hands, apparently not wanting to let them go.

"These poignant goodbyes are hell," he muttered. "And we're having far too many of them."

"It's for a good cause," she whispered as she slipped away.

Michaela hurried to the front of the church. Once outside, she took a ragged breath. Tears of emotion stung her eyes. No matter how often she told herself she had to keep her head, Reed Lakesly made her want to break all the rules. The question was, If she listened to her heart, would she wind up paying for it?

CHAPTER SEVENTEEN

As she made her way from the fountain where Pablo had said goodbye, Michaela considered her feelings about Reed. For all intents and purposes he'd told her he loved her. The notion made her spirits soar, but at the same time she had doubts, wondering if she was a fool to put stock in what he said. Quite simply, she was afraid to trust him.

In a moment of candor Chelsea Osborne had once told her that the only reason she had never envied Michaela her looks was that she would constantly be uncertain about men's true motives. "It must be hard believing anyone saying something special to you when everyone you meet lusts over you," she'd said.

"I want to be loved for myself, the same as everyone else," Michaela had told her. "I guess guys do project on me more than on most women. And you're right—it isn't pleasant when you know it's not you they want, but some image in their head."

But Michaela also knew she wasn't the only pretty girl in the world. Others she'd known didn't have the same problem with trust. Her insecurity had as much to do with the hardships she had endured in childhood as the way men related to her.

She and Reed had discussed that and he seemed to understand. Yet in spite of that, she'd been racked with doubt ever since her visit with Susana. She didn't know whether his relationship with Susana was the real problem, or only an excuse to pull back from him.

And yet, amid her distrust and uncertainty, her heart kept pushing her back to Reed. In the past, when her mind and heart had pulled her in different directions, she'd always gone with her head. This time, it was different. The same passionate fit of courage that had brought her to Pangonia was keeping her from making a clean break with Reed.

As Michaela rounded the last corner on her way back to the hotel she noticed a man near the door, reading a folded newspaper. That seemed odd, considering that it was dark, but even so she wouldn't have thought anything of it if Reed hadn't told her she might be watched. She scrutinized him. He was wearing a suit, but no tie. He was presentable enough to wait in the lobby, if waiting for someone was what he was doing.

Hearing her heels clicking on the sidewalk, the man glanced up. Michaela noted the faintest sign of recognition, though his eyes immediately returned to his paper. He didn't look at her again, which was unusual in itself, especially since this was Pangonia, where redheads were a novelty.

Michaela entered the lobby and went to the desk. Seeing her approach, the clerk turned to get her key. She casually glanced back toward the entrance and saw the man from outside coming in the door. He went to a chair across the lobby, where he sat down.

"Good evening, Miss Emory." The clerk handed her the key.

"It's a lovely evening." She spoke loud enough to be heard throughout the lobby. "I've been out to enjoy the balmy air."

"Montagua is a good town for walking, most assuredly," the clerk said, "but you must be careful where you go at night. It is the same back in the United States, I am sure."

"Most cities are like that," she said, turning. "Thanks."

As she spun around she caught the eye of the man across the lobby. He stared at his newspaper as she strode to the elevator. It wasn't until she was in the car and the doors were practically closed that she saw him glance her way.

"Give my regards to General de Falcón," she muttered to herself. "And for heaven's sake, do tell him I went for a walk."

MICHAELA DID NOT SLEEP well that night. She was concerned what would happen when Bernardo whisked her off to his country home for a "sexy" weekend. Reed had told her not to worry, saying that she should trust him. That wasn't easy, considering that in the next breath, he'd urged her to play along with Bernardo.

Having been awake much of the night, Michaela greeted the morning with relief. She was up by six and put in an hour of editing before getting cleaned up. After eating breakfast, she put the finishing touches on her project.

There was nothing in the second installment that directly betrayed the fact that she'd been in contact with the MAP, though a careful reader might develop suspicions. But in light of what Reed had said about General de Falcón checking up on her, and then having been watched by the man in the hotel lobby, discretion seemed the better part of valor. She decided not to fax her article from the hotel. Since she had to go out anyway to pick up her dress, she'd send her dispatch then.

Michaela was prepared to use the last of her traveler's checks to pay for the dress, but shortly after ten she received a call from the Pangonian National Bank informing her that they had received a nine-hundred-dollar credit for her from Washington. Good old Jack had come through—albeit with the minimum.

Shortly before she was to leave her room, she had a call from Bernardo.

"How is the loveliest angel in the firmament?" he crooned.

"Looking forward to tonight," she cooed back, hating herself for sounding so convincing.

"Don't forget to pack a bag for the weekend. After dinner we'll go by the hotel to pick your things up," he said, sounding giddy. "We'll have a glorious time, my love. I don't think a minute has gone by that I haven't dreamed of us together again.''

"It's been on my mind, too." That, at least, was true.

"I only wish I could escort you tonight. Knowing I can't touch you until after we leave the palace will be utter torture."

"The expectation will make it all the better," she said disingenuously. "Tell me, Bernardo, have you gotten your father to agree to an interview?"

"Yes, I have arranged it, just as you wanted," he replied, sounding very self-satisfied.

Michaela gulped with surprise. "When?"

"Tuesday."

"Tuesday?" That meant she'd have to endure the weekend. And if she had to spend it with Bernardo, it would seem like a century. "Is that the soonest it can be arranged?"

"I thought you would wish to rest Monday," he replied. "I plan to exhaust you, my little dove." He tittered as though he fully expected her to receive the news with elation.

"Couldn't we do it today, Bernardo?"

"Impossible."

"Why not after the dinner?"

"I don't understand the urgency," he said. "Anyway, stimulating as my father is to talk to, nothing can compare with the ecstasy you will find with me, dear heart. Worry about your interview next week, for heaven's sake."

Michaela sighed. Reed had told her he would know of the plans of the general and his son before she did. She hoped he had something worked out for her salvation.

"All right," she said, resigned. "But I'll have to bring my computer with me. I don't have many more days in Pangonia and my editor is waiting for my dispatches."

"Bring it if you must," Bernardo said, "but I doubt you'll think about work once you're alone with me."

"You don't know how conscientious I can be, Bernardo, dear."

He laughed and they said goodbye.

After her telephone conversation, Michaela left to do her errands. Entering the lobby, she felt a little paranoid. She glanced around and immediately spotted a potential tail. Her suspicions were confirmed when the man followed her out of the hotel, lingering to watch as she got into a cab.

Michaela looked back when they were half a block away. She saw a car pull up to the hotel entrance and pick up the man. She was certain she was being followed.

She was at the dress shop for only twenty minutes. The seamstress had done an excellent job and the gown fit perfectly. She was lovely in it, but the realization gave her no joy. What did it matter that Bernardo saw her at her best? It was Reed's admiration she craved.

The man tailed her to a photocopy shop where she faxed the second installment of her article. To make her errands seem routine, Michaela bought a postcard in a nearby bookstore, jotted a greeting to Chelsea, then mailed it. Next she went to a small café and bought a light lunch.

From time to time she would catch a glimpse of one or the other of the men who'd been following her, but mostly they kept a low profile. Since she'd done nothing suspicious, she could only assume there would be nothing negative in their report.

When she'd finished lunch, Michaela picked up her money at the bank, then returned to the hotel. She was opening the door to her room when she heard the phone. She grabbed it.

"Mike, it's terrific," came the voice. It was Jack.

"You liked it?" she said, pleased.

"First-rate, sugar. I'm not kidding."

"Does that mean I'm getting a five-hundred-dollar raise instead of two-fifty?"

He laughed. "You don't miss a trick, do you?"

"Well, am I?"

"Yes," he replied. "But I'd hoped to surprise you. You just won't give a guy his pleasure, will you?"

Jack chuckled, but he didn't have to for her to know he'd made another of his sexual puns. They were as inevitable as his passes. But bad as Jack was, he almost seemed like a choirboy beside Bernardo de Falcón.

Of course, Jack Ellison had never had the leverage over her that Bernardo wielded. Her job was always on the line, true, but with Jack she'd decided early on not to bow to pressure. She'd taken a firm stand and it had worked, though some people might have said she was lucky. The situation with Bernardo was more complicated. It involved not only Susana Riveros, but Reed Lakesly, as well.

"I'm pleased that you like my story, Jack," she told him. "I consider this assignment just the beginning."

"Have you gotten your interview with Juan de Falcón?"

"Yes. It's set for next Tuesday."

"Great! You're dynamite, kid. This could be even bigger than I thought."

"I'm glad you've come around to my point of view," she said, unable to resist tossing a barb his way.

"I'm thinking maybe you could use some help down there, Mike, What do you think?"

"Jack, this is my story and I've got it well in hand. I don't need help."

"Not even from your managing editor? I'd love to help my newest star reporter."

"Jack, this is a very sensitive situation and it's built on relationships I've forged with great difficulty."

"What kind of relationships are you referring to?" he asked, his tone suggestive.

"Get your mind out of the gutter, Mr. Ellison. I get my stories straight." No sooner had she said it than a pang of guilt went through her. In a way what she said was true, but in another way it wasn't.

"I have no intention of stepping on your toes, Mike," he replied. "This is your baby, and you'll get full credit. I just want to help if I can." His voice shifted down half an octave. "And I wouldn't mind seeing you."

Michaela rolled her eyes, wanting to scream. "Thanks, Jack, but I'm really doing fine."

"Give it some thought," he said. "Will you do that much?"

"All right, I'll give it some thought."

"You know, Mike," he said, "the only problem with doing good is people start expecting it all the time. I'm eagerly awaiting your next installment."

"If that's pressure, I'm ignoring it," she said.

"I'd really like to come down there and join up with you, so to speak," he said, with another of his trademark chuckles. "Don't dismiss me out of hand."

"I always remember who signs my paychecks, boss. But I also never forget there's more than one guy in the world willing to pay me to write news stories."

"Emory, you're going far."

"I hope so," she said.

"I'll talk to you at the beginning of the week," Ellison said. "Have a nice weekend. Don't do anything I wouldn't do."

"Bye, Jack."

She hung up, thinking his last comment was a suitable warning, considering the situation she was in. With luck, she *wouldn't* do anything he *would* do. Jack and Bernardo were two of a kind and she seemed to be hanging precariously between them.

After an unsuccessful attempt at a nap, Michaela got out her laptop and tried to write, but it was no use. She simply couldn't concentrate. She was worried sick that she'd get stuck with Bernardo, though she'd been telling herself that she absolutely, positively was not going to sleep with him— no matter what. The problem was, she didn't have a clear notion of how to avoid him—without telling him to go to hell, thus blowing everything.

Michaela was hoping to hear from Reed, but by midafternoon she'd had no word from him. She decided to make a last-ditch effort to warn him about what was coming down. She wrote a note saying that her interview with Juan de Falcón wasn't going to take place until Tuesday, and that Bernardo was determined to take her to Rancho Delgado for the weekend. She ended it with a simple question: "What are we going to do?"

She hadn't seen Rosita that afternoon and decided to look for her. Seeing a maid's cart at the end of the hallway, she found her changing the sheets in a vacated room.

"¡Holá, señorita!" Rosita said, seeing her at the door.

"Hi, Rosita. I saw your cart, so I thought I'd say hello." She walked over and handed the maid the envelope.

Without looking at it, Rosita stuffed it in her pocket. "There is a rumor you are going to have dinner with the president this evening," she said. "You must be very excited."

"More than you can imagine," Michaela said.

"You have a pretty dress?"

"Yes, to look good for Señor Snake," she said ironically.

"Do you need some help getting ready this evening? I can stay after, if you want that I do it."

"That's kind, Rosita, but I wouldn't want to put you out."

"No problem, señorita. For you, I would be happy to stay."

"Thank you," she said. "I could use a friend."

"What time should I come to your room?"

"Would six be okay?"

"I'll be there, señorita."

Michaela went back to her room. She sat and paced and tried to read. She would have called Chelsea, but there was no point since the phone might be bugged. So she agonized, hoping against hope that Reed would come through, but fearing that he wouldn't.

She had a long soak in the tub. She washed her hair. While she was doing her makeup she gazed in the mirror and cried. For the first time in a long time, she thought of her parents, which made her feel especially lonely.

At six o'clock Rosita came, but she had no messages from Reed, no word, nothing by way of encouragement except her smiling face. Michaela knew there was no point in ask-

ing what Reed was thinking. As Rosita herself said, she was
only the honey bee.

Michaela had gotten her dress out of the closet and they
were admiring it when Chelsea called.

"I can't tell you how good it is to hear your voice," Michaela said, her eyes glossing.

"I've been dying of curiosity, Mike. How's it going with
the new disciple?"

"The what?"

"Luke."

"Oh, him." She wondered how she could explain what
had happened without saying something that might get her
in trouble, should there be an eavesdropper.

"Don't tell me he's history," Chelsea said, breaking the
silence.

"Yeah, that's as good a way to put it as any. It was sort
of like a summer romance—fun while it lasted, but over
now."

"That's a shame. You sounded happy when we talked."

"I'm happy, Chels. You know me."

"I take it that editor, Señor Snake, has been put in a cage,
or did you drown him in champagne?"

"That sobriquet was not mine and it was ill-advised.
Bernardo's definitely in the picture. As a matter of fact, I'm
going away with him for the weekend."

"You're what?"

"It's a long story," she replied. "I'll tell you when I get
home."

"It sounds like a tragedy to me," Chelsea said. "The
dreamboat's gone and you're spending the weekend with
the . . . editor?"

"It's a topsy-turvy world, Chels. Bernardo has his virtues and his connections, let me put it that way. But I'd
rather not talk about it now. Not on the phone."

"I don't suppose you've seen Susana yet."

Michaela realized she hadn't called Chelsea after seeing
their friend. It was a terrible oversight and she was really
embarrassed. "Yes, I did, as a matter of fact. Just the other

day. I meant to call you but didn't. Things are at a delicate point right now, if you know what I mean."

"Well, is she okay?"

"Yes, she's all right, Chels. Better than I expected, in ways. Her spirits are good. She's a fighter. That may be the most important thing. She said to give you her best."

"I can't wait to hear more." Chelsea must have understood that they couldn't talk freely. "When are you coming home?"

"I'm not sure. Late next week, probably. Maybe as early as Wednesday. It depends on what I'm able to turn up."

There was a silence on the line. "Mike, you aren't going away with that editor for Susana's sake, are you?"

"Not exactly."

"Listen, girl, there are limits. Don't get yourself in a mess over a problem that isn't yours. If you report what you've seen and heard, you'll have done more than your share."

"Thanks for saying that, Chels. But I know what I'm doing, even if I'm not quite sure how it's going to come out."

Another long pause. "Will you be careful?" Chelsea asked.

"You know me. Impetuous at times, but I'm no fool."

"Let your head guide you, not your heart."

Michaela smiled at the comment. She didn't tell her friend, but it was probably already too late for that.

CHAPTER EIGHTEEN

MICHAELA PASSED THROUGH the gate at the palace, feeling like Cinderella going to the ball. When the limousine arrived to pick her up, she'd hoped that the driver would be Santos Moreno. The chauffeur turned out to be a stranger. She began to worry in earnest then, because there had been no word from Reed.

Would he forsake her? Over and over she kept thinking of his plea—"Trust me." But she also thought of him telling her to play along with Bernardo. Did he mean to the bitter end? Had Reed sold her down the river? He risked his life daily for what he believed in. Would he rationalize that it wouldn't be the end of the world if she endured a weekend with Bernardo, so long as it was for the good of his country? As they both knew, she would have compensations—a dynamite story.

When the door of the limousine opened, and Michaela alighted, a dozen heads turned her way. She knew she looked good. After she'd put on the dress at the hotel, Rosita had been awestruck, staring at her with her hands clasped to her breast. *"Un ángel,"* she'd murmured. "Right from heaven."

An officer offered Michaela his arm and escorted her into the palace. A majority of the guests had arrived. Some fifty or so were gathered in a large salon where drinks were being served. The men wore tuxedos, the women, like Michaela, had on formal gowns. The crowd was mostly older, with only a few women close to her in age. The four or five who were under forty were, by all appearances, second wives.

One of the white-gloved waiters brought Michaela a glass of champagne. Looks were cast her way as she moved toward a corner of the room where she might be less conspicuous. A tall, elderly man with a gray beard who was standing by himself turned to her. He was the Finnish ambassador and, like her, had come alone.

"It's unusual for a journalist to be invited to these affairs," he said after they'd introduced themselves. "Inhibits conversation." His English was perfect.

"I'm acquainted with the president's family," she said noncommittally. Michaela was struck by her own euphemism. "Would-be mistress of the heir apparent" would have been more accurate.

They chatted as the guests glanced their way. "You attract a lot of attention," the ambassador observed. "I suspect, if I may say so, it's your lovely face, not your occupation that intrigues them."

Michaela laughed good-naturedly. "You're kind to say so, sir, but I'd rather people were aware of me for what I did."

"By day, that's a valid philosophy. By night, enjoy your beauty." He gave her a grandfatherly smile. "The wisdom of an old man."

It was probably good advice, but Michaela did not relish the attention. In fact, it struck her as far less agreeable than the scrutiny she had endured back in her days as a beauty queen. At least then, there were lots of pretty girls around.

She sipped her champagne, conscious of the matrons observing her—some with envy, some with admiration, many simply watching their husbands watch her. She listened to the ambassador as she cast her eye about the crowd, wondering if Bernardo was secretly observing her. If he was there, she hadn't yet spotted him.

Guests were still arriving and Michaela began watching them come in the door. She saw Bernardo's wife first—the woman she'd seen at the hospital. She wore a severe yellow satin gown that made her skin look sallow. Bernardo, an expectant look on his face, came in right behind her. His tuxedo looked as if it had been made fifteen pounds and a number of cases of champagne earlier.

Bernardo spotted her almost immediately. His mouth fell agape and he stared wistfully. The Finnish ambassador was holding forth, relieving her of the burden of carrying the conversation. Still, she felt like a rabbit, aware that a fox was sniffing around the hutch.

Bernardo put a drink in his wife's hand, injected her into a conversation, then, without waiting a decent interval, excused himself. From the corner of her eye, Michaela watched him circle the room, making his way to where she stood.

As she figured it, it wouldn't hurt to give ol' Bernardo a little grief. "Mr. Ambassador," she said, sensing the editor approaching from behind them, "would you be so kind as to accompany me to the bar for more champagne?"

"Allow me to get it for you, my dear."

"Come with me instead," she pleaded.

"Delighted," he said. "My pleasure."

As they went off, Michaela felt Bernardo's hot breath on her back—or imagined that she did. Escaping him was a triumph, even if it was to be short-lived. Far more important was how she was going to avoid being trapped in his bed at the rancho.

The ambassador got her another glass of champagne and seemed more than willing to continue talking with her. Bernardo, hot on the scent, was working through the crowd, again heading in their direction. He was trying to appear casual, but he was doing a poor job of it.

"Don't you think it's rather close in here, Mr. Ambassador?" Michaela suggested. "A stroll in the hall might be pleasant. Could I interest you in accompanying me?"

"Assuredly, Miss Emory. How often does a gentleman get such a charming invitation?"

She took his arm and once again they made their escape. Michaela chuckled as they went off, though she feared any victories later in the evening would be harder won.

Fifteen minutes later, when they returned to the salon, all the guests had arrived. General Juan de Falcón, in full dress uniform, was receiving them in a reception line. Out of nowhere, Bernardo pounced on them.

"Mr. Ambassador," he said, taking both their arms, "the chief of protocol is looking for you. They want you in the reception line. I'll occupy Miss Emory in your absence."

"Quite right," the ambassador responded, a bit befuddled.

He went off and Bernardo, slightly red-faced, turned to Michaela. "Are you avoiding me, my love?" he said under his breath. "Or am I blinded by the fires of jealousy?"

"I thought you would be tending to your wife," she replied, showing surprise, "so I'm fending for myself."

"With an old goat?"

She gave him a look. "I assumed chatting with an elderly gentleman would be less offensive to you than if I were to round up some handsome young man, Bernardo."

"I'm sorry," he said, chastened, "but I simply cannot bear the thought of you in the company of another man—even one not so gallant as me."

"Should we be talking?" she asked from the corner of her mouth.

"Talking?" he said, agitated. "It is all I can do to keep from dragging you off to an anteroom and making passionate love to you. You are the most unbelievably exquisite creature to roam the earth." His voice rose with his last words, his fingers sinking into the soft flesh of her arm. "If I could take you away this instant, I would."

Michaela blanched, shocked by his fervor. "Bernardo!" she exclaimed under her breath, but sternly.

"I don't know how I'll be able to wait, my sweet dove."

She groaned, wondering if there was enough champagne in Pangonia to quench his fire. Why hadn't Reed sent her some knockout drops, a can of mace... anything?

About then, she caught the eye of Señora de Falcón. "Your wife sees us talking," Michaela said through her smile. Then, extending her hand, she said, "It's been nice talking to you, Mr. de Falcón. I believe I'll go through the reception line now."

Before he could protest, she was gone.

By supreme irony, Michaela was seated between the ambassador from Finland and the editor of *La Pensa*. As they all took their places, Bernardo introduced his wife. Michaela shook hands with the woman, surprised that Bernardo had had the presence of mind to cover the truth of their acquaintance with such a deft ploy.

The guests were seated at a long banquet table in the wood-paneled room. Waiters were spaced along the walls, waiting to start serving. Before they began to eat, General de Falcón rose to make a toast, which turned out to be a speech. Since the ambassador had been paired with her, he took it upon himself to discreetly translate the gist of the president's remarks—more self-laudatory bombast.

As soon as the toast was finished, the dinner conversation began. Michaela talked with the ambassador, ignoring Bernardo, who, to her relief, was speaking with his wife. She wondered if she would get through the meal unscathed, when suddenly she felt a hand on her leg. Bernardo was groping her under the table while chatting with the mother of his children.

Michaela pushed his hand aside, but he was persistent, pulling up her gown in search of the soft flesh of her thigh. She would have hauled him off and whacked him, except that the scene would have been more humiliating than the liberty he was taking. Bernardo knew that, too, and it galled her that he was taking advantage of the situation.

Michaela glanced around. No one seemed aware of the battle going on under the table. She happened to shift her gaze to the waiters. A large, heavyset bearded man caught her eye. She blinked. It was Father Tucino, the man who'd been with Reed that first day, and again at the Rancho Delgado. He wore the white coat of a waiter, and was smiling at her.

Stunned, Michaela scanned the faces of the other waiters. Many were familiar—men she'd seen at the rancho. Glancing over her shoulder she saw Santos Moreno directly behind her. He sported a handlebar mustache. When their eyes met, he winked.

Michaela's heart began to race. Her next thought was that Reed, too, might be among them. She quickly peered up and down the table, almost oblivious to the fact that Bernardo was now squeezing her thigh.

A handsome man with a neatly trimmed beard and gorgeous blue eyes, stood behind the general. It was Reed Lakesly.

"My God," she murmured aloud, though only the Finnish ambassador seemed to hear her.

"What's wrong, my dear?"

At that moment Reed pulled a pistol from under his coat and placed the muzzle to General de Falcón's head. Simultaneously two dozen waiters produced guns. There were startled gasps, then a stunned silence. Bernardo's hand clamped tight on her leg.

"*Señores,*" Reed declared loudly. "We have one further piece of business before the repast can begin. Wouldn't it be fitting if we say a prayer for our countrymen languishing in the prisons of Juan de Falcón—citizens held without a trial, tortured for no greater crime than their desire to see the return of their duly elected president?" He leaned close to the general's ear. "What do you think, my dear generalíssimo? A prayer for your victims?"

Juan de Falcón went chalky white. His mouth dropped open.

"Shall we bow our heads, *señores?*" Reed intoned.

One man at the far end of the table tried to get to his feet, but was rudely shoved down into his chair. The guests bowed their heads. Michaela glanced from under her brows at the people around her. Some were on the verge of panic, others frozen with fear. Bernardo, who'd let go of her leg, was trembling, mumbling Hail Marys.

"Thank you, *señores,*" Reed continued. "You are generous with your prayers. Now be generous with your purses. We are going to collect donations for the less fortunate. We will accept money, jewelry and watches—anything of value you care to donate."

He gave a signal and two of the cadre started coming down each side of the table with small sacks. Murmuring spread through the room as the diners began shedding their jewelry and emptying their wallets.

Reed began walking slowly down Michaela's side of the table as the collection progressed. "My apologies to the foreigners among you," Reed said over the low rumble of voices. "If you document your contributions before leaving this evening, I'm sure General de Falcón will be pleased to compensate you for your generosity."

"Señor, por favor," one woman said to him. "This is my wedding ring. I have had it for forty years."

"We will see that it is in safekeeping, *señora,*" he replied. "Perhaps General de Falcón will be good enough to buy it back with the money he has stolen from the people." He signaled to the cadre collecting the valuables. "Keep the ring separate." Then, to the others he said, "We will honor similar requests."

Reed came to where Michaela and Bernardo were seated. He put his hand on the editor's shoulder.

"Ah, Señor de Falcón, you look in good health. Could it be because you are seated between two such lovely women? Let me see, which one is the mistress and which one is the wife?"

There was a murmur and Bernardo's wife leaned forward to glare at Michaela. Michaela didn't move. Then she heard the sound of dripping water. Looking down, she saw that it was trickling off Bernardo's chair. He whimpered so violently, she thought he was going to fall off his seat.

She jumped to her feet and spun around to face Reed. "How dare you!" she said through her teeth. "What kind of man are you to insult women under the point of a gun?"

He reached out and pinched her cheek. "Ah, Bernardo, you've got yourself a fiery one! And American, too. What did she cost you—five peasants' wages for a year?"

Michaela slapped Reed hard across the face. Blinking with surprise, he slapped her back, almost as hard.

"You bastard!" she cried, and hit him again—this time as forcefully as she could.

There were cries of surprise. Reed shook his head to clear it, then grinned. "I never hit a woman more than once," he said. "The second blow is free, but I warn you to stop while you are ahead." He turned to the head of the table. "General, here is one with balls, perhaps you will compensate her double for her contribution." Then to Michaela he said, "What have you donated to the cause?"

She opened her purse. He peered inside, then smiled.

"Looks like you could be a recipient of our charity." He leaned over close to Bernardo's ear. "You should be more generous with your lady friends. The poor girl scarcely has two nickels. And by the way, if you'd told me, I'd have let you go to the *juan*." Winking at Michaela, he moved on down the table.

She sat down, her heart racing, her expression grim, though she was filled with elation. When the collection was over, Reed expressed his thanks, then he and his men filed toward the kitchen door.

Before he disappeared, Reed turned and said, *"Gracias, señores. ¡Bueno provecho y buenas noches!"*

For a second after they'd gone, there was a stunned silence. Then General Juan de Falcón, his face flushed, slammed his fist on the table, making the china clatter.

MICHAELA SAT IN THE limousine outside the palace, waiting for Bernardo. He'd vetoed her suggestion that she go on back to the hotel, insisting they had to leave together. The poor man was so humiliated that she almost felt sorry for him.

After Reed and his men left, locking the doors behind them, it took a while before the security people arrived to let them out. Somehow an erroneous order had been passed along and all the guards had been sent outside. General de Falcón was so enraged that he made only a brief apology to his guests before stomping off. Bernardo slipped out to change his clothes, having "accidentally spilled wine" all over himself. After putting his wife in a limousine, he had Michaela served dinner and went off to confer with his father, saying that afterward he would take her to the hotel to get her things.

As she waited, she realized that Bernardo wasn't going to let Reed Lakesly spoil his weekend. The real question was whether Reed had assumed that the burglary would put an end to Bernardo's designs. If so, it hadn't worked. She could only hope that Reed had something further in mind.

Then she began to worry. What if Reed didn't really care what happened to her? What if his sole intent was to establish their mutual hostility so that later, when she went to the general with misinformation, she'd be believed? Under those circumstances, Reed wouldn't have planned another intervention. Would he use her that way? She didn't know.

Michaela agonized, not knowing what to think. Susana was in jail. That had been her reward for serving the revolution. Was Michaela's reward to be a "sexy" weekend with Bernardo? She didn't want to think so.

As the minutes wore on, she got more and more agitated—not only with Reed, but with Bernardo, as well. Men, it seemed, had but one thing in mind—to use her. All of them were the same—Jack, Bernardo, even Reed. She'd seen it so often.

Michaela was contemplating getting out of the limo and going back to the hotel on her own, when Bernardo arrived. He ordered the driver to take them to the Hotel El Presidente.

"I'm sorry for the delay, my love," he said. "I had to speak with my father."

"He must be very upset. That was a cowardly thing for the MAP to do."

"He is outraged. They will pay. He is determined." Bernardo took her hand. "Father spoke of you with admiration, my sweet. He said you were very brave."

"I was angry at that man for what he said. It was an outrage."

"You know who that was, don't you?" Bernardo said. "It was Lakesly. He was in disguise, but I recognized him immediately."

"*That* was Reed Lakesly?"

"Yes. The villain. Father is determined to have him in jail within a week. He's tripled the reward for Lakesly's head, and ordered raids and a roundup of suspected sympathizers."

"I hope they catch him," she said. "I've never been struck by a man before."

"I shall avenge the blow," Bernardo said, drawing himself up. "Never doubt that for one moment."

Michaela patted his hand. "You're very sweet. But, Bernardo, I've been thinking. We've had a very traumatic evening. Why don't we delay our trip to your country home?"

"No, I've been looking forward to it with great expectation, my love. After your bravery you deserve a pleasant sojourn with the man who adores you above all others." Smiling, he kissed her hands. "But I have a surprise, as well."

She was afraid to ask. "What's that?"

"My father was impressed with the way you challenged Lakesly. He plans to honor you with a special commendation when you visit the presidential palace for your interview on Tuesday."

"How nice."

"And another thing. I confessed to my father my love for you, Michaela. I told him I wanted to give you a gift you would treasure above all else—Susana Riveros's freedom."

"Bernardo! You mean Susana is going to be freed?"

"It's not certain yet, but my father has agreed to consider it. On Monday after we return from the country I will meet with him and we will discuss it further."

Michaela had a sudden letdown from her brief elation. Was this more bait—another inducement to give him what he wanted at the rancho? She bristled. She'd been praised and promised rewards, but when you got right down to it, they were treating her like a whore.

But what could she do? Maybe they *would* release Susana. One thing was certain. If she told Bernardo to go to hell, the chances of them releasing Susana would evaporate. Bernardo de Falcón, fool that he was, was apparently guileful, after all. As they neared the hotel, she had a feeling that maybe, just maybe, she'd been had.

CHAPTER NINETEEN

MICHAELA MADE BERNARDO wait in the limousine while she went inside to change and get her bags. As she entered her room she was hoping against hope that Reed would be waiting. He wasn't. There were no messages. Nothing. Either he'd sold her down the river, or he didn't care.

Her moment of truth had arrived. In a real sense, Susana's freedom was at stake. Even so, Michaela couldn't stomach the thought of prostituting herself. This was the Hobson's choice she'd dreaded. She paced, running her options through her mind. She would go with Bernardo, but take along a couple of bottles of champagne. Once at the rancho, she would do her level best to keep him drunk.

Changing quickly, Michaela grabbed her things and went to the lobby. The clerk at the desk had two bottles of champagne brought from the restaurant for her.

Bernardo's eyes widened when he saw the wine. "What's this?"

"My gift to you, Bernardo. We should toast the weekend."

"You are a temptress," he said with a devilish smile.

They drove off, Bernardo immediately opening the champagne. He imbibed with relish. Michaela endured a few sloppy kisses, but as they neared the edge of the city, he was already half drunk.

But half drunk was not enough. When she tried to pour more into his glass, he pushed the bottle away. "No," he said, "I shall satiate myself with you." Then, plunging his face to her breast, he inhaled her scent, snorting like a hog after a truffle.

"Bernardo!" she cried, trying to push him away.

"Have you ever made love in a limousine?" he asked. "It's wonderful, believe me. Especially on a bumpy road."

"Oh, my God," she mumbled. She'd been naive at best, stupid at worst, to think she could handle him. "Can't we wait?"

"No!" he exclaimed, actually sounding angry. "I shall have you now, my dove. You'll love every bump."

Bernardo pounced, tearing at her clothes. Michaela fought him, but he took her defiance as play, pro forma resistance.

When she gave him a whack, he laughed, thinking she enjoyed the game. "Being a gentleman," he said, pulling down her bra, "I won't hit back, like that bastard, Lakesly."

Michaela grabbed the champagne bottle and was about ready to clunk him on the head when the limousine suddenly screeched to a halt, throwing them both to the floor.

"¿Qué pasa?" Bernardo said, lifting his head to peer out.

Suddenly the limo was flooded with light. From where she lay, with Bernardo kneeling between her legs, Michaela saw half a dozen flashlights shining in at them. She heard shouts outside.

"Dios mío, Dios mío," Bernardo mumbled. "It's an ambush!"

The car doors flew open. There was a moment of silence, then the laughter of several men.

"Well, well," came a familiar voice. "What have we here? A game of post office?" It was Reed.

At that instant, hands reached inside and Bernardo was jerked out of the vehicle. He began whimpering in Spanish, pleading for mercy. Another hand came in, to help her. Michaela looked up at Reed, her eyes wide with astonishment.

"Are you all right?" he asked gently, and with concern.

She stood, her heart pounding, her chest heaving as much from shock as from tussling with Bernardo. Michaela caught sight of the editor in the beams of light. He was blubbering.

Reed put his arm around her waist. "I'm sorry you had to endure that, but I thought the sonovabitch would wait."

"What's happening? What are you going to do?"

"Play along for a few more minutes, darling," he whispered. "It's important we make this look authentic. You don't have to resist, but try not to look too happy about being abducted."

He led her around the limo. "Well, Señor de Falcón," Reed said, "I see you prefer the company of the mistress to the wife. I hope Señora de Falcón will not be upset that you were taken prisoner with a beautiful girl. You will be kept in separate cells... unless you would be too lonely by yourself."

The men laughed.

"I take it you have luggage. Where is it? In the trunk?"

Bernardo nodded, his eyes wide with fear. Reed signaled for one of the men to get their things.

"Well, enough joking," he said. "The people of Pangonia have two prisoners. Get them in the van, *amigos.*"

A signal was given and a van roared up. The rear door was opened and the luggage was put inside. Michaela was told to get in. Reed climbed in after her. They sat on one of the banquettes on the sides of the cargo space. Michaela looked out the back at Bernardo, seeing his terrified face in the glare of the flashlights.

Suddenly a siren went off. More lights flooded the scene. Shots rang out. There were shouts.

Michaela gasped as two men near Bernardo dropped to the ground. There were more shots. Bernardo was standing alone. The guerrillas were picking up their fallen comrades and tossing them into the van.

Horrified, Michaela looked at Reed. He had a big smile on his face. When Bernardo continued to stand there, frozen, Reed cursed under his breath. "What an idiot," she heard him say.

He moved to the back of the van. "Quick, somebody grab de Falcón before he gets away!" he shouted.

The cry awakened Bernardo from his catatonia. He took off like a wounded jackrabbit, running up the road in the direction of the approaching police vehicles.

"He's gotten away!" Reed called. "Let's get out of here!"

The doors to the van slammed closed and they roared off. Reed put his arm around her shoulders. The "wounded" men got off the floor and sat down across from them, laughing. For thirty seconds Michaela sat stunned, speechless.

"What in God's name happened back there?"

"That, my dear," Reed said, "was a feigned, partially successful abduction. We got the mistress, but not the pig. Bernardo was very fortunate tonight."

"How did you know the police would show up?"

Reed kissed her temple, holding her close. "They were ours," he said. "A friendly patrol shooting blanks. Bernardo won't know the difference. And his father will give our boys medals for saving his son's life."

"You mean you had this planned? You were going to let me get right to the point of being raped, then feign an abduction?"

"Like I said, I thought Bernardo would be better mannered."

"Why didn't you tell me?" she demanded, her voice taking on an edge. "I was sure you'd thrown me to the wolves."

"I couldn't divulge our plans. What if you slipped, or they got suspicious and beat it out of you? This way, we didn't force you to act."

"You took a darn big chance. What if I'd told Bernardo to go to hell and gotten on a plane for home?"

The lights from passing cars alternately illuminated their faces and cast them in shadow. "Maybe I was presumptuous, but even if your love was in doubt, I thought I had your trust."

She scoffed, folding her arms over the front of her torn dress. "Love? Trust? You're living in a make-believe world, *Lucas*. You've been playing Robin Hood too long."

He took her hand and rested it on his knee. "Michaela, the last thing I intended was to take you for granted. I really thought we were on the same page."

The emotion in her brought tears of anger. "You might as well know the truth," she said, trying hard to keep from crying. "The only reason I went with Bernardo was because he told me that his father might release Susana. I thought if I gave Bernardo the brush-off, she'd be the one who would suffer."

"They're going to release Susana?"

"Bernardo said they might. I don't know whether to believe him or not. But I couldn't dismiss the possibility out of hand."

Reed was silent for a minute. "I see."

She tried to read his expression, to see how the news about Susana affected him, but she couldn't see him well enough. "Sorry to deflate your balloon," she said, the tears flowing, "but you were hardly a factor at all."

He ran his thumb over the backs of her fingers, sending a shiver up her spine. She glanced at the other men, who were talking among themselves.

"I know this whole business has been upsetting," Reed said softly. "Putting you through it has been rough on me, as well. The easy thing would have been to let Bernardo take you off for the weekend. But I couldn't do that. He's a bumbling fool, I know, but he's dangerous in his way. And selfish. A number of people have suffered because of him, including his own family."

"Yes, I know," she said. "I hate Bernardo, and yet a part of me pities him."

"If it was in me, I could have had him killed. Tonight I had a gun to the head of the general himself. Killing is not the solution. Our purpose was to humiliate. In the long run that's more effective. Besides, if we'd resorted to violence, innocent people could have been hurt, not the least among them you."

"How important was our confrontation at the dinner table?"

"It was the main reason we snuck into the palace and thumbed our nose at ol' Juan."

"You took that risk in order to make it easier for me to deceive them?"

Reed gave her a quirky smile. "That, and I was jealous. I had no invitation to the party, so I crashed it."

Michaela laughed.

"How else was I going to see you all dressed up?" he said. "You looked absolutely beautiful, by the way."

They stared into each other's eyes in the light of the passing traffic. She put her hand to his cheek. "Thank you."

"Be honest," he said. "Were you glad to see me at the palace?"

"It was a surprise," she admitted. "And there was one truly gratifying moment."

"What was that?"

"When I slugged you. It was worth the whack you gave me."

"I tried to pull my punch," he said. "I had to be convincing, though. It didn't hurt too much, I hope."

"No, and it didn't matter. The second one I gave you was practically orgasmic."

"Michaela," he said, cuffing her playfully, "are you saying ours is a love-hate relationship?"

She fell silent. The question was really more serious than he'd intended it, and it gave her pause. "There have been times the last few days when I *have* hated you," she told him.

He touched her lip. "And times when you've loved me?"

She smiled with embarrassment. "No, just times when I hated you less."

Reed took her into his arms and held her close. He didn't kiss her. He just hugged her, and stroked the back of her head.

Michaela was a bit stiff at first, but then her body started melting into his. She felt herself letting go. And then, as if someone suddenly turned on the spigot, she began to sob, all the tension of the evening pouring out.

Reed kissed the tears on her cheeks, then took her face in his hands. "Don't worry, darling," he murmured. "You're safe."

She hugged him back, their faces pressed together. "Where are we going?" she asked.

"To our command center in the mountains. I thought you could use a few days' rest."

"Then what?"

"We don't need to discuss that now, darling. There's plenty of time." He lightly kissed her lips.

Michaela looked into his eyes. She wanted to tell him not to let her down. She needed to trust him. She wanted to believe in him, but she couldn't, quite. Not yet. She was too afraid.

THEY DROVE FOR AN HOUR. Michaela and Reed were the only ones who didn't fall asleep, though she rested with her head on his shoulder. They finally stopped at a little *cantina* at the edge of a village up in the mountains.

Reed helped her out. The air was cool and fresh. Carlos Tucino and Santos Moreno emerged from the front of the van, greeting her. Reed excused himself and went inside. As he walked away, she noticed that there was a pistol stuck in his belt. It struck her for the first time that she was actually off in the hinterland with a real revolutionary hero.

She turned to Santos, whose earnest smile evoked his love for Susana. "We keep meeting in the strangest places," she said.

"I was curious what de Falcón was serving tonight," he said with a laugh. "But the next time I see you there, I hope it will be to welcome Corazón de León back. And, God willing, I pray Susana will be with us."

"That would be wonderful," she said as they headed for the entrance to the cantina.

Inside, Reed was speaking with a barefoot man wearing an undershirt and baggy trousers. Michaela glanced around at the simple room with a dirt floor and a few tables and chairs. It was lit by a single light-bulb hanging from the ceiling.

Michaela and Santos sat at a table while Reed continued conversing. She looked at her watch. It was nearly midnight, but seemed later. Finally Reed joined them.

"We'll stay here until dawn, then we head for the command center. There aren't any army patrols in the area, so there's no need to make the trek in the dark." He grinned. "Besides, you look like you could use some rest."

"I hope I don't look as tired as I feel, because I'm bushed."

"Come on, then," he said, getting up. "The accommodations are modest, but you should be able to rest."

Reed took her into a room where a couple of cots were set up. There were blankets, but no sheets. Michaela didn't care. She did need to visit the ladies' room, however.

"Are there any facilities?" she asked.

"Not with plumbing. But a crusty journalist like you has probably endured worse."

He took her out back, using a flashlight he took from a shelf by the back door. Reed led her by the hand.

"Are there snakes in Pangonia?" she asked.

"Only little ones."

"What do you mean, 'only'?"

"Well, I don't want you thinking there are fifteen-foot pythons waiting for wary foreigners around every outhouse."

"Shut up, Reed Lakesly, that isn't funny!"

They came to the privy. "Shall I wait?" he asked.

"No, just give me the flashlight," she said, taking it. "You can go back inside."

"You're sure?"

"Go on," she said, giving him a playful shove. "Right now I'd rather deal with the snakes than you."

A few minutes later she made her way back along the path, and found Reed waiting for her at the rear of the cantina. He was sitting on a log, gazing up at the night sky. He got up as Michaela approached. She handed him the flashlight.

"No snakes and no plumbing," she said. "A fair trade-off."

Reed chuckled and set the flashlight down on the log, then put his arms around her waist. "I was just sitting here, Mike, thinking how glad I am I decided to abduct you."

"Why's that?"

"Because whether you believe it or not, I've gotten very fond of you."

"I know you're a passionate man, Reed. You're passionate about women, and passionate about your revolution."

"I feel a lot more for you than just passion," he said earnestly. "And in my eyes you're not just another woman."

She put her head on his shoulder. "I'm rather fond of you, too. But these are extraordinary times. Being in a guerrilla camp with a leading revolutionary is hardly a normal situation. This trip is an adventure to further my career. I left my personal life back in Washington."

"Your personal life goes with you wherever you go, Mike."

She shook her head. "No, this isn't real."

"Why? Because you don't want it to be?"

Michaela thought for a moment, running her finger over the cleft in his chin. "I'll be heading home soon, and the problem will take care of itself."

"I don't regard this as a problem," he said.

"Maybe I'm too tired to argue the point. In the morning I plan on becoming a journalist again."

Reed ran his hands up and down her back as he gazed at her. "All right," he said gently. "But I'd like to give you something to dream about."

He lifted her chin and kissed her mouth. Despite herself, Michaela leaned into him, liking the feel of his chest against her breasts, the warmth of his arms as he held her. The kiss deepened and their tongues swirled against each other. A rush went through her and her heart tripped.

He excited her. She would have dreamed about him whether he'd kissed her again or not. Reed Lakesly was the kind of man who tormented a woman's soul. But the sad part was, other women were dazzled by him, too. Including her friend. And try as she might, Michaela couldn't get Susana and Reed out of her mind.

CHAPTER TWENTY

MICHAELA SLEPT ALONE in the back room of the cantina, though Reed told her that in the middle of the night he'd piled down on the cot next to her for a couple of hours. It was barely light when he gently shook her awake.

She sat up, momentarily disoriented. Seeing Reed's face in the soft glow of dawn, she threw her arms around his neck. "Oh, it's you. Thank goodness."

"Did you have a bad dream?" he asked, holding her close.

She nodded.

"I trust it was about Pangonian snakes, not me," he said.

"You'll have to wonder."

Reed stroked her cheek. "I hope you brought some pants or shorts. We're going to the camp on horseback."

"My God, where is this place?"

"In a remote mountain valley. It's really quite lovely. It might even be the highlight of your trip."

Michaela put on jeans, then joined the seven men in the main room of the cantina. She took the chair between Reed and Carlos Tucino. Tucino said good-morning and broke her off some bread. There was honey and jam and rich black coffee in tin cups. She ate with a good appetite.

Michaela had no sooner washed down the last bite than Reed said it was time to go. Outside she saw that the area was lush with dense vegetation. There were emerald mountains all around. The road that passed in front of the cantina was a dirt trail.

The van was gone, and across the way were eight saddle horses and a couple of pack mules. The owner of the cantina was tending the animals.

"Do you ride?" Reed asked her.

"Nice time to ask, *jefe*," she replied. "Fortunately I do."

"We could always tie you on one of the pack mules," he teased.

"I bet you're not kidding."

Reed, who also wore jeans, only smiled in response.

"Do we have my bag and my computer?" she asked.

"Already aboard." They went to the horse that was to be hers and Reed offered her a knee to mount. Michaela took the saddle horn and swung herself onto the saddle.

Reed adjusted the stirrups and tightened the cinch. He got on his horse and, giving the signal, led the way up the road. The proprietor waved goodbye.

Half a mile up the road they branched off. They were soon climbing a trail that switched back and forth up the side of the mountain. The higher they got, the thinner the vegetation was, and with the sun above the ridge to the east, the cool air began to get hot.

After an hour they stopped to rest by a stream. It had been years since Michaela had ridden and she knew she'd be sore later. She sat on a rock next to Reed, sipping water from a cup one of the men brought her. "How much farther to the camp?" she asked.

"Just a bit. Most of the climbing is over," Reed said.

"What exactly is the plan? Am I going to escape so that I can tell General de Falcón about your dastardly intentions?"

"Something like that." He took a handkerchief from his pocket and dabbed her damp brow and lip.

"No one would believe I could get out of here on my own."

"I'll be providing you with an accomplice."

"Considerate of you," she teased.

"We try to think of everything. Any more questions?"

"How long will I be here?"

"For a while. Your credibility will be diminished if you're with us too long, though." He waited for her next question.

"Is there running water and plumbing in this secret base?"

"No, but there's a nice waterfall not far."

Her eyes widened with delight. She recalled the article in the travel magazine—the one that had gotten her to daydreaming in the committee hearing the day Chelsea had read her Susana's letter. Michaela had fantasized about making love by a tropical waterfall. Was fate trying to tell her something? Despite the heat, a shiver went down her spine.

"Don't you like waterfalls?" he asked.

"As a matter of fact, I like them a lot," she said. "Maybe more than I should."

He didn't understand, but seemed to sense he wasn't intended to. "If we get going, there'll be time for a swim before lunch. There's a beautiful pool by the falls."

Michaela had a sudden premonition and it wasn't altogether unpleasant.

The rest of the ride was easier. They dipped down the back of the mountain into a small valley, where the camp was located. Twenty minutes through a leafy forest with a high canopy and ferns and they came to the camp.

It wasn't as primitive as she'd expected. The half-dozen-or-so buildings surrounded a pleasant glen. Everyone dismounted and their horses were taken away. It looked to Michaela as if there was a resident population of twenty or thirty. She saw three women among those who came out to greet them.

Reed led her to a small building that was set apart from the others. "I share quarters with the communications center. There are two beds, so you're welcome to stay with me."

"What's the alternative?"

"The barracks."

They stopped in front of the building. "So it's either you or twenty men.

"There's a separate section for women. There are normally six or eight here at any given time. The staff is rotated. If you prefer, you can stay with the women."

Michaela put her hands on her hips. "Can I ask a pointed question? Do you normally choose one of the women and invite her to your quarters when you're here, or do you bring the lucky lady with you?"

He turned serious. "You're very cynical, aren't you, Mike?"

"I notice you aren't answering the question."

"I haven't always slept alone, I'll admit that. But many of the women who work here are married, and they're often with their husbands. I'm usually too busy for play. The average bachelor in Washington probably leads a racier sex life than I do."

She scrutinized him. "How do you manage to sound so believable?"

He shrugged, his palms up. "It could be my inherent honesty, Mike."

The door to the communications center opened and a voluptuous brunette in a peasant blouse and skirt strolled out. Michaela didn't recognize her until she saw the fiery look in her eye. It was Cecilia, the waitress from the restaurant.

She greeted Reed in Spanish, appearing happy to see him. "So," she said, switching to English, "you brought our new secret agent along." She offered Michaela a thin smile. "*Buenos días, señorita*. Welcome to our humble guerrilla camp. I hope you enjoy your stay, but I warn you, here there is no French champagne."

Michaela gave Reed a look.

"You remember Cecilia, don't you, Mike?" he said with a weak grin.

"Yes. Good to see you, Cecilia."

The woman cocked her hip, nodding. "Likewise."

"Cecilia is going to be your collaborator in the escape," Reed said.

"It will be interesting to see if I make it back to town alive," Michaela said under her breath.

Reed had a woebegone expression on his face.

"Lucas," Cecilia said, descending the steps, "I hope you don't mind, but I've been using one of your beds. Should I stay now, or should I go?"

There was an awkward silence. Reed looked embarrassed.

"I think you should stay in the barracks, Cecilia," he said.

The woman looked back and forth between them. "Oh. I begin to understand now. The secret agent is a *special* secret agent." With that, she turned on her heel and went back into the building.

Reed wore a pained expression. Michaela stared directly into his eyes. "So much for your inherent honesty," she said caustically.

"It's not what you think."

"That's kind of become your slogan, hasn't it?"

"Cecilia has expectations and she has desires. That doesn't mean I share them."

"Maybe not at this particular moment."

"I slept with her a couple of times, I admit it. But that was a long time ago. Long before I met you."

"Save your breath, Reed. And tell Cecilia she doesn't have to leave. I'm sleeping in the barracks." She started to turn away, but he grabbed her arm.

"Mike, I would have sent her to the barracks even if you weren't here. I decided a long time ago that it was unfair to Cecilia to take advantage of her feelings."

"Why should I believe you?"

"First, because it's true. Second, because I'd have been a fool to select her to work with you if I thought this was going to happen. I've made my feelings clear in the past and I thought she and I understood each other."

Michaela thought it over, deciding what he said made sense. Still, she felt uncomfortable. "Maybe Cecilia and I both should sleep in the barracks."

He gave her an intense look. "I want you with me, Michaela."

The door of the building flew open and Cecilia stomped out. She had one bag in her hand and another, smaller one, slung over her shoulder. Michaela watched her stride across the compound, feeling sorry for her.

"I apologize for letting that happen," Reed said. "I miscalculated. It's my fault."

Michaela felt uncertain. "Any more surprises?"

"No." He looked at his watch. "We've got the better part of three hours till lunch. Why don't you rest while I meet with my staff? Then I'll take you to the waterfall for a swim." He took her arm and they started toward the building.

"A swim sounds delightful," she said, "but I'm afraid I didn't pack a suit."

"No problem," he said, holding the door for her. "Nobody up here uses them."

MICHAELA LAY ON THE BED, listening to the birds singing outside the window. She was tired from the ride, and the short night, but she couldn't sleep. She agonized over what to do.

Reed wanted her—in his bed, at least. She'd slept with him once. She had strong feelings for him. And she was fairly certain his feelings for her went beyond lust. But that didn't mean she should let go, follow her desires.

She was afraid to trust him. Yet the problem went beyond not wanting to be used and made a fool of. In the past she'd found it easy to avoid emotional commitments because the men she met weren't men she really wanted. In Reed Lakesly she'd found everything she'd hoped for. And he claimed to want her. So why was she catatonic with fear? Why couldn't she follow her heart?

The simple truth was that she was afraid of being hurt. Everyone she'd ever loved had abandoned her, if only by their death. She'd known she'd had this problem for a long time, but until Reed came along, it hadn't really mattered. After all, she couldn't love just any man to prove to herself she wasn't afraid of commitment. With Reed she was being put to the test, and that wasn't easy.

When she'd talked to her aunt about her fears, Gayle had said, "What's the worst that could happen if things go wrong?" The advice had helped her take up challenges, do some pretty gutsy things. If she could risk her job and her financial well-being by going off to Pangonia, she ought to be able to love a man she cared for and let the chips fall where they may. Yet she was terrified at the very thought. To give of herself, to truly let go, was much harder than it looked.

What's the worst that can happen? she asked herself now. You can spend a few days in paradise with this man, say a tearful goodbye and go home to Washington and your life. Or he can sleep with you, then tell you he really loves Susana Riveros, or some other woman you've never heard of. It would be a crushing blow, but would you die? Would your life come to an end because once, just once, you let yourself want a man as much as he wanted you?

What a crazy week it had been. She'd had the guts to turn a fantasy into reality and now she was on the verge of opening her heart. She was telling herself to live the emotions she felt, without fear of the consequences.

Michaela dozed off, sleeping for half an hour before Reed came in and sat on the edge of the bed. The face she saw when she opened her eyes was rather dear.

He smiled at her and she touched the corner of his mouth. "Is it time to go swimming?"

"Yes," he replied, sounding pleased by her cheerful tone. "It'll be the best bath you've ever had."

Michaela nodded. "You know, Reed, you just might be right."

He kissed her hands and she felt her heart soar. There was a new resolve rising from deep inside her. She wasn't sure what had done it, but something fundamental, something important, had happened. She had Reed to thank for it.

She got up and followed him to the next room. Reed grabbed a small rucksack, saying he had towels for them both. "Is there anything else you'd like to bring?"

She shook her head.

They went off together, following a faint trail almost overgrown with ferns. "I take it this is sort of a communal bath," she said, lightheartedly.

"There are times when a couple wants a little privacy and the rest of the camp respects it."

"Is this such a time?" she asked.

"Yes." Reed reached back and took her hand. They walked side by side. "There's something I want to discuss with you, Mike."

The seriousness of his tone sent a wave of trepidation through her. "What do you want to talk about?"

"A couple of days ago you asked what was in the note you carried to Susana, and I told you I couldn't say."

"Yes..."

"I can tell you now."

She waited. "I alerted her that we were going to launch a countercoup in a matter of days. I couldn't let you know that while you were still in the arms of the enemy, so to speak. It not only would have been dangerous for you, as I've said, but also for Susana."

"Are you saying there wasn't a personal message?"

"There was a personal message, too. I sent my love. Susana and I are very good friends. We've had an affair of the spirit. I respect her and I believe she feels the same about me."

"My impression is that she loves you, Reed."

"Maybe our feelings for each other aren't exactly parallel. I can't speak for Susana. But we've never been lovers."

He looked at her questioningly, as though he was uncertain whether she would accept his explanation. Michaela smiled to let him know that she did. "I appreciate you telling me."

"I couldn't before. As it was, I was risking that they'd succeed in torturing it out of Susana."

"I know that now."

"And you'll know a lot more before you go back. I'm going to put you in a position to tell them everything you learn—except of course, that you're a double agent. That will be your only secret." He firmly squeezed her hand. "And between you and me, I don't want any secrets—not about our feelings."

"You want to hear something funny? It wouldn't have mattered what you'd told me about you and Susana. I'd like to believe you're being truthful about her, but the only thing that really matters, Reed, is that I don't do something to hurt her. She's been through so much."

He stopped walking and faced her. "And I've come to realize how important being forthright truly is."

"You're a slow learner, Father O'Laughlin," she said, feigning an Irish accent. "It certainly took you long enough to come 'round, laddie."

Reed threw back his head and laughed. "For as long as you know me, Mike, you'll never let me forget that."

She shook her head. "Especially not around St. Patrick's Day."

They laughed, then looked into each other's eyes. Emotion filled Reed's face and he kissed her tenderly.

"Do you think a man can know a woman for as little as a week and be in love with her?" he asked.

"It's possible, I suppose, but it'd be risky to draw any conclusions."

"All I've got to say is we'd better do a lot of living the next few days, Michaela Emory, because I want to believe in this feeling I have."

"You are a terrible romantic," she said, kissing his chin.

He took her hand and started pulling her along the path. "Mike, honey, you ain't seen nothing yet."

CHAPTER TWENTY-ONE

REED SENSED HER excitement as they neared the waterfall. Something about Mike had changed. It was subtle, but unmistakable. There was a freedom, an openness he hadn't seen before. It was hard to know what to make of it.

"How much farther? I can hear the roar. It must be close." She had moved ahead and was pulling him along by the hand.

"Just beyond the next rise."

"Come on." She pulled his arm with childlike impatience.

"You can run ahead if you like."

"I think I will." She moved on briskly, brushing aside the lacy ferns that overlapped the trail.

"Watch out for pythons, lass," he called after her. "Especially the big brown one. He's a mean son of a gun."

"Shut up, Father O.," she called over her shoulder. "We already know you're full of blarney."

Lakesly laughed, feeling more lighthearted than he had in months. The woman had had an enormous effect on him, and not just emotionally. For some reason she had him reassessing his life and asking questions of himself he hadn't asked before.

He pushed his way through the ferns. Michaela was standing on the little rise, gazing down at the pool in awe.

"My God, Reed, it's beautiful," she said.

It was. He never tired of the place, finding every visit to the site a spiritual experience.

The surrounding trees were tall, covering the pool with a lacy canopy, filtering the light. The waterfall spilled over a rock ledge at the far side of the pool, dropping some forty feet into the water. Patchy sunlight formed a muted rainbow in the mist at the base of the falls. Birds flew back and forth across the space, their cries echoing above the roar of the water.

"I've never been here," she said, "but I've dreamed about this place. I know I have."

She moved down the slope. He followed, watching her, taking delight in her joy. When he came up beside her at water's edge, she was staring into the clear depths of the pool.

"Is it cold?" she asked.

"Not really. Most people find it refreshing."

Michaela swished her hand in it. "Feels good."

"People who like showers stand under the fall. I prefer the pool, myself."

"I think I'll have a closer look," she said, rising.

"For the next couple of hours, the place is all yours, Mike."

He slipped the rucksack from his shoulders and sat down on the mossy bank, watching her move around the perimeter of the pool, stepping from rock to rock, pushing aside the fronds of the ferns that grew to the water's edge. She was so lovely, it made his heart ache. He didn't fully understand the hold she had on him, but her effect was undeniable.

That morning, in the first light of dawn, he'd stood beside her cot as she slept, staring at her face, asking himself how he could possibly allow her to leave his life. And yet, he saw no way it could be avoided. He'd sensed that her attraction to him was practically as strong as his own, but she'd been holding back, unwilling to trust him, to really let go.

He could hardly blame her. He wasn't the sort of man to inspire a woman's confidence. He'd made no attempt to hide his carefree ways. He did like women, it was true. Susana Riveros had been his intellectual soul mate and friend, just as he'd told Michaela. Others had aroused him, fired his passions. But Mike Emory spoke to a side of him he didn't know well himself.

She was almost directly opposite him now, and near the falls. She seemed totally absorbed, like a child in wonderland. He observed the long slender lines of her body, savoring the fact that he'd known it intimately, that he'd experienced the softness, the warmth and scent of her flesh. He knew what it was for her to yield to his strength and his desire.

He wanted her again, but he wanted her more than physically. He wanted to embrace her spirit and to know her love. He wanted to feel at one with her. He wanted her to know his devotion and feel hers. It had become an obsession—one he feared a little because it was so unique in his experience.

Michaela faced him, her hands on her hips. "I want to go into the waterfall," she called.

"Go ahead."

"Aren't you going to turn around so I can get undressed?"

"Modesty is against the rules," he called back.

"I've never been much for rules," she replied.

She stepped back into the ferns so that he could only see her head and shoulders. His pulse picked up, knowing she was undressing. He smiled as he stared at her. The combination of spunk and elegance in her manner very much appealed to him.

She emerged from the ferns totally naked, but didn't linger, moving directly to the torrent, skipping the few feet she had to traverse with the grace of a ballerina. Through the mists and opaque sheet of water he was able to see her gauzy silhouette. He could make out the curve of her hips and waist, and when she turned, he could see the swell of her breasts. It was a breathtaking sight—not simply because it was the naked form of a beautiful woman, but rather because it was *her*, the woman he desired above all others.

He swallowed hard. He felt his loins swell, and his heart thunder. It was the delightful torture of desire, the want of a woman—this *particular* woman.

Seeing her in profile, lifting her face to the cascade, her torso arched, her arms lifted as she smoothed back her hair, his eyes filled with tears. It was a vision for the gods. The utter majesty of it was almost too much to bear.

He got to his feet, stripped and plunged into the pool. It felt cool at first, stimulating his blood. But after a few strokes, he became aware of the sensuality of the water.

He gazed at Michaela as she turned and twisted under the deluge. The sight of her mesmerized him and he trod water, unable to take his eyes off her.

After a few moments, she peeked around the curtain of water for a better look at him, her hair plastered down her face and onto her chest.

"Come on in," he called over the steady thunder of the falls. "The water's wonderful."

She hesitated briefly before diving into the pool, surfacing several feet from him. She looked at him through wet lashes, but didn't speak. They faced each other, their limbs undulating gracefully in the water.

Lakesly stared into her eyes, feeling as though his very being might be drawn right inside her, only to be lost for all eternity in her perfection. At that moment he understood the meaning of worship—what it meant to lose one's soul to a goddess.

He circled around her as if to measure the boundaries of her aura. Michaela didn't move until he'd made a full circuit. The magic of the moment seemed to have captured her as much as it had him. He wondered if this might be the path to a perfect death; if, when an exceptional moment in life such as this came along, one quietly slipped into the bliss of eternity. Reed Lakesly couldn't imagine an experience more sublime, unless it was the ultimate blending of two souls, the merger after the dance.

Then, without saying anything, Michaela slowly swam around him, headed for the shore. He watched her climb onto the rock shelf at the edge of the pool, near where he'd left the rucksack. She got a towel from the bag, holding it modestly in front of her as she dried her face.

He swam toward her and she watched him approach. When he neared the bank, she spread out the towel and lay on it, peering up at the verdant boughs.

He climbed up on the rock as she had, and retrieved the other towel from the sack. Michaela didn't look at him, but continued to stare up at the sky.

He spread his towel next to hers, on the soft bed of moss. It wasn't until he lay beside her that she rolled her head toward him and touched his face. He kissed her fingertips. Michaela closed her eyes and let her hands drop to her sides.

Reed knew at that moment, that perfect moment, that he couldn't wait much longer. He needed to touch her skin, revel in her silkiness, her heat. He wanted her to come alive for him.

He turned to her, tracing her lower lip with his index finger, then drawing it over her chin, down her throat and between her breasts to her waist. Seeing her nipples harden, he lowered his mouth to her breast and sucked. His penis rose against her hip. He wanted to be inside her, but he made himself wait, knowing she had to be as ready for him as he was for her.

But Michaela did seem ready. She arched when he bit her nipple—not hard, but enough to make her moan. He moved his hand between her legs and stroked her, slowly at first, and then faster as she moistened.

Soon he was able to slip his finger inside. She was hot and smooth and wet. She scooted down, against his hand, and he knew she wanted more of him. He put a second finger in her. But even that wasn't enough because Mike put her hand on his wrist and stilled him.

"Not like this, Reed. I want you in me."

He moved over her then and she spread her legs wide. He watched her face—her beautiful, expressive face—as his sex bumped up against her. He paused, rubbing the tip of his penis against her opening. And when Michaela's lips parted and she took a deep breath, he plunged into her.

He told himself to go slowly, to make it last. But dear God, he couldn't. Each time he entered her he wanted to thrust harder, go deeper, move faster. Michaela seemed to understand his need and share it. She moved with him, taking everything he had to give.

He felt a tingling at the base of his spine and knew he was about to explode. Michaela was panting, taking in little gulps of air with each of his thrusts. Then she held her breath and pushed against him a little harder. He came then, calling out her name.

He collapsed onto her, utterly exhausted, his force spent. He had surrendered to her, as she had to him. There was no anger in that realization, only fulfillment, a feeling of completeness, of being at one with her. As his body melted into hers, he could still feel her pulsing around him. Her fingers caressed the back of his neck and he shivered. She touched his ear and sighed.

"That was wonderful, Reed. Fabulous."

He groaned, unable to speak. He never wanted to move. If only they could stay like this, always joined, where her very existence was a part of him.

They lay like that for a long time, listening to the inner silence of their contentment. He was vaguely aware of the rush of water cascading into the pool, the call of the birds in the trees and the soft hush of breeze blowing over them; but mostly he knew he'd never felt this way before.

Finally he rolled off her, but he took her hand and held it, feeling with all the certainty of his being that he had found his soul mate, a woman understanding of his particular spirit and mind, a woman who could love him for the man he was. This was new to him, and the wonder of it, a miracle.

He heard Michaela take a deep breath. "You know what the saddest part is? Knowing this day, these hours must end."

"But there'll be others, darling," he said softly.

"Maybe. But they'll be part of the same dream. And dreams always end."

He propped his head in his hands and looked at her. "Why the dark view? Isn't it better to enjoy every second of this?"

She sighed. "I don't mean to sound negative. I guess I'm thinking it's too good to be true."

"Oh, it's true, all right, Mike. There's nothing false about this."

"Are you saying the life I left behind, the one I had before I came into these mountains with you, wasn't real?"

"Oh, it was real, but this is going to change it."

She turned to him, searching his eyes. Then she put her finger to his lips. "Don't talk about the future, Reed."

"Why not?"

"Because I know who I am, and I know this isn't me."

"It *is* you."

"Then it's me for the time I'm here. But it'll be better if we don't try to push it into the future where it won't fit. Promise me, Reed, you won't talk about the future. Just the present. I don't want this tainted in any way."

"I'm not so pessimistic as you, Michaela. That won't be easy."

"Do it for me," she pleaded. "Let's live minute to minute, hour to hour. It will be better that way. I know it will."

He leaned over and kissed her swollen lip. "You aren't a woman typical of your sex, are you?"

"I'm just me. And at the moment I'm very, very happy. I don't want to think of anything else."

"All right," he whispered. "If that's really what you want, we'll do it your way."

CHAPTER TWENTY-TWO

FOR THE NEXT SEVERAL days Michaela did her best to do what she'd asked of Reed—to live each day, unmindful of the future. Sometimes she succeeded. Other times, especially when she was alone, she couldn't help brooding. She tried to convince herself that she would have her memories, and that she would have grown emotionally from the experience. That was rationalization, but it was the best she could do.

Their love showed no sign of fading. Their first night together they slept naked in each other's arms. They made love with patchy moonlight streaming in the window, but it was a quiet love because the radio operator was in the communications room at the front of the building. There wasn't much privacy, even in the dead of night, so Michaela stifled the sounds of her ecstasy just as she stifled her anguish over the future.

Most of the cadre found an hour or two for a siesta in the heat of the day. A few times she and Reed napped, dozing in each other's arms after making quiet love. They returned to the pool on half a dozen occasions, including once in the middle of the night when the moon was bright enough to illuminate the trail.

They made love in the water that night. Michaela cried out at the moment of ecstasy, her scream absorbed by the never-ending sound of falling water. She gasped for air as wave after wave of sensation rippled through her. Even as her breathing returned to normal, the pulsing continued on, leaving her a slave to the pleasure Reed gave her.

Reed was as good as his promise. He didn't discuss the future, except when he made reference to her mission. But he often spoke of his love, of the happiness she gave him.

They both sensed that they had to compress a great deal of living into a very few days, so there was an urgency to their lovemaking. Michaela came to know Reed's body as she'd never known another's. Their common pleasure had truly made them one.

There were many hours when they couldn't be together. Michaela used that time to work on her computer. But once she'd exhausted both sets of batteries, she was forced to use pencil and paper. "I've almost forgotten how to write long-hand," she complained to Reed.

"Is that what it means to be a modern woman?"

"No," she said, tapping his chin. "Being a modern woman means learning to keep your work out of your heart and your heart out of your work—like men have been doing for centuries."

When she wasn't with Reed, or writing, Michaela socialized, becoming friendly with almost everyone in camp except Cecilia. But the woman's hostility lessened as the days passed, partly because Reed had had a long talk with her. He'd insisted that there couldn't be ill feeling between them if they were to succeed and the people of Pangonia were to win their freedom.

The other women in the camp were friendly, especially a tall, slender clerk named Lupe, whose husband and brother were both in Juan de Falcón's prison. But apart from Reed, it was probably Santos Moreno whom Michaela felt closest to.

One evening, while Reed was in a meeting with his operations chief, she and Santos talked for hours about Susana Riveros. They compared notes, exchanging anecdotes.

They sat on the steps of the communications center. Santos stared off across the compound. "Whenever I think of her in that cell, I die a thousand deaths," he said. "Not being able to help Susana has caused me the most suffering I've ever known."

"She'll be free soon," Michaela said. "And she'll need a friend. Your love will help heal her. She'll welcome it."

"I don't believe she even thinks of me."

"Perhaps not now, but she will. I can't say for sure what the future will bring—you must tell her of your love."

"You think so?"

"You're a caring person, Santos, and you have a good heart. That doesn't go unnoticed. The main thing is not to be afraid of your feelings. It's a lesson I've recently learned myself."

"Lucas loves you, Michaela. Everyone sees it on his face. He is a different person from before you came to Pangonia."

"I love him, as all of you do," she admitted. "But Reed and I are from very different worlds."

"There is only one world," Santos said. "And it is not the world that matters, but the hearts of the people in it."

She smiled at him. "That is a very nice sentiment."

"I thought you might stay with us, even after the victory of the revolution," he said.

"After the revolution is like a distant star. The only period of time I can think of is from today until I go."

"And for me it is the opposite. Today means nothing. All that matters is what happens after the prison doors are open."

"That will be a pivotal day for us both, then, won't it?" she said sadly.

"I hope it will be the first day of my life."

Michaela wondered if it would seem like the last of hers. That was what she'd come to fear most.

THE NEXT EVENING BROUGHT a surprise visitor—Luke Hammond. A thin, blond man with rimless glasses and a wry sense of humor, Hammond greeted Michaela affably.

"You are the talk of the hemisphere, Miss Emory," he told her as he unloaded his document case. He presented her with a stack of newspapers. There were a couple of issues of *La Pensa*, the *New York Times*, and Michaela's own paper, the *Daily News Bulletin*.

The headlines read, Reporter Abducted In Pangonia, Kidnap Attempt Of Editor Thwarted, and Police Nearly Foil Kidnapping. The front page of *La Pensa* featured a large picture of Bernardo. Hammond gave her a synopsis of the lead story.

"It seems de Falcón was on his way to a meeting when he was ambushed by the MAP guerrillas. According to the report, an American reporter who had hitched a ride with him was abducted by rebels, despite de Falcón's gallant effort under a hail of bullets to rescue her." Hammond chuckled. "Quite a brave fellow, according to his own paper."

"How do they treat Michaela?" Reed asked.

"The press is billing her as a heroine, an innocent victim."

"That's just what we want," Reed said. He scanned the page. "It seems General de Falcón has his troops scouring the country for you, Mike."

"Really?"

"Not really. They wouldn't spare any troops from defending the capital, but saying it makes them look macho." He smiled. "Like Bernardo the night of the abduction."

Luke Hammond pushed his glasses up off his nose. "Seems the time is right to spring our trap, Reed," he said. "When are you going to push the button?"

Reed glanced at her. "Soon, I guess."

"The opportunity won't last," the Canadian said. "If we wait too long, it will be hard to convince them she's for real."

"Yes, I know. Tomorrow morning we'll brief her and Cecilia. They can be in Montagua tomorrow night."

They were talking about her, and the mission that was the whole point of her being there. But to Michaela, the discussion seemed unreal, somehow. Detached.

Reed got up from the table. "I need some air," he said. "Mike, do you want to go for a walk?"

"Sure." She stood and they went outside.

Dusk had come and the sky was imbued with a strange luminosity. They strolled. Michaela slipped her arm through his.

"I know you're worried about sending me back to Montagua," she said, "but don't be. It's why I came here."

"I can't help being worried. Now that I love you, this mission is going to be a thousand times harder on me."

"You can't let your personal feelings interfere," she said. "If the cause is just and the plan is sound, it should be done. If you have to think of anybody, think of Susana."

"Yes, I know you're right."

"Even if I'm found out, they won't torture me. There's been so much press about my abduction, they'd just boot me out of the country."

"Maybe. But much as I don't like the danger I'm putting you in, that's not the worst of it."

"What is the worst?"

He took a deep breath and sighed. "I'm concerned about what happens to us."

"You promised we wouldn't talk about the future."

"At some point it can't be avoided," he said. "I've held my tongue and we've had a wonderful, idyllic week. But neither of us knows where we're headed, and I think we need to talk about it. We won't have many more chances."

Michaela pulled Reed off into the shadows. She took his face in her hands. "This has been a fantasy...a dream," she said, her eyes glistening. "We must deal with reality now. What's happened to Susana, and the people you've been fighting for, isn't a dream. It's real. You've dedicated your life to rectifying an injustice and I've agreed to help, in my own small way. Until we've finished the job, Reed, what happens to us doesn't matter."

"You're saying we should discuss this after the war."

"In a sense, I guess I am."

"I just want to know one thing. Have you already made up your mind about us?"

"I've tried not to think about it," she replied. "That's the truth."

He ran his hands down her arms, making her shiver. "When you do think about us, keep in mind one very important thing, Mike. I love you. I love you with all my heart.

And I don't want this to be the end. I want it to be the beginning."

Michaela pressed her face to his neck, and tears started to flow. "You don't want to make it easy for me, do you?"

"Promise me you'll think about what I said."

"I can't. Not and keep my wits about me."

"Table it, if you wish," he said, "but at the other end, my smiling face will be waiting for you, Michaela. My smiling face and my love."

MICHAELA LAY AWAKE in Reed's arms, listening to the sounds of the forest. They had made love with the poignant tenderness of lovers about to part. She had dreaded the end of their time together, and now it had finally come.

This was the most difficult night of her life. There had been other occasions when she'd suffered more, struggled to deal with loss and disappointment, but never had she felt so torn. For the first time in her life she'd let go and allowed herself to really love. It had been blissful, it had been sheer ecstasy. But it couldn't last. Romantic love was only a beginning, the prelude to the committed love that carried a couple through the years. What followed the initial days of joy depended on the people involved, and the circumstances.

Michaela turned to Reed. She could tell by his breathing that he was asleep. She kissed his shoulder, then squirmed closer to him, trying to ignore the fact that it could be the last time she would ever sleep in his arms. As the tears flowed, she told herself that no matter what happened, she'd won—she'd found happiness. Her memories could never be taken away from her. She drifted off with that thought in her heart.

Morning came with the realization of a new challenge. Reed was dressed and putting on his boots when she awoke.

"I was going to let you sleep in," he said. "You're going to have a very long day."

Michaela sat up on the bed, looking at him. "Let's let last night be our goodbye, Reed. From this moment on, I'm a MAP cadre. It's all business between us. Okay?"

"Is that what you want?"

"It'll be easier that way. For us both."

"Whatever you want," he said, his voice tinged with sadness.

Michaela got dressed and they had breakfast with the rest of the cadre in the dining hall. Luke Hammond sat at their table.

After eating, Michaela was briefed by Hammond. Reed sat in on the discussion. The story she would give General de Falcón was that she had been taken to the MAP's headquarters where she was lectured on the virtues of their cause in hopes that she would write their side of the story.

She resisted at first, then pretended to buy their arguments. Her friendliness won her their trust and gave her the opportunity to roam the camp freely. Sitting outside a window where a top-level meeting was going on, she learned that the MAP had secured the army's defense scheme and response plans. They would launch an offensive in two weeks.

Realizing that could spell disaster for General de Falcón, she continued to eavesdrop as the commanders discussed how to best thwart the government's defensive scheme.

"I understand the concept," she said. "I only hope I can remember the details."

"That's not important," Reed replied. "Just give them enough facts to be credible."

Hammond reiterated the army's defense plan, focusing on a few key points. "Only a dozen of their highest-ranking officers know the priority given to the key installations in the city," he said, after listing them for her. "That and the code perameters will convince them that we in fact have the plan, and therefore a spy at the highest levels of the army's command structure."

"Won't General de Falcón simply change his plan when he realizes it's been compromised?" she asked.

"Yes, but unless he captures the spy, no plan will be safe. Knowing that, your disclosure will throw him into a panic. The ol' boy is paranoid as it is."

"But you obviously do have a spy at the highest level. Can't you use your information to outsmart the army?" she asked.

"Yes, and that was our original plan," Hammond told her. "But Reed decided that our advantage would be greater still if we were able to throw the enemy into confusion at the critical moment. That way we not only have the element of surprise, we have an enemy whose command structure is unable to respond effectively when we attack. It could mean far fewer casualties."

"It *is* clever," she said, with an admiring glance at Reed.

"It all depends on your ability to convince them you're for real," Reed said. "After seeing you in action at the state dinner, I know you can do it."

"But won't they wonder how I managed to escape?"

"That's where Cecilia comes in," Hammond said. "Her story is that Reed rejected her romantically, so she decided to help you escape, and thereby get her revenge."

Michaela glanced at Reed. "That strikes a little close to home, doesn't it?"

"Cecilia has her passions," he replied, "but they are for our cause."

"How can you be sure?"

"She might be miffed at me, but a few years ago she was gang raped by an army patrol. Her sister was killed. Who would you hate more?"

"Besides," Hammond said, "being upset with Reed won't hurt her credibility."

Michaela nodded. "Will she know the plans, as well?"

"No. Cecilia's out of the command structure. She isn't aware of what we know, or what we intend to do after you've given de Falcón the misinformation."

"What *do* you intend to do?" she asked.

Reed patted her cheek. "If you don't know, you can't tell them and there's no way they can beat it out of you."

"What if they want to know where your camp is?"

"Go ahead and tell them. Give them the directions, if you wish. Feel free to tell them everything you know except that we gave you the information you're passing along and that you're really on our side."

She thought about it. "There's hardly anything I can tell them. I didn't see how we got to the cantina. I don't even know what part of Pangonia we're in."

Reed smiled broadly.

"But what about Cecilia?" she asked. "She knows. And she'd be able to tell them."

"She's going to tell them where the camp is, Mike. The only trouble is, it will be our alternate headquarters, the one not in use at the moment. By the time they discover that, it will be too late."

"You're a tricky devil," she said.

"I've been told that before," Reed replied with a wink. He looked at his watch. "There's not much time. Carlos will take you back to the cantina on horseback. In theory you and Cecilia could have walked out, but there's no point in making you do it. We'll also provide transportation to the edge of town. The story is you hitched rides."

"You've certainly thought it through," she said, as they got up. "I hope I can carry it out."

Reed put his arm around her shoulders as they went out the door. "Just think of the fabulous story you'll write."

"You'll save my computer and my notes, won't you?"

"If you'll promise to treat us well in your articles, we'll see that you get it," he teased.

"I'm a journalist, Reed. I tell the truth to my readers, no matter what."

He squeezed her shoulder. "I guess I'll have to take my chances, then, won't I?"

Michaela got a few of the things she was going to take with her from Reed's quarters, then returned to where Reed, Cecilia, Luke Hammond and Carlos were waiting with the horses. As she approached, she saw the first crack in Reed's demeanor.

Michaela shook Luke Hammond's hand and said goodbye. Then she turned to Reed. He took her hand in both of his.

"Well, me child," he said in his phony Irish accent, "it all started with an urgent call from Mother Nature, and now here we are, a million miles later, parting with an urgent call to duty."

"It's been quite a ride, Father O'Laughlin."

He smiled, his eyes glistening. "The luck of the Irish be with you, lassie." Then he gave her a big hug. "Break a leg, Mike," he whispered. "Take damned good care of yourself."

She nodded, biting her lip to keep from crying. "You, too, Reed. You, too."

They mounted their horses then, and Carlos Tucino led the way to the trail head. As they neared the edge of the forest Michaela glanced back, her eyes flooded with tears. She was able to make out Reed. He stood with his hands on his hips, watching her, unwavering, until she could see him no more.

CHAPTER TWENTY-THREE

MICHAELA SAT NEXT TO Cecilia in the back of the battered old pickup as they sped along the bumpy road, their hair tossed by the wind. They hadn't spoken much and the tension between them was palpable. Michaela decided the time had come to clear the air.

"I can't blame you for hating me, Cecilia," she said. "But believe me, I certainly had no intention of hurting you."

"Don't worry, *señorita*, already I stopped thinking about it. You, too, will get over Lucas when your time comes."

Michaela wasn't sure whether Cecilia was taking a last shot—trying to make her feel insecure—or if she truly believed that Reed would throw her over for someone else. He had seemed sincere enough, but honesty and good intentions at any given moment were hardly a guarantee for the future.

She sighed. Trust, again. The same old issue—did she love Reed enough to trust him, really trust him? And even if she did, was that a guarantee that things would work out for them? A new day invariably changed one's perspective. And when Pangonia was liberated, it would be a new day—not only for the country, but for Reed.

"What do you think Lucas will do after the revolution?" she asked Cecilia.

"It is a good question. His heart is here with us, but he is a *norteaméricano*, too. After a war tradition says a man takes a wife and he has children and grandchildren to tell his stories to. Is it also like this in your country?"

"Not in the same way, I don't think."

"Lucas, he was once in a bank or something in New York. If he does not go to his rancho to live a quiet life, maybe he will go to the bank again. I cannot say."

Michaela smiled at the thought. "Somehow I can't see Lucas in a three-piece suit spending his days on Wall Street." The realization didn't make her sad, exactly, but she knew it didn't auger well for them. "If you're right about him wanting a wife and children and grandchildren, then it will probably be here in Pangonia."

Cecilia looked at her. "What about you, *señorita?* What will you do?"

It was the question she'd been asking herself. The answer seemed obvious, Reed's professions of love notwithstanding. "I'm a journalist," she said. "I'll do what journalists do. Find a story and write it. The only thing certain is I won't be staying here."

Michaela fell silent. She'd promised Reed they'd talk about the future "after the war is over." But what could he say that would change things? It was no more in her to make a career out of having children and grandchildren than it was in Reed to return to Wall Street. Why was that only now apparent? What could she have been thinking?

"I must tell you something, *señorita,*" Cecilia said. "For a time it was hard for me to think this, but it is very generous of you to do what you do for my country. We are all grateful."

She reached over and touched Cecilia's hand. "Thank you for saying that. But your cause is just. No one should ever deny doing what is right. I guess that's true of many things, though we don't always see it."

Cecilia didn't respond. Michaela decided it was time to put the future out of her mind—at least until the dangerous hours ahead had passed. So much was riding on her. Pangonia and Susana Riveros deserved her full attention.

The truck began to slow and the driver called out something. Cecilia turned and looked through the window at the road ahead.

"What's happening?" Michaela asked.

"There is a roadblock, *señorita*. I think we are about to be 'saved' by the army of General Juan de Falcón."

Cecilia gave the sign of the cross. Michaela contented herself with a silent prayer. They would need all the help they could get.

MICHAELA WAS JUST finishing a light dinner at the table in Juan de Falcón's private dining room when Bernardo arrived. He swept into the ornate room with the gold-leaf ceiling and crystal chandelier, his hands lifted in praise.

"Thank God!" he exclaimed. "You're safe, my love. I came as soon as I heard." He planted a big kiss on her temple before joining her at the mahogany table. His cologne was overpowering. "My precious, I was afraid I would never see you again. Was it terrible? Did they abuse you?"

"They didn't hurt me, Bernardo. I'm fine."

"But how did you escape?"

Michaela repeated the story she'd given General de Falcón and the intelligence officers who had questioned her. She'd asked for Bernardo as soon as she got to the palace, figuring that an ardent ally might discourage any excesses. As things turned out, she had gotten through the interrogation without arousing suspicion, as best as she could tell.

Predictably, Bernardo seemed to care little about what she'd learned, though he was eager to take his share of credit.

"My failure to save you during the abduction has turned to good fortune," he said. "Look how we have been rewarded! I have you back and my father has information about the enemy."

"Reed Lakesly is a bastard, Bernardo," she said. "He said so many unkind things about you and your father. I don't know how he would expect me to believe them when I know you as I do."

The editor drew himself up. "The man's a coward," he said with a huff, "trying to brainwash an innocent woman. I should have killed him with my bare hands when I had the chance." He leaned close and put his arm around her shoulder. "Thank God, you're back with me, safely in my arms."

"Your father wants me to stay here until tomorrow, in case he has more questions." She eased away from him as she spoke, then got up from the table, hoping to get some distance from Bernardo.

"Yes, I spoke to him. Your news has been very upsetting. He now has proof of a traitor in the highest levels. He's determined to find the culprit."

"What is he going to do?" she asked, sounding innocent.

"He's calling in all the commanders to interrogate them."

Michaela was secretly elated. The ploy had worked, exactly as Reed had planned. "I'm relieved to be back here," she said, practically gagging on the words.

"The whole world worried for you," he said. "Your editor, Mr. Ellison, was most concerned. I believe he's on his way to Montagua."

"Jack is coming here?"

"That's what I've been told."

Just what she needed—another complication. Bernardo was gazing at her with lust in his eyes. He left the table and came toward her. She wondered if he would have the gall to try to hit on her.

"I'm exhausted," she said quickly. "I wonder if my things have arrived from the hotel?"

"There was a bag in the entry. It must be yours."

"Good. I think I'll go to bed. It's been a trying day."

Bernardo sent for her luggage, then insisted on escorting her to an upper-floor guest room.

"Good night," she said when they came to the door, hoping he would take the cue and leave.

But he went right in. "I must make sure my little pigeon is comfortable in her nest," he said.

After the footman brought her suitcase, Bernardo closed the door. He slowly walked toward her. It was apparent he intended to pick up where they'd left off.

"Bernardo, I don't want to be unkind, but romance is the furthest thing from my mind right now."

He looked wounded. "I planned to stay with you to-night, Michaela, to comfort you. But if you don't want my company, I can leave."

"It's not you," she said, biting her tongue. "It's the circumstances. Anybody in my shoes would feel the same."

"Then let's talk, my pet."

Michaela relented. Being stuck with him wasn't quite like being jailed, but it wasn't much better. Bernardo went on and on about how he'd suffered over her. His incessant yammering became a kind of torture and, as the minutes passed, Michaela regularly got up to pace, looking out the window at the city, wondering what was going on in the general's command center.

"What do you think's going to happen?" she asked him.

"My father will resolve matters. He's a very good military man," he assured her. "Thanks to you, he'll beat Lakesly."

"I hope your father knows that I want him to beat the MAP, rid the country of those scoundrels."

"Most certainly. You've proven your fidelity. And Father knows of our love."

That wasn't as reassuring as Michaela would have liked. Juan de Falcón was no fool. At some level, the general had to wonder how sincere she was about his son. She saw the insipid grin on Bernardo's face and realized he didn't have a clue. She let him babble for a few more minutes, then insisted she had to go to bed.

"Are you sure I can't persuade you to let me stay the night and comfort you, my love?"

"No, Bernardo. Not tonight."

"Maybe tomorrow, then?"

Michaela saw a struggle looming. "We'll see."

He got to his feet. "Since we're having a crisis of state, I'll stay here at the palace tonight," he announced. "If you need me, my dove, tell the footman and I'll fly to your side."

He embraced her then and Michaela let him kiss her. She closed the door and leaned against it after he'd gone, her eyes filling—as much in frustration as for any other reason.

She was almost ready for bed when there was a blackout, reminding her of the first time Reed had come to her room. She went to the window and looked up at the carpet of stars—the same stars she'd seen in the mountains. Closing her eyes, she thought of being naked in the pool with Reed. She thought of making love with him, an ecstasy she might never know again. Why, suddenly, did she feel such desperation?

MICHAELA WAS AWAKENED by a loud explosion that rattled the windows and shook the bed. It was barely dawn. Listening, she heard more explosions in the distance.

She went to the window. On the horizon she saw flashes and columns of smoke. In the courtyard below soldiers were scurrying about. She heard random shots. My God, she thought, could this be the offensive? Already?

Moments later there was pounding on her door. She opened it and Bernardo rushed in, wearing a bathrobe. "They're attacking, they're attacking," he said, his eyes wide, his hands trembling. "Get dressed and come downstairs. We must escape to safety." He was gone without waiting for a reply.

Michaela stood there, dazed. Then her heart leaped. This was it! Reed's countercoup!

She wasn't sure what to do. Was she better off going with Bernardo or staying where she was? Then it hit her. If she was with Bernardo, she'd more likely be in the middle of the action—exactly where every self-respecting reporter wanted to be.

Michaela got dressed as fast as she could, slipping on her yellow cotton dress and white leather flats. Outside she heard the rattle of machine-gun fire. She hurried downstairs. The place was in pandemonium.

This was the chance of a lifetime—getting to witness a coup d'état from the inside. Resolved to make the most of it, Michaela began searching for the general. Had he al-

ready escaped, or was he still at the palace, directing his
army in a last-ditch effort to defend his regime?

She walked down the corridor where most of the offices
were located. Then, over the din, she heard his voice. Peek-
ing in an open doorway, she saw de Falcón by his desk,
stuffing documents into a case. Bernardo was at his side, his
shirttails hanging out, pleading about something. They
spoke Spanish, so she couldn't understand a word until she
heard her name. They were arguing over her!

When General de Falcón started out of the room, Michaela ducked around a corner. The men hurried out of the
office and along the hall. Bernardo trailed behind his father, still imploring, though seemingly with little effect.

Michaela took off in pursuit, staying far enough behind
that they wouldn't notice her. The men disappeared down a
stairwell. She followed, arriving at the basement level. She
saw a situation room with maps covering the walls, a communications center and several offices. All were empty. It
was like a ghost town.

Around the corner, just ahead, she heard a door close.
When she reached it, she put her ear to the door and listened. It was quiet. Easing it open, she was greeted with a
rush of cool, damp air. There was another stairwell. This
one was dark except for a dim bulb sticking out from the
wall. Below, she could hear the sound of feet on the metal
steps.

Michaela slipped off her shoes and silently crept down the
stairs. She could hear muffled voices. The subbasement was
very dank. Bernardo and his father were at the far side of
the room, still arguing and, thankfully, oblivious to her
presence. Finally, the general seemed to lose patience and
ordered his son to be quiet. Bernardo hung his head.

Michaela watched as the general opened a locker and removed two long robes, handing one to Bernardo. They
slipped them on and Michaela realized that the president of
the republic and his son intended to disguise themselves as
priests. The irony amused her.

But the palace was surrounded. How could they avoid
capture, even in disguise? Apparently, Juan de Falcón had

prepared well, because he pulled aside an old cupboard, revealing a hidden door. They were going to make their escape through a secret passage.

Taking a flashlight with them, the men disappeared into the passageway. Michaela hurried over. The tunnel was about four feet wide and high enough to stand in. In the darkness, she could see their flashlight some eighty or a hundred feet ahead.

Michaela searched the locker, hoping to find a flashlight, but there wasn't one. She decided to follow anyway.

She entered the tunnel, shivering from the coolness of the air. The floor was relatively even, but it felt cold to her bare feet. She kept one hand on the wall and started walking, all the while focusing on the bobbing light ahead. She was careful not to get too close.

When the light suddenly disappeared it nearly threw her into a panic. Then she saw a faint glow ahead and realized there had been a bend in the tunnel. Michaela quickened her pace, thinking it would be better to stay closer. Finally the men came to the end of the passageway. She crept closer. They were trying to open a door with a key. Once past it, would they lock it behind them? If so, the only way out was back the way she'd come—through a hundred yards of utter darkness. Her skin crawled at the thought.

She edged closer. They went through the door. It closed solidly behind them. It was pitch-black. Michaela fought back her panic, her heart pounding as she strained to listen for the sound of a dead bolt turning. She heard nothing.

She had to feel around for the handle, but once she located it, she pressed her ear to the metal door and listened. Nothing. How long should she wait? After counting to one hundred, she tried the handle. To her relief the door opened.

On the other side there was a hint of light, though it was dim. The air seemed different, too. She could make out bare walls and wooden stairs on the opposite side of the room. It looked like a cellar. The light was coming from the staircase, as were the footsteps. She realized then that the two men had gone up the stairs.

She hurried over, fearing the light would go out. No sooner was she there when she heard still another door open. The light became brighter for a second, then went out when the door clanked shut.

Michaela started up the stairs in pursuit, but stubbed her toe. She fell, dropping her shoes. The noise sounded thunderous to her, but would they have heard it? She waited, so scared that she nearly forgot to breathe. She was sure that the door would fly open and the general would flip the light switch, spotting her. It didn't happen.

Feeling around for her shoes, she slipped them back on, then carefully negotiated the last few steps. She eased the door open and saw that she was in a storeroom. There were crates and old wooden chairs. The only light came from a small window. The place had a musty smell.

She closed the heavy door and turned around just as a robed figure popped up from behind a box, startling her. Michaela gasped.

"Don't move!" he shouted. It was Juan de Falcón and he was brandishing a gun.

"No, Father!" came a cry from the other side of the room. "It's Michaela. Don't shoot!"

She turned to see Bernardo moving toward her.

"Idiot!" the general said. "I can see who it is. She followed us. We have been discovered."

Bernardo was quickly at her side. "She wanted to escape also, Father. She's no friend to the rebels."

Juan de Falcón moved from behind the box, his gun still pointed at her. He stood directly in front of a door, shaking his head. "No, you are wrong, Bernardo. It is no accident that she comes from Lakesly's camp only hours before an offensive is launched."

"But Father, she came with proof of a traitor. You were fortunate to learn of it."

"It was not fortunate. Lakesly wanted me to panic. It's obvious to me now, but I was blind. A fool. This woman is an agent for the MAP."

"Impossible!" Bernardo said, drawing himself up. "Michaela is as devoted to me as I am devoted to her. She wants to escape with us." He turned to her. "Tell him it's true, my love."

"Don't be an imbecile," the general said. "Did she call out, asking to come with us? No, she followed us secretly. She intends to warn her comrades the first chance she gets."

"You are mistaken, Father. You don't know her as I do."

Juan de Falcón gestured with the muzzle of the weapon. "Move away, Bernardo. There is only one way to ensure her loyalty."

"What do you intend to do?" Bernardo demanded.

"Shoot her, of course! What do you think I'm doing with this gun? Directing a choir?"

Bernardo stepped in front of her. "I will not allow you to kill the woman I love. She would give her life for me. And I would give mine for her!"

Michaela listened in shock. Her pulse was pounding so hard she could hear it in her ears. Juan de Falcón turned bright red. "*¡Dios mío!* How could your mother have delivered me such a moron? Step aside!"

"I refuse!"

The door behind de Falcón suddenly flew open, knocking him forward. The gun discharged and Bernardo de Falcón fell against Michaela, dropping at her feet.

She looked up to see Carlos Tucino struggling with the general, easily disarming him. A couple of other MAP guerrillas hurried into the room. Michaela looked down at Bernardo, who stared up at her, his eyes wide with fear.

"Are you all right, *señorita?*" Tucino asked.

"Yes," she said, kneeling at Bernardo's side. "But Señor de Falcón is wounded."

Bernardo's lip trembled as he stared into her eyes. "I'm dying," he moaned. "I hear the angels singing."

Michaela was filled with compassion. She lifted Bernardo's head onto her knee. "I'm so sorry," she whispered. "I didn't intend for this to happen."

After a couple of the guerrillas had hustled Juan de Falcón out the door, Carlos Tucino knelt down and pulled open Bernardo's clerical robe to check the wound. There was a smear of blood on his shirt. Tucino peeled back the fabric as Bernardo cried out in pain. Tucino shook his head, rolling his eyes. He looked at Michaela. "It's only a scratch, *señorita*. The bullet, it barely broke the skin."

Michaela gave Bernardo a look and got to her feet, letting his head clunk on the floor. "How did you to find us?" Michaela asked Carlos Tucino.

"Our spy said there was a secret passage to a nearby building. We didn't know which one, so we watched them all."

"Where are we?" she asked.

"In the cellar of a wine merchant," Tucino replied. Opening a carton, he took out a bottle of champagne. Then, looking down at Bernardo, he said, "We can take this one to the hospital. Even mosquito bites can get infected. Our Santos is not so lucky, unfortunately."

"What happened to him?" she asked.

"He led the assault on the prison and was wounded. He wouldn't go to the hospital until Susana was liberated. They are at the hospital together now. Perhaps you would like to go in the ambulance with this one so that you can see them."

"Yes," Michaela replied, "I would."

"Come," Tucino said to Bernardo, tapping his haunches with his boot, "maybe you will need a transfusion."

Bernardo got to his feet, acting bewildered. Michaela patted his arm. "You were very brave, Bernardo. I won't forget how you tried to save me."

He stared at her numbly. Tucino handed Bernardo the bottle of champagne and gave him a gentle nudge toward the door. "Ride in style, editor," he said. "You will find we treat our prisoners better than your father did."

They left the stockroom.

"So the coup was successful," Michaela said as they walked through the building.

"Yes," Tucino replied. "The casualties are very light on both sides. The operation was almost flawless. Lucas is very busy, but he told us to take you to your hotel when you were found. He will come as soon as possible."

"Good," she said. But in her heart of hearts, she wasn't really pleased. It was over now. Her fantasy had come to an end; the real world was waiting. But could she be happy there, after living a marvelous adventure with Reed? Could everyday life ever measure up? Michaela didn't think so.

CHAPTER TWENTY-FOUR

THERE WERE TWO OTHER wounded in the ambulance. Michaela sat on the jump seat, near Bernardo's stretcher. He was still in a daze. As they moved through the crowds in the street, the siren wailing, Bernardo rolled his head toward her.

"Then it's true, you don't love me?" he said.

Despite herself, Michaela had begun feeling sorry for him. His defense of her against his father had won her gratitude, and she felt badly now about deceiving him. But even so, she had to be honest with him. "It's true, Bernardo."

"Were you working for the MAP all along?"

"At first I was simply trying to do my job as a journalist. After I saw Susana, I knew I had to help her and the people of Pangonia."

"Then my father was right. I am a fool," he said.

"Your only mistake was in being selfish," she replied. "If you'd thought of others first, you wouldn't have gotten into this mess."

"Maybe I've been greedy," he said woefully, "but I really loved you, Michaela."

"You couldn't have, Bernardo, because you didn't know me. You loved a pretty picture you'd painted in your head. You'd have been much smarter to devote your energy to the people who love you—like your wife and your children."

Bernardo got all teary eyed. His lip quivered and he couldn't speak.

"You did something very brave today, though," she told him. "If you show the same courage at home by being honest with your wife, you'll be a happier man."

Bernardo began weeping and Michaela took his hand. She held it the rest of the way to the hospital. When the attendants took Bernardo away she got misty-eyed herself. Then she grinned. Chelsea would never believe it—her lover from hell.

The emergency room was packed with wounded. A nurse told her there were only half-a-dozen seriously injured combatants, Santos Moreno being one. His prospects were good, though he did require surgery. She was shown to his room. Susana Riveros was at his bedside.

Seeing her, Susana, still in her prison garb, got up and they embraced. Santos was sleeping, so they went over to the window where they could talk without disturbing him.

"It's so good to see you free," Michaela said, squeezing her friend's shoulders.

Susana shook her head, wiping away a tear. "I can't tell you how wonderful it is, Michaela. I heard what you did. I am so grateful—not for myself, but for the people of my country."

"I really didn't do anything special—certainly not like you. Everybody I talked to has such respect for you, Susana. You're the heroine of the revolution."

"Juan de Falcón made me a martyr by putting me in jail, that's all."

"There's a man who admires and loves you very much," Michaela said, glancing over at Santos.

"He is a dear friend. I will never forget how he fought to free me. Coming here in the ambulance, he told me he could die now, knowing I am free. But I told him I didn't want him to die. I begged him to live."

Michaela got choked up, just hearing the account. Santos was so passionate about Susana, she could easily picture the scene. "I must put that in my story about you, if you don't mind," she said.

"You'll write about me?"

"I already have. And I've written about Reed, as well."

Susana took Michaela's hands. "Santos told me how Reed loves you, how he is a different man than before."

"Different? I don't think Reed is any different."

"Yes," Susana said. "We always knew he lived for the moment. He was not serious about anything but the revolution. Santos said the passion burns more quietly now, that his heart is full of love for you—and that when you go his joy goes with you."

"I'd hate to think that was true."

"It shows where his feelings lie."

"These have been unusual times," Michaela said. "I told Reed that. Now he must learn the life of a rancher and forget the revolution. He must go back to the real world."

"You have not seen him today?"

"No, but I will soon, I imagine," she replied, feeling strangely wistful about it. A sadness filled her. It was partly fear, but also her conviction that the dream was over. "Well, Susana, I must go. I wanted to see you and Santos. I was very concerned when I heard he was wounded, but I'm glad to see he's okay and that you're here with him."

"I'll stay until I'm sure he's all right."

They embraced again.

"You aren't leaving Pangonia for a while, I hope," Susana said.

"I don't know. I haven't decided for sure. In case I do, I'll be sure and give Chelsea your love."

"I hope you don't leave," Susana said, looking disappointed. "Not yet."

Michaela kissed her cheek. "Life is unpredictable." She smiled despite her friend's look of concern, then left.

Michaela was walking through the hospital reception area when she saw Jack Ellison rushing through the door.

"Mike!" he cried, seeing her. "Thank goodness you're all right." He gave her a big bear hug before she could register her surprise. Bernardo had said her editor was on his way, but she hadn't expected to run into him so soon.

"Jack, why did you come all the way down here?"

"When an editor's star reporter is abducted by a band of revolutionaries, he can't exactly ignore it."

"It wasn't a real abduction. It was creative investigative reporting."

Jack grinned. "I figured you were up to something. But I had to get my butt down here to show concern." He beamed, looking her over. "Glad I did. Seems I got here in time for all the action."

"I really should be in the street, getting this story."

Ellison waved off the notion with a gesture of his hand. "I've got two people in town covering the coup. Brought them with me, thinking we'd be covering your abduction. What I want to know is, what's happening to that series?"

"It's in my computer," she said, walking toward the door. "As soon as I find it, you can have it. The last installment's in my head. I only need a few hours to write it."

They went outside.

"I've got a taxi," he said pointing. "Make that last installment the top priority, Mike. As soon as I saw the coup would be successful, I phoned Washington and had them run the first piece. You can't imagine what hell it's been, sitting on that for a week."

She gave him a look as he opened the door of the taxi. "I imagine it's been just awful for you, Jack."

"Nothing compared to what you've been through, of course," he said lamely. He went around and got in the other side. "Where to? The hotel?"

"Yes."

Ellison told the driver to take them to the El Presidente. "So, what now? You want to cover postcoup Pangonia? The word is Ricardo Corazón de León could be flying in as early as tomorrow."

She stared out the window of the taxi, thinking.

"Mike?"

"I don't know, Jack. I'm inclined just to go home, not to drag things out. I want to finish writing my story and I could do it at home. Since you've got somebody here, I wouldn't be letting the paper down." She glanced over at him to see his reaction. He was contemplating her.

"What's the problem, kid? Something's wrong."

"Nothing's wrong. I'm just tired."

"No, there's a problem. Did something happen while you were with the guerrillas? I mean, you weren't . . . hurt or anything."

"No, it's nothing like that."

He rubbed his chin, studying her. "Anything I can do?"

"Yeah. Find me another assignment. Somewhere else. Something really big that'll keep my mind occupied."

"You deserve it, there's no denying that."

The streets were full of people celebrating. It was like a holiday. Michaela couldn't help feeling satisfaction. She'd played a small part in the success of the day. But her mind was preoccupied with Reed. She knew what she wanted to say to him, but she was afraid she wouldn't be able to express herself successfully.

They arrived at the hotel. Most of the staff was in the street, enjoying the festive mood of the city. Rosita saw Michaela emerge from the taxi and hurried over to greet her.

"¡Señorita! ¡Señorita!" she exclaimed. "You are back! It is so wonderful to see you."

Michaela embraced her. "It's a happy day, isn't it, Rosita?"

"The best in the whole world!"

"I don't suppose Lucas has been here."

"Not yet, but they say he is coming, señorita." She grinned. "To see you, I think."

"I guess I'll go upstairs and wait."

"A man came earlier and brought your things. He tells me Lucas is coming later. As jefe, he is very busy, of course."

"Yes," Michaela said. "I know."

Ellison had paid the driver and came to join Michaela on the sidewalk.

"My computer's here," she told him. "I'm going up to my room."

They went inside. On the way up in the elevator Michaela leaned against the side of the car, blowing a strand of hair up off her forehead. She was more emotionally wrung out than physically exhausted.

Ellison looked her over, admiring her as a woman. "You know, you're even more appealing than before, Mike. The experience of being a foreign correspondent has added a maturity and grit I find appealing."

"Jack," she said, shaking a finger at him, "don't hit on me. I've had enough the past couple of weeks to last a lifetime."

"I was trying to pay you a compliment," he said. "I see something new, and it's appealing. That's all."

"I'd like to be appreciated for my journalistic skills. Period."

"Yes, I've gotten that impression. No harm in paying a lady a compliment, though, is there?"

"No," she said, smiling faintly, "as long as we leave it at that."

The door opened and Michaela walked out. Jack Ellison followed her to her room.

All of her things were there—her computer, even the bag that had been taken to the presidential palace. She went over to the window to look at the city, sorry her mood prevented her from enjoying the day more.

Ellison stretched out on the bed, his hands behind his head. "You can just about name your ticket at the paper," he said. "I might as well tell you that. And there won't be any conditions. Of course, if you wanted me to take you to Bermuda I would, but it's not a condition."

"*Your* newfound maturity is gratifying, Jack." She continued to stare out the window, pondering the situation. Then it hit her. A face-to-face conversation with Reed wasn't necessary. Turning to her boss, she abruptly said, "There's something I would like for you to do for me."

"Name it."

"Get me on the first plane back to Washington."

He contemplated her. "You want out of here, don't you?"

Michaela nodded.

"Mind some company? This story's covered, and now that my star reporter is out of harm's way, I've got no reason to stay."

"Suit yourself."

Ellison hopped up and immediately got on the phone. There was a lot of chaos and confusion, so it took him a while to make arrangements. While he was working on it, Michaela sat down to write Reed a letter, explaining that he had a lot preoccupying him at the moment and didn't need another distraction.

She wrote that their week together in the mountains was the most beautiful closing chapter she could possibly imagine, and she had no desire for a tearful farewell. Her feelings for him, her love—ran very strong, and she wanted her last recollections to be of him as the dashing revolutionary hero who had taken her prisoner and stolen her love. "It was the perfect fantasy, Reed," she wrote, "one that will live on forever in my heart."

THE CHAOS AT THE AIRPORT was worse than Michaela could have imagined. Officials sympathetic with the old regime were replaced by others loyal to the rebels. Papers were closely checked to make sure that Juan de Falcón's cronies weren't able to slip out of the country with booty belonging to the people. A number of arrests had been ordered. Customs and flight departures were moving at a snail's pace.

Their flight had been delayed. They sat in the gate area, waiting impatiently. When the flight was finally announced they got up with a sigh of relief. Paramilitary police supervised the boarding, but at last they were on the plane.

Michaela sat in her seat, gazing out the window at the terminal building, thinking of her arrival only a few weeks before. She'd been excited, hopeful and naive, then. In an emotional sense, it seemed a hundred years ago. She'd changed so much it was almost frightening.

But even though she was returning home with sadness, it was also with a vague hope for the future. Whatever the coming weeks must bring, things would somehow be better for her. She would be looking at the world differently, especially her relationships.

At last the boarding was complete, the doors closed and the ramp withdrawn. The pilot started the engines and the

plane began taxiing. Michaela's thoughts were on Reed.
Tears ran down her cheeks. She wiped them with the back
of her hands, sniffling so much that Jack had to give her his
handkerchief.

At the head of the runway the jet poised for takeoff, its
engines rising in a high-pitched whine. The pilot released the
brakes and the plane lurched forward. But it hadn't gone
twenty yards before the engines suddenly cut out and the
huge aircraft braked to a stop. A murmur went up in the
cabin as people began looking around.

The pilot then pulled the jet back onto the taxiway and
again brought it to a stop. Over the loudspeaker system he
announced that an irregularity had been discovered by
Customs. Their departure would be delayed.

"Some colonel and his mistress must have sneaked on
board," Jack said, ennui evident in his voice. "The poor
bastard is really squirming now, I bet."

The passengers were fidgeting, probably having similar
thoughts. Michaela hoped it wouldn't take long. It was difficult containing the intense emotion she felt, not to mention the fact that she needed to go to the bathroom and
would have to wait until they were airborne. She looked out
the window and saw that a couple of vehicles were approaching. Moments later, the front door of the plane was
opened and Michaela could see that the ground officials
were coming aboard.

There was mumbling throughout the cabin. Visas. They
were rechecking visas. Jack Ellison groaned and leaned out
into the aisle to see. "Hell," he said, "I hope they make this
quick."

Michaela rested her hand on her chin and looked out at
the tall grass swaying in the breeze beside the taxiway. In the
distance she could see the bluish-tinted mountains, marveling that she'd actually been there with Reed by that waterfall. Those days and nights would live forever in her mind.
For her, it would always be the most sacred place on earth.

The official was moving along the aisle, checking passports. When he drew close to where they were sitting, she
turned and her mouth dropped open. Despite the hat of the

custom's official, there was no mistaking who it was. Reed Lakesly.

"Passports, *por favor,*" he said in a thick Spanish accent.

Michaela was speechless. She stared incredulously. Grumbling, Jack took his passport from inside his coat pocket and handed it over. Reed glanced at it and handed it back.

"*Señorita, pasaporte,* pleeese."

Michaela fumbled for her purse, finally handing Reed her passport. He looked at it and shook his head with disgust. "Uh-oh, thees ees not good, *señorita.* You have no exit visa."

"Exit visa?" Jack said. "Nobody said anything about an exit visa being required."

"A new regulation, *señor.* Eet's about fifteen minutes old. I'm sorry, *señorita,*" he said to Michaela. "I'm afraid you will have to come with me."

She gave him a look and he wagged his finger at her.

"Eet will be easier for you if you do not cause the trouble."

"This is ridiculous," Jack said, as Michaela climbed past him. "I don't have an exit visa, either."

Reed scrutinized him. "No, *señor,* but you have the honest face. The *señorita* is much too beautiful to be trusted." Waving to the rest of the passengers, he said, "A thousand pardons, *señores.* Please enjoy your flight. *Adíos.*"

Moments later, Michaela was seated in the back of the jeep as Reed, who'd taken a moment to chat with the pilot, finally made his way down the boarding ladder and walked to the vehicle. He climbed in beside her.

She felt more guilty than annoyed as she looked down at her folded hands. "Wasn't that a bit heavy-handed?" she asked, struggling to find her dignity.

"Extraordinary measures are required when dealing with a sneaky woman."

"Didn't you get my letter?" she asked, turning to him.

"Yes. It was a nice letter. I liked everything about it except your conclusion."

"I thought it would be easier that way. You shouldn't have taken me off the plane, Reed. We could have talked on the phone if you had something to say."

"You already know I love you, so telling you again isn't the point."

"What *is* the point?"

"We'll discuss it at the terminal building." He directed the driver to proceed and the vehicle started up.

They drove back, parking beside the building. The driver went inside. Reed put his arm behind her on the back of the seat.

"My life is at a turning point, Mike," he said. "I'm going to be living differently from here on, and I want it to be with you."

"How can you be sure? Only hours ago you were a guerrilla leader and now you're a conquering hero. It'll be days before there's normalcy in your life."

"I want to find my normalcy with you."

She bit her lip, her eyes shimmering. "I'm not the housewife type, Reed. I love your rancho, but I can't spend my life there having children and grandchildren. There are women who want that. You should be looking for one of them."

He took her chin in his hand. He shook his head disapprovingly, then kissed her tenderly. "I don't recall asking you to live there and bear my children."

"That's what you want, isn't it—in the long run, I mean?"

"What is it *you* want, Michaela?" he asked, his voice growing serious.

"My career. A normal life. Children maybe someday, but not as a career."

"That doesn't sound unreasonable."

"But Reed, I have to go home for that."

"The States is my home, too. I've neglected it of late because of pressing obligations here, but I'm my father's son as well as my mother's."

"You wouldn't leave Pangonia."

"I'd come back a lot. I'd live here part of the time," he said. "Would that be a problem?"

"You sound like you're proposing marriage."

He looked deep into her eyes. "I have a very serious question and I only want you to answer it if you can be a hundred-percent truthful."

"What question?"

"Why did you get on that plane?"

She swallowed hard. "Because I was afraid."

"All right, here's another question that demands total honesty also. Do you love me?"

"Yes, of course I do. Too much for my own good."

"No," he said. "About that, you're wrong. Listen to me, Mike. There are going to be some fun and interesting times here in the coming weeks. I want you to enjoy them with me. Write about them if you want to. And when the dust has settled, we'll figure out a plan for us."

She blinked back her tears. "That sounds too good to be true."

"It's not. Believe me." He kissed her then, deeply.

Michaela savored the kiss for a long moment, then she groaned with discomfort.

Reed's brow furrowed. "What's wrong?"

She turned bright red. "I didn't go to the bathroom before getting on the plane. I was going to wait until we were in the air. It was a mistake."

Reed chuckled. "What am I to do, lass?" he said in his Irish accent. "There's no changing you, is there?"

"No, Father O'Laughlin," she replied. "You'd better like me the way I am. But could we please discuss this after I find a bathroom?"

"Come on, me child," he said, taking her hand. "The *juan* is this way."